DEDICATION

A modern plaque fixed to the wall of the gate-house of Exeter's Rougemont Castle, directly below Crowner John's chamber, reads:

THE WITCHES OF EXETER
In memory of Temperance Lloyd,
Susannah Edwards and Mary Tremble of
Bideford, who died in 1682 and Alice
Mollard, who died in 1685.
The last people in England to be executed
for witchcraft. Tried here and hanged at
Heavitree. In the hope of an end to
persecution and intolerance.

The Witch Hunter

The Witch Hunter

Bernard Knight

W F HOWES LTD

This large print edition published in 2004 by
W F Howes Ltd
Units 6/7, Victoria Mills, Fowke Street
Rothley, Leicester LE7 7PJ

1 3 5 7 9 10 8 6 4 2

First published in the United Kingdom in 2004
by Simon & Schuster UK Ltd
A Viacom Company
Copyright © Bernard Knight 2004

A CIP catalogue record for this book is available
from the British Library

ISBN 1 84505 685 X

Typeset by Palimpsest Book Production Limited,
Polmont, Stirlingshire
Printed and bound in Great Britain
by Antony Rowe Ltd, Chippenham, Wilts.

HISTORICAL NOTE

People variously described as 'witches, wizards, sorcerers', and so on have been recorded for millennia, but they were rarely persecuted until after the medieval period.

Though the established Church generally disapproved of any competition in the occult and magical sphere, it tended to ignore village sooth-sayers and spell-casters unless they displayed frankly heretical or sacrilegious behaviour. Similarly, the secular powers showed little interest, unless such activities led to criminal damage.

All this changed in 1489 after two German monks published their notorious *Malleus Maleficarum* (The Hammer of Wrongdoers), a handbook for torturing inquisitors, which was taken up by the Inquisition and began a centuries-long persecution that led in England to the witch-hunt hysteria of the sixteenth to eighteenth centuries and at least 300,000 burnings and hangings across Europe. It even spread across the

Atlantic, leading to the well-known scandal of 'The Witches of Salem'.

In the twelfth century, the time of our story, this morbid hysteria was far in the future and both ecclesiastical and secular attitudes were quite relaxed. King Henry II openly stated his disinclination even to believe in magic, let alone hound such persons.

The term 'witch', which can be applied to both male and female, was then less common, the more usual name being a 'cunning woman' for the widow or wife who practised her art in almost every village. They were part of the social fabric of medieval England, where physicians, other than compassionate monks, were almost unknown outside the largest cities and even apothecaries practised only in towns. The vast majority of the static population lived in villages, and here the woman with a rudimentary knowledge of herbal remedies, first aid, animal care and midwifery was an indispensable part of the community. Some of these enlarged their repertoire to offer love potions, cures for impotence and infertility, or found lost objects and procured miscarriages, whilst others might gain a reputation for putting a spell on a rival to make him impotent or come out in boils, or for cursing the cows of a hated neighbour so that their milk dried up. Only occasionally in the early medieval period were such cunning men and women vilified by the Establishment. This story tells of one such episode.

The most common language spoken by the citizens of Exeter in 1195 would have been early Middle English, quite unintelligible to us today. The Norman aristocracy spoke French and the language of the clergy and almost all written documents would have been Latin. In the countryside, many would still have spoken Western Welsh, the aboriginal Celtic language that persisted as Cornish. Only about one in a hundred people could read and write, the majority of these being priests and clerks. The only English money was the silver penny, though some foreign gold coins were in circulation. The terms 'pound' and 'mark' were notional values, not coins, the pound being 240 pennies or 20 shillings and the mark being 160 pennies or 13 shillings and 4 pence (just over 66 decimal pence). Silver pennies were cut into halves and quarters for convenience, as a penny was about half a day's pay for most workers.

PROLOGUE

August 1195

The old woman sat on the cold stones of the ledge that ran around the walls of the little church, waiting her turn to take the sacrament. The rest of the congregation stood on the earthen floor of the bare nave, which was barely twenty paces long and half that wide. They were few in number, as the priest of St Martin's was not popular and there were another twenty-six churches within the walls of Exeter to compete with his ministrations.

Theophania Lawrence could sit down because of her age and presumed infirmity, though in fact she was quite spry for her sixty-six years. As in many other matters, she was crafty and full of guile and 'going to the wall' in church was a convenience, rather than a necessity. She sat and watched the dozen communicants shuffle towards the chancel, which was little more than a raised platform. It carried a simple altar, a table covered with a white cloth, on which was a cross of Dartmoor tin and two pewter candlesticks. Theophania was in no hurry and she let the last few townsfolk get near the priest before hoisting herself up and walking with an exaggerated hobble to stand at the end of the queue. Her face was round and smooth, with a pair of mischievous little eyes which stared out below the headband of a frayed linen cover-chief that enveloped her head and hung down the back of her much-darned brown kirtle.

As she stood behind the tall back of a pious cloth merchant from Southgate Street, she could hear the priest muttering the unintelligible Latin as he doled out the wafers and wine. Thin and fair haired, Edwin of Frome was unique in Exeter, as he was the only Saxon priest in a solidly Norman enclave. His sermons were laced with half-concealed diatribes against the invaders, though they had been here for well over a century and none of his parishioners was now likely to rise up in rebellion.

As the three people at the chancel step rose and returned to the nave, Theophania followed the pair in front. With a grunt, she lowered herself to kneel on the edge of the wooden dais. Her eyes darted around and settled with satisfaction on Father Edwin as he took a couple of steps towards the altar to replenish his paten. He refilled the shallow metal dish for holding the wafers from a new supply kept in the pyx. This was a carved wooden box, in which he stored the small pieces of pastry he bought at a cook-stall in High Street. He held the paten up to the cross and mumbled some more Latin to bless them. The old woman glowed internally, as freshly sanctified, they were all the more powerful.

The priest came back to the step and bent over her, mouthing more phrases as he placed a wafer in her supplicant palm. Edwin scowled at her suspiciously, knowing her of old. He waited until she had lifted the scrap to her mouth and made swallowing gestures, before moving on to the clothier. Theophania waited patiently until the priest came around again to offer a sip of cheap wine from the chalice, which she pretended to take. Then she stood up, crossed herself and unobtrusively walked out of the church without waiting for the completion of the Mass.

St Martin's was at the corner of the cathedral Close and she looked around in the early morning air to make sure that no one was watching her, before putting a hand to her mouth. Spitting out the consecrated Host, which she had kept stored inside her cheek, she carefully wrapped it in a scrap of cloth taken from a small pouch on her girdle, before replacing it and stepping out quite briskly up Martin's Lane, past the coroner's house. It was the first step towards an appointment with a noose that would be thrown about her wrinkled neck.

1

In which Crowner John finds a strange doll

Robert de Pridias was feeling out of sorts on this hot Tuesday afternoon. He rode his big bay gelding slowly along the high road towards Exeter, wondering uneasily what he might have eaten to give him this burning under his breastbone and the frequent belches that erupted from his belly. He had left Buckfast Abbey that morning, but the good breakfast that the monks had given him in the guest hall was surely as wholesome as one could wish. He had settled a mutually-satisfying deal for two hundred bales of new wool from the abbey's famous flocks and the abbot's satisfaction had been reflected in the hospitality he had been given.

No, it must have been that damned inn where he had eaten some dinner an hour ago. He had thought then that the pork was over-spiced, probably to conceal the fact that the meat was going off in this hot weather. Robert belched again and tried to ignore the fact that he had had these pains on and off for some weeks. He was forty-eight years old, comfortably rich and considerably overweight. Red of face and short of neck, the fuller had inherited his woollen mill on Exe Island from his father. He had built it up into a good business during the long years of peace that was turning Exeter into one of the most prosperous towns in England. As well as turning the raw wool into yarn, he now had a dozen looms working for him around the city, making the cloth that sold so well at home and abroad.

As he jogged along the dusty road, he tried to ignore the ache across his chest, which felt as if an iron band was being tightened around his ribs. Instead, he diverted his thoughts to his beloved wife Cecilia, who, as with so many successful men, was a powerful spur to his ambitions. A strong character, there was no doubt of that, and she was handsome even in her middle age. She had borne him three strong daughters, but unfortunately not a single son. He supposed that one day he would have to pass on his business to the eldest son-in-law, who was decent enough, though rather stupid – but he would have preferred to see a de Pridias as mill-master. The alternative, which he vowed would happen only over his dead body, would be to sell out to Henry de Hocforde, his main rival in the fulling trade and as obnoxious a man as ever trod the soil of Devon.

The thought of Henry seemed to increase the ache in his chest – now he fancied it was even spreading up into his throat. Though the city was now only a couple of miles away, he felt the need for a rest and something to drink, even if it was only the poorest ale. The afternoon was hot, but surely not enough to cause this sweat that was beading on his forehead and sticking his under-shirt to his skin?

He was passing through Alphington, a hamlet on the west side of the river, within sight of the cathedral towers. It was little more than a score of thatched wattle-and-daub cottages, a wooden church and a larger hut with two old barrels and a brewing-pole outside to mark it as an alehouse. He pulled the horse to a halt in front of its door and stared down groggily at two old men sitting on a plank placed across two large stones against the front wall. They had earthenware pots in their hands and were staring up uneasily at this well-dressed stranger on such a fine horse. He was not the usual type of client for this mean tavern – and he certainly looked unwell.

The aged peasants knew their place and waited for him speak first – but all they heard was a gargling noise from his throat as he bent forward in his saddle and clutched his arms around his chest. Suddenly, he felt violently sick; the pain had increased to an intolerable degree and radiated like lightning down both arms into his fingers.

He fell across his horse's neck, but his feet stayed in the stirrups, preventing him from falling off. Alarmed, the old men got to their feet, one stumbling towards the distressed man, the other going to the door of the inn to call in a quavering voice for the ale-wife. A buxom woman hurried out and between them they freed his fine leather boots from the stirrups and managed to slide him off to lay him on the ground, his horse champing and pawing unhappily alongside. The ale-wife also acted as the village nurse and layer-out of corpses, so had no difficulty in recognising a new client when she saw one.

'He's dead . . . dead as a salted ham!' she proclaimed, after holding a capable hand over the place where a light summer tunic covered his heart. For good measure she thumbed up his eyelids and looked at the sightless orbs staring at blue sky.

'But he can't be – he rode up on this horse not three minutes ago!' protested one old man.

'I know a corpse when I see one, Wilfred Coe!' the widow snapped. 'He's had an apoplexy or a visitation of God. But dead he is and you'd better get the reeve and the priest, for he looks like a rich man – and that can only mean trouble for the likes of us if it's not handled properly!'

The ale-wife was right in her gloomy foreboding, for the complex demands of the law could eventually cost the village many precious pennies in fines by the time the King's coroner had finished with them.

The dead man lay in the dust at the edge of the road while the reeve was sent for, the priest being away in Exeter for the day. A reeve was the villager who represented the manor-lord and who organised most of the activities in Alphington, especially the work in the fields. As the manor was a royal one, belonging to the King himself, there was no local lord, the demesne being managed by a bailiff, who had several similar villages to oversee.

The first problem for the reeve was to discover who the dead man might be. There were parchments in his saddle-bag with writing upon them, but as no one in the village could read, apart from the absent priest, these were of no help. Luckily the next rider to come along the high road from the direction of Plymouth, within a few minutes, was a merchant from Exeter, who recognised the victim. Seeing the knot of people clustered around the door of the tavern, he reined in his steed and slid from the saddle to investigate.

'This is surely Robert de Pridias, of the weavers' guild,' he exclaimed in concern. The pallid features looked very different in death and he squinted at them from several angles, then bobbed his head in confirmation. 'No doubt about it, it's de Pridias, poor fellow.'

The reeve, an emaciated fellow with a skeletal face and a hacking cough which suggested he had the phthisis, offered the parchments to the newcomer, but he shook his head.

'I can't read those, I do all my trading on tally sticks! But it's him alright, he owns a fulling mill on Exe Island.'

This was the large area of flat, marshy ground just outside the city. Exeter was built on a marked slope, running down from its castle on the east side to the river on the west. The swampy island was cut through by leats and gullies and after heavy rains up on Exmoor, these often over-flowed to flood the low-lying ground and the mean huts of the wool workers perched upon it. However, the many fulling mills that cleaned and prepared the raw wool needed great quantities of water and the site was ideal for industries such as those of the late Robert de Pridias.

When the traveller was told how his fellow-citizen had fallen dead across his horse, he offered to take the sad news to his family. 'I can be at his house in well under the hour,' he said solicitously. 'Where shall I tell his family to seek his body?'

The reeve looked at the ale-wife, but she shook her head firmly. 'No, I'm not having a corpse in my taproom, it's bad for trade. The church is the place for him.'

With an assurance that the fuller would be handled reverently, the merchant rode off with his doleful message. The reeve called two younger men from the nearest strip-field and they went to fetch the village bier, a wooden trestle with handles at each end, which was kept hanging from the roof beams of the church. On this they carried Robert into the small building and left him lying before the altar until the priest returned. However, the family arrived first, within two hours of the messenger leaving Alphington. The first was the son-in-law, Roger Hamund, whose feelings of grief were secretly allev-iated by the unexpected prospect of inheriting de

6

Pridias's business. He had cantered ahead in his enthusiasm, but within a few minutes his wife and mother-in-law appeared, sitting side-saddle on their palfreys, escorted by their household steward. They were all well dressed and well fed, contrasting markedly with the threadbare inhabitants of the village, as they stalked past them into the church.

The new widow, Cecilia de Pridias, marched towards the tiny chancel and stood looking down at her dead husband, more in anger than desolation.

'I knew it, I knew something like this would happen!' she snapped, sounding as if her husband had dropped dead purely to annoy her.

Roger Hamund stared at her, habitually open mouthed because of his adenoids. He was not an intelligent man and his mother-in-law's strong personality always overawed him.

'He must have had a stroke, Mother,' he ventured tentatively. 'The apothecary said he was in poor health.'

'Nonsense, boy!' grated Cecilia. 'He was done to death by that swine Henry de Hocforde and I'm going to call the coroner.'

Though by August the long summer days were beginning to shorten, there was still plenty of time for Roger Hamund to ride back to the city and fetch Sir John de Wolfe. He found him in his dismal chamber at the top of the tall gatehouse of Rougemont Castle, listening to his clerk reciting some inquest proceedings from a parchment roll.

The soldier on guard duty at the gate had directed him up the steep, winding staircase inside the tower and when he pushed his way through the sacking curtain that hung over the low doorway at the top, he found himself in a small room with rough stone walls and two narrow unglazed windows. The furniture consisted of a crude trestle table flanked by a couple of stools, which were occupied by a little man with a slightly humped shoulder and a tall, gaunt figure dressed in a grey tunic. The light from one of the windows was blocked by a giant of a man sitting on the sill, pouring ale from a large pot into his mouth, which was just visible beneath a huge ginger moustache which matched a wild thatch of hair.

The visitor knew all three by sight, as did most of the inhabitants of Exeter, for the coroner's team was a familiar and usually unwelcome sight about the city. Wherever a King's crowner appeared, it usually meant either a death or a lightening of the purse – and often both.

Roger stood hesitantly inside the doorway and addressed himself to the lean, forbidding figure behind the table, whose swept-back ebony hair and dark-stubbled cheeks made it easy to believe that the troops in his campaigning days had nick-named him 'Black John'. Now he was known as 'Crowner John', and beneath the beetling brows, the deep-set eyes that used to rove over battle-fields now sought out the crimes and tragedies that beset Devonshire.

'Sir John? I have come with a sad request for you to attend the body of my father-in-law, who has died suddenly and most unexpectedly.'

Three pairs of eyes swivelled around to stare at him. He was a podgy fellow of about twenty-eight, amiable but indecisive. His wife, a younger version of her formidable mother, directed his life from the security of their home near the East Gate, though she acted meekly and demurely enough when out in company.

The coroner aimed his predatory hooked nose in the man's direction and scowled at him ferociously. 'Why should his death concern me, sir? Was he beaten, kicked or stabbed?'

Roger shuffled his elegantly clad feet uneasily.

'He fell dead across his horse, Crowner. I would think some form of apoplexy was the most likely cause, but his wife is insistent that he was put under a malignant spell.'

The little clerk's eyebrows rose and he rapidly made the sign of the Cross. 'A spell? Nonsense, there is no such thing, it is against the precepts and teachings of the Holy Church!' he squeaked indignantly.

Roger recoiled slightly at Thomas de Peyne's vehemence. Although he had seen the clerk about the town, at close quarters he even more strongly resembled a priest, in his threadbare black cassock and the shaved tonsure on top of his head. A pair of bright little eyes darted intelligently from a thin face, which carried a long pointed nose and receding chin.

9

'My mother-in-law is convinced he was done to death. There have been threats uttered against him and she claims it is murder.'

John de Wolfe rumbled in his throat, his usual way of expressing disbelief. 'I have been the King's coroner for almost a year now, but this is the first time that witchcraft has been alleged as a cause of death.'

He managed not to sound sarcastic and Roger Hamund was encouraged to carry on, mindful of the tongue-lashing he would get from Cecilia if he failed to return without de Wolfe.

'There was certainly bad blood between him and another merchant,' he said carefully, not wanting to name another influential citizen whose patronage might yet prove useful. 'Perhaps it were best if my mother-in-law explained the situation herself.'

'So who is the dead 'un?' demanded the untidy giant from the window sill. This was Gwyn of Polruan, a former Cornish fisherman who had been Sir John's squire, bodyguard and companion for almost twenty years of fighting from Ireland to the Holy Land and who now acted as the coroner's officer. He was not renowned for his sensitivity and Roger cringed at the description of his father-in-law as 'the dead 'un'.

'It is Robert de Pridias, Crowner, the master of the guild of weavers in this city.'

John's black brows rose at this. He knew de Pridias slightly, as he had done some business with him over the last year or so. Since hanging up his

10

sword after returning from the Third Crusade, de Wolfe had ploughed much of his campaign plunder into a wool business. He was a sleeping partner to his friend Hugh de Relaga, a prominent burgess and one of the two portreeves that ran the city council. Though they exported most of their wool purchases to Flanders, Brittany and the Rhine, they sold some locally to the fulling mills and Robert de Pridias had been one of their customers, so John felt that perhaps he should indulge his widow's fantasies about murder. Rising from behind the table, he stood with his characteristic slight stoop and looked down at his little clerk.

'Get on and finish those other rolls, Thomas, they'll be needed at the Shire Court tomorrow.'

With a jerk of his head to Gwyn, he left Thomas reaching thankfully for his pen and ink. The clerk disliked both corpses and sitting on a pony to get to them. De Wolfe ushered Roger to the stairs and Gwyn lumbered after them.

The newly bereaved son-in-law explained where de Pridias was lying and on reaching the arch of the gatehouse the coroner led them across the inner ward of the castle to one of the lean-to sheds where their horses were tethered. Though it had been a very wet summer, the last two weeks had been unusually dry and the almost grassless mud of the ward had dried into hard rough-cast, churned by the hoofs of horses and oxen, wagon wheels and soldiers' boots.

Rougemont took its name from the red sandstone from which it had been built by William the Bastard soon after the Conquest. It occupied the high north-east corner of Exeter, in the angle of the city walls first built by the Romans and improved upon by both the subsequent invaders, the Saxons and the Normans. The inner ward was demarcated by a high wall, pierced by the gate-house, which guarded a drawbridge over a deep ditch. This led out into the much larger quadrant of the outer ward, bounded by another ditch and an embankment topped by a palisade. The Conqueror had torn down over fifty Saxon houses to make space for his new fortifications. Three buildings stood inside the inner walls – the tiny chapel of St Mary, the bare stone box of the Shire Hall and the larger two-storey keep near the far end, where the sheriff and the castellan lived. All around the inside of the walls were sheds and lean-to buildings, which housed forges, stables and living quarters for soldiers and a few families.

An ostler saw them coming and with a boy, led out Odin, de Wolfe's retired warhorse, together with Gwyn's big brown mare. Roger's gelding was hitched to a rail outside the stable and when all three were mounted, they trotted back out beneath the portcullis and down into the outer ward. This large area was part village and part army camp, where most of the garrison and their families lived in huts and shanties behind the outer line of defences, which had not been needed for the past fifty years since the civil war between Stephen and Matilda.

At the bottom of Castle Hill, the road joined the high street, which ran from the East Gate to Carfoix, the central crossing of the streets that joined the four main gates of the city. Beyond that, Fore Street dipped steeply down towards the river. They pushed their way through the crowded narrow streets, jostling aside townsfolk lingering at the stalls and booths along the sides of the main thoroughfare. Porters pushing barrows or bent double under bales of wool stumbled out of their way and beggars shrank back out of reach of the hoofs of the three horses.

Near the bottom of Fore Street, the West Gate let them out on to Exe Island. There was a wooden footbridge across the main channel of the Exe, but the grand new stone bridge lay half completed, as the builder, Nicholas Gervase, had run out of funds. With the tide out and the water at a low level from the recent dry weather, they splashed across the ford with their stirrups clear of the surface and went up the far bank to complete the mile to Alphington. Roger Hamund seemed reluctant to enlarge upon the circumstances of the death and was relieved to see his wife and mother-in-law waiting with a small knot of people at the entrance to the churchyard.

Willing hands took the reins as they slid from their horses and the sickly manor-reeve came forward to knuckle his forehead to the coroner. He had never had dealings with this official before and was vague as to his functions – but all he had heard by way of gossip seemed to indicate that unless you trod very carefully you risked getting both the length of his tongue and a hefty amercement.

'The cadaver's in the church, Crowner. We sent for you straight away, though there's no call to think it was anything but a seizure.'

He said this deliberately, as if the death was not natural, a 'hue and cry' should have been set up to chase any possible culprit and the failure to do so might be grounds for the first of the unwelcome fines. However, his words were brushed aside by the advancing figure of the widow, Cecilia de Pridias. She was a formidable woman of ample proportions, with a bust like the prow of a ship.

'Nonsense, my poor husband was done to death by some cunning means!' she snapped, in a voice that reminded John of the crack of a whip. 'There have been omens these past few weeks. I know the signs, someone has caused a spell to be put upon him. He told me he had presentiments of death.'

De Wolfe sighed, as it was obvious that she was going to be a difficult woman to placate. Like her daughter, who stood behind her, and her son-in-law, she was round of face as well as body, showing that the de Pridias family were affluent enough to over-eat. She wore a dark red kirtle of light wool, with a gold tasselled cord wrapped around her full waist. Instead of a wimple and cover-chief around her head and neck, she had a tight-fitting helmet of white felt, tied firmly under the chin. A short summer cape of fawn wool hung around her shoulders.

14

'Perhaps I had better view the body first, then you can tell me what you know,' he said with a mildness that Gwyn felt was uncharacteristic. John had just remembered that Cecilia attended St Olave's Church, where his own wife Matilda was a devout supplicant. They knew each other quite well and if he trod too heavily on Cecilia's toes, he would suffer a verbal lashing at home when the complaints reached Matilda.

The reeve led the way into the little church, which had been built in Saxon times and was in dire need of repair or preferably rebuilding in stone. Architecturally, it was little different from a barn, but had a gabled entrance on the south side, through which they now trooped. John marched across the earthen floor to the flagstoned area at the other end, which served as the chancel. He stopped at the bier, which was like a wooden stretcher with legs, and looked down at the still figure, fully dressed, with his dusty riding boots hanging over the end. The ale-wife had crossed his hands over his chest and had closed his eyelids with her fingers before the stiffness of death set in.

'Tell me what happened,' demanded the coroner, fixing the reeve with his deep-set eyes. The two old men from outside the tavern had tentatively followed them into the church, along with the ale-house keeper. Between them, they gave an accurate account of the sparse facts of de Pridias's demise, but his widow remained adamant that he had been done to death by magical means.

'I saw five magpies cross his path a week ago, when we visited my sister in Topsham,' she snapped. 'That's certain sign of bewitchment. And not two days ago, my husband dropped his knife and horn spoon from the table and they fell to form a cross at the ground near his feet.'

She voiced these occult manifestations with rock-hard certainty, as if defying anyone to query them as harbingers of doom.

'You said your husband thought himself to be under some . . . some noxious charm?' rumbled de Wolfe, cautious as to how he should approach this nonsense. If it had been a man offering this foolery, he would have given him a buffet around the head and told him not to waste his time, but a guildmaster's wife was another matter, especially one who would have the ear of Matilda.

'Indeed, he began having tight sensations in his throat every time he walked past a certain house in Fore Street, where a certain cunning man lives.' Her son-in-law restrained himself from pointing out that this was the steepest part of the hill coming up from Exe Island.

'Anything else?' demanded the coroner.

'For many weeks he has been waking in the early morning with a terrible headache, after dreaming morbid thoughts. He agreed with me that some hag somewhere was putting a curse on him.'

'Was his health good? Did he take any pills or potions?' asked de Wolfe.

'He was a hale and hearty man! Perhaps he had a little shortness of breath, but he indulged at table a little too liberally. As master of his guild, he had to attend many feasts and I had told him that he needed to watch the size of his belly.'

John noticed that the daughter and her husband looked a little askance at these protestations of rude health. 'Did he take any medicaments, I asked?' he repeated, gazing sternly at the weakest party, Roger Hamund.

'He was attended now and then by an apothecary, it's true,' mumbled Roger.

'Which apothecary would that be?' snapped the coroner.

'Walter Winstone, who has his shop in Waterbeer Street,' said Roger. 'But he merely gave him regular potions for his indigestion. As my wife's mother says, he was overweight and often had eructation of wind and an ache in the upper belly after a heavy meal. This Walter gave him some foul liquid for it – though the only good it did was to the apothecary's purse.'

Cecilia became impatient. 'This is all of no consequence, Sir John! My husband was done to death by witchcraft.'

John blew out a long breath in muffled exasperation. 'Why should anyone wish to harm your husband?'

Her pugnacious face, which reminded him too readily of his wife, glared up at him. 'I know fine well who has commissioned these evil acts! It is

17

Henry de Hocforde, who wishes him dead so that he may take over the mill.'

Gradually, de Wolfe pieced together the accusation, explained disjointedly by Cecilia and the daughter and her husband. It seemed that de Hocforde, who owned an adjacent fulling and carding mill, had long wished to buy out de Pridias, partly to remove competition and also to gain a better site on Exe Island, as the leat that drove Robert's mill-wheel was larger and more powerful than his own. He had made many offers of purchase and used every means of persuasion without success, until the matter became acrimonious in the extreme.

'And you claim that de Hocforde has resorted to attempted murder to gain this mill?' demanded the coroner, unable to keep incredulity out of his voice.

Cecilia glared back at him, entirely unabashed. 'And why not indeed? Men have killed for far less – a crowner like you should know that better than most!'

John shook his head in disbelief, then turned to the son-in-law. 'Do you think the same way, young man?'

Roger squirmed as his gaze shifted uneasily between his dominating mother-in-law and the masterful coroner. 'Well, I know that de Hocforde has become most aggressive about the matter these past few months. What started as a merchant's offer drifted into a fierce dispute.'

The daughter chipped in with her own forceful opinions. 'In the end, he came to the mill and to our house, shouting and raving at my poor father, threatening to put him out of business if he didn't see reason and sell up.'

'But did he threaten his person, as well as his business?'

The new widow glowered at de Wolfe. 'Perhaps not in so many words, but the threat was plain to see. The bad blood between them became so vicious that I forbade my husband to go out at night without a servant to accompany him with a cudgel.'

John waved a hand towards the bier. 'As you see, there's not a mark upon his body – and we have witness to the fact that he had a seizure, madam!'

Cecilia de Pridias remained scornful of his dismissive attitude. 'Of course there are no wounds, man! These cunning women spell their curses in occult ways. For a few pence, they will work any manner of mischief, from stealing your neighbour's husband to killing a rival's sheep.'

The coroner sighed. There was obviously no way of shifting this obstinate woman from her conviction that her husband had been magicked to death. However, he was damned if he was going to distort the system of justice just to pander to her delusions.

'You are entitled to think what you may, goodwife,' he said as reasonably as he could. 'But I cannot see any reason to bring this sad event within the jurisdiction of the coroner and hold an inquest. There is no wound, the death was witnessed by several people as a seizure – and now I learn that he was under the care of an apothecary for pains in his belly.'

Cecilia glared at him and already he could feel the nagging that he would get from Matilda when she heard of this slight against her friend. 'If you'll not look into the matter, then I'll go to the sheriff! Sir Richard will have a more sympathetic ear than yours seems to be.'

John shrugged. 'It's none of his concern, lady. I was appointed by the King to record all such matters in the county. A sheriff has no jurisdiction, unless you can show that a killer is on the loose and needs apprehending.'

'Well, one is, you stupid man!' she said shrilly. 'Henry de Hocforde!'

De Wolfe regarded her sternly. 'I'd be careful of proclaiming that too openly, madam. De Hocforde could take you to law for defaming his name if you persist in an accusation that you have no means of proving.'

He said this with the best of intentions, as he felt that a newly bereaved widow might declaim things in her grief that at other times would be left unsaid – though he had to admit to himself that she seemed more angry than distressed.

Gwyn sidled up to him and muttered in a low voice, 'Are we staying, Crowner? This seems a waste of time.'

'We'll go through the motions, just to humour her fantasies,' replied John, stepping away a few paces to avoid being overheard. 'I'll have a quick look at the corpse, to reassure them that he's not been stabbed. You go and look at his horse and search through his saddlebags, just to make it appear as if we're doing something.'

As Gwyn shambled off down the nave, the coroner turned back to the family, who were grumbling indignantly among themselves.

'I'll examine the body myself, to put your minds at ease. You must wait outside, please. It's not seemly for me to undress the cadaver in your presence.'

Still protesting that he was wasting his time in looking for wounds, when the death was due to a malignant spell, Cecilia de Pridias stalked out of the little church, the others trailing behind her. John called to the reeve as he reached the door. 'Shut that and come back here to help me, man. My officer is looking at his horse.'

Between them, they took off Robert's wide belt and hoisted up the dead man's long tunic, of best-quality brown worsted. Underneath, he wore long black hose tucked into a pair of leather riding boots. An undershirt of fine linen was pushed up to his armpits for John to examine his belly and chest, which were unremarkable apart from the size of his paunch. Turning him over, John confirmed that there was no injury on his back, then they restored his clothing to make him decent and stood back.

Death stiffness was beginning to appear and

the coroner reached out to close his half-opened mouth before it set fast in that unbecoming position. As he did so, he noticed that although Robert still had most of his teeth, the gums were in a very bad state, being discoloured and darkened along the edges. He idly contrasted them with the perfect teeth of Nesta, his Welsh mistress, and recollected that during his visits to Wales he had seen many people cleaning their teeth with the chewed end of a hazel twig dipped in wood ash, a habit de Pridias could have adopted with advantage.

He straightened up and stood broodingly over the reeve. 'Nothing here, so let the family arrange for a cart to take the poor fellow home for burial.'

As he stalked towards the door, it opened and Gwyn came in, his red hair as tousled as ever, the ends of his ragged moustache drooping to his collar-bones. His brow was furrowed and he came to meet the coroner with a hand outstretched, something clutched in his ham-like fist.

'Don't understand this, Crowner!' he boomed. 'It was pinned underneath one of the saddlebags. I only found it because I lifted the bag and the damned pin stuck in my finger.'

He opened his hand and showed his master what lay across the palm – a small corn-dolly, no more than four inches long, with recognisable arms, legs and head, though it was crudely made. Stuck to the head was a small clump of what seemed to be human hair and around the body was a torn scrap of green cloth, secured to the dolly by a thin metal spike which transfixed the chest.

The reeve sucked in a sudden breath and crossed hinself rapidly, a gesture that the coroner and his officer associated with their own clerk, who did it a dozen times a day.

'That's a witch's effigy, Crowner!' he hissed in a frightened voice and edged away from Gwyn's proffered hand.

'Yes, that's what I thought,' grunted the Cornishman. 'I remember a cunning woman in Polruan when I was a lad. She made one of these once when she wanted revenge on a man who had stolen one of her sow's litter. Didn't work, though.'

DeWolfe took it from his officer's hand and examined it more closely. It was little more than a bundle of straw stalks, bound up into the crude shape of a man.

'That hair, it looks like a match for the dead 'un, I reckon,' said Gwyn, pointing at the bier. John took the little effigy across and held it next to the corpse's head. The fine, sandy hair did indeed appear to be identical with the fluff of hair on the dolly.

'What about this bit of cloth? I wonder where that came from,' said de Wolfe.

'I can tell you that straight away,' snapped a triumphant voice. Turning, John saw that the widow and her family had come back into the church. 'It's a shred from an old tunic of my husband that the moths had ruined. I threw it out some weeks ago.'

'How can you tell that it's his?' demanded the coroner.

'I know that pattern. It was made from our own wool by a weaver in St Sidwell's to my own requirements. Some wicked person has salvaged part of it to use against him. So now will you believe that a spell was cast upon him?'

'I believe, lady, that this thing was found under his saddlebag. That's a long way from believing that it had anything to do with his death.'

Cecilia's round face flushed with anger. 'Then you are a stubborn, stupid man, Sir John! You hold in your hand an effigy that is clearly of my husband, carrying his hair and his clothing, with a lethal weapon stuck through its chest like a chicken on a spit – and you say it's nothing?'

De Wolfe could see that he was in for a hard time from his own wife after this, but his sense of duty overcame any personal problems.

'Calm yourself, madam. Let's take this a step at a time. How would anyone come by this rag and this hair, which I do admit looks uncommonly like that of your husband?'

This time the daughter spoke up. 'I remember throwing that moth-infested tunic on to our midden in the back yard. We pay a man with a barrow to collect our night-soil and other waste every few days. He takes it to the river and tips it in, downstream of the bridge.'

'Anyone could have stolen the cloth or even just torn a piece from it,' volunteered Roger, anxious to back up his mother-in-law's case.

'What about the hair?' objected Gwyn.

'My husband was very particular about his appearance,' snapped the widow. 'Every few weeks, he used to attend the barber who keeps a stool outside St Petroc's Church. Any evil person could lie in wait and then pick up some trimmings from the ground as they pass.'

This woman has an answer for everything, thought John peevishly, but he admitted that he could not fault her explanations.

'And who do you think was responsible for this flummery?' he demanded, still obstinately opposed to giving any credence to Cecilia's convictions.

'You're the law officer, it's your job to discover that!' she retorted. 'But whoever did the actual deed was but an agent of the true culprit, that devil Henry de Hocforde.'

They argued the issue back and forth, the mother and daughter becoming more and more shrill and vituperative as the coroner dug in his heels more deeply and refused to hold an inquest.

'How can I assemble a score of men here as a jury to examine a corpse without so much as a pinprick upon him and ask them to decide if he was murdered?'

'Most sensible men believe in the powers of cunning women,' railed Cecilia. 'They see it often enough in spells for good weather, for fertile cattle, foretelling fortunes, banishing the murrain in their livestock and the like! So why are you so set against what is common knowledge to most people?'

The reeve was nodding his agreement and John could sense that even Gwyn, who came from the fairy-ridden land of Cornwall, was disinclined to dismiss the widow's claims. However, de Wolfe remained adamant, as he could not square this situation with the letter of the law, which he had sworn to uphold on behalf of his hero, King Richard the Lionheart. He held up his hand to try to stem the torrent of indignation that was still pouring from the lady's lips.

'That's my last word, madam. Bring me some concrete proof that your husband was done to death and I'll surely listen. But until then, I suggest you try to come to terms with your grief and set your unfortunate husband to rest in the cathedral Close as soon as can be arranged, given this hot weather.'

With this practical advice, he beckoned to Gwyn and made for the door and his horse.

2

In which Crowner John meets the archdeacon

When John de Wolfe went home to his wife that evening, he decided that attack was the best form of defence against what he could foresee would be a burning issue when Cecilia de Pridias next met Matilda at church. He would get his story in first and hope to moderate the inevitable tongue-lashing that would come in the next day or two.

He rode past the new Guildhall in the high street and turned right into Martin's Lane, a narrow alley that was one of the entrances to the cathedral Close, the episcopal enclave around the great cathedral of St Peter and St Mary. Halfway down the short lane he slid from his stallion and led Odin into the farrier's yard on the left, where the beast was stabled. Directly across the way were three almost identical houses, the one on the left being his own. It was a tall, narrow building of weathered timber, with a peaked slate roof. A heavy oak door and a shuttered window were the only breaks in its blank face.

With a muted sigh, he lifted the iron latch and stepped into the vestibule, a small room with a row of hooks for cloaks and belts hanging on the back wall. He slumped on to a bench, its only furniture, and pulled off his riding boots, groping under the seat for a pair of leather house-shoes.

As he pulled them on, there was the padding of paws from a passageway to his left, which led around the side of the house to the back yard and a large brown hound appeared. Brutus was as pleased as ever to see him and licked his hand as his great brush of a tail wagged slowly back and forth.

'Got to face the dear woman now,' he whispered to the old dog, as he stood up and went to the door of the hall, at the opposite end of the vestibule from the passage entrance. Brutus watched him, then decided that he preferred the back yard and vanished as de Wolfe pushed open the inner door and stepped into the main room of the dwelling.

Inside was a wooden screen to stop some of the draughts that in windy weather moaned around the sombre hall, which rose right up to the bare roof beams high above. The dark timber was partly covered by faded tapestries, except on the inner wall, which was of new stone. This was where he had had a large fireplace built with a conical chimney tapering up to roof level, a device he had seen in Brittany. Before this innovation, the smoke from a central fire-pit used to cause an eye-watering fog to fill the hall, as it sought to escape by seeping out under the eaves.

On this hot summer evening there was no fire, as their maid Mary did all the cooking in a hut in the yard. But as he trudged past the long oaken table with its stools and benches, he saw that one of the cowled chairs facing the empty fireplace was occupied. His wife was staring at the cold stacked logs as if they were crackling cheerfully on a cold winter's night.

'You're late, Mary has been waiting to bring the supper in,' she grated, without any word of greeting. John was so used to this that he took no notice and went to a side table to pour some red wine from a pitcher into a pewter cup. He saw that Matilda already had one in her hand.

'I had to ride out to Alphington to see a corpse,' he said with studied indifference. He brought his drink to the hearth and sat in the chair opposite his wife. Looking at her, he remembered that she had been almost comely when they married, some sixteen years earlier. Now her stocky frame had filled out and her square face had thickened, with loose skin under her eyes and throat. She was forty-four, his senior by four years, but looked a decade older. Her thin-lipped mouth was turned down at the corners in permanent disgruntlement. He admitted that his own behaviour had done nothing to make her nature more amiable, but neither of them had wanted to marry in the first place, having being pushed into it by their ambitious parents. His father, Simon de Wolfe, was a modest landowner with two manors at the coast and saw marriage into the much richer de Revelle family as a way of advancement for his second

29

son. Matilda's parents had hoped that a dashing young knight who was carving out a name for himself in the Irish and French wars, was a good way of getting their youngest and least attractive daughter off their hands, so the bride and groom had little say in the matter and had regretted it ever since. They had never had children, which was hardly surprising, as John had made every effort to stay away from home for most of their married life. Only in the last two years, since he had returned from Palestine and had run out of wars to fight, had they lived together for more than a few months – and although they now slept together, sleep was the operative word, for neither felt the slightest inclination to indulge in marital congress.

'So what was this body that kept you from your supper?'

Her voice jerked him out of his reverie and he remembered his plan to forestall Cecilia de Pridias's inevitable complaints about him.

'Someone you knew, I'm afraid. It was Robert de Pridias, the fulling and weaving merchant. I think you know his wife quite well.'

Matilda sat up abruptly in her chair, her small eyes alert at the news.

'Robert dead? Poor Cecilia, I saw her only yesterday at St Olave's. How did he die? Why were you called? Was it some accident – or worse?'

'He died of a seizure, on the back of his horse. A natural death, but sudden. It seems he had pains

30

in his chest for some time and was under the care of an apothecary.' He deliberately emphasised the natural aspect, to defuse the coming criticisms.

'So why were you called?' she snapped. Whatever her faults, no one could ever accuse the sharp-witted Matilda of any lack of perception.

John sipped his wine as he thought about the safest answer.

'His wife – now his widow – has some strange idea that he was done to death through being cursed. Extraordinary idea, I had considerable difficulty in trying to convince her otherwise.'

'Henry de Hocforde!' she exclaimed, much to her husband's astonishment.

'What about him?' he said feebly.

'She has spoken to me in confidence about the trouble between the two fullers. I have the ear of many influential folk in this city, John.'

Matilda's two weaknesses – apart from food and drink, which accounted for her heavy appearance – were fine clothes and social snobbery. As sister to the King's sheriff and wife to the King's coroner, she considered herself amongst the elite of the county hierarchy. It galled her to find that John had not the slightest interest in social advancement and she had to prod him mercilessly to take part in prestigious events in the city. The de Pridias family were rich merchants, Robert having been master of his guild, so his wife had been someone worth cultivating.

'Cecilia told me that de Hocforde had been

31

putting pressure on her husband to sell his mill. It seems that the affair was becoming quite oppressive and that Robert's health was suffering from it.'

This was quite different to the widow's claim that he was 'hale and hearty', thought John. Aloud he said, 'But that's a long way from murder by witchcraft, which she accused de Hocforde of perpetrating!'

He meant this to sound jocular, but Matilda's granite face showed no amusement. 'Never mock what you do not understand!' she snapped sententiously.

This surprised him, as Matilda was pathologically religious, spending half her waking hours at either the nearby cathedral or in St Olave's Church in Fore Street. Indeed, very recently, after he had offended her even more than usual, she had taken herself to Polsloe Priory, intending to take the veil – until she found that the poor food and dowdy raiment was not to her liking. For her now not to dismiss outright any un-Christian practices like witchcraft, seemed at variance with her faith – though on reflection he decided that after many centuries of acceptance, magic was so deeply ingrained in most people's minds that a veneer of religious belief was not sufficient to extinguish it.

Matilda demanded more details and he described the finding of the effigy under the dead man's saddle. 'Cecilia de Pridias was very loath to accept that his death was from some stroke seizing his heart, even though he had had these chest pains and had been attended by Walter Winstone for some time,' he concluded, determined to get his version of events firmly in place.

His wife glowered at him and sniffed her disdain. However, for once her scorn was not directed at John, but at the mention of the apothecary.

'A scoundrel, that man Winstone! I advised Cecilia to seek a better dispenser, such as Richard Lustcote. Winstone's reputation is dubious in the extreme. If he was supposed to be treating Robert, he made little success of it, if the poor man fell dead from his horse!'

John noted that Matilda's mental gymnastics had now allowed her to leave witchcraft in favour of the apothecary's medical negligence.

'So what will happen now?' she demanded, as Mary came in to start setting out their supper.

'Nothing, as far as I am concerned,' grunted John, fetching the wine jug to take to the table. 'A witnessed death from natural causes is no concern of a coroner, much as his widow might demand it.'

'I trust that you were considerate and civil to the poor woman, John,' grated Matilda, as she heaved herself from her chair.

'I was diplomacy itself, wife,' he replied coldly. 'Though no doubt she will voice her complaints to you in due course.'

The man and wife sat at opposite ends of the long table, perhaps symbolic of the emotional distance that separated them in life. Mary, their handsome cook and maid-of-all-work, brought in wooden platters of cold meats, which included the remains of the dinner-time goose and some slices of boiled ham. A few hard-boiled eggs and a dish of onions fried in butter completed the meal, apart from a dessert of fresh red plums. They ate their main meal at noon, but Matilda's robust appetite had expanded their supper repast beyond what most people ate in the evening. There was silence for a while as she got down to the serious business of eating and as soon as she had finished she left the table, muttering that she was retiring to the solar. This was the only other room in the house, built on to the upper part of the hall at the back, reached by outside stairs from the yard. As she lumbered into the vestibule, heading for the passageway, she started screeching for Lucille, her personal maid.

Sighing with relief, de Wolfe refilled his wine cup and went to sit by the hearth to fondle the ears of Brutus, who had slunk in when the mistress had left the hall. He listened to the familiar sounds that came faintly through a slit in the wall high up on one side of the chimney, where the solar communicated with the hall. His wife was chiding Lucille, a snivelling French girl from the Vexin, north of Rouen. The evening ritual of getting prepared for bed was being played out, with Matilda snapping at the maid for brushing her hair too roughly or being too clumsy in undressing her.

The coroner knew that all this would eventually subside, when his spouse would say her lengthy prayers before getting into bed. As soon as he decided that she was asleep, he would take Brutus for a walk – and it might just so happen that their feet might take them in the direction of the Bush tavern in Idle Lane.

The sun was setting as Henry de Hocforde strode along the upper part of High Street, away from his fine house in Raden Lane, near the East Gate. The rays reddened the buildings on each side as he walked almost directly towards the fiery orb, now low in the western sky. There were still many folk ambling along, gazing at the few stalls that remained open this late – and more than one drunk rolled out of an alehouse door into his path. But no one hesitated to get out of the way of this tall man as he stalked along with a face like thunder. Well dressed and with an arrogant swing to his shoulders, he was not a person to obstruct, especially as the ivory-headed staff that he carried looked as if it was more for use than ornament. As he reached the Guildhall, one of the city's finest buildings which had been rebuilt in stone not many years before, he turned right, then left again into Waterbeer Street, which ran behind the high street. It was an unsavoury lane, several low drinking dens and brothels doing nothing for its reputation. However, there were a few respectable houses and shops there as well and it was for one of these that he was aiming. Halfway down on the right was an old timber building, squeezed in between two newer dwellings in stone. It was narrow and roofed with wooden shingles, some of which were missing, thanks to a storm a month earlier. At street level, there was a door alongside a wide window, the shutter of which was hinged down at right angles to form a display counter for the apothecary's stock-in-trade. It carried a meagre array of pots and jars, the tops covered in parchment tied down with cord. In addition, there were a few crude glass vials of coloured liquid and some small bundles of dried herbs. Inside the window, the apothecary's apprentice, a runny-nosed lad of about twelve, sat rolling pills on a grooved board, keeping one eye on the counter to see that no light-fingered passer-by lifted any of the unimpressive items. De Hocforde marched through the door, dipping his head to avoid the low lintel. He glared at the boy and demanded to know where his master was.

'Out in the yard, sir. Hanging bunches of rosemary out to dry.'

Hocforde didn't care if Walter Winstone was hanging up his dirty hose to dry and rapped on the apprentice's pill-board with the head of his staff.

'Go and get him, boy. Quickly!'

The lad looked up at the imperious visitor and saw a stern face below dark hair shaven close around the sides and back, leaving a thick cap on top, in the style beloved of many aristocratic Normans. His dark red tunic was plain, but reeked of quality, as did the intricate silver buckle on a wide belt that carried a handsomely tooled leather pouch and an ornate dagger. He had seen him in the shop before, but did not know his name, as his master always took this customer upstairs for private consultation. The apprentice dropped his board and scurried away through a door at the back of the shop, leaving Henry to scowl at the musty shelves filled with earthenware pots of all sizes, many with crude Latin or alchemaic lettering painted on them. One wall was lined with ranks of small wooden drawers, again labelled with incomprehensible symbols. Hanging from the ceiling, from nails driven into the roof beams, were faded bunches of dried vegetation and some dusty, leathery objects that seemed to be desiccated lizards or snakes. A moment later, the boy hurried back and slipped hastily on to his stool to continue rolling his grimy pills.

'The master will be with you now, sir,' he piped, keeping his eyes down to appear industrious when Walter came in. The apothecary appeared in the dooway and bowed his head obsequiously to his visitor. He was a small man, with a marked limp in his left leg due to a childhood illness. A sallow face with projecting yellow teeth gave him the look of a large coney, an appearance that was strengthened by his large stuck-out ears. A frizz of short sandy hair was matched by a narrow beard that rimmed the edges of his face. He wore a nonde-script tan tunic over cross-gartered leggings, a long leather apron hanging from his neck. Walter opened his mouth to greet his esteemed customer, but Henry de Hocforde cut him short.

'Upstairs – now!' he snapped, crossing to the inner door and almost shoving the apothecary back through it. In the storeroom behind, there was a wide wooden ladder going up to the next floor and Winstone clambered up ahead of his visitor, apprehensive at his obvious ill temper.

At the top was a work-room, with benches where ointments and potions were made, and behind it were the apothecary's living quarters, a dismal room with a straw mattress on the floor in one corner and a table, stool and cooking utensils along the far wall. An unglazed window, its shutter half open, looked out on to a yard where more herbs were drying on lines stretched between poles.

Walter Winstone nervously indicated the stool, but de Hocforde ignored him and perched on the edge of a table, where he was still taller than the other man.

'I want to know why I wasted my money on you. In fact, I want it back, as you did nothing for me!'

The apothecary squirmed at the harsh, uncom-promising tone of the merchant. 'Give it time, master! I will devise some other means, never fear.'

Henry gave a humourless laugh, almost a bark. 'You haven't heard, then? You're too late, you useless worm. The man's dead!'

Walter gaped, then a false smile cracked his face, pushing his teeth even farther out. 'Then it did work! I told you to be patient.'

'No thanks to you, you charlatan! Fifteen shillings I've paid you altogether, over the past months – and for what?'

'But he's dead – which is what you wanted all along!' protested the smaller man. 'My tampering with his medicaments had the desired effect in the end.'

De Hocforde leaned forward threateningly. 'You're changing your tune now. The last time I was here, to complain that nothing had happened, you said you had stopped the poison, as it was without effect. You were working on something else. So how has he just died, when you ceased your efforts four weeks ago, eh?'

The apothecary wrung his hands in agitation. 'I told you, sir, this is a slow poison, it had to be to avoid any suspicion. Its action is cumulative. It continues to reside in the body long after the dosing has ceased.'

'Nonsense, man! The fellow stayed as fit as a fox after two months of your pathetic efforts.'

Winstone shook his head emphatically. 'Indeed not. I attended him weekly and he showed certain signs of the plumbism I was inducing. He had belly-ache and was almost totally costive – his wife told me that he spent hours in the privy with no result.'

Henry de Hocforde went red in the face. 'I don't

give a damn whether he could shite or not! I paid you to kill him and you failed dismally. So just give me back my fifteen shillings and I'll not darken your door again!'

Although Walter was a timid man, the thought of handing over a hundred and eighty silver pennies provoked some desperate defiance. 'So why then did he die, if it wasn't from my efforts?' he bleated.

'Because I took other measures, my patience with yours being exhausted!' hissed the fulling master. 'Last week I sought out a witch to place a curse on de Pridias – at a fraction of the cost that I wasted on you!'

Walter's watery eyes opened wide in astonishment. 'A curse? Surely you can't believe in that old witch's nonsense?'

'This old witch did the trick. This afternoon the fellow fell from his horse, stone dead !'

'Sheer coincidence. It was the long-term effect of my *Plumbium acetas*, without a shadow of doubt!' stammered the apothecary.

For answer, Henry held out his hand menacingly. 'My money– now!'

Walter Winstone backed away slightly, but his defiance remained, mixed with cunning. 'It would go ill with you if the news leaked out that you had done away with a rival merchant . . . all Exeter knows that you have been trying to wrest the ownership of his mill from him!'

De Hocforde's hand shot out and grabbed the smaller man by the shoulder. He dragged him close and bent so that his inflamed face was inches from the man's nose. 'You little rat! Who was it who had been feeding poison to the man for weeks? D'you think anyone would take you word against mine, you miserable little tyke? You'd hang from the gallows tree and I'd be there to see you off!'

He shoved the apothecary away and Walter staggered back and fell heavily against the far wall.

'Now give me that money – or you'll wake up one morning soon and find your throat's been cut! I know men in this city who'll kill for a shilling – a pity discretion stopped me from employing them on de Pridias.'

Defeated for now, the apothecary fumbled at his belt for some keys and went reluctantly towards a locked chest in the corner.

When John de Wolfe strode out into Martin's Lane with his hound, he had intended to go straight down to the Bush tavern, but he was accosted by a familiar figure as he entered the Close. As he began walking between the mounds and grave-pits of the burial ground towards the huge bulk of the cathedral, he saw a lean, cassocked figure approaching from the direction of the West Front.

It was John de Alençon, Archdeacon of Exeter, one of the four archdeacons who under Bishop Henry Marshal, administered the various parts of the large diocese of Devon and Cornwall. Though de Wolfe was by no means an enthusiastic church-goer, the two Johns were firm friends, their main

41

bond being mutual loyalty to King Richard and antipathy to his treacherous brother, Prince John, Count of Mortain.

The priest waved a greeting and the coroner waited for him to approach, as he was obviously heading for his dwelling in the row of canons' houses that formed the northern side of the cathedral Close. He was a thin man, not overly tall, but erect. Some years older than John, the shock of wiry hair that surrounded his shaven tonsure was iron grey. A bony, somewhat sad face was relieved by a pair of clear blue eyes, which twinkled as he grasped his friend's arm in greeting.

'Another fine evening, after all those terrible weeks of rain. Let's hope the harvest will be saved, God willing.' The words were spoken fervently, not as a casual remark. The awful growing season of that year might mean starvation for many next winter, unless the crops could revive within the next month. That the day was unusually hot was demonstrated by the absence of the archdeacon's hooded cloak, an almost obligatory part of a senior priest's outdoor dress.

'Come over for a cup of wine, John. I have some new Poiteau red I'd like you to try.'

John de Alençon was an ascetic man, unlike many of the twenty-four canons of the Exeter chapter, some of whom revelled in luxurious living. But his one weakness was fine wine, which he appreciated for its quality, rather than quantity.

The two Johns walked together through the mess

42

of the Close, weaving along paths of hardened mud between heaps of rubbish strewn among the graves. Beggars, cripples and drunks squatted on their haunches and pedlars rattled their trays at them as they passed. Urchins and louts ran across the resting-places of the dead, playing ball or tag and ignoring the screeches of protest from mothers and old crones when the infants in their charge were pushed over.

'This place is becoming a disgrace,' grumbled the coroner, glowering at the incongruity of these squalid acres, compared to the majesty of the cathedral that soared above them.

His friend agreed, with a sigh of frustration. 'With only a couple of men working under our proctors, it's impossible to control it. And it's the only open space in the city where the people can escape the squalor of the streets.' The cathedral Close was an enclave belonging solely to the Church, where only canon law applied, even the sheriff and coroner having no jurisdiction here, except along the main pathways.

They passed the treasurer's house, built against the north wall of the cathedral and reached Canons' Row, the narrow road that bounded the north side of the Close. There they made for one of the central houses of the dozen or so that stretched from St Martin's Church across to the city wall. It was an old two-storey structure of timber, with a thatched roof. A side passage went around the back, where the usual stable, kitchen-shed, privy, wash house and pigsty were set in a muddy yard, alongside a small area that the archdeacon kept as a private garden.

John commanded Brutus to wait outside as they went up to the iron-bound front door. They were met by John's steward-cum-bottler, one of only three servants that the austere priest employed. They went into his study, a small room on the ground floor, where de Alençon spent most of his time. A table, two stools and a low cot in one corner were the only furniture, apart from a large wooden crucifix on the wall. The rest of the house was occupied by his two vicars-choral, who deputised for him at some of the nine services each day – and several secondaries and choristers, young men who were prospective priests in training.

John waved his guest to one of the stools and sat on the other, pushing aside a pile of leather-bound books on the table to make way for a flask of wine and two goblets that his servant brought in. The goblets were another luxury, being of heavy glass, instead of the usual pottery or pewter. When they had sampled the French wine and commented on its taste, the archdeacon turned to current events, especially his friend's recent activities. He always seemed fascinated by the coroner's work and liked to be kept up to date with happenings outside his sheltered ecclesiastical world.

After relating a few tales about various inquests and cases at the last Shire Court, de Wolfe told him about the death of Robert de Pridias that day.

'I met him several times,' mused the canon. 'Both at guild feasts and when our treasurer purchased a large consignment of cloth for garments for our secondaries and servants. He had many weavers working for him, as well as his fulling mill, so he must have been quite a rich man.'

When the coroner told him of the widow's accusations against Henry de Hocforde – and the finding of the pierced effigy – de Alençon frowned. 'Defaming a man like that is unseemly, even allowing for the distress of a bereaved wife,' he said sadly. 'But this business of the straw figure is a sign of the Church's failure to banish magic from the common mind. I despair of ever completely wresting superstition from our flock.'

John gave one of his rare lopsided grins. 'Isn't religion just a different kind of superstition, John? We worship a God that none of us has ever seen and we revere his son who was a Jew living in a distant land a thousand years ago!'

If the archdeacon hadn't known his friend's penchant for teasing him on the subject of his faith, he would have been shocked – might even have accused him of heresy. As it was, he smiled gently.

'I know full well you don't mean that, John de Wolfe! But seriously, the efforts of priests like myself over centuries have only managed to lay a thin skin of Christianity over most of our population.'

He stopped to savour his wine, then continued. 'Many find it hard to distinguish between the

45

mysteries of the Holy Sacrament and the antics of the old wives and witches who cast spells for a wench to get a good husband or to make their neighbour's cattle fertile.'

'So you don't think that de Pridias was done to death by necromancy?' asked the coroner, half jokingly.

'It's too ridiculous even to contemplate,' said the archdeacon, rather sharply. 'You did right in refusing to pander to the woman's nonsense, though of course I'm sad for her in her loss, God rest his soul.' He made the sign of the Cross, reminding de Wolfe again of his own clerk's irritating habit.

'If the Church so disapproves of the widespread belief in magic and the casting of spells, why does it not proscribe it more severely?' asked John, the wine putting him in a ruminative mood. 'Your masters in Rome have always been quick enough to pounce drastically on any whisper of heresy or other activity which is not to their taste.'

De Alençon smiled wryly at his friend's deliberately provocative cynicism. 'That day may come, John, but at present we have more pressing enemies at the gates of God's kingdom, as you should well know, having been a Crusader yourself.'

The coroner continued to worry at the topic like a dog with a bone. 'But such widespread superstition surely cuts at the heart of your teachings that there is only one God. If he is the jealous God that the Scriptures describe to us, then should not his servants – the Church – be trampling these witches and wizards underfoot?'

The archdeacon, warming to a theological debate, raised his eyebrows at his friend. 'Where does all this philosophical talk come from, John? You always pretended to be a rough, blunt soldier. You must have been listening too much to that strange relative of mine.'

Thomas de Peyne, the coroner's clerk, was de Alençon's nephew and it was through his influence with de Wolfe that the disgraced little priest had at last been given a job. Once a teacher in the cathedral school at Winchester, he had been defrocked when a girl had accused him of interfering with her. Only 'benefit of clergy' had prevented him being hanged for attempted rape, but he had almost starved after being ejected from holy orders, until he walked all the way to Exeter to throw himself on his uncle's mercy.

De Wolfe drank the rest of his wine and refused another glass, as he intended drinking ale at the Bush. Before he left, he made one last assault on his friend's implacable faith.

'So you're not going to round up and hang all the cunning women in Devon? They can continue to compete with the bishop and all his minions in working miracles, without any challenge?'

The archdeacon prodded him hard in the chest with a finger. 'You're trying to provoke me, John. You must be short of other challenges this week.'

As they walked to the front door, the priest had

47

the last word. 'These old wives – though not so old, some of them – do little harm and quite a lot of good, John. Many folk cannot afford to visit an apothecary and, anyway, there are none to visit out in the countryside. Many a croup or constipation has been cured by their harmless herbal potions. And if people are gullible enough to pay a ha'penny for a spell to make their lover more potent or to get a better crop of beans, who are we to deny them?'

De Wolfe had to be satisfied with this moderate and civilised comment, and it gave him something to think about as he whistled for his dog and set off for the tavern.

The archdeacon's words were still on his mind when he reached Idle Lane, a short track joining Priest Street to the top of Stepcote Hill, which led down towards the West Gate. The name came from the waste ground that surrounded the alehouse – several years earlier, a fire had destroyed the surrounding wooden houses, leaving the stone-built inn standing, and as yet only weeds and bushes had reclaimed the scorched area.

He pushed open the front door, over which a large bundle of twigs hung from a bracket, perpetuating the old Roman sign for a tavern. The big room that occupied the whole ground floor was crowded with drinkers, this being a popular place, famed for its good ale, decent food and relatively clean mattresses in the loft. Thankfully, the warm summer evening did not require a fire in the large stone hearth against the end wall, which made the atmosphere redolent only of the smell of spilt ale, sweat and unwashed bodies, without the eye-watering swirl of wood smoke from the chimney-less fireplace. Benches around the walls and a few rough tables surrounded by stools formed the amenities for patrons, all set on a rush-covered earth floor. At least the rushes were clean, being replaced every few days – unlike in the nearest rival tavern, the notorious Saracen on Stepcote Hill, where the filthy straw was more a nest for rats than a floor-covering.

John advanced to his favourite place against a wattle screen set at the side of the hearth. A couple of young men seated at the small table immediately rose and, bobbing their heads in respect, found stools elsewhere. All the regulars at the Bush knew that this was the coroner's spot and yielded it to him with good grace.

He sat down and Brutus slid under the table after a longing look at two patrons opposite, who were sharing a pig's knuckle on a thick trencher of gravy-soaked stale bread. The old dog knew that with luck, the bone would come his way when they had finished.

De Wolfe settled his back against the screen and looked around contentedly. For once, his life was fairly stable. Matilda was her usual grumpy self, but was not in any particularly belligerent mood – at least, not until Cecilia de Pridias stirred her into action, as she surely would. His mistress was neither pregnant nor having another affair with a younger man and even Thomas seemed to have abandoned his efforts at suicide. Gwyn, of course, was the same as ever – gruff, amiable and constant in his fidelity.

Feeling at peace with himself, John looked around the crowded taproom, nodding to several aquaintances, who touched their foreheads in a respectful salute to a man almost everyone admired and not a few feared. As the second-most powerful law officer in the county, he was looked upon with some awe by many, yet most acknowledged him as a fair-minded man with an honourable record of serving their king in many a campaign, from Ireland to the Holy Land.

His eyes roved about, but he could not see Nesta, his beloved Welsh mistress. At the back of the chamber was a row of casks propped up on stands and wedges, from which old Edwin, the potman and one of the serving-maids, drew the ale and cider that had made this establishment famous in the city. As soon as Edwin's one remaining eye saw that the coroner had come in, he filled a clay quart pot from the barrel of 'best', and limped over with it, dragging his war-wounded leg through the rushes.

Banging the jar on the table, he beamed a crooked grin at John, the white of his dead eye rolling horribly, a legacy of a spear-thrust at the Battle of Wexford. He greeted John, using his old military title.

'Evening, Cap'n! The mistress is out in the brew-shed, stirring the mash. She'll be in shortly.'

Nesta was the genius behind the quality of the ale, having learned her trade in her native Gwent before moving to Devon some years before. She was the widow of Meredydd, a Welsh archer who had served under John, until they had both given up campaigning. He had bought the inn with his accumulated booty from years of warfare, but within twelve months was dead of the yellow jaundice, leaving his wife almost destitute with debt and with a tavern to run alone. De Wolfe had come to her rescue with a loan and gradually a business relationship had grown into affection and then love. It was no secret in the city, where most affluent men had a leman or two – and it was certainly no secret to Matilda, who bore the burden of his infidelity with abrasive ill grace, though she could not bring herself to abandon her marriage to such a senior member of the Norman hierarchy.

John took a deep draught of the ale, a slightly cloudy brew flavoured with oak galls, then stared again at the back of the taproom. A wide wooden ladder gave access to the upper floor, which was mainly an open loft where straw-filled pallets provided the accommodation for overnight lodgers. However, one corner had been partitioned off as a small bedroom for the landlady, in which John had installed a French bed, a novelty in a city where most folk, even the well-to-do, slept on a mattress at floor level. He had spent many a passionate hour in there and even a few nights, when either his boldness or circumstances allowed. Tonight was not going to be one of them, he mused ruefully, his eyes still roaming around for a sight of his mistress.

Eventually he was rewarded, at the same time as his hound was rewarded by the coveted knuckle-bone being thrown down into the rushes by the grinning pair on the next table. The back door of the inn opened and Nesta entered from the yard, where the cook-shed, the brew-house, the pigsty and the privy were situated. She shouted a last command over her shoulder at one of the maids, then scanned the room eagerly with her hazel eyes. When they lighted on John, her heart-shaped face lit up with delight and she hurried across to him, though not failing to give a smile and a touch on the shoulder to her favourite patrons as she went. De Wolfe's heart warmed as he watched her coming, yet part of his mind stood aloof and cynically asked why a middle-aged old soldier was acting like a callow lovesick youth, for at forty he was twelve years older than the ale-wife. Nesta came up to the table, gave him a quick peck on the cheek and slid on to the bench alongside him.

'And how is Sir Coroner this evening?' she asked softly, with her usual bantering affection.

'All the better for seeing you, *cariad*! And even better after a few mouthfuls of this good ale – you've excelled yourself with this last brew.'

They spoke in Welsh, her native language and

one that John had learned at his own mother's knee. Even Gwyn spoke it with them, as his own Cornish tongue was very similar – to the eternal annoyance of Thomas de Peyne, who came from Hampshire.

Nesta took a drink from John's pot and nodded her approval of her own handiwork, then they went on to speak lightly about the day's events and the increasing trade at the inn. Because of his financial stake in the Bush – though he took no profits from it – he was always interested in its fortunes. Lately it had been sharing in the increasing prosperity of the city, which because of the wool trade and the tin exports was going from strength to strength.

As she talked, he looked down at her, this petite woman coming only to his shoulder. Her light gown of pale yellow linen was tightly girdled at her waist, which emphasised her shapely breasts. A felt helmet, laced under the chin, failed to hide all the deep auburn curls that peeped out across her high forehead. Her large hazel eyes were set wide above a snub nose and when her slightly pouting lips parted, they revealed an almost perfect set of white teeth, unusual in a woman of twenty-eight.

John was totally entranced by her and, in spite of the vicissitudes that they had suffered in past months, he felt closer to her than ever before. They continued to talk for a few minutes, Brutus even forsaking his new bone to lay his slobbering mouth on the hessian apron that she wore over her kirtle.

Like Gwyn, she was fond of all animals and they responded in kind. Every few minutes, however, some minor crisis in the inn caused her jump up and go off to harangue either one of her serving maids or a customer who had become obstreperous. Even then her decisive voice and pithy commands avoided giving deep offence – John saw again how well she was suited to handling what could become a fraught or even violent situation.

He managed to decline her offer of another meal, having not long risen from his own supper table. As he drank a few more jugs of the weak liquor, John followed his usual practice of keeping her up to date with his cases, as not only was he flattered by her genuine interest, but sometimes both her common sense and her fund of local knowledge were helpful to him. The Bush, being the most popular inn in Exeter, accommodated a steady stream of travellers seeking a pallet in the loft and more than once, the gossip Nesta picked up from these, as well as from her regular customers, had been of considerable value in his investigations. He related the story of that day's excursion to Alphington and the death of Robert de Pridias.

'Did you know him at all, dear lady?' he asked.

Nesta shook her head. 'I think he frequented the New Inn, it was nearer his dwelling. But of course I know of him. He was a fuller and weaver, master of his guild.' She paused and looked thoughtful for a moment. 'I heard something else, too. Wasn't there bad blood between him and another fuller? I remember some of the weavers who come in here talking about it several weeks ago.'

'Henry de Hocforde, that would be. The widow is accusing him of murdering her husband by witchcraft!' John related the full story, ending by mockingly describing the pierced corn-dolly. He had expected Nesta to be amused, but she looked strangely serious.

'Don't dismiss it too easily, John. There are many things that defy explanation.'

'You sound like Matilda!' he said in a surprised tone. 'And even my friend the archdeacon declined to pour scorn on the possibility. Do you believe that these cunning folk have the power of life and death?'

'We are Celts, John, you and I. At least, your mother had a Welsh father and a Cornish mother. The tradition of spells and charms is strong amongst us, but even the pure English have plenty of faith in occult matters.'

He looked down at her curiously. This was the first time he had ever heard her speak of such things.

'This is what John of Alençon said, in different words. I had thought as a churchman he would have condemned all such beliefs out of hand, but he was remarkably tolerant of them. He said that the mass of our peasantry had little else to aid them when they were in trouble.'

Nesta pulled off her hot and restricting coif and shook out her luxuriant red hair, which fell to her shoulders.

'Where else can they turn, with little money and no apothecaries? The parish priests are often of little help. They are either drunks or corrupt or just plain ignorant.'

She glared at him almost defiantly, challenging him to contradict her.

'I seem to have touched a raw spot in you over this issue,' he said mildly.

'Maybe because I have a little talent in that direction myself,' she said unexpectedly. 'Not so much these days in the city, but when I was at home in Gwent, I did what I could to help those who needed it.'

De Wolfe was intrigued – this was something she had never mentioned before. 'You mean that you had some gift yourself?'

'It was nothing important, but my own mother had taught me a little about herbs and various means of treating small illnesses and other problems. She said that her mother and grandmother were quite notable healers in their day, so maybe it runs in families.'

'What kind of miracles did you perform?' he asked, half seriously.

Nesta pinched his arm, quite painfully. 'Don't mock me, Sir Crowner! Our little village had the same troubles as everywhere else. Sickness, palsies, fits and seizures . . . though probably there were more problems among the animals and crops. Pigs without litters, fields with strips where the oats always failed.'

She hesitated, her eyes seeing a scene a hundred miles and five years away. 'Then sometimes, a wife would want a man-child, or any child at all to please her husband – while another poor weak woman could not face being with child yet again. Those of us who had the gift tried to help. The village was like a big family, everyone did what they could.'

John nodded, although he could not fully appreciate what she was saying. Though he had been born and brought up in the Devon village of Stoke-in-Teignhead, he had been comfortably raised in the manor house that owned the village and most of the villagers, so his empathy with the lower reaches of the feudal system was limited.

'Do you still practise the black arts?' he said, trying to lighten the mood a little. Nesta gave him a ferocious scowl, which was not entirely feigned.

'There is black magic as well, John – be assured of that! But what village folk attempt to do against cruel nature is far from that. I have tried to help a few people here, yes. My maid's mother had a tumour on her neck two months ago, which I tried to assuage with poultices, a potion and a few charms.'

'Was it successful?' he asked, soberly now.

Nesta shook her head sadly 'She died three weeks past. There are many things that only God can deal with. Even an expensive apothecary or the monks at St John's could not have done anything for her.'

John had a niggling query, but it was a sensitive issue.

'Nesta, dear, when you were with child yourself not long ago, I know that you wished to be rid of it, mainly for my sake. Yet you went elsewhere for the purpose.'

She sighed and her eyes became moist. He kicked himself for his insensitivity in bringing it up, but Nesta seemed willing to explain.

'You cannot treat yourself, John. Much of the power is in the mind, not the herbs. You have to convince the other person that what needs to happen, will happen. You cannot do that to yourself. That is why I went to Bearded Lucy – not that she was successful.'

The woman that Nesta mentioned was an old crone who lived in a hovel on Exe Island and who had a wide reputation as a cunning woman.

De Wolfe felt that this conversation was taking a morbid turn and steered it away to other topics. He was helped by a sudden commotion at the back of the room, where stools were being thrown over and a fist fight had erupted between a pair of tinners who had drunk too much. Nesta streaked away to deal with it and with the help of Edwin and a couple of dependable customers, the most aggressive miscreant was manhandled out into the lane, Nesta's strident voice following him with pithy advice not to return until he was sober.

John grinned to himself, not intervening as

experience had told him that his mistress was more than capable of dealing with such episodes.

The dusk was now well advanced and after one more jug of ale, he kissed the landlady goodnight and with a last regretful look at the ladder to his French bed, called to Brutus and made his way home.

3

In which a new widow visits an old canon

Early the next morning, which was a Wednesday, Cecilia de Pridias forsook her usual church in Fore Street and walked to the cathedral. She went just before the eighth hour to attend prime, the third service of the episcopal day which began with Matins just after midnight. The new widow was swathed in a black mantle, secured at the shoulder with a circular silver brooch, the hood pulled up over the white cover-chief and wimple that enveloped her head. In spite of her sombre attire, her face bore a flinty expression that suggested determination rather than mourning.

Her daughter Avise and podgy son-in-law Roger trailed behind her as she climbed the steps of the West Front and entered the small entrance set in the massive doors, which were opened only on ceremonial occasions.

Inside, the huge nave was almost empty, the only sound apart from their feet on the flagstones being the chirruping of birds as they flew in and out of the unglazed windows high on the walls. Ahead in the distance was the pulpitum, the carved wooden choir-screen that seperated the priests from the common folk. It crossed the nave just before the two side chapels in the bases of the great square towers that formed the arms of the crucifix-shaped building.

Cecilia marched down the centre of the echoing nave, to where a dozen people, mostly women, stood a respectful distance in front of the ornate screen, between the two small altars of St Mary and St John the Baptist. The service was just starting, as with no clock nearer than Germany, everyone's time-keeping was approximate and the chanterel bell had started ringing before the de Pridias family had turned into Martin's Lane.

Beyond the screen, the prayers and chanting seemed remote to the small congregation, the clergy and their acolytes being seen and heard indistinctly through the intricate woodwork. This was a choral service, not a Mass and the priests were indifferent to the small audience outside. In the cathedral, the numerous daily offices were not primarily for the benefit of the public, but were held as perpetual acts of worship to God, offered by the complex hierarchy of canons, vicars and secondaries. The lay population was served by more than two dozen churches scattered around the city and it was a matter of indifference to the chapter of the cathedral whether anyone turned up to listen in the nave, other than on special days, when pomp and ceremony required an audience.

Prime droned on for about forty minutes, with psalms, chanting, prayers and responses being orchestrated beyond the choir-screen by the precentor and his assistant, the succentor. Some of the other people dropped to their knees on the cold stones at appropriate moments in the service, but devout as Cecilia was, she had no intention of prostrating herself on the grubby slabs in her best cloak. At St Olave's, she always took her own padded kneeler, but here she contented herself with a bowed head at the more solemn moments.

The formalities ended with a blessing given in high-pitched Latin by one of the archdeacons, after which the choristers, secondaries and priests processed out of their stalls and dispersed, most to get some refreshment before terce, the next service held at around the ninth hour. This was what Cecilia had been waiting for, and with Avise and Roger trailing behind, she went to the north side, where a passage went through to the crossing of the cathedral, at the base of one of the towers. A stream of boys and young men hurried past in their black cassocks, followed at a more sedate rate by their seniors, most draped in their cloaks as the heat of the day had not yet arrived. The lady stood respectfully with her head downcast, but her sharp eyes were scanning each figure as they emerged from the gloom behind the end of the screen. After a few moments, she saw the person for whom she had been lying in wait and moved forward towards him.

Canon Gilbert de Bosco was her cousin, though a dozen years older than her forty-five summers.

He had Cecilia's forceful manner which bordered on arrogance, probably inherited from their mutual grandfather, who had been a knight in the service of the first King Henry, before becoming embroiled in the civil war between Stephen and Matilda.

Gilbert was a large man and could have been a soldier like his ancestor, rather than a priest, as he was powerful and muscular, though good living was making him run to fat. A thick neck and a red face were topped by bristly hair of a sandy colour with still no grey to be seen. His fair colouring had made him prey to the recent scorching sun and his bald tonsure glowed like a brazier.

He was stalking along oblivious to his surroundings, his mind on a leisurely breakfast, as his vicar was standing in for him at all the later offices until the evening compline. The sudden touch on his arm jerked him into awareness and a scowl was hastily converted to a sympathetic smile when he saw it was his cousin Cecilia. Although they were by no means close, he had approved of his cousin marrying into money and kept on good terms with her and her husband, in case one day some useful legacy might come his way. He had heard of her husband's death only that morning and hastened to express his sympathy, clasping her hand and managing to look mournful.

'I was going to seek you out later today, dear cousin, to offer my deepest sympathy and to pray together for the repose of poor Robert's soul.'

His deep, booming voice managed to sound

totally sincere, as if his mind had been filled with sorrow, rather than the anticipation of breakfast.

The widow brusquely acknowledged his concern, then cut straight to the point. 'There are matters concerning his death which I must urgently discuss with you, Gilbert.'

His big face bent towards her and his rather watery blue eyes sought hers to exude commiserations. 'Of course, Cecilia, the funeral arrangements. Be assured that I will see to it that a requiem Mass will be conducted with all due dignity . . .'

She cut him off with an impatient shake of her head. 'I thank you, Gilbert, but my parish priest at St Olave's is seeing to that aspect. I need to talk to you of the manner of his death. Is there somewhere more fitting that we can go?'

Mystified and somewhat reluctant to get involved in something which might divert him from more lucrative pursuits, the benign smile on the priest's ruddy face faded somewhat.

'Manner of his death? What help could I possibly give you there?' he rumbled, lowering his voice as some of his colleagues were passing. They were looking curiously at the sight of their fellow canon with his head together with that of a well-dressed woman.

'I cannot speak of it in public, Gilbert,' said his cousin sharply.

He looked around the wide, cold nave and sighed. He had no wish to take her to his comfortable house in the Close, as it might interfere with his breakfast. In any event, women, apart from the odd washerwoman or skivvy, were banned from priests' lodgings – though this was a rule that was regularly ignored by some of his fellows.

'Very well, cousin, let us go back into the robing room. It will be empty now.'

For the first time, he seemed to become aware of the daughter and her husband, who stood indecisively behind Cecilia. With a grunted acknowledgement, he turned and led them back past the end of the choir-screen, where the last columns of the nave gave way to the massive buttress of the north tower. The high, square chamber at its base had a small altar at one side, dedicated to St Radegund, a sixth-century queen of the Franks, but opposite was a curtained-off area used by the clergy and their acolytes for changing vestments. Canon de Bosco stuck his head through a gap in the drapery to confirm that everyone had departed, then held it aside for the other three to enter. They stood in the centre and with the two younger persons hovering awkwardly behind her, Cecilia de Pridias fixed her cousin with a gimlet eye.

'My husband was done to death, Gilbert! I know how and I know by whom, but that stubborn coroner will not take me seriously.'

Initially reluctant to get involved, the canon's well-developed sense of self-advancement stirred within his brain. Although in late middle age, he was still ambitious and so far had climbed from being a lowly parish priest near Tavistock to attaining a coveted prebend near Crediton and thus becoming a canon of the cathedral. He still wanted to go farther and though he was realistic enough to know that a bishop's crozier was forever beyond his reach, he had his eye on one of the more senior posts in the chapter, preferably that of an archdeacon or treasurer, when one should fall vacant. His ears had pricked up at the mention of the coroner, as de Wolfe was well known as a zealous supporter of the King, whereas the bishop was well disposed towards Prince John. In fact, Henry Marshal, though brother to William, the Marshal of England, was well known to have been actively sympathetic to John's abortive rebellion when Richard Coeur-de-Lion was imprisoned in Germany. Gilbert de Bosco had no political leanings either way, but being associated with anything that confounded or discredited the coroner might improve his own standing with the bishop, which could do his hopes of advancement no harm at all. All this passed rapidly through the mind of the devious priest as he waited for his cousin to enlarge on de Wolfe's failings.

'He refused to investigate the death or even hold an inquest,' complained Cecilia. 'He treated my accusations with contempt, even in the face of the evidence!'

'And what was that, cousin?' Gilbert was now attentive and solicitous, the oil of self-interest lubricating his manner.

'You will have heard of the feud between my poor Robert and Henry de Hocforde, over Henry's desire to acquire our mill?'

The priest had heard no such thing, but he nodded sagely. He could soon catch up on the gossip, if needs be.

'Well, failing to persuade Robert to sell by legal means, he arranged for his assassination! But that fool coroner will have none of it.'

Gilbert's interest began to waver. If this silly woman had some obsession about a murder conspiracy that would lead nowhere, he wanted to keep well clear of it. But her next words reclaimed his attention immediately.

'He was done to death by witchcraft. An effigy was hidden under his saddle, with a spike through its heart!'

Ecclestiastical politics apart, Gilbert de Bosco had a deep, unshakeable devotion to Christianity and the doctrines of Rome, free from some of the doubts and crises of faith that were admitted to by some of his colleagues. One manifestation of this dedication to the Church was a fierce hatred of any competitor to Holy Writ. This included the manifold remnants of paganism and pantheism which pervaded the countryside, in spite of many centuries of Christian influence in the islands of Britain. In the years when he had been a village priest, his sermons had often contained vehement condemnations of the everyday practice of super-stition and rural magic, with demands to his flock to abandon the ancient customs of folk medicine, spell-casting and sooth-saying. The fact that his exhortations fell on the deaf ears of folk who had no alternative but to turn to their cunning men and women, did little to dampen his crusading efforts. Since he had moved to the city with its slightly more sophisticated community, his ardour had subsided, but now Cecilia's words ignited the slumbering embers into sudden flame.

'Witchcraft! Tell me more of this,' he commanded.

His cousin had little more to tell, but she repeated and embellished the few facts, then called her daughter and the abashed Roger forward to confirm her story, especially the discovery of the corn-dolly under her husband's saddlebag.

'Leave this with me, cousin,' he snapped, after some very quick thinking. 'I will look into this matter at once. The archdeacon should be told and perhaps even the bishop himself. When is the funeral to be held?'

Cecilia, gratified that her relative was taking this seriously, told him that Julian Fulk, the priest of St Olave's, was holding a service the next morning and after that, the burial would take place in the afternoon, following a Mass in the cathedral. As the family was relatively rich, they had bought the right to bury Robert under the flagstones at the back of the nave, rather than out in the chaos of the Close outside, where most of Exeter's dead had to be deposited. In spite of the multitude of churches in the city, none had the right to bury their parishioners; this was jealously guarded by the cathedral, which collected all the fees for the funeral formalities.

Gilbert de Bosco nodded sagely. 'As this is a family matter, I will deliver an oration at the requiem – and I will make sure that your concerns are voiced in the strongest terms.'

As well as his own genuine crusade against necromancy, he saw an opportunity to bring himself to prominence over this issue. It was a timely move, as one of the archdeacons was in poor health and there were rumours of his post soon falling vacant. Becoming a champion for the Church against what he considered the powers of darkness, should help to persuade the bishop and chapter to consider him more energetic and enthusiastic than the other twenty-three canons. The fact that he had not the slightest evidence that Robert de Pridias had died from anything other than a seizure or stroke hardly occurred to him, for he had the single-mindedness of an obsessive personality.

'I must go now, I have important business,' he said solemnly, thinking of his breakfast cooling on the table. 'I will take action this very day and see you at the sad occasion here tomorrow.'

He ushered them back into the nave and then hurried away importantly, leaving Cecilia well pleased with her morning's work.

For very different reasons, the apothecary Walter Winstone was even more opposed to the activities of cunning folk than was Canon Gilbert de Bosco. Still smarting from the pain of giving back the money to Henry de Hocforde, he marched around his shop that morning in a foul temper. The apprentice had already felt the rough edge of his tongue and the palm of his hand across his head. Sitting low over his pill-board, the lad was trying to look as inconspicuous as possible as Walter finally tore off his apron and went to the door.

'I'm off to Northgate Street to speak with Richard Lustcote,' he snarled. 'Behave yourself whilst I'm away or it'll be the worse for you.'

With this happy valediction he hurried away down Waterbeer Street, muttering curses under his breath at the idlers who got in his way. His oaths worsened as he dodged the contents of a chamber pot thrown from the window of a brothel, while he headed for the shop of his nearest colleague. It was a man he disliked, but at the moment he had need of him. There were four other apothecaries in Exeter, too few to have a proper guild, though they paid a small fee once each year to a visitor from London, who kept their names on the register of the Company of Apothecaries and brought any news concerning their craft. Walter was not an enthusiastic member and grudgingly attended their 'feast' each Easter, which, owing to their small number, was held in one room of the New Inn.

As the small man pattered testily towards the North Gate, he reflected on the reasons for his dislike of Richard Lustcote. They were mainly based on jealousy of the older man – his seniority in the craft, his long-established and more

70

successful business and his popularity with the townsfolk, mainly because of his pleasant nature. Although their rudimentary guild had no warden, Lustcote was looked on by the other apothecaries – and by the populace – as the father figure of the healing art in Exeter. There was no secular physician nearer than Winchester, and as monks and nuns provided all that was available in the way of hospital care, the apothecaries dispensed medicines and visited the paying sick in their homes. This function they jealously guarded, as it was their livelihood. Now Walter felt threatened – cunning women not only competed with his healing herbals, but were usurping his illegal trade in surreptitious poisonings and abortions.

His hurrying feet had taken him around the corner and on towards the North Gate in the city walls, where the road went out towards Crediton. The buildings lining the narrow street were the usual mixture of styles in this thriving city. New houses were being squeezed between the old, taking over garden plots and progressively replacing the ancient timbered structures with stone. There was a whole range of roofing, from mouldering thatch through wooden shingles to thick tiles. The height and width of every dwelling were different and some projected over the road as new-fangled solars became the fashion. One thing that did not change was the smell – the packed-earth street had a central gutter of crude stones, down which a stream of filth oozed towards a conduit alongside the gate, which was

71

downhill from Carfoix, the central crossroads of the city. As Walter walked along, he unthinkingly avoided the stinking trench, keeping away from both the middle of the road and the edges, where the perils of waste water – and worse – thrown from doorways and windows were another hazard. However, he reached Lustcote's shop without undue soiling and pushed aside the thick leather flap that hung over the doorway. The establishment was twice the size of his own, with display shutters lowered from windows on either side of the central door. The interior was roomy and no fewer than three apprentices sat working behind counters, one of them dealing with a pair of matrons who were seeking relief for their aching joints. Apart from its size and tidier appearance, the place was very similar to Walter's – and almost every other apothecary's shop in England – but he still felt envy creeping over him as he asked one of the young men for his master.

'In the store behind, sir,' was the reply. The lad knew Walter by sight and reputation, though he was an infrequent visitor.

The room behind the shop was again similar to his own, but much larger. Here he found Richard Lustcote hunched over a small charcoal stove, boiling a copper pan containing a quart of some liquid that smelled strongly of vinegar. He was a round, chubby man with white hair that hung down to the collar of his green tunic, over which was a tabard of thin leather, stained with several years' worth of splashed medicines. His amiable face smiled a greeting, which was not something that the miserable Walter Winstone often received. After a guarded conversation, mainly about the novel brew that Richard was preparing as a treatment for dropsy of the legs, Walter came to the substance of his visit.

'This is a guild matter, Richard and you are the acknowledged leader of our small band here in Devon. We need to be united on this, as it affects our trade and our purses.'

The old apothecary moved his pan from the trivet over the glowing embers and looked quizzically at his visitor. 'Do you wish us all to raise our prices?'

Walter shook his head irritably. 'Nothing like that. I am talking about competition – and unqualified competition at that. It's not only against the interests of our guild, but dangerous to the public.'

Richard looked uncomprehendingly at Winstone. Not for the first time, he considered him to be a strange man – resentful, ungrateful and envious. He had never heard anything against his ability as an apothecary, but he was certainly not a personable character. No wonder he was unmarried and lived in rather squalid loneliness over his shop, even though he could obviously afford better. He had arrived in Exeter about seven years ago, from Southampton, so it was said, but no one knew anything about him before that. The guild-man from London said that he had not previously been registered with the Company of Apothecaries in Southampton and had told him some vague story about having served his apprenticeship in Brittany. The older apothecary waited for some fuller explanation, which tumbled from Walter's lips as bitter as the vinegar that simmered on the stove.

'These self-appointed healers are meddling more and more in our business,' he complained. 'Most are what we know as "cunning women", though there are some men as well. I have lost customers to them and that means money lost. They charge far less, but provide nothing but ridiculous charms and spells, which are nothing more than attempts at magic.'

Richard Lustcote smiled indulgently. 'Many of the things that we sell are little more than attempts at magic, brother! We rely heavily on the faith our customers have in us, so that they feel we are doing them good. In reality, we keep them occupied while we wait in hope that God and time will alleviate their sicknesses.'

Walter Winstone looked shocked at this cynical, if realistic view of their noble craft. 'You cannot really believe that, Richard!' he brayed. 'We have been trained and have studied the precepts of others learned in the art, from Galen onwards. These interfering impostors are charlatans, casting their spells and gibberish, little better than witches!'

His indignation made him gabble and flecks of spittle appeared at the corners of his mouth.

Lustcote tried to soothe him a little. 'Come now, Walter, there is room for all in trying to do good for the sick and distressed. We have no quarrel with the monks at St John's Hospital and St Nicholas – nor with the good sisters at Polsloe Priory. Beyond a few miles from our city walls, we have no patients – and they have no apothecaries, so they must fend as best they can. Name me a hamlet between here and Totnes or Tiverton that boasts an apothecary's shop?'

Winstone would have none of this argument. 'I give not a fig for those peasants in far-flung villages. I am concerned with this city and the few miles around it, where we are increasingly losing business to what is little better than irreligious witchcraft! It is a danger not only to us, but to the sufferers, who are exposed not only to God knows what harmful potions, but to forces of the Devil, which is what some of these harridans rely upon.'

His eloquence deafened the sound of his own hypocrisy, considering that he had been feeding Robert de Pridias the poisonous sugar-of-lead for weeks on the pretext of treating the ache in his chest.

They argued the matter for some minutes, although Robert turned back to his copper dish, which had gone off the boil, while they spoke. He was a mild-mannered man and played down Walter's fears, saying that he had not noticed any falling-off of his trade. Furthermore, he thought that the clientele that could afford the services of an apothecary, was generally unlikely to seek the more dubious offerings of cunning women.

However, his colleague from Waterbeer Street continued to rant about the iniquities of common good-wives interfering in their noble profession. 'It should be a matter for the law!' he snapped. 'The guilds were strengthened by old King Henry and they should be looked on as a monopoly, exclusive to those trained in the art. Think what would happen if some damned peasant masquerading as a mason came and offered to build a cathedral on the cheap! Or a goldsmith or draper usurping the established companies. There would be a riot and the guilds would drag such an impostor away and hang him! So why should we be different, just because we purvey medicinal knowledge, rather than stones or gold rings?'

The even-minded Richard had to admit to some logic in this and finally he reluctantly agreed to bring the matter up at the meeting of their tiny guild to be held the following week – and also to discuss it with one of the portreeves. These were the two prominent burgesses who ran the city council, though there was talk of replacing them with a mayor, a new idea imported from the Continent, which had already been adopted in London four years earlier. Both of them were wardens of their own guilds and were knowledgeable about such matters.

With that Winstone had to be satisfied and he eventually left, still muttering under his breath about unfair competition.

Later that morning, a pale-faced young woman turned off Fore Street, just down the hill from the

Carfoix crossing. She entered a short lane called Milk Street, which crossed the head of Smythen Street, noisy with the banging and hammering of the smiths' forges. There was no mystery about the name of Milk Street, as the dozen huts and cottages were almost all occupied by dairiers, purveyors of milk and cream. Halfway along, she hesitantly approached a lopsided hut of wattle and daub, crowned with a tattered thatch roof. In the dozen square yards of dung-strewn earth that formed the front yard, she saw a patient donkey chewing on a pile of cut grass, with two large churns slung across its back, formed of dented and tarnished copper. They were empty now, but the handles of two ladles stuck out of each container.

The young woman, dressed simply in a patched linen kirtle bleached by innumerable washings, had her hair swathed in the usual linen head-rail, tucked closely around her face and under her chin. She appeared nervous as she went up to the open door in front of the windowless shack and tapped on the scarred boards, the bottom few inches of which were frayed with dry rot.

There was no response from the dark interior and after a few moments she plucked up enough courage to walk around the back of the dwelling. Here she found a larger yard backing on to the buildings at the upper end of Southgate Street. Although in the centre of one of England's major cities, it seemed full of cows, bony dun-coloured beasts with great udders. There were at least eight of them filling the small area, tethered by ropes to a ramshackle fence, munching away like the donkey at piles of freshly cut green grass. Beyond the side fences, the visitor could see similar groups of cows in the adjacent properties.

In the middle of the yard, squatting on a tiny stool, was an elderly woman, pumping away at a cow's teats as she directed a stream of warm milk into a leather bucket gripped between her knees, her head jammed against the beast's flanks. Alongside, a small calf cowered against its mother's legs.

The new arrival watched for a few moments, fascinated in spite of her own troubles by the almost artistic flourish of the milker's hands, as the little fingers spread upwards and outwards at every stroke.

The jets from the udder gradually diminished and with a grunt, the old lady pushed back her stool and stood up, becoming aware of the spectator.

'Looking for me, dear?' Her sharp eyes peered out from beneath the grimy helmet of felt that covered her head, its front soiled from rubbing against her cows.

'If you be Avelina Sprot,' answered the woman, diffidently.

The good-wife nodded, then pointed to the bucket half full of milk that she had in her other hand. 'Let me just give this to the orphan first.'

She waddled bent-backed across the yard and

poured the milk into a trough made from a hollowed-out log, placed in front of another, larger calf tied to the fence.

'Primrose has too much milk, she needs some taking off her that her own babe can't drink. This one needs it more, since its mother died.'

She came back towards the hut and dropped the bucket, motioning the woman to come to the back door of the cottage. As they went into the dark interior, Avelina asked what had brought her visitor here. 'Is it the usual, my girl?'

The meaning was clear, but Gertrude shook her head, two spots of colour appearing on her pale face. 'It is quite the opposite, good dame.'

When her eyes grew more accustomed to the dimness after the bright summer sun outside, she saw that there was just one room beneath the thatched roof. A wicker screen partitioned off one end, where straw mattresses lay on the floor. The other part was occupied by a circular fire-pit in the centre, ringed with stones embedded in dried clay. Beyond this was a wide wooden tray on legs, filled with milk which was settling so that the cream could be skimmed off.

'Sit down there, girl, you look fragile. Your blood is obviously thin.'

Avelina pointed to a low bench near the fire-pit and when Gertrude was seated, she squatted on her haunches opposite. 'So you don't need to bring on your monthly courses?' she said bluntly.

The younger woman, who looked about twenty

79

years old, shrugged. 'Yes, I do – but not because I'm with child.'

Avelina frowned as she scratched at her left armpit, where a flea was biting her. 'You wish to have a child, is that it?'

Gertrude hesitantly explained her problem. 'I have three children already – and have lost two more by miscarriage. But all of them were girls – and my husband is becoming impatient for a son to carry on his business, as he is a master carpenter. He has a workshop near St Nicholas' Priory.'

Avelina began to understand. 'You wish to conceive a boy? Well, maybe the next one will be.'

Gertrude shook her head. 'I was married at fourteen and have been pregnant every year until last year. Now I have seen no monthly flow since last Advent, yet I am not with child. My courses have dried up and I cannot conceive.'

'Do you wish to become gravid again?' asked Mistress Sprot, almost aggressively. These poor girls were like her cows outside, never free from either pregnancy or lactation.

'Only if it would be a male child,' Gertrude said softly. 'Else my husband would be very angry. And he is a big, strong man.'

The older woman took her meaning and looked covertly at Gertrude's face for signs of bruising.

'I was told that you were a wise woman, expert in these matters, so I have come to you. I have very little money, but can give you what I have.'

Avelina shrugged as if to dismiss the idea of a

fee, then leaned forward and, with a dirty finger, pulled down one of Gertrude's lower eyelids. 'You are as pale as death, girl!' she exclaimed. 'Do you eat well – or give it all to your big husband?'

'We have three hungry girls as well and this year has been a very bad one, for carpenters as well as those who live off the land.'

The cunning woman wagged a finger at Gertrude. 'Tell your man that if he wants a son, he must stop eating all the meat himself. You need blood to start your courses, you have drained yourself with five pregnancies.'

'I need a son, not just another child,' countered the woman, with a trace of desperation in her voice.

Avelina hauled herself to her feet and went over to a wall, where several crude shelves were fixed above a table that carried a pestle and mortar, together with a couple of pewter dishes. Now that her eyes could see better, Gertrude noticed that many bunches of dried vegetation hung from the roof beams and that the shelves were filled with pots and packets of all shapes and sizes.

'Take one of these every morning with a mug of small ale,' Avelina commanded, offering a small packet wrapped in a scrap of parchment, tied with twine.

'Will they induce a boy-child?

'Not at all, but they may persuade your courses to return, without which you'll not give birth to as much as a mouse, let alone a boy-child. They are for thickening the blood.'

Gertrude's face fell. 'Is there nothing else you can do for me?' she asked plaintively.

Avelina clucked her tongue. 'Patience, girl, patience! Listen while I tell you what to do.'

Ten minutes later, Gertrude came out of the cottage with a smile on her face, one hand clutching the cloth purse which hung from her girdle, making sure that the collection of herbs and oddments it contained were safe. The three pence that she had saved from her housekeeping were now in a stone jar on Avelina's shelf, but the young woman considered that it had been money well spent.

Up at the top end of the city, the county court was in session within the walls of Rougemont Castle. Often known as either the Shire Court or the Sheriff's Court, it was held once a fortnight and usually lasted at least a whole day. However, this August session was quieter than usual, which John de Wolfe attributed to the previous weeks of bad weather, which had slowed down most outside activities and reduced the number of people travelling, giving less opportunity for robberies and assaults.

He sat in his usual place on the low dais at the end of the bare hall, which lay inside the inner ward of the castle. The coroner was obliged to attend every session, to record any matters which had a bearing on cases that might go to the royal courts – and to present various matters to the sheriff, who now sat in the only decent chair in the middle of the platform. To either side were a few benches and stools, on which sat a representative of the Church and one of the more prominent burgesses of the city. A couple of trestle tables gave writing space for the clerks and, at one of these, Thomas de Peyne was perched. His parchments were spread out before him and his quill waggled furiously as he inscribed them with his impeccable Latin. Farther back, Gwyn of Polruan stood gossiping in a low voice with his friend Gabriel, the sergeant of the garrison's soldiers.

Today's token priest was Brother Rufus, the portly monk who was the castle's chaplain, who now seemed be dozing on his stool in the heat of late morning. On the other side of the sheriff from the coroner was Ralph Morin, the Viking-like constable of Rougemont – another friend of de Wolfe and a covert antagonist of Sheriff Richard de Revelle.

The latter was posturing in his chair, showing off his latest costume, which he had bought on his last visit to Winchester. The dapper guardian of Devonshire wore a long tunic of bright green linen, with gold embroidery around the neck and hem, which was slit back and front for riding a horse. A loose surcoat of fawn silk was kept open to display his splendid new tunic and a wide leather belt, secured by a large burnished buckle. His feet were encased in soft calf-length boots with ridiculously long, curled toes, padded inside with teased wool – and at the other end of his slim body, a pointed beard had been freshly trimmed and perfumed. Above it, his narrow, foxy face sneered out at the world, especially despising the accused and supplicant folk that were paraded in front of the judgement seat.

'How many more this morning?' he snapped in an aside to his senior clerk, who hovered just behind him.

'Just a few, sire. We should finish by dinner-time today, no more this afternoon.'

Richard sighed with relief. It was hot and he was looking forward to a jug of Anjou wine and the dishes of grilled fish and cold pork that awaited him in his chambers in the keep. He dragged his attention back to the next case, as two men-at-arms thrust forward a sullen youth to stand before him on the beaten earth below the dais. He was dressed in filthy rags and had blue and yellow bruises all down one side of his face, a legacy of two weeks in the burgesses' prison in one of the towers of the South Gate. Of those confined there awaiting trial or execution, a sizeable proportion died of disease or from assault by other prisoners – though quite a few managed to bribe the warders and escape.

The chief clerk stepped forward with the ends of a parchment roll grasped in each hand. He read out the details of the youth's case, as a shifting audience of a score of citizens and peasants listened from where they stood at the back of the barren chamber.

'This is Stephen Aethelard, an outlaw. He was

recognised as such in the vill of Dunstone, and captured by the men of that place.'

The man glowered up at the sheriff, who turned languidly to his brother-in-law.

'John, have you details of the exigent?'

The coroner stood, unwinding his tall body from his stool and reaching back to take a roll from Thomas, who had it ready to hand to him. He opened it, but did not look at it, as he was unable to read more than a few simple words, laboriously learned from his tutor in the cathedral. However, Thomas had primed him beforehand about the essential facts.

'This man lived in the said Dunstone and was appealed by John de Witefeld for breaking into his house, stealing fifteen shillings and assaulting his daughter Edith on the eve of the Feast of St Michael and All Angels last September. Attached by two sureties to attend this court, he made himself scarce and did not answer. His name was called at the four subsequent sittings of this court, but he still did not answer and was declared exigent on the fifth day of November last.'

He sat down and handed the roll back to Thomas. The sheriff sighed to express his boredom and looked down at the bedraggled figure below him. 'Have you anything to say for yourself, fellow?'

The bruised face rose briefly. 'Whatever I say will be of no account. But I did not harm that girl.'

'Did you steal that money?' asked John, more out of curiosity than for anything relevant.

'That's never been proved,' said Aethelard sullenly.

'Because you never showed up in court to plead your innocence,' observed the coroner.

'Stop wasting my time!' cut in the sheriff irritably. 'It's of no interest to me whether you were guilty or not. You were legally declared outlaw and now you have been recaptured. The only penalty for that is death! It would have saved the time of the court – and my patience – if someone had seen fit to cut off your head at the roadside!' His stomach rumbled to remind him of dinner-time. 'Take him away and hang him tomorrow. Bring in the next case.'

Half an hour later, John de Wolfe sat down at his own table, having forgotten all about Stephen Aethelard, although he would see him again briefly the next day, when he was pushed off a ladder at the gallows, with a rope around his neck – one of six hangings scheduled for the Thursday executions. Even then, the outlaw would be of little concern to the coroner, as he had no land nor chattels for him to confiscate for the royal treasury, which was the main purpose of the coroner's attendance at the gallows-beam on Magdalen Street, out of the city towards Heavitree.

De Wolfe had dismissed the youth from his mind and was concentrating on the mutton stew that Mary had set before them. It was too liquid to be served on trenchers of bread, so they had wooden bowls and horn spoons, with small loaves alongside. A large jug of ale stood between John and his wife, who sat at either end of the oaken table and Mary bustled in frequently to ladle more stew into their bowls and to refill their pottery mugs from the jug. As usual, the meal was a silent occasion, apart from the slurping of the stew, especially from Matilda's end, as she was a voracious eater. When they had eaten their fill, Mary appeared with a slab of hard yellow cheese to accompany the remainder of the bread. John hacked some slices off with his dagger and Mary carried the platter up to her mistress. When she left, de Wolfe tried to start up some conversation to break the strained silence.

'I hear that the funeral Mass of Robert de Pridias will take place tomorrow afternoon.' He chose something to do with the Church to catch her attention.

Her face lifted towards him and he waited until her jaws had finished champing the hard bread. Though she still had most of her front teeth, albeit yellowed, most of her molars had either crumbled or had been wrenched out by the itinerant tooth-puller.

'I know that. I shall be there to support poor Cecilia. But we also have a private memorial service in St Olave's beforehand – the widow was a faithful attender there, though like you, Robert himself came but seldom.'

She managed to squeeze a reprimand even out of a stranger's death, thought John sourly. He waited for the expected complaint about his failure to hold an inquest and was not disappointed.

'My poor friend tells me that you were less than helpful yesterday, when she called you, John.' Her eyes were like gimlets and her lips like a rat-trap, he thought, as she glowered at him down the length of the table.

'There was no call to do otherwise! The man was seen to clutch his chest and fall dead across his horse.'

'You know of the feud between de Hocforde and Robert. Could you not take it more seriously?'

'I didn't know then. But it would have made no difference, the law is not for giving credence to old wives' tales.'

As the words left his lips, he knew he had said the wrong thing.

'Old wives, are we? I'm glad I know what you think of me. No wonder you go chasing young whores, Welsh or otherwise.'

Her chair grated on the flagstones as she stood up. With a glare that should have turned him to a pillar of salt, she swept out of the room, slamming the door behind her.

The old hound, lying near the empty hearth, showed the whites of his eyes as he looked mournfully up at his master. John got up and took his mug of ale to his favourite seat alongside the fireplace, bending to fondle the dog's soft ears. 'She'll be in a foul mood until tomorrow, Brutus. But a good requiem Mass will cheer her up again, never fear.'

★   ★   ★

The coroner dozed for an hour, seduced by the oppressive heat and humidity that penetrated even the dank hall of his gloomy house. Although the sun still beat down from a pale blue sky, a bank of cloud was building up on the western horizon and a distant rumble of thunder threatened the return of the rain that had plagued the country all summer. Mary let him sleep as she quietly removed the debris of the meal, but by the middle of the afternoon he roused himself and stretched his arms above his head, feeling his undershirt sticking to his back with sweat. Although all he wore over it was his usual drab grey tunic with no surcoat, it was still uncomfortably hot. He had even forsaken his long hose in favour of knee-length stockings and, like everyone else, wore no undergarments on the lower part of his body, yet still felt as uncomfortable as he had been in the heat of Palestine.

He walked around to the back yard and relieved himself against the fence, as in this hot weather the privy stank so much that even his insensitive nose baulked at going inside.

'When is the night-soil man due to shovel this place out?' he called across to Mary, who was washing a pan in a bucket of murky water hauled from the well in the middle of the yard.

'He's two days late – everyone is having their privies and middens cleared more often in this heat.' She tipped the dirty water on to the ground and dropped the leather bucket back down the well. 'We need some rain again soon to bring the water level up, there's little better than mud in it now.'

They stood together to look down the narrow shaft and John, after a quick look up at the stairs to Matilda's solar, slid an arm around the maid's waist. They had had many a tumble in the past, but the handsome woman, a by-blow of an unknown Norman soldier and her Saxon mother, had recently refused him, being wary of Matilda's suspicions, strengthened since the nosy body-maid Lucille had arrived to spy on them.

Now Mary smiled and twisted away from him. 'What would your mistress Nesta do, sir, if she saw you? To say nothing of your wife – and the pretty woman from Dawlish?'

The mention of John's other paramour down at the coast was enough to make him grin sheepishly. His childhood sweetheart Hilda was now married, but that had not stopped them from an occasional bout of passion when it could be managed. As Mary went back to her kitchen-shed, where she not only cooked, but slept on a pallet in the corner, John was aware of a distant crash as his front door slammed shut. Heavy footsteps followed and Gwyn hurried out of the narrow passage at the side of the house. His dishevelled ginger hair was wilder than usual and the armpits of his short worsted tunic were dark with sweat, as he had been trotting across the city in the sultry heat.

'Crowner, d'you recall that outlaw in the court this morning – the one the sheriff sent to be hanged?'

John stared at his perspiring officer – it was unlike the normally imperturbable Gwyn to exert himself, unless there was a fight on offer.

'What about him? Has he cut his own throat to cheat the gallows?'

'No, he's done better than that. He's escaped from the South Gate and he's gained sanctuary. He's calling for the coroner to take his confession so that he can abjure the realm.'

De Wolfe's hawkish face creased in doubt. 'I'm not sure an outlaw can do that,' he growled.

'Don't see why not. Convicted felons can seek sanctuary,' objected the Cornishman.

John rubbed his black stubble, a mannerism he had as an aid to thought, just as Gwyn scratched his crotch and Thomas made the sign of the Cross. 'True. I know nothing against it, though I've never heard of it being done before.'

'The sheriff will be against it, so soon after sentencing the fellow to death!' observed Gwyn, craftily.

His master took the bait immediately. 'Then that's a good reason for me to grant it! Where has he taken refuge?'

Gwyn grinned impishly. 'You'll like this, Crowner. He ran straight to St Olave's!'

John burst out laughing, a rare phenomenon for the dour knight. 'God's guts, man, my wife will have a fit!' Then he quickly sobered up, giving another anxious glance up the steep stairs to Matilda's solar, as a new thought occurred to him. 'There's to be a special service there tomorrow, for Robert de Pridias. My wife will be in a frenzy if she finds some ruffian clinging on to the altar cloth – or if we have to lay siege to the building to keep him inside. And it'll be all my fault, no doubt!'

'If we hurry, maybe we can get rid of him before then,' suggested the ever-practical Gwyn. It was a faint hope, considering all the legalistic ritual that went with abjuration of the realm, but the sooner they started, the better.

The pair hurried out into Martin's Lane and down the high street towards the tiny church dedicated to St Olave, the first Christian king of Norway, where Gwyn said that he had told their clerk Thomas to meet them. De Wolfe had recently had some acrimonious dealings with its priest, Julian Fulk, which had not endeared him to his wife, who revered the man only slightly less than the Pope or Bishop Henry Marshal.

Outside the door, which opened directly on to Fore Street, they found a small crowd gawping at the unexpected drama that had enlivened their afternoon.

Blocking the door was one of the two city constables, a bean-pole of a Saxon named Osric. Alongside him was Thomas de Peyne, Gabriel, the grizzled sergeant of the castle guard and two of the gaolers from the burgesses' prison, from where the outlaw had escaped.

The crowd, a score of old men, grandmothers, urchins and cripples who had little else to divert them, parted to let the coroner and his officer through.

'It's that fellow Stephen Aethelard,' grunted Gabriel. 'I'll wager he had the gaolers bribed, though these fellows deny it.' He jerked his head at the two warders, brutish men with short necks and glowering expressions.

'Weren't us, Crowner,' grunted one of them. 'We only came on duty an hour ago and when we checked on who was being hanged tomorrow, this bastard was missing.'

'And as usual, nobody knew nothing about it!' added the other.

John ignored them and went through the small door into the church, Gwyn close behind. Thomas bobbed his knee and crossed himself repeatedly as soon as he entered this diminutive house of God. St Olave's was little more than a large room, with a tiny chancel at the far end. This contained an altar, covered in an embroidered white cloth on which were a metal cross and candlesticks.

It now also contained a sanctuary-seeker, who looked even more scruffy that he had in the Shire Court that morning. Stephen Aethelard was sitting dejectedly on the step below the altar, staring at the floor and scratching at some sores on the side of his neck. Halfway down the nave, the resident priest, Julian Fulk, was standing with his back to the door, glaring at the intruder with a marked lack of Christian compassion.

'Let's get this over with,' snapped John, after taking in the scene.

'Be a damned sight easier just to let the fellow run back to his forest where he came from, to save all this rigmarole of abjuring,' growled Gwyn.

Though privately he may have agreed, the coroner was a stickler for the law and shook his head. 'It must be done properly – the quicker the better.'

He moved into the body of the church, which had the luxury of a paved floor and the sound of his footsteps caused Fulk to swing around. He was a short, rotund man in early middle age, without a clerk's tonsure, for he was as bald as an egg. His round face with its waxy complexion usually bore a fixed smile, but today he looked anything but pleased. 'Ah, Sir John, I'm very pleased to see you. This fellow has lodged himself in my chancel at a most inconvenient time.'

Julian was nominally the coroner's own parish priest, as it was to St Olave's that Matilda dragged him about once a month. He was a reluctant worshipper, to say the least, as although actual atheism had never occurred to him, he found the rituals of the Church dull and meaningless.

'I have heard that you have a service for Robert de Pridias here tomorrow,' he responded. 'I will do my best to get the fellow out of here before then, but it cannot be earlier than the morning – assuming that he collaborates.'

94

Leaving Fulk standing forlornly in his bulging black cassock, the coroner loped down towards the chancel, Gwyn and Gabriel following behind.

The fugitive had by now clambered to his feet and groped behind him to put one dirty hand on the altar, causing the priest to cluck with annoyance at the soiling of the fine lace cloth worked by one of the richer ladies in his congregation. Fulk assiduously cultivated the wives of burgesses and knights with his obsequious manner and false smiles, which was the main attraction of the place for Matilda de Wolfe.

'You needn't grab the altar, fellow,' snapped John. 'The whole church is a sanctuary – the churchyard would be equally safe, if there was one.' St Olave's, like many of more than two dozen city churches in Exeter, was built directly on to the street and had no land around it all.

'You were in the court this morning,' said the outlaw, in a coarsely aggressive voice. 'But you can't throw me out, I know my rights!'

John gave him a twisted smile. 'As an outlaw, you don't have any rights! That's what the name means, you don't exist in the eyes of the law. I'm not even sure you can claim sanctuary. I could probably drag you out now and get my officer to cut off your miserable head!'

Gwyn leered happily at this, and rattled his huge sword ominously in its scabbard. 'Right, Crowner, I could use the five shillings' bounty!'

Both of them knew that they were play-acting,

but felt that this man should suffer some grief for the nuisance he was causing.

'If you want to abjure – assuming I agree – then you will have to confess your guilt,' grated de Wolfe.

'How can I confess to something I didn't do?' objected Stephen, running thick fingers through his matted hair.

The coroner shrugged. 'Please yourself, man. Either confess or stay in here for the allotted forty days and then be slain.'

There was a howl of protest from Julian Fulk, who had padded up to the chancel step. 'I'm not having this creature sitting before my altar for forty days! Do something, Crowner – get rid of him!'

John looked down his big hooked nose at the indignant priest. 'What happened to your Christian charity, Father? It was the Church that invented sanctuary, not the King's justices.'

He turned back to the ragged prisoner, who was now squatting on his haunches. 'For forty days from today, you can stay in here, with guards on the door. You will have bread and water at the burgess's expense and be provided with a bucket. If you so much as put your head outside the door, it will be cut off! If you fail to confess to me in that time, the church will be boarded up and you will be starved to death. Is that clear?'

Stephen Aethelard gave a surly nod, but Julian Fulk uttered another squeal of protest at the prospect of his beloved church being boarded up for a long period. 'Confess, you evil man and get yourself away from here!'

After a moment's cogitation, the fugitive decided to co-operate. 'What do I have to do, then?' he muttered.

'First of all, we need a jury,' replied John. He told Gwyn and Gabriel to go outside and call in all the men over twelve years of age from the crowd outside. More must have drifted to the church since John had arrived, as within a few moments a dozen men and boys sidled into the nave, driven by the two officers like sheep before a dog.

They were marshalled into a semicircle around the chancel step and the tall, brooding figure of de Wolfe gave them their orders. 'You are here to witness the confession of this man, who has sought sanctuary and wishes to abjure the realm – so pay attention!'

He turned back to Aethelard, grabbed him by the shoulder of his soiled tunic and pushed him to his knees on the flagstones. 'This is supposed to be done at the gate or stile of the churchyard, but as we don't have one, this will have to do.' He looked across at the priest. 'We need the use of a holy book, Father.'

Only too pleased to help in getting rid of the unwelcome intruder, Fulk hurried across to his aumbry, a carved wooden chest against the north wall of the chancel, and took out a heavy book bound in leather-covered boards. 'Here is my copy of the Vulgate. Be careful with it, I beg you.'

De Wolfe took the testament, laboriously hand-written on leaves of parchment, and handed it to Thomas, who, after crossing himself once again, held it out to Stephen.

'Place your hand on that and repeat my words,' commanded the coroner.

Haltingly, the outlaw muttered a confession to having broken into the dwelling of John de Witefeld in the vill of Dunstone on the eve of the Feast of St Michael and All Angels and stealing fifteen shillings. He stubbornly refused to confess to having assaulted his daughter Edith, but the coroner decided that a longer confession would make not the slightest difference to the process, so did not pursue the matter.

'Now repeat the oath of abjuration after me,' boomed de Wolfe and Stephen stumbled through the ritualistic words.

'I do swear on this holy book that I will leave and abjure the realm of England and never return without the express permission of our lord King Richard or his heirs. I will hasten by the direct road to the port allotted to me and I will not leave the King's highway under pain of arrest or execution. I will not stay at one place more than one night and I will diligently seek a passage across the sea as soon as I arrive, delaying only one tide if that is possible. If I cannot secure such passage, then I will go every day into the sea up to my knees, as a token of my desire to cross. And if I cannot secure a passage within forty days, then I will put myself again within a church. And if I fail in all this, then may peril be my lot.'

At the end of this, Thomas handed the vulgate back to the priest, who with obvious relief locked it back in his aumbry.

Now John had to issue instructions to the abjurer. 'Tomorrow, you will leave this place, casting off your own clothing.' Looking at the man, who had spent months in the forest and weeks in a filthy gaol, John felt that the loss of his rags would be a blessing. Legally, they should have been confiscated and sold for the benefit of the Crown, but it was doubtful that a beggar would have bothered to pick them from a midden. 'You will wear a garment of sackcloth and walk bare headed, carrying a cross of sticks which you will make yourself. You will tell passers-by what you are and you will not stray by so much as a foot from the highway. I charge you to go to Topsham to seek a ship and you will be given sufficient coins to pay for a passage to France. If you ever set foot in England again, your life will be forfeit.'

Thomas thought that his master was being too magnanimous in nominating Topsham as the port of exit, as it was only a few miles down the river. He knew that many coroners acted perversely in sending their abjurers vast distances – some from the North Country had been sent all the way to Dover, for example. But John himself knew that it was irrelevant which harbour he nominated, as he had a shrewd suspicion that as soon as Aethelard was out of sight of the city, he would throw away his cross and vanish back into the trees to make his way back to his outlaw comrades, which probably happened to more abjurers than actually reached their ports. As Gwyn had suggested earlier, it would have saved all this trouble if the fellow had been allowed to run out through the city gates and vanish into the forest.

While Thomas fumbled pen, ink and parchment from his shoulder bag to record the event and get the names of the ad hoc jurors, Julian Fulk approached him. 'So how soon can we get rid of this fellow?' he asked peevishly.

'As soon as you can find him a length of hessian and two sticks for him to make his robe and his cross. I'll leave that to you, as you're so keen to see the back of him.'

'And who is going to give him his passage money to Cherbourg or St Malo?' huffed the priest, suspicious that the burden might fall on him.

John winked, keeping a straight face. 'I should forget about that. I'll wager that Topsham will not see hide nor hair of him. But once he's out of the city, our duty is done.'

4

In which Crowner John goes to a funeral

John de Wolfe managed to avoid a return visit to St Olave's the next morning, although his wife pestered him to accompany her to the private obsequies over the body of Robert de Pridias. He claimed that his official presence at the Thursday hangings was inescapable, which was almost true – but he had to compromise by agreeing to attend the funeral service at the cathedral later that day.

He had risen at his usual early hour and made his way to his chamber high in the castle gatehouse. Here Gwyn assured him that Stephen Aethelard had been seen off from the church in his sack-cloth at dawn, leaving on the road to Topsham as soon as the city gates were open. The fact that the abjurer had not even asked for his passage money confirmed John's suspicions that the man would melt into the woods before he had gone a mile from the city, but that was of no concern to him. He had not yet told the sheriff of Stephen's escape, keeping that until after his second breakfast, looking forward to it as a comforting item with which to irritate his brother-in-law.

It was the custom of the coroner's team to gather

each morning in their barren room, to arrange the day's work and to have a little sustenance, especially as Gwyn seemed unable to survive for more than a few hours without refuelling his large body with food and drink. The usual fare was a fresh loaf of coarse rye bread and a hard chunk of cheese bought from a stall at the bottom of Castle Lane, washed down with either ale or rough cider from a gallon jar that the Cornishman kept in the office. Thomas usually nibbled at the food, but avoided the drink. In better days he had been used to wine, but now, in his near-destitution, he reluctantly had to make do with ale at his lodging in the Close, but baulked at the cruder liquid that Gwyn purchased from a nearby tavern, which to him was a cross between vitriol and horse piss, with shreds of what looked like rotted sea-weed swirling at the bottom.

'Is that widow still pestering you to hold an inquest?' asked Gwyn, between mouthfuls of bread.

'No doubt she will this afternoon, unless I can keep clear of her,' replied the coroner glumly. 'Though I doubt I'll manage that, with Matilda hovering over me, anxious to aid and abet her.'

Thomas's beady eyes settled on his master's face. 'I have seen some strange things over the years, Crowner. I'd not dismiss witchcraft too readily,' he said uneasily.

'That goes for me, too,' boomed Gwyn. 'In Cornwall, there are many fey women – and some men, too! I could tell you stories that would make your hair stand on end.'

The coroner glared sourly at his acolytes. 'What are you two trying to do – scare me into taking this death under my wing? We've all seen strange things, but I'm damned if I'm going to turn up at the next Eyre and present the King's justices with a death by magic! I'd be the laughing-stock of the county.'

Gwyn wiped ale from his luxuriant moustache, then shook his head. 'Most folk would agree with you, if you did. Especially when they heard of that stabbed straw figure.'

De Wolfe bristled. The more he was pushed, the more he dug in his heels. 'Damned nonsense! I'm surprised at you, Thomas – a man of the cloth like you. Doesn't your Church condemn all this pagan belief as heresy?'

They argued back and forth for a while, until all the bread and cheese had gone, but the coroner was adamant about keeping de Pridias's death at arm's length. When the good-natured bickering faded, John announced that he was going over to the keep, to goad the sheriff about the loss of his felon, before the trio went out of the city to attend the executions.

As John crossed the inner bailey, he saw that the weather was threatening rain again, but although there had been more thunder, the black clouds were still holding back the inevitable deluge. The air was still and sultry and people seemed enervated as the cloying atmosphere stuck their clothes to their perspiring skin. In the crowded main hall of the keep it was even more of an effort to breathe and John was glad to escape though the small door into de Revelle's quarters, away from the stench of sweltering humanity.

In the outer chamber, where the sheriff conducted his official business, he found the dapper man checking piles of money that his chief clerk had set out on a side table. As John barged in unannounced, Richard whirled round, his hand going to his dagger, as if he was afraid that some robber was about to steal all the taxes of Devonshire. 'Oh, it's only you!' he snapped ungraciously, turning back to his counting. The clerk, an old grey-haired man in lesser religious orders, had set out orderly rows of silver pennies in piles of twelve, arranged in islands of twenty, so that the sheriff could count them as pounds, an accounting device that, like marks, had no actual coin. Alongside the table was a massive oaken chest, bound with bands of black iron. At the moment it was open and empty, but when the money had been replaced, it would be sealed with a pair of locks, to which only de Revelle had keys.

De Wolfe watched as his brother-in-law continued to count, using one forefinger to tap the piles of coins, while in the other hand he held a sheet of parchment, covered in columns of figures provided by the clerk. De Revelle was quite literate, having been educated when young at Wells Cathedral –

a fact that he never failed to rub John's face in, the coroner never having had any learning other than the hard school of battle.

'Have you come into a fortune, Richard – or have you taken to highway robbery?' asked de Wolfe sarcastically.

The sheriff held up a hand for silence until he got to the last row of coins, his lips moving silently as he counted. Then he motioned to the clerk to start replacing the money in the treasury and turned to his sister's husband.

'It's part of the county farm, John. I have to keep a strict check on it.' His voice conveyed the importance of his office and the depth of his responsibility, although John suspected that his auditing enthusiasm was mainly driven by a desire to see how much he could siphon off into his own purse.

'I thought that your next submission was not due until Michaelmas?' commented the coroner. Twice a year, on alternate Quarter Days, every sheriff had personally to deliver the 'farm', the taxes squeezed from each county, to the King's treasury, which was an even larger box kept at Winchester. Originally, payment was made on to a chequered cloth derived from the chessboard, to help the poorly numerate officials make an accurate count, hence the name 'exchequer'.

Richard ignored John's question and stalked back to his chair behind the main table which he used as his desk. Today he was attired in a long tunic of dark red silk, with a large silver buckle on his leather belt and a chain of heavy silver links around his neck. His mid-brown hair had been freshly cut into a new style, a thick pad on top surmounting an almost shaven neck and sides. John thought his head looked a little like a mushroom, but he kept his opinion to himself.

'What brings you here, John? I trust my sister is well?'

'Matilda is in robust health and is looking forward to a good funeral this afternoon,' answered John, anticipating with relish the moment when he would tell Richard of the outlaw's escape.

'Ah yes, poor de Pridias, I heard of his demise. Some form of stroke, I was told.'

'Something of that nature,' agreed John. 'But another life has been saved today in compensation.'

Richard frowned at his brother-in-law. He knew his warped sense of humour from many previous experiences. 'Whose life?' he asked suspiciously.

'The fellow you sentenced to death yesterday – the outlaw Aethelard,' John said casually. 'He escaped to sanctuary and I've sent him off to France, though I doubt he'll get as far as Topsham.'

De Revelle's foxy face reddened with anger and he launched into a tirade of recrimination, against the prison guards, his soldiery and, obliquely, the connivance of the coroner. 'He was an outlaw, he couldn't claim sanctuary! What were you thinking of, damn it?'

Although privately John felt this might be true, he was not going to admit it.

106

'Show me the law that says he couldn't, Richard. Did you want me to keep him for a few months until the royal judges next arrive? The priest of St Olave's was on the verge of apoplexy at having him in his church for just one night.'

De Revelle fumed on for a while until there was nothing left to say and, his satisfaction achieved, John turned to leave.

'Will you be at the cathedral later today?' he asked at the door.

The sheriff nodded irritably. 'Yes, the man was one of our guildmasters, I must show my respects. Though God knows when I'll get the time, with all this to attend to.' He waved a hand at the scatter of parchments across his table and the clerk hovering in the background with more documents.

Glad for once that he was unable to read and therefore free from such labours, John went back to the gatehouse and joined the waiting Gwyn and Thomas for the walk to Magdalen Street, to see five miscreants shuffle off their mortality and to confiscate any property they might own.

The sight of a row of felons kicking at the air in their death-throes did nothing to spoil John's appetite for his noon-time dinner and he and Matilda did full justice to Mary's boiled fowl with leeks and turnips. Afterwards, imported dried apricots were washed down with wine from the Loire and, once again, John blessed his partnership with Hugh de Relaga, whereby they shipped wool and cloth abroad and brought such luxury goods on the return trips from both France and Flanders. The ship they most frequently chartered belonged to Thorgils of Dawlish, the elderly husband of the delectable Hilda. He thought wryly that the fruit might taste less sweet in Matilda's mouth if she knew that it was from a box that Hilda had given him on his last clandestine visit to Dawlish, when Thorgils had been away on the high seas.

'Mind that you wear your best tunic this afternoon,' snapped his wife, eyeing his crumpled grey outfit with distaste. 'Though why you must always insist on such drab blacks and greys, I cannot understand! Other men let themselves be noticed in bright colours.'

John sighed as he recalled her brother's gaudy outfit. Matilda never failed to berate him for his reluctance to push himself forward in the county hierarchy. 'Black is surely the most suitable for a funeral,' he muttered.

'Well, I'm certainly not wearing black today. I have a fine new blue kirtle. It's a shame the weather is so hot, or I could show off my new mantle as well.'

An hour later, as one of the large bells tolled monotonously overhead, John escorted his wife the short distance to the cathedral, his tall, black figure stalking slowly alongside her, head thrust forward like that of some huge bird. They joined a small procession of other mourners as they reached the door in the West Front, mostly burgesses and guildmasters all in their best clothes, some as gaudy as peacocks. The beggars and cripples in the Close stared curiously at them and a few urchins and louts made cat-calls, until one of the proctor's servants chased them away with his staff. Requiem Masses were usually held in the mornings, but the prominence of Robert de Pridias among the commercial community of Exeter – and the fact that his wife's cousin was one of their canons – had ensured that enough of the cathedral clergy would turn out after their dinner to see the burgess safely into heaven.

His body was already lying in the building, having been brought on a cart from St Olave's some hours ago. The coffin lay in the side chapel of St Mary in the base of the south tower, the lid nailed down securely, given the hot weather and the couple of days which had elapsed since his death. The service was to be held there, as the choir and high altar were used only for sanctifying the departure of barons and churchmen.

About fifty people stood in the high, square chamber, and John recognised both the city's portreeves, one of whom was his partner Hugh de Relaga. Virtually all the guildmasters and guild officials were there together with many of the more senior tradesmen of Exeter. He saw several apothecaries, including Richard Lustcote and Walter Winstone, but one person who was conspicuous by his absence was the rival fuller and weaver, Henry de Hocforde.

Several of the cathedral canons were present, including the archdeacon, John of Alençon and the precentor, Thomas de Boterellis, although this pair took no part in the celebration of the Mass. This was said by another canon, William de Tawton, assisted by his vicar and secondaries and the chanted responses were provided by some of the choirboys, who had been paid a penny each by the widow to forgo their afternoon games to attend.

The coroner stood glumly at the back, in spite of Matilda's efforts to prod him to a more prominent position near the front of the congregation, where Richard de Revelle was making sure that he was seen by everyone, especially the rich and influential. John saw Canon Gilbert de Bosco at the side of the altar, in his cassock, surplice and maniple. He had expected the widow's cousin to have conducted the Mass in person, but it transpired that Gilbert was saving himself for later.

The ritual droned on for half an hour and eventually, the congregation partook of the Host before the office ended. Then they stood aside to allow four vergers to carry the bier out past the end of the choir into the empty, echoing nave. Towards the south corner, a deep hole had been dug and a new six-foot slab of stone lay to one side, ready to place on top of the grave. No doubt Cecilia would have Robert's name chiselled on it in the near future.

For the moment, the dead man had a short respite before being consigned for eternity to his subterranean claustrophobia, as the coffin was left on the edge of the pit while Canon Gilbert delivered his homily. He advanced to the opposite side of the grave, flanked by his vicar and secondary. The large man looked very imposing in his ecclesiastical robes as he glared around to still the murmurs and whispers before he began to speak. The first five minutes of his obituary were a conventional tribute to Robert's honesty, charity and industry. He was a devout and caring husband and father, boomed the canon, as he delivered the usual platitudes in his fine, deep voice. Then abruptly, his tone changed and he began to harangue the audience with missionary zeal.

'Fine man that he was, Robert de Pridias met his untimely end in a way which should shock true Christians into action! Though our law officers have seen fit to ignore what stares them in the face, I tell you that our brother Robert lies here dead today from the evil deeds of the Devil's disciples!'

He threw out his arm and pointed a quivering finger at the coffin. A stir of anxious surprise rippled through his audience and John's brow furrowed as the import of Gilbert's words began to sink in.

'We should be ashamed to admit it, especially the priests amongst us, but witchcraft is alive and well amongst us today! Cunning women, crafty menfolk, evil-doers using the power of Satan to pervert our lives! All this and more, is under our noses and we do nothing about it!'

He glared around his audience, everyone now hanging on his words, as this was a sermon unlike any of the dry, dreary homilies that they were used to receiving from the bored clergy of their parish churches. And Gilbert de Bosco had by no means finished with them.

'Our king has not long returned from the Crusades and half Christendom marches across the known world to fight the Mohammedans. This is right and proper, commissioned by our Holy Father in Rome. But we need our own crusade much nearer home! A crusade against the pagan superstition and black magic that exists all around us. We call ourselves Christians, yet we use these purveyors of the black arts ourselves without a thought!'

He changed from the 'we' to a more accusative style as he continued to glare around the assembled faces. De Wolfe caught John de Alençon's eye and saw the expression of concern on the archdeacon's face as he listened to the fiery diatribe from his brother canon.

'When you want a wart removed from your eye, you visit some old crone who mumbles spells over it and rubs it with toad slime. When you wish for a boy-child, you seek out a cunning woman and give her silver to spin some evil ritual over your belly! Those of you who have land outside the city pay for a potion to cure the barrenness of your best cow!'

The big, beefy priest swung his head from side to side like a bull confronting baiting dogs, as he fixed his audience with an accusing grimace.

'Yes, most of you pray to God to help you – then next morning go off to find some witch to perform pagan rituals that Our Lord died to abolish from the earth. You are betraying your faith when you sink to dealing with these evil crones!'

There was a shuffling of feet and twitching of shoulders among his listeners, as some felt shame, others embarrassment, especially those who in the last few days had sought out the help of the very agents he was now castigating,

'I call upon you, you who are leaders in this community and thus persons of influence – seek out these disciples of Beelzebub, the servants of the arch-fiend! Root them out, condemn them and return to the paths of righteousness!'

Before he finished, he once more glared around the throng as he delivered his clarion-call in the new crusade.

'I am myself found guilty for waiting so long before attacking this evil – but now I will petition the bishop and his senior brethren to declare war on these who mock our faith with their magic. And I also call on the law officers to cast off their apathy and hunt down these creatures of the night and bring down the full penalty of the law upon them!'

He drew himself up to his considerable height for the finale.

'For keep in your minds what the Book of Exodus commands us – "*Thou shalt not suffer a witch to live*"!'

There was a stunned silence, as this was not

what the comfortable burgesses and their wives had expected at a burial service. Then Gilbert de Bosco seemed to deflate as, dropping his eyes, he began muttering the rituals of committal as he motioned to the verger to lower the coffin by its ropes into the grave. The widow seemed unmoved by the final exit of her husband, as her face was upraised to her cousin, bearing an almost triumphant expression. She hurried around the pit to him and grasped his arm, followed more slowly by a rather abashed daughter and son-in-law.

'Gilbert, bless you! That was magnificent. I could not have hoped that you would take on this cause so readily and energetically!'

As she gabbled her thanks, another figure sidled up behind her and when he could get a word in, added his support to the proposed crusade against the cunning women. It was Walter Winstone, still smarting at the way he had been bypassed by Henry de Hocforde and full of malice for the folk healers who were depriving him of some of his trade.

'Reverend sir, you have said at last what has long been needed to be shouted abroad!' he whined. 'I am an apothecary and I know the damage these evil folk can do, pretending to offer cures and usually making matters far worse.'

Cecilia turned to him quickly, gratified to find such a ready recruit so soon. The three of them began gabbling together, virtually ignoring the thumping of earth behind them, as the vergers shovelled soil back into the grave-pit. Others gravitated towards the trio, some impelled by the herd instinct, feeling that any new cause with influential members was worth latching on to. Matilda was one, though her friendship and support for her friend Cecilia were added incentives. But one other quick-witted person rapidly weighed up the political and personal advantages of a new campaign and with only momentary hesitation, stepped across to insinuate himself into the group around the burly priest.

'I can assure you, Canon de Bosco, that as far as it is in my power as the chief law officer in this county, you will find the forces of law and order entirely on your side,' brayed Richard de Revelle.

Gilbert's mention of Henry Marshal had tipped the balance for de Revelle, as, like the bishop himself, the sheriff was a covert supporter of Prince John in his aspirations to displace Richard Coeur de Lion from the throne. When Richard had recently been incarcerated in Germany for eighteen months, open rebellion had ensued – until March the year before last, when Richard returned and quashed the revolt. Foolishly, he was far too lenient with his brother, so that John was still at liberty to continue his plotting.

Now the sheriff saw another chance to consolidate his position with the bishop, who was also the younger brother of William, Marshal of England. If the King fell, as he was daily likely to do in his incessant battles against Philip of France – or if another more successful revolt took place – then de Revelle, who had long-standing political ambitions, wanted to be on the winning side.

John de Wolfe watched this development with a sense of foreboding. Anything that brought a crusading priest into an alliance with his brother-in-law was a matter of concern, as the coroner knew the sheriff of old and was sure that he would manipulate any issue to his greatest advantage. As the crowd began to disperse, muttering and whispering among themselves, he caught the eye of his archdeacon friend. Leaving Matilda in the cluster of people around the de Bosco, he moved across to John de Alençon. 'And what did you make of that?' he asked sombrely.

The ascetic priest shook his head sadly. 'I know Gilbert only too well. He either does nothing at all – or he goes off on a rampage, if the issue takes his fancy.'

'So now he has appointed himself witch-hunter to the county of Devon, by the looks of it.'

The archdeacon nodded, his thin face looking more worried than ever. They began walking behind the throng towards the door and the daylight beyond.

'What view will the bishop have of this affair?' asked the coroner.

'I doubt he has ever considered the matter before, but I am sure that he will not be against it. Strictly speaking, he has no direct authority over the canons of the cathedral, as his remit is the diocese – though few members of the ecclesiastical community would ever care to challenge him.' He stood aside for de Wolfe to pass through the door on to the steps of the West Front. 'Yet the Church in the West of England has been in the doldrums lately, and Henry Marshal may see this as an opportunity to stir up some episcopal activity to impress Canterbury and remind them that the See of Devon and Cornwall is still alive and well.'

The two friends walked on in silence for a few yards.

'What of Richard de Revelle's sudden enthusiasm for seeking out cunning women?' asked de Alençon, although he knew the answer well enough.

'As usual, he wishes to keep in with those in the cathedral who lean towards John, Count of Mortain,' said John bitterly. 'We both know whom they might be – and the bishop himself is Richard's main target, you may be sure.'

In the cathedral, the precentor, the canon responsible for the organisation of services, was Thomas de Boterellis, another supporter of the Prince. Several other canons also favoured the younger royal brother and only John de Alençon and the treasurer, John of Exeter, were declared royalists like the coroner himself.

They caught up with the knot of people at a junction of the paths across the Close, just as Gilbert de Bosco took himself off towards his house in Canons' Row and the rest dispersed in various directions. The archdeacon excused himself hurriedly as he saw Matilda making for him, but de Wolfe had to stand his ground as his wife beckoned him vigorously towards her. She was standing with her brother, the widow Cecilia and her family close beside them.

'John, I hope you took to heart what the good canon had to say just now!' she snapped, fixing him with her cold eyes. He knew that however he replied it would be twisted against him, so he merely nodded and kept his mouth shut.

'I'd like to talk this over with you, John,' brayed the sheriff, still resplendent in his red tunic with the silver trimmings. 'Come to my chamber in the morning and we'll work out a plan of campaign against this creeping evil. You'll need to hold that inquest now, as you should have done in the first place.'

De Wolfe glared at his brother-in-law. 'What plan of campaign? I'm a coroner, not a persecutor of old wives! And since when does a priest order an inquest in his sermons? I take my orders from the King's Council and the Chief Justiciar, not cathedral canons!'

Incensed beyond measure, he grabbed Matilda's arm and almost dragged her towards Martin's Lane. He was well aware that he would pay for his flash of temper very soon, when she gave him a tongue-lashing, but for the moment, anger made him foolhardy. He would regret it later.

5

In which a canon speaks to the chapter

In the Bush that evening, John de Wolfe related
that day's events to Nesta as they sat together at
his table by the empty hearth. Although the ashes
were cold, the room was stifling, as the threatening storm had not yet broken and the whole
city was perspiring in sullen stillness.

'So your dearly beloved wife gave you a hard
time?' said the Welsh woman. Although she tried
hard to hide her jealousy of John's spouse, sometimes she could not resist some mild sarcasm.

'She played merry hell with me,' he answered
feelingly. 'Both for dragging her off from her friends
so abruptly – and for turning down the sheriff's
demand for an inquest.'

'But Matilda is surely under no delusions about
her brother these days,' objected Nesta. 'You've
told me that his endless misbehaviour has embit-
tered her against him.'

De Wolfe ran a finger around the inside of his
neck-band, easing it away from the sweaty skin.

'True, his repeated transgressions, especially his
near-treachery, have destroyed the rosy picture she
once had of him,' he answered. 'But it was my

119

refusal to go along with these fanciful suspicions of the widow that really caused Matilda to shout and snarl at me.'

Feeling the heat as well, Nesta pulled off her trailing head-rail and shook out a cascade of shining auburn hair. The tavern was fairly quiet this evening, the sultry weather too enervating to bring many people out of their dwellings. Refilling his ale mug from a large jug on the table, she picked her words carefully, knowing his short temper.

'D'you think it might be politic to make a few more enquiries into his death?' she asked gently. 'After all, there was that doll with a spike stuck through it. Someone meant him ill will, even if it didn't cause his death.'

De Wolfe took a long draught of her best ale before replying. 'It's true that that thing showed that some person must have wished some evil to come to de Pridias,' he conceded grudgingly. 'But I don't know of any law that forbids placing a straw dolly in a man's saddlebag! What am I supposed to do about it?'

She sensed that his resolve was weakening a little. As long as John de Wolfe was not challenged head-on, she could sometimes win him around by persuading him that the suggestion came from himself.

'Someone must have been stalking him, to obtain a bit of his hair and a shred of his clothing. Is that sort of behaviour something the law condones?' she asked with false innocence.

For once, he saw through her stratagems and grinned lopsidedly as he nipped her smooth thigh under the table. 'You're a cunning woman yourself, Nesta of Gwent!' he murmured in the Welsh they always used together. 'I think you must have put a spell on me, to be able to twist me around your fingers, as you do.'

Her heart-shaped, open face smiled back at him with undisguised affection. 'I'll be putting another spell on you very soon, *cariad*, one that will make you go with me up that ladder in the corner.'

She raised her fine eyebrows and inclined her head towards the wide steps at the back of the taproom which led up to her little room. His fingers were encouraged to explore a little farther under the table, as they sat close together on the bench.

'Maybe it's just that bit too hot tonight, Nesta,' he teased. 'I'm already in a sweat, just sitting quietly here.'

She pretended to pout and pulled away from him. 'Then sit and drink your ale, old man, if you're that feeble!'

'I'll just finish this quart and then see if I can manage to climb those rungs. Meanwhile, tell me something of these cunning women, if you're really a witch yourself.'

'Oh, John! You know as well as I do that everywhere there are old wives – and younger ones – who carry out a bit of homespun magic. And there are men too, the women don't have a monopoly of the art.'

'Do you know any of these people yourself?' he asked.

'Most of them keep it within the family, like grandmothers who boil a few herbs and mutter a few spells when the babe has the croup or the house cow goes dry.'

'But some go much farther than treating the family. There are those who make a living from their art, surely?'

Nesta took a sip from his mug and shook her head. 'Very few make a profession of it. Those who try to help outside their family usually keep it to their friends and others in the village.'

'What about the towns? We must have them here in Exeter as well? This must surely be where the corn-dolly came from, as de Pridias was a city man.'

She looked up at him looming over her, his black hair curling around his neck. Fierce though he usually looked, she loved this big stern man with an intensity that was as strong as it was hopeless. He was a Norman knight, a respected Crusader and a senior law officer of the King. And what was she but a lowly ale-wife and a foreigner from Wales into the bargain? What could life hold for her, other than frustration and disappointment for as far ahead as she could imagine? With a sigh, she forced herself to pay attention to what he was asking.

'In the towns? Well, there are cunning women here as in every other borough and city. You know

122

that for yourself, you called on Bearded Lucy at one time, remember?'

John certainly did recall the poverty-stricken old woman who lived in squalor in a tumble-down shack on the marshes of Exe Island – and Nesta had plenty of cause to remember her, too.

'But there must be many more in Exeter, a great city with over four thousand souls,' he objected. 'Are they more likely to ply this as a trade than the ones out in the countryside?'

The red-headed landlady prodded him with her elbow. 'Why look on me as an authority, Sir Crowner?' she snapped, using the parody of his title to poke fun at him. 'I'm not the warden of the Guild of Witches, you know! You'll be getting me into trouble if this pompous canon launches a campaign against cunning women.'

Perhaps Nesta did possess a sixth sense, for her careless remark was to be proved all too prophetic.

The chapter house was an old wooden building, planted against the foot of the southernmost of the two great towers of the cathedral. Exeter was a secular establishment, like eight of the other nineteen English cathedrals, the rest being monastic institutions. It was run by the 'chapter', comprising the twenty-four canons who ran every aspect of cathedral business.

The lower floor of the chapter house was used for their daily meeting, the upstairs housing the library and scriptorium, as well as accommodating

123

the clerks who toiled over the treasury and accounts. The building was becoming too small and inconvenient, and negotiations were slowly going ahead for the acquisition of part of the garden of the bishop's palace, further along the south side of the church, where a new stone building would be erected. Although officially the palace was Henry Marshal's main residence, he was more often absent than present. The bishop had many manors of his own where he preferred to stay – and was frequently in London, Winchester or Canterbury, leaving his diocese in the care of his archdeacons.

At about the eighth hour on the morning after the remarkable funeral service, the canons and clergy assembled as usual after prime at the chapter house. Sitting in their black-and-white vestments on benches around three sides of the bare room, they listened as a chorister stood at a lectern and read out the daily calendar – including the date as given by the Roman calendar, the age of the moon in the month and the saints to be commemorated that day.

A secondary, a young priest in training, next announced the rota of duties for the following day, then another read a chapter of the Rule of St Chrodegang, the strict code of behaviour adopted by Leofric, the last Saxon bishop, who founded the cathedral. Then, after prayers for the King, the relatives of the clergy and the dead, the lower orders and choristers departed to celebrate their capitular Mass, leaving the canons to deal with their official business. Jordan de Brent was this week's convenor of the chapter, as it would be another quarter of a century before Exeter appointed a dean to officiate. He rose to introduce a few financial matters, then a rather bitter discussion took place between the precentor and succentor about the choral arrangements for the feast of Epiphany. A short disciplinary hearing followed, when a downcast secondary was brought in by a proctor and sentenced to a month of almost continuous duties for being found incapably drunk in the Close. Jordan de Brent then asked whether there were any further matters for discussion and immediately Gilbert de Bosco lumbered to his feet. John de Alençon, sitting on the right hand of the convenor, groaned inwardly, as he guessed what was to come.

'Brothers in Christ, I rise to put before you an issue which should long ago have exercised our hearts and minds,' he began in his powerful voice. 'In all humility, I am as guilty as any of us, as I had never considered the matter seriously until it was forcibly brought to my attention this very week.'

Chapter was not always very attentive to the usually dull business before them and canons often whispered together or even dozed as the discussion droned on. But today every ear was cocked towards the speaker. Almost all had already heard of the outspoken obituary speech the day before, the grapevine being even more active in the incestuous community of the Close than in the city generally, where it was certainly highly efficient.

'In this diocese, in this county, in this very city, we have a legion of evil-doers who practise their black arts under our noses – and we hardly notice them, let alone do anything to stamp them under-foot!'

Gilbert slowly swung his big head around to encompass the three sides of the chapter house with his glaring eyes and his powerful presence. Although the archdeacon disliked the launching of a pogrom against harmless folk, he had to admit that Gilbert de Bosco was a highly effective orator, able to seize and hold the attention of his audience.

'Only yesterday, we laid to rest under the stones of our beloved church, the body of a man done to death by satanic means. Though the custodians of the King's peace – or at least some of them – stubbornly refused to take action, I have no doubt that he was deliberately killed, the black arts being used to effect his death.'

Once more he stopped for effect, his eyes seeking out every third or fourth face in the congregation and drilling into their eyes with his almost hypnotic stare.

'Brothers, we have a community riddled with prac-titioners of sorcery, who blatantly ignore, despise and revile the teachings of God's word. Cunning women, witches, wizards – call them what you will – they are perverting the fabric of our Christian way of life. Now that the scales of ignorance have

126

been cast from my eyes, I am appalled to realise that for centuries we have done nothing about this heresy. The time has come to rise up and enforce the might of the Holy Church against them. They must not prevail or their increase will lead us to the apocalypse, the coming of the Anti-christ!'

His voice gradually rose to a booming crescendo and de Alençon saw that a number of his fellow-prebendaries were nodding enthusiastically and a few were making the sign of the Cross as if in harmony with his exhortations.

Gilbert carried on his diatribe for a some time, now becoming more specific about the transgressions of the servants of Satan. He listed some of their evil deeds, their placing of curses on men and beasts, their tampering with the love lives of honest folk, their perversion of the healing arts – and their procuring of miscarriages, all against the will of God and the tenets of the scriptures, the Holy Father and his Church. John de Alençon, who had been present himself when the canon had made his now notorious requiem sermon, realised that overnight de Bosco must have done some very quick research into the alleged activities of cunning women. He thought that probably the widow Cecilia and the disaffected apothecary must have fed him much of the material, but whatever the source he had certainly got an excellent grasp of the issue in a very short time.

Gilbert came to the end of his harangue with a final flourish, a clarion call for immediate action.

'I have already spoken to our Lord Bishop, who thankfully was in residence last evening. He thoroughly supports my desire for action against these disciples of Beelzebub and intends to spread the message to his fellow-bishops and indeed, to Canterbury, to make this an all-England crusade! And I have the full support of Sir Richard de Revelle, who agrees that when these evil people break the King's peace, then the might of the law must fall upon them.'

He raised his brawny arms, the folds of his black cassock falling like the wings of some great bat.

'Every one of you, my brother canons, must preach against this evil – and those who employ vicars in your livings, you must instruct them to constantly deliver the same message to their flocks. I would implore the archdeacons to do the same in respect of all the parish priests in the whole diocese of Devon and Cornwall.'

His stentorian voice reached a new peak as he raised his right hand and made the sign of the Cross in the air.

'In the name of God, we must root out this hidden evil, once and for all. Remember what the scriptures exhort us – *thou shalt not suffer a witch to live*!'

He sat down heavily on to his bench, to the accompaniment of much foot-tapping and murmurs of approbation.

The convenor, who was the oldest canon as well as the archivist and librarian, stood up and held his hands out for silence. De Alençon could see by the expression on the old man's face that he had the same uneasy reservations about Gilbert's ranting as the archdeacon himself.

'Is there any discussion of this matter?' asked Jordan, in a tone that suggested he hoped the issue was closed. The hope was short lived, as a dozen canons scrambled to their feet to speak. Although a few urged caution about upsetting what was mostly harmless folk tradition, most endorsed Gilbert's crusade and related stories of their own about the wicked activities of sooth-sayers and sorcerers. Cynically, the archdeacon felt that most of their tales were second or third hand, rather than from personal experience. Listening to them, he rapidly came to the conclusion that the chapter was equally divided, as far as supporters and doubters were concerned. Generally, the younger canons were keen to follow de Bosco, while the older and wiser men knew enough about life, especially in the countryside, to doubt the wisdom of this proposed campaign.

He felt obliged to rise himself to try to dampen down what was in danger of becoming a hysterical response to Gilbert's powerful oratory.

'Brothers, we must not be hasty in this matter,' he said above the continued murmur of voices. 'Of course, I can but agree that where any person transgresses the law, be it secular or religious, then the appropriate censure must be applied.'

His frail figure, topped by the wiry grey hair that

fringed his shaven tonsure, seemed insignificant compared to de Bosco's bulk, but his voice was clear and penetrating.

'But let us be clear about what is at issue! Does our brother Gilbert wish us to hound the old woman who gives her neighbour a potion to soothe her quinsy? And are we to pursue the goodwife who murmurs some words over her brother's cow to ensure it gives birth to a she-calf? Or the yeoman who chants an old rhyme and scatters some sycamore ash to increase the yield of his oat field? We must keep a sense of proportion about this. The traditions of the countryside are rooted in antiquity and most do no harm and often some good.'

There was some muted foot-tapping and muttering of agreement from a section of the chapter, but others frowned at John for pouring the cold water of reason on this latest diversion.

Gilbert de Bosco scowled at the archdeacon. 'Anything not done in the name of the Father, the Son and the Holy Ghost is either sterile or frankly blasphemous,' he snapped. 'I am surprised at your lack of support, Brother John. I am reminded of the text, "*He who is not with me, is against me*"!'

And with that almost threatening parting shot, he stalked out of the chapter house.

The split in the attitude of the canons soon overflowed into the general population, as the Friday meeting of chapter was soon followed by Sunday sermons at churches all over Exeter and the rest

130

of the county. John de Alençon, who was responsible for the priests in the city, tried to play down the issue and conveniently omitted to instruct the incumbents of Exeter's twenty-seven churches to preach on the evils of witchcraft and folk magic. However, as with every other facet of life in the city, news travelled as fast as if it too, was imbued with magic and quite a number of the parish priests seized upon the intriguing topic for the subject of their sermons. Their congregations also found it a welcome change from the usual dull exhortations droned from the chancel steps. The novel proposition to hound down cunning men and women led to many discussions and even heated arguments outside church doors after the services were over. The issue was seized upon with almost hysterical fervour and within a few days the city was divided into two camps – those who wished to let the spell-binders and sooth-sayers well alone and those who wished to hang them all or cast them into the Exe, bound hand and foot.

Not all the vehemence was spontaneous, however, as it was helped along by some underhand scheming by the apothecary, Walter Winstone. Incensed by the way that he had been humiliated by Henry de Hocforde, he plotted over the weekend both to get even with the merchant and to strike a blow against the magicians who were under-cutting his trade. Walter hired a sly rogue from one of the quay-side alehouses, a fellow he knew from some previous dubious tasks he had carried out for the apothecary. The man was Adam Cuffe, a slaughterer from the Shambles at the top end of Southgate Street. He was sent by Winstone on Sunday afternoon to a woman in Rock Lane, which ran up from the new Watergate pierced through the southern corner of the city walls. She was known to offer cures for various ailments for a few pence. Adam pretended that he had ringing in the ears, dizziness and a splitting headache and staggered about the woman's small cottage to add substance to his story. The goodwife was Alice Ailward, a benevolent widow of fifty-eight who treated people more from a genuine desire to help, than for the trivial payment. She listened to Adam's fabricated symptoms, looked in his mouth and eyes and poked in his ears with a piece of stick. Then she went to her table in the corner of the single room that was her home and pounded some dried seeds in a mortar, adding a sprinkling of herbs. Folding the powder into a scrap of cloth, she gave it to the impostor in return for a penny, instructing him to take a large pinch four times a days, washed down with ale. There were no spells or incantations involved and by next morning Alice had almost forgotten the incident.

She was truly astounded, as well as terrified, when at about the ninth hour on Monday morning she heard a fusillade of knocks on her front door and a chorus of angry shouts in the narrow street outside. The knocks were from stones thrown at the house and, as she opened the door, another rock crashed through the flimsy shutter covering her single window. Outside were a score of people, all shouting and making threatening gestures. Alice knew none of them, as they were not from Rock Lane and she was petrified with fear to find a mob inexplicably clustered in front of her house.

Thankfully, the noise had rapidly brought a dozen of her neighbours to her assistance and both the local women and their husbands gathered outside her door to face the noisy throng in the dusty road.

'What in God's name is going on here?' roared her next-door neighbour, a burly porter built like an ox. A man half his size pushed forward, his bravado bolstered by the greater number of demonstrators in the road. It was Walter Winstone, the secret architect of this performance.

'It's none of your business. We have come to denounce this wicked woman here,' he brayed, pointing dramatically at Alice Ailward. 'She is a witch and a consort of the Devil.'

There was renewed shouting and gesticulating from the people behind him, one of whom was Adam Cuffe. He came forward on cue, as he had been instructed by the apothecary earlier than morning and flung up an arm to point accusingly at the bemused widow.

'She put a spell on me, with the aid of the Horned One himself,' he yelled and then, to validate his bewitchment, fell to the floor where he twitched for a moment before getting up again. It was a transparently false performance, and the porter from next door, who recognised him, gave him a hefty kick to help him to his feet.

'You damned fool, Cuffe! What mischief are you up to this time?'

Walter Winstone shrieked in his high-pitched voice at the woman still standing distraught at her own front door. 'I am an apothecary and this fellow came to me last night bidding me to treat his curse! You communed with Satan, woman, and your evil caused this poor man to have fits.'

Alice found her voice at last. She was no wilting violet and anger was rapidly replacing her fear. 'What nonsense are you talking, man?' she shouted. 'He came to me yesterday with a headache and dizziness, probably from some suppuration inside his ear – together with too much ale the night before.'

'You conjured up the Dark Angel to help you, I saw him in the room with you!' yelled Adam, his acting skills now stretched to their meagre limit.

Before Alice and the porter could contradict him, there was a shout from the road and the tall, thin figure of Osric appeared, staff in hand. The Saxon was one of the city's two constables, paid by the burgesses to keep order on the streets. Attracted by the racket, he had hurried to Rock Lane and now pushed his way through the small crowd to reach the figures arguing on the doorstep.

The apothecary got in first with a rapid accusation concerning the widow's collaboration with the Devil himself. 'She is one of those whom Canon Gilbert warned us against!' he screamed. 'This man unwisely came here for help and was cynically bound with spells by this evil woman. She called on the forces of darkness to aid her wicked desires.'

Osric was a conscientious official, but one not over-imbued with brains. He gaped at the main antagonists, bewildered at events. 'What are you accusing her of, then? Did she wound him or attempt to slay him?'

'Don't be so bloody daft, Osric,' snapped the neighbour, to whom plain speaking was a way of life. 'For some reason this pig's ass wants to cause trouble for the poor woman. You should lock him up, together with this scum from the quay-side, Adam Cuffe.'

The forthright common sense of the brawny porter, together with the constable's obvious reluctance to do anything, had almost silenced the small crowd and if the matter had been left there, the whole episode might have faded away, in spite of Walter's efforts to keep it alight. However, at that moment – and not by coincidence, for the apothecary had tipped them off – Cecilia de Pridias and her cousin Gilbert de Bosco appeared in Rock Lane.

The big priest, wearing his voluminous black cloak over his cassock, in spite of the sultry weather, strode down the slope, his cousin pattering alongside to keep up with him. Behind him came a thickset man carrying a heavy staff capped with silver, the symbol of authority of a proctor's servant. These were the men who enforced order and discipline within the cathedral enclave, acting as ecclesiastical constables and even gaolers for the occasional errant priest or other offender detained in the cells in one of the buildings on the north side of the Close.

Gilbert marched up to the crowd around the door and addressed himself to the bemused Osric. 'What's going on here?' he demanded of the skinny official.

Before the constable could reply, Walter cut in and tugged Adam Cuffe forward. 'Your reverence, this man has been bewitched by this depraved woman! He came seeking a cure for a trivial ailment, which I could have treated properly, but out of spite the cunning woman used the forces of the Devil to curse him. She must be stopped from committing further evil, sir.'

Winstone covertly kicked Adam on the ankle and on cue he dropped to his knees and grabbed his throat, muttering in a half-strangled voice that he could not breathe and was in mortal fear of dying.

'I did no such thing,' yelled Alice, her anger now tinged with fear that some ghastly plot was being hatched against her. 'I gave him but a few herbs to soothe his head, nothing more!'

'This man says you called down the Devil, he saw apparitions in your dwelling,' yapped the apothecary excitedly.

'A great red-and-black monster with horns and cloven feet, hovering behind her!' cried Adam, his voice miraculously recovered. There were murmurings and faint moans from the crowd clustered closely around.

136

'You're a liar, Adam Cuffe,' roared the burly neighbour, grabbing the actor by the shoulder and shaking him. 'This man is a well-known trickster, the dregs of the taverns down by the river. You can't believe a word he says!'

'Why should he lie? He has nothing to gain from it,' bleated Walter Winstone, turning to the big priest for support.

Gilbert de Bosco, who had been silent until now, turned to the plump good-wife, trembling on her front doorstep. 'Did this man come to you yesterday and ask for help?' he grated ominously.

'Yes, but only for a potion for his headache . . .'

'Just answer my questions, woman, nothing more,' snapped the canon. 'And did you give him something and take money from him?'

'A few dried herbs – and only for a single penny! Is that a crime?'

Gilbert started at her coldly. 'A crime? We shall see, woman.'

He turned to Adam Cuffe, who had decided to twitch one shoulder. The apothecary was beginning to worry that his accomplice's enthusiasm for over-acting might ruin the whole performance.

'What took place when you came here yesterday?' demanded the canon.

Cuffe stopped jerking and a crafty look came into his small eyes. 'I told her my symptoms, but she didn't look at my head nor body, just began canting some strange spells and dancing around me.'

The idea that the rotund middle-aged woman

would be likely to dance around a stranger in the cramped confines of her small dwelling should have been ludicrous, but a chorus of gasps and angry murmurs from the audience told of their willingness to accept anything that supported their preconceptions.

'What happened then?' grated Gilbert de Bosco, his bulk hovering threateningly over the small man.

'She first demanded money from me . . . six silver pennies, no less!'

There was a hiss of disapproval from the crowd at the mention of this extortionate sum.

'Liar, it was but one penny!' In her anger, Alice unwisely added, 'May you be damned for such mischievous untruths!'

'Hear that, she curses him again, even in the presence of a man of God,' screeched Walter triumphantly.

'What then?' demanded Gilbert, implacably.

'After I paid her all I had, she chanted more spells and weird verses, in some language I could not understand,' answered Adam, having been carefully coached beforehand by the apothecary. 'And the room went dark and there was the flutter of satanic wings. I saw this apparition behind her, it was Beelzebub himself. I fainted and when I came to, she was dragging me to the door. I staggered home and then was sick. I suffered shivering and fits like the ague until I dragged myself to this good apothecary here for help.' He ended with another bout of twitching, this time with the opposite shoulder.

Alice hotly denied his allegation and her neighbours joined in until there was a rising cacophony of voices. Walter, Adam and even Cecilia now yelled and gesticulated as vehemently as the residents of Rock Lane staunchly supported their besieged neighbour. Osric looked on helplessly, wishing himself far away, until the heavily built canon decided to bring the matter to a head.

'Be quiet, all of you!' he bellowed in a bull-like voice. It had the desired effect as the squabbling rapidly subsided and all faces were turned to the priest. He glared back at Osric. 'This is a public disturbance, constable! The root cause is obviously this woman here, so I charge you to take her into custody until the matter can be properly investigated.'

Dim though he was, Osric knew enough about his duties to resist being ordered about by someone from the cathedral. 'I can't do that, sir! I know of no offence she has committed. She stands at her own door and has done nothing apart from deny some accusations!'

There was a roar of approval from the locals and the porter slapped the thin Saxon on the back in admiration. 'Well said, Osric, you're not as stupid as you look!'

Irritated by the stubborn rebuff, Gilbert de Bosco turned to the servant with the silver-topped staff, who had been standing stoically in the background all the while. 'William, seize this woman and take her to the proctor's gaol. If this oaf will not act

139

on a breach of the peace, then she must be arraigned under canon law, on suspicion of blasphemy and sacrilege.'

Amid howls of protest, the proctor's servant stepped forward and grabbed Alice Ailward not too gently by the arm and pulled her into the road. Her next-door neighbour, with a roar of anger, launched himself at the man, but received a smart blow across the head from the staff. The other inhabitants of Rock Street surged forward, and for a moment it looked as if there would be a free fight in the lane, but Osric, clear at least about his duty not to allow brawling in the streets, seized the porter by the shoulder to restrain him from further violence.

'Leave it, Henry!' he shouted in his ear. 'You cannot prevail against the bishop's men. Let the law sort this out.'

With the canon, Cecilia, Adam Cuffe and the apothecary clustered around her, poor Alice was led away, wailing and weeping, with a trailing crowd of supporters and antagonists tagging along behind, still shouting and scuffling.

As they went up Rock Street to Southgate Street and then across through Beargate into the cathedral precincts, the crowd grew larger as, like a snowball, it gathered up more townsfolk, who themselves then took sides.

When they discovered what was going on, there were shouts of 'Shame!' and 'Let the old woman go free!' mixed with more hysterical yells of 'Witch, she's a witch!' and 'She's in league with Satan!'

By the time they reached the church of St Mary Major, one of the six small churches dotted along the west side of the Close, some fifty people were trailing behind, the two factions still shouting abuse at each other. The proctor's man dragged the still-protesting Alice to a door in a building opposite St Mary's, which backed on to the houses in the high street. This was the office of the proctors, a pair of canons responsible for keeping law and order in the episcopal enclave, any physical work being delegated to their servants, of whom William was one. He thrust the wailing widow inside and vanished, followed by Canon Gilbert, who slammed the door behind him.

The mob, abruptly deprived of their entertainment, rapidly dispersed, leaving a few of Alice's friends to round on Walter, Cecilia and Adam, blaming them loudly for the scandalous way in which the widow woman had been treated. The apothecary took fright at the threatening attitude of the burly porter and hurried away in the direction of Martin's Lane, while Adam also thought it wise to quietly slip away to the nearest tavern to spend some of Walter's bribes on ale. Only Cecilia de Pridias stood her ground and haughtily declaimed her intention to hound every cunning woman out the city, to avenge herself for the death of her husband.

Having said her piece, she turned and stalked away towards her home near the East Gate.

6

In which Crowner John handles gold

The sky, which had been holding its hot and humid breath for days, eventually decided that it had had enough. Later that morning, the heavens split above the city in a crashing peal of thunder and black clouds loosed a torrent of vertical rain that fell like a waterfall into the dusty streets.

Thomas de Peyne was caught by the downpour just as he was limping from the cathedral up to Rougemont. Within seconds, his threadbare black tunic was saturated and his mousy hair was plastered in lank strands around his thin face. He was soon so wet that there was no point in sheltering or trying to run the rest of the way, so he ambled along, the rain streaming off his eyebrows and long nose. On either side, tradesmen were cursing as they struggled to cover the goods displayed on their flimsy stalls, the rain drumming on the striped fabric of the awnings over the booths. By the time Thomas got to the bottom of Castle Hill, the high street was already a morass of fine mud. The central gutter was pouring filthy water down towards the river, and he had to stretch his short legs to cross it, as a flotsam of rubbish, including a decaying cat, careered past.

As he passed into the outer ward of Rougemont, he saw that some wives were chasing after their urchins, who were dancing gleefully in the rain, while others were desperately collecting their washing, which had been drying on bushes. At the inner gate, the solitary guard was sheltering under the arch of the gatehouse, thinking dolefully that he would later have to take sand and a rag to his round iron helmet to polish off the new rust that the rain would cause. He nodded at the familiar figure of the coroner's clerk as Thomas passed behind him to climb laboriously up the steep steps to the upper chamber.

'We've got a drowned rat, Crowner!' cackled Gwyn from his usual seat on the window ledge. 'For Christ's sake take those wet clothes off, or you'll catch the ague.'

Thomas pulled his black cassock-like garment over his head and stood shivering in his patched undershirt. The rain had brought welcome relief from the heat, but his soaked body now felt cold.

'You'd better take it all off, Thomas,' recommended de Wolfe, from behind his table.

'We've seen naked bodies before, lad,' said Gwyn. 'I doubt that yours will drive us crazy with lust!'

Thomas blushed and refused to undress altogether, his modest upbringing at odds with their rough military humour. Gwyn, whose teasing of their little clerk was a mask for his kindliness, took an old riding mantle from a wooden peg driven between the stones of the wall and draped it over Thomas's shoulders.

'There's been quite a commotion in the lower town, Crowner,' said the clerk, as he perched himself on his stool at the table. 'Canon Gilbert has had a witch locked up in the proctors' cells, after Osric the constable refused to arrest her.' Thomas was exceptionally well connected with the city grapevine and seemed to hear gossip ahead of anyone else. His remarkable gift for intelligence-gathering was another reason why he was so valuable as a coroner's assistant, apart from his talents in reading and writing.

De Wolfe's ears pricked up at this latest titbit and he rapidly drew out from Thomas all that he knew about the affair in Rock Lane.

'So that damned apothecary and the de Pridias widow were there with that interfering canon!' he grunted. 'That seems too much of a coincidence. I smell some sort of conspiracy in this.'

'What can you do about it, Crowner?' asked Gwyn, tugging at one side of his drooping moustache.

John shrugged helplessly. 'Not a thing, as it stands. I've no jurisdiction over allegations of sorcery. Osric was right for once, refusing to have anything to do with it. If there was no violence or damage to property, then it's none of the business of the law officers.'

He looked at the hunched figure of his clerk, swathed in the oversized brown cloak. 'You're the

144

authority on matters ecclesiastical, Thomas. Has a canon the right to drag some poor wretch from her home and incarcerate her in the church dungeons?'

Thomas looked up with a rather hang-dog expression. He felt guilty on the rare occasions when he was unable to be of help to his master. 'The matter has never arisen before, to the best of my knowledge,' he admitted. 'Though there is a clear admonition in the Book of Exodus that witches should be put to death, the Church has never enforced it in living memory. In fact, I doubt if it has even addressed the problem.'

'Looks as if this bloody canon is stirring it up for his own ends,' growled Gwyn, in his usual blunt fashion.

John sighed as he uncoiled himself from his stool. 'I'm sorry for the poor dame, but there's nothing I can do at the moment. I'll seek out the archdeacon later and see what he feels about it. I know he was unhappy with Gilbert de Bosco's performance last week.'

He stretched his long arms and straightened his back after being hunched over his Latin lessons for the past hour. Going to the window opening, he peered out at the rain.

'Easing off a little, Crowner,' observed Gwyn. 'But still coming down steadily enough. It'll last all day, a poor look-out for the harvest if it keeps on.'

'If you're right, we're going to get a wetting this afternoon. We have to ride to Cadbury, whatever the weather.'

Usually it was Gwyn who brought new cases to John's attention, as the castle guards normally directed reeves and bailiffs to his officer when they arrived at the castle to report deaths, assaults, rapes and other assorted disasters. This time, de Wolfe happened to be coming out of the keep when he heard a dusty rider asking for the coroner. He made himself known to the man and found that, unusually, this was no murder or mayhem, but a discovery of treasure trove, another event that fell under the jurisdiction of the coroner. The man was the manor-reeve of Cadbury, a small village eight miles north of Exeter, about halfway to Tiverton. John listened to his brief story, then sent him off to feed and water both himself and his horse, with instructions to meet them at the North Gate soon after the cathedral bells tolled for vespers, which was a couple of hours after noon.

It was midday now and John announced that he was seeking his dinner at the Bush, as Matilda was spending the day with her sickly cousin in Fore Street. It was an opportunity for him to sneak away to his mistress without suffering the abrasive recriminations of his wife. Thomas decided to stay in the chamber and dry off, claiming he had some cases to copy on to the parchment rolls that must be presented to the justices when they came to the Assize of Gaol Delivery in a couple of months' time. John privately thought that the clerk relished the chance of his own company and the opportunity to read in peace from his precious

Vulgate. He lived on sufferance in one of the canons' houses in the Close, sleeping on a straw mattress in the passageway of the servants' quarters, where there was no privacy at all.

Gwyn went off to eat, drink and play dice with the off-duty men-at-arms in the guardroom below and the coroner strode off towards Idle Lane. It was raining steadily, but not the drenching downpour that had soaked Thomas. He had borrowed Gwyn's tattered shoulder-cape with the pointed hood, the worn leather keeping most of the rain off, though the skirt of his long grey tunic and his boots were soon wet and muddied.

At the tavern, he found that Edwin the potman had just lit a fire in the stone hearth, as a number of other patrons were in varying stages of dampness and needed to dry off, even though the summer afternoon was still warm, in spite of the change in the weather.

John stretched out his legs to the blazing logs and watched as steam began to wreathe up from his clothing. Almost immediately, Nesta appeared with a jug of ale and sat down on the bench alongside him. 'Your boots will split if you dry them too quickly!' she warned, giving him a quick kiss on his stubbled cheek.

'It's a waste of time anyway, they'll be wet again soon enough.'

He explained about the journey to Cadbury that afternoon, to examine an alleged find of coins. After assuring him that his dinner was on its way, she asked him to explain about treasure trove. Nesta was an intelligent woman, with a healthy curiosity about a whole range of matters and John delighted in pandering to her inquisitiveness.

'Why should a coroner be involved?' she asked. 'I thought your task was to investigate deaths and evil things like that.'

He took a pull at his ale and shook his head. 'It's mainly about money, good woman. Though it's true that death and injury is a big part of the work, that's because there's silver to be gained out of it for the King.'

He explained again that Richard the Lionheart was always short of money, especially since Henry of Germany had demanded the vast ransom of a hundred and fifty thousand marks for Richard's release from capture. John still felt guilty about this, as he had been one of the small bodyguard that had travelled with the King through Austria, when their ship had been wrecked on the shores of Dalmatia, coming back from the Holy Land. They had been ambushed at an inn in Erdberg and John had never forgiven himself for having been absent, looking for fresh horses, when the Mayor of Vienna had burst in with his men and captured Richard.

'So the Chief Justiciar, Hubert Walter, was given the job of raising the money – and he has to keep on finding it, now that the King wages these incessant campaigns against Philip of France. One of the ways he invented – apart from taxing the barons, the Church and everyone else – was to bring back the old Saxon office of coroner, to drive more cases into the royal courts, instead of them going to the county courts, the manor courts and the rest. And as you well know, any fault in the process of dealing with the legal process leads to fines, all of which goes into the King's treasury.'

Nesta had heard most of this before, but still wanted to know more about treasure trove. Just then, one of her maids arrived at the trestle with a wooden board on which was a thick trencher of yesterday's bread supporting a slab of boiled bacon, with two fried eggs on top. A wooden bowl contained cooked beans and peas, which John heaped on to slices of the meat which he cut off with his dagger. Between chewing and swallowing ale to wash it down, he explained about finds of treasure.

'There's a great deal of valuable metal hidden about the countryside, especially since the Battle of Hastings. Very many Saxons hid their wealth to keep it from us Normans – then they were either killed or died before they could recover it.'

He wiped the back of his hand across his mouth to remove the bacon fat.

'I have heard of much older coinage being found, even going back to the Romans. But whatever it is, it has to be either gold or silver to be reckoned as treasure trove. Jewel stones don't count, unless they are set in precious metal.'

'But who does it belong to?' persisted Nesta, her big eyes round as she looked up at her dark and angular lover.

'That's why there must be an inquest on the finds, to decide if the finder or the owner of the land or the King gets the value. There are rules, but I rely on Thomas to put me right on the details. You know what a mine of information he is, I'd be lost without him when it comes to fiddling details.'

Some ripe plums and an apple rounded off the meal and as there was no time to climb the ladder for a dalliance in the loft, he had to be satisfied with another quart of ale and a relaxed gossip with his mistress – though she was constantly interrupted by either Edwin or the maids to settle some dispute in the kitchen or a problem among the patrons.

He asked her whether she had heard anything about the strange arrest of Alice Ailward by the cathedral proctors, but Nesta had no more information than himself. 'It will be a dismal day if any good-wife who gives a potion or a poultice to a neighbour, gets herself locked up for it.'

She sounded worried, and John wondered whether her own activities in that direction were more extensive than she had admitted to him. Nesta was a tender-hearted soul and he knew that she often went out of her way to help those less fortunate than herself. Beggars were often to be found around the back gate, where she unfailingly let them have the old trenchers and scraps of food left over from the kitchen. He suspected that the families in nearby Smythen Street and the upper part of Priest Street were quite familiar with her Welsh folk cures for a wide range of illnesses.

'You be careful yourself,' he admonished her. 'Lay low with your cunning-woman activities, until this stupidity has blown over.'

He left the alehouse before the vesper bell and was helping Andrew the farrier to saddle up his great horse Odin when it finally pealed out from the cathedral tower. The rain was now an intermittent drizzle and there were gaps in the cloud where scraps of blue sky suggested that maybe it would clear up towards evening.

When he reached the North Gate, Gwyn was waiting on his big brown mare and, just outside, Thomas was perched side-saddle on a small cob, all Gwyn's efforts to get him to ride like a man having failed. Alongside him was Henry Stork, the reeve from Cadbury, a leathery, taciturn man of about fifty, who spoke only when it was absolutely necessary. He had said little about the discovery, other than it was on the land of Robert Hereward and had been found in a mound by one of Robert's villeins.

The four set off northwards along the road to Crediton, the rain causing little problem to men used to travelling in all weathers. The main problem was the surface of the track, which after a couple of weeks of drought, had now been converted into a sticky red paste by the recent downpour. The mud was not yet deep but was slippery and occasionally one of the horses would slide and lose its footing in the rutted surface. Even at a cautious trot, the eight miles did not take long to cover.

They left the Crediton road soon after leaving the city and followed narrow tracks to the village of Thorveton, then on through mixed forest and cultivated land to Cadbury, a small hamlet in deeply undulating country just west of the River Exe.

The rain had stopped by the time they arrived and broken cloud allowed shafts of sunlight to draw steaming wreaths of vapour from the pasture land around the village.

'It's but a small place, Crowner,' grunted Henry Stork, as they walked their horses into the grassy area in the middle of the hamlet, where the track divided into two, the right-hand one going on to Tiverton, a few miles farther on.

'You say the manor is held by Robert Hereward?' asked de Wolfe, as he slid from Odin's high back.

'Indeed, but he doesn't own the land. He has Saxon blood on his grandmother's side, they used to hold it. But they became Norman when William de Pouilly's son married into the family a century ago.'

'So who owns the freehold?' persisted the coroner. This was not just idle curiosity; the resolution of a find of treasure trove needed all the information available. His black eyebrows went up sharply when the reeve told him that the ultimate landlord was Sir Richard de Revelle, sheriff of the county and a substantial landowner around Tiverton. His wife, the glacial Lady Eleanor, lived in his main manor near there, refusing to stay with her husband in the grim and draughty castle of Rougemont.

'Does the sheriff know of this find?' he asked curtly.

Henry shook his head. 'I was charged by Sir Robert's bailiff to give him a message, but at Rougemont I was told that he had just left Exeter for Revelstoke and will be away for at least four days.'

Revelstoke was one of Richard's manors near Plympton, on the coast in the far west of Devon.

They had stopped outside a small alehouse, a hut of wattle and daub with a ragged thatched roof, slightly larger than the dozen tofts clustered around the centre of the village. A steep hill rose behind, with some ancient walls hidden in the turf at the top. On each side, strip fields ran up the sloping sides of the valley, the oats and rye beginning to brown up after a week of hot sun, though still not ripened sufficiently for harvesting. Strips of green alternated with the grain, where beans and peas were looking healthier. As John stretched his aching back, his gaze travelled around the horizon, where dark forest began beyond the waste ground that surrounded the cultivated areas. About a quarter of a mile to his left, he saw a hump in the pasture, just before the trees began. It was about the height of a cottage, smooth and covered in grass.

'Is that the mound?

The reeve bobbed his head. 'It is, Crowner. Maybe you'd like a drink and a bite to eat while you talk to the man who found the valuables?'

Gwyn was through the door of the tavern before John could answer and with a wry grin, the coroner beckoned to Thomas and followed the Cornishman inside. Already a few curious villeins had gathered around the door and the reeve directed a few of them to take the horses to water. In the single room of the alehouse they sat on benches around the dead fire-pit while a young girl in a ragged smock fetched them pots of indifferent ale from a shed at the back.

Henry Stork came back inside and in the dim light of the windowless room they saw he was followed by a muscular youth of about sixteen, who had a disfiguring purple birthmark covering one side of his face. He seemed a bright, intelligent lad, his eyes flitting from one to the other of these strangers in his village.

'Simon, this is,' said the reeve. 'He found the stuff yesterday, when he was digging out a badger sett.'

John caught Gwyn's eye and he grinned. It was an unlikely tale, as mound digging was a common but illegal activity, invariably undertaken in the hope of finding treasure. De Wolfe wondered why this village had reported it, rather than keeping quiet, but maybe the surprise of actually finding treasure had unnerved the digger. He decided to bait the young man a little.

'Why dig for a badger in the middle of an open pasture, boy?'

Simon looked back innocently. 'We've had our turnips dug up at night – some with claw marks on them. I saw a hole, so I thought maybe I could raise a badger if I made it a bit bigger and sent the dog down there.'

John believed this as much as he believed that the moon was made of cheese, but decided to give the youth the benefit of the doubt. Just then, the silent girl padded barefoot into the room with a grubby board on which was a loaf cut into half a dozen chunks, together with a heap of sliced mutton. She wiped her running nose with her fingers, then handed out the bread to each of the visitors, leaving the meat board on the ring of stones around the fireplace.

'So what did you find instead of your badger?' demanded de Wolfe.

The young man hawked in his throat and spat on the floor before replying. 'The turf had fallen in, because there was a hollow underneath. All that bloody rain had made holes everywhere, washing out the soil below. I stuck my spade in and straightway it hit something hard.'

'An old box, it was,' broke in Henry. 'A bit rotten, but it was oak with some iron bands, so it kept together, just about.'

'Where is it now?' asked Gwyn.

'In the church, only safe place we've got. The parson is guarding it himself.'

The coroner had less faith than the reeve in the honesty of parish priests, but recognised that there were few secure places in a remote hamlet like Cadbury. He drank down the rest of his ale and put the remnants of his crust down, together with the mutton, conscious that the little girl was eyeing it hungrily, waiting for them to go in the hope that something would be left for her.

He rose and jerked his head at Thomas and the still-champing Gwyn. 'Let's go and look this great treasure, then.'

Across the village green, the little Saxon church stood forlornly within its ring of old yews. It was stone built, but hardly more than a large room, with a small arched belfry perched on one end of the roof, which was made of overlapping flat stones. The inside was almost bare, a hard-packed earth floor leading up to a small apse where a table covered with a cloth did service as an altar, supporting a bronze cross and a pair of wooden candlesticks. The walls were whitewashed and some crude coloured paintings of biblical scenes were placed between the slit windows. More recent coatings of white lime had blurred the edges of some of the pictures, where the brush of a careless painter had slipped.

Squatting on the edge of the wooden platform that supported the altar was a thin figure dressed in a rough hessian smock, belted around his waist so that the hem came above his bandy knees. Wooden-soled working shoes were on the ends of his spindly legs and the only indication that this was the parish priest and not another villein from the fields was his shaven tonsure. A long-handled shovel, its wooden blade edged with an iron strip, leaned against the wall near by, increasing the impression that this was just a bald-headed labourer.

He climbed to his feet as the coroner's party entered. Thomas was in the rear, crossing himself as he genuflected to the altar.

'This is Michael, priest of St Mary's, Crowner,' said the reeve. 'He has cared for this box since it was found.' The priest was a slender man of about thirty, who to John's eyes looked chronically ill, his eyes sunken in deep sockets above a wasted face where the cheekbones stuck as if in a skull.

'Forgive my appearance, sir,' he said in a surprisingly deep and firm voice. 'But my pastoral duties in a place like this are light and I must work in the fields with my flock if we are to avoid starvation next winter, after this terrible year.'

De Wolfe was well aware that many priests, especially in tiny parishes with a scanty living, had to work hard to feed themselves, but this man seemed to be killing himself with toil. However, this was none of his business, although he determined to ask John de Alençon when he returned to Exeter, why the inordinately rich Church seemed indifferent to the poverty of many of its servants.

'You will want to see the thing that young Simon discovered. I have placed it in the aumbry for safe-keeping. It is the only place in the village that possesses a lock!'

He led them to the north side of the semicircular apse where there was a large chest, made of blackened planks secured with large iron nails. He fished a large key from a pouch on his belt and opened the crude lock, pushing back the lid with a creak to reveal what was inside. A chalice, paten and cruet of a poor-quality mix of tin and silver were stored there between celebrations of the Mass, along with a breviary and a manual, the only sacred books the priest possessed. These had been pushed to one end of the chest and de Wolfe saw that most of the space was taken up with a battered box, with crumbly soil still adhering to its rough sides.

He motioned to the brawny Gwyn, who lifted it out with a grunt and dropped it on the edge of the dais.

'Bloody heavy, that!' he said, getting a poisonous glance from Thomas for using such language in the house of God.

He squatted alongside the box, almost nose to nose with the coroner on the other side. Usually they adopted this pose across a corpse, so this made a novel change.

'It's just a box, not a proper chest,' observed the Cornishman.

The object that the lad had dug from the side of the mound was about four hands-spread long and three wide and deep. It seemed to be made of thick boards, now brittle and split, but was held together by two bands of thin beaten iron, almost completely rusted through. The remnants of a few nails were visible at the edges, where the boards had originally been butted together to make a rough box.

The reeve stooped above them, pointing at one end. 'We saw silver coins through that broken part, so we didn't go any farther.'

John again thought that the honesty of the Cadbury inhabitants was remarkable, but the next words of Michael the priest tempered his opinion a little.

'I was up at the top of the fields when Simon came running from the mound. I stopped him and he took me back to show me what he had found. When we walked back to the road, we found that Robert Hereward was drinking ale after visiting his mill to collect the dues. He was the one who first saw the treasure through that crack and told us to report it straightway to you, Crowner.'

De Wolfe wondered whether the villagers, including their priest, would have been so honest if the manor-lord had not happened to be on the scene.

'Where is Robert now?' he asked.

'He said he would come down here as soon as you arrived,' replied Michael. 'I sent a boy up there to tell him when I heard your horses coming.'

John turned his attention back to the box. A gap in the clouds must have passed overhead at that moment, as a shaft of sunlight struck through one of the narrow window slits and illuminated it in an eerie fashion.

'Can you get the top off, Gwyn?'

His officer reached behind to his belt and pulled

out a large dagger. Putting the thick blade flat under one of the fragile bands, he levered up and the parchment-thin metal snapped in a shower of rust. He did the same to the other one, then prised up the rotting remains of the top boards. Shreds of a decomposed linen bag failed to hide the closely packed coins that filled the box. Most were tarnished to a deep grey colour, but when the coroner disturbed them with his fingers, those beneath, which had been lying tightly face to face, showed the brighter glint of silver.

'There's another bag underneath,' said Michael, jabbing a finger at the mass of coins. Where John had moved some aside, the top of a more intact pouch could be seen, tied with a thong. When de Wolfe pulled, it ripped, but enough material came up to reveal a leather purse.

Inside were several dozen bigger coins showing the yellow glint of gold.

'Keep that aside, then tip the rest out of the box,' he commanded.

Handing the leather bag up to Thomas, the fount of all knowledge as far as he was concerned, he demanded confirmation of their identity. 'Look like bezants to me. What do you think?

The little clerk, his thin nose almost twitching with excitement, pulled the opening to the full extent of the purse-string and ferreted inside with his fingers. 'These are indeed, Crowner! All gold *solidii* from Byzantium. Each is worth about six shillings today!'

Gwyn whistled. He had never seen half as much money in one place before. 'How many are there, Thomas? And don't go slipping a few up your sleeve when we're not looking!'

Thomas flushed indignantly, though he knew Gwyn was teasing him. 'I'll lay them out in a row, before your very eyes, you ginger oaf!' he retorted and proceeded to tip the bag on to the wooden platform.

'May as well count the silver ones, too,' ordered John, getting up from his crouch, his back reminding him that he was not getting any younger. 'The two priests can do that. They can read, write and do their sums.'

He stood back with Gwyn and Henry to watch the other pair put the coins into small piles. Behind them, at a respectful distance, a dozen men and women of the village stood awe-struck at this display of wealth that was far beyond their comprehension. The average wage of a freeman farmer was about two pence a day, so to them one bezant was almost three months' earnings. The villeins and serfs worked for nothing but the occupancy of their toft and what they could grow and breed on their croft.

'There are fifty-two gold coins, master,' declared Thomas, looking up from his little piles of money. The bezant, though minted in Asia Minor, had been a standard gold piece throughout Europe for hundreds of years and this little bagful was a small fortune in itself.

161

Thomas went to help Michael count the far more numerous silver pennies, the only English coin in circulation, all of these minted by the Saxons before the Conquest. After another fifteen minutes, during which the spectators appeared hypnotised by the chink of coins being put into piles of ten, the local priest announced that there had been four hundred and eighty-six pence in the box. Calculation was beyond de Wolfe, a soldier not having the computing power of a merchant, but his clerk rapidly had the answer.

'Altogether, that's about three hundred and twenty-eight shillings. That's more than seventeen pounds, Crowner!'

'And this!' said the parish priest, suddenly. He held up a glinting object. 'It was at the bottom, under the last of the pennies.'

He handed it up to the coroner, who turned it over admiringly in his fingers. It was a gold brooch, as long as his forefinger, an oval of delicate moulding, with a dragon-like heraldic beast across the open centre. On the back were two small loops with a thick gold pin between them, to fix it to a cloak or tunic. Of obvious Saxon design, it weighed as much as a dozen of the bezants, but was more valuable than its sheer mass, because of the exquisite workmanship.

De Wolfe handed it back to Michael. 'Find a length of cloth and wrap everything up again and put it back in the box. Thomas, make a careful inventory on one of your rolls, with the names of

162

the witnesses who were here present. I don't want any accusations that some of this has gone missing later on.'

The reeve sent one of the villagers to find some wrapping while Thomas unpacked his writing materials from the bag that he carried on his shoulder. By the time he had written down all that the coroner had demanded, an old sack had been produced and the pennies, bag of gold and the brooch had been wrapped up and replaced in the old box, which was then secured with some cords to prevent it falling apart.

'I want to see the place where it was found,' announced de Wolfe. 'So for now, can you lock the box back in your aumbry to be safe?'

The priest agreed and when the key had vanished back into the scrip on his belt, they all trooped out into the fitful sunlight. Henry Stork led the way and after the coroner's trio and the priest came a straggling bunch of locals, all agape at this novel intrusion of the outer world into their monotonous lives.

The procession crossed the track and walked up a muddy lane at the side of a dry-stone wall, built more to accommodate loose stones from the adjacent strip fields than as a partition. It enclosed lines of crops grouped in sections belonging to different villagers, so that everyone had their share of good and bad soil. Oats, rye, peas and beans seemed the main crops, although farther away, the green heads of turnips and cabbage could be seen. In the centre, where the root crops had already been lifted, a pair of patient oxen were dragging a plough, with a bare-footed villein leading them and another leaning on the handles to keep the coulter in the ground.

On the other side of the path, fallow land stretched away for two hundred paces, part of the three-field system that rested the ground for a year, after two of cultivation. At the end of this, the path opened on to a dozen acres of pasture land, where sheep and a few lean cows grazed, along with a small herd of goats, watched over by a small boy.

The meadow rose gently towards the edge of the forest and the reeve marched up this towards the tump in the ground, just before the trees began. They followed him to a spot at the base of the mound, where the soil was disturbed, forming a red scar in the green grass.

'This is where it was found, Crowner,' declared Henry, with a flourish of his hand towards a hole in the ground. He beckoned Simon and the youth came sheepishly forward, standing awkwardly before the ring of spectators. 'Tell them, boy!' commanded the reeve.

'Not much to be told, sirs. I was up here looking for a stray heifer two days ago and saw a hole. So yesterday I brought up a shovel and had a poke around – in case it was a badger sett,' he added hastily, recalling his original lame excuse. He squatted alongside the hole and pointed down. 'Just in there it was, barely covered in earth, once the top turf was off.'

De Wolfe peered in, then looked up at the mound, which close up, looked larger than it had from a distance. It was twice as high as a man and roughly circular, being about fifty paces around.

'You know everything, clerk!' said Gwyn to Thomas with mock sarcasm. 'So what is this poxy lump?'

The former priest gazed up at the smooth grass-covered cone and crossed himself. 'No one rightly knows, but they are pagan temples of some kind, built by the ancients, long before the Saxons came. There are many more in Wiltshire, where some have bones hidden in crypts of stone in the centre.'

The coroner had no interest in such antediluvian monuments, but had heard that many had been dug into in the hope of finding ancient treasure, which had sometimes been fulfilled. But this particular treasure was not all that ancient, as the silver coins were Saxon.

There was nothing more to be seen and he was just about to leave when there was a cry from across the pasture and two men could be seen hurrying up to them.

'Who the hell is this?' growled Gwyn.

'It's our landlord, Robert Hereward,' said the reeve.

The tenant lord arrived, somewhat out of breath, his stocky bailiff close behind. Robert was younger than de Wolfe had expected, a man of about thirty, with thick fair hair swept back off his face. He had a beard and moustache of the same colour which, with his rather ruddy complexion and blue eyes,

165

betrayed his Saxon blood, even though it had been diluted by four generations of Normans.

'Sir John, I am glad to see you!' He sounded genuinely pleased to have the coroner on his land, a somewhat uncommon sentiment, as a visit from officials of the King usually meant trouble or expense – often both. The two men exchanged some civil words of greeting and explanation, then Robert Hereward peered down at Simon's excavation. 'I presume you have already examined what this youth discovered?' he asked.

John described the contents of the box and Robert was keen to see inside it for himself. The whole party went back down the meadow and into the village, the coroner and the manor-lord walking together behind the bailiff and the reeve. John took the opportunity to discover the exact status of Hereward's tenancy of the land, anticipating problems ahead over the ownership of the find.

'I rent this village from de Revelle for a fee each year,' explained Hereward. 'I have the manor that I inherited from my father over in the next county at Hillfarrance, but it's too small to provide a comfortable living, so five years ago I took on this manor, which is about ten carucates. The place has a special meaning for me, as it once formed part of my ancestor's lands.'

They were approaching the church now, as de Wolfe carried on with his questions. 'Why would our noble sheriff want to part with it?'

Robert shrugged. 'He has very large estates, some from his family and the rest from his wife, the Lady Eleanor. That's why he married her. It certainly wasn't for her looks or her charm!'

His tone was sarcastic and the coroner guessed that he was no great friend of the de Revelle household.

'With so much land, I think he became impatient with its management, even though his bailiffs did most of the work. Cadbury was run down and poorly productive, so he preferred to get a steady rent, rather than try to bring it back into profit.'

As they marched up the path to the church door, John asked a last question. 'And has it done better since you took the tenancy?'

'It's certainly improving. I have a good bailiff and reeve – but these last two years have been disastrous for the crops. I hope to God the weather lets us have at least some sort of harvest or there'll be empty bellies and full graves come the winter.'

Robert Hereward seemed a sensible, practical man and de Wolfe took a liking to him. He reminded him of his own brother William, who prudently administered their two manors down near the coast, at Stoke-in-Teignhead and Holcombe.

Michael the priest was still in the church and took the box from his aumbry to show to his manor-lord, upon whom he was dependent for his tithes. Robert looked at the coins with interest, but it was the brooch which really captured his attention.

'For all I know, this may have belonged to one of my Saxon forebears!' he said forlornly. 'They were ejected from the land when William de Poilly was granted it by William the Bastard.'

He put it back rather reluctantly into the box, but before the treasure was put away, the coroner took the precaution of getting Thomas to recount all the coins in the presence of Robert Hereward and then adding his name to the parchment that certified the exact amount discovered. Only then would he allow the box to be tied up again and placed in the priest's chest.

'What happens now?' asked Robert.

'There has to be an inquest, but in this case I can see no way in which I can declare who is the owner, other than to formally seize it for King Richard. But I can decide whether or not it is treasure trove.'

Robert Hereward looked puzzled and decided to seek enlightenment in more comfortable circumstances. He invited the coroner's team to the manor house for refreshment and with the bailiff and Thomas in attendance they began walking up the track from the village green. The coroner sent Gwyn with Henry the reeve to assemble a jury for the inquest in an hour's time, confident that his officer would pass most of that time drinking ale in the tavern opposite the church.

The manor house, a few hundred paces along the Tiverton road, was a small and rather dismal dwelling, for which Robert apologised. 'I only wanted the land here, as I live at my other place in Somerset,' he explained. 'Certainly my wife refuses to stay here and I only sleep here about once a fortnight when I visit.'

The house was a wooden structure with a thatched roof, sitting in a circular compound within a fence of stakes built on a low earthen bank. There were several rooms off the draughty hall and inside the palisade there was a barn and outhouses for animals, cooking and storage. It was more a barton than a manor house and Robert explained that his bailiff lived there with his family. They sat at a table in the hall, where the bailiff's rosy-cheeked wife brought them fresh bread, cheese, slices of cold meat and some passable wine, as well as good ale.

'Crowner, explain this treasure trove business to me,' pleaded Hereward. 'Who does the stuff actually belong to?'

De Wolfe was not all that clear on the law himself, although he had held a couple of inquests on discovered valuables in the ten months in which he had been coroner.

'This case is more complicated, because you are not the freeholder of the land. Knowing Richard de Revelle as I do, he's going to fight tooth and nail to get his hands on it.'

As they ate and drank, John did his best to explain the rules as he understood them. 'Putting aside that complication for the moment, everything hinges on whether the valuables were deliberately

hidden with the intention of recovering them later
– or had just been lost accidentally.'

He saw the puzzlement on Robert's face and
tried to explain more fully.

'Look, if a man walks across a field and a gold
coin drops unnoticed from a hole in his purse, that
would be an accident. He had no intention of either
hiding it or recovering it later.' De Wolfe took a
large swallow of ale while Robert digested this situation. 'But if a man was in fear of being robbed –
or probably, in this case, if he anticipated a troop
of Normans riding up to his door to dispossess
him – then he might gather up all his treasure and
hide it in the ground, with the intention of
reclaiming it secretly at some later time.'

Hereward nodded. 'That's obvious, but what
difference does it make to ownership?'

'Firstly, the treasure must be deliberately
concealed to be treasure trove. If it just falls on
the ground, then it is the property of any finder.
It's only hidden gold and silver that is considered
to be treasure trove – and the purpose of my inquest
is to decide that first.'

'Pretty simple in this case, buried in a box under-
ground!'

'Yes, but it has to be done officially,' replied John.
'Once I've decided, it becomes a felony to retain
the treasure, under pain of hanging.'

'That still doesn't settle to whom it belongs.'

Thomas, who had been sitting farther along the
table, opposite the bailiff, had been listening

170

intently and now couldn't resist airing his undoubtedly large store of knowledge.

'It goes back to Roman times. They called treasure *thesaurus inventus* and divided it equally between the finder and the owner of the land.'

De Wolfe shook his head. 'Not so now in England, though I think some countries abroad still adhere to that. The theory here is that the King owns the whole country and that though he doles out parcels of it to his barons, he still retains the basic ownership. That's why they are called "tenants-in-chief" and "free-holders" – they only hold it at the King's pleasure. So anything found hidden belongs to him, unless he waives the right.'

Thomas nodded eagerly. 'It says in the Holy Gospel of St Matthew that a man who knew there was treasure in a field, sold all his worldly goods to raise the money to buy the field, so that he could claim the treasure.'

He crossed himself devoutly as he mentioned the gospels, but John scowled at him. 'What's that got to do with it? We're in Devon, not Palestine.' He turned back to Robert Hereward. 'I'm going to leave the knotty problem of who owns the treasure to the King's justices when they next come to hold the Assize of Gaol Delivery in a couple of months.'

An hour later, de Wolfe held the inquest at the gate of the churchyard, with a jury of about twenty men and boys gathered from the fields by Gwyn and the reeve. Behind them, along the hedge that surrounded the churchyard, a score of wives, old men and widows, together with a gaggle of children, watched the proceedings with slack-jawed fascination, as an inquest was something none of them had ever heard of before.

John once more had the box taken from the church and placed at his feet, before he stood in front of the half-circle of jurors as Gwyn bellowed the inquest summons at the top of his voice, something he always enjoyed doing. '*All you who have anything to do before the King's coroner for the county of Devon, touching the finding of this treasure, draw near and give your attendance!*'

With Robert Hereward, his bailiff and Michael the priest at one side and Thomas squatting with his pen, ink and parchment on a stool on the other, the coroner called for the finder to step forward. Gwyn helpfully pushed the young Simon, who stood sheepishly before de Wolfe for his brief moment of fame. He repeated what he had said about the discovery and thankfully melted back into the jury line. Henry Stork, the manor-reeve, then confirmed that Simon had reported the matter to him without delay and that he had consulted the bailiff, who stepped forward to say that he had sent to Exeter to notify the coroner, as he had heard was the proper thing to do since last year.

John then got Gwyn to untie the bonds around the box and fold back the cloth so that the contents could be seen. The jury then filed past, gaping at the sight of more money than they would see in a score of lifetimes. Standing back in their ragged line, they listened bemused as de Wolfe concluded the proceedings.

'I have to pronounce on three matters, when such wealth is discovered. Firstly, is it gold or silver? In this case, both are present and I have no hesitation in declaring that this is treasure.' He scowled around the throng before continuing. 'Secondly, where was it found and who was the finder? Obviously, it was this Simon, who unearthed it in a mound in the vill of Cadbury.'

For the finale, he stood with his thumbs hooked into his either side of his wide sword-belt, his tall, spare body slightly stooped. With his long dark grey tunic, his black hair and his predatory nose, he looked like a great crow standing guard over the box of precious metal.

'Next, was this treasure deliberately hidden or merely lost? There is no doubt that it was secreted by intent – no one can just lose a box of this size and weight. And was it abandoned or was there the intention to recover it at some later date?' He glared around again, as if challenging anyone to disagree with him. 'Of course it was not abandoned. No one in their right mind would discard gold and silver! And if it was hidden, then there must have been the desire to reclaim it one day, else there would be no point in hiding it.'

There was no demur from the jury, who were not going to bandy words with this forbidding official from far-away Exeter.

'Lastly, who did it belong to and who hid it? We

173

will never know, though the fact that none of the coins was minted after the arrival of King William in this land, suggests that the owner was a Saxon.' John shot a quick glance towards Robert Hereward, but there was no sign that he wished to claim his ancestors as the original owners. 'As we can never be sure that there are legitimate heirs or successors to the unknown owner, the matter ends there and all that remains is for me to declare that the find is treasure trove and it will be so recorded in my rolls.' He jabbed a finger towards Thomas, who was busy scratching away on his stool. 'The amount has been accurately recorded and witnessed by several persons. I therefore seize this treasure in the name of King Richard and will cause it to be held in safe-keeping in Exeter until the royal justices confirm that it should be sent to the King's treasury in Winchester.'

Gwyn marched forward to close the proceedings by shooing away the jury and picking up the valuable box, which he re-tied once again.

'What's to be done with this, Crowner?' he boomed.

'I want you to take it straight away back to Rougemont and give it into Ralph Morin's hands, to be locked up somewhere safe. I'm staying here for a few hours, as Robert Hereward has kindly invited me to eat with him at the manor house. I'll ride back this evening with Thomas.'

It was a decision that was to cause de Wolfe considerable aggravation some time later.

7

In which Thomas de Peyne hears exciting news

Although Walter Winstone lived a frugal existence in the dismal room above his shop, he was a moderately rich man, mainly because he added considerably to his legitimate business as an apothecary by his more dubious activities in procuring miscarriages and the occasional killing. The last was usually of animals, when some disgruntled person wished to get even with an enemy by poisoning his horse, cow or pigs – but sometimes, as with the attempt on Henry de Pridias, he undertook the occasional murder. As he begrudged every penny he was forced to spend, his wealth had steadily accumulated and his locked chest upstairs now contained quite a few pounds, quite apart from the box buried in his backyard, which held another large hoard of silver pennies. Thus, although he was the meanest man in Devon, he felt able to cast a little bread upon the waters by bribing agents to discredit his rivals, the cunning women whom he obsessively blamed for undercutting his business.

So far he had scored a spectacular success with Alice Ailward, the widow of Rock Lane, who was now securely locked up in the proctors' cells near the cathedral. This emboldened him to repeat the escapade, after doing some intelligence work to discover the names of a few more alleged witches in the city.

On the evening of the day when John de Wolfe rode out to Cadbury to inspect treasure trove, a porter called at the cottage of Theophania Lawrence, in one of the mean lanes of Bretayne. This was the south-western corner of the city, called after the remnants of the original Britons of the Dumnonia tribe, who gave their name to Devon. These Celtic people were pushed into this ghetto when the Saxons arrived hundreds of years earlier to settle within the old Roman walls. It remained Exeter's poorest area, a warren of narrow lanes, shacks and hovels, populated by the lowest class of manual workers.

Theophania's hut was marginally better than those of her neighbours, but was still a dismal one-room dwelling, with wattle and daub walls and a tattered roof of straw thatch. Her visitor aimed a kick at a large rat that was nibbling at some offal in the gutter that oozed past the rickety door and shouted her name through the cracks in the warped boards. He was Edward Bigge, from St Sidwells, the village where Gwyn of Polruan lived, just outside the East Gate. A wide, squat man of thirty, he had cropped ginger hair and a square, pugnacious face that was deeply pitted by old acne scars. He had almost no neck and his arms seemed too long for his short body, but he was immensely strong, almost muscle-bound, from his occupation of carrying goods on and off the ships at the quay-side.

He shouted again and was answered by a yell from inside to wait a moment, as the woman of the house was occupied. Theophania was dealing with another client, a sailor who was about to take ship to Flanders, carrying tin and silver bound from Dartmoor to Cologne. Such cargoes were often preyed upon by pirates, who came from as far afield as the Barbary Coast or even Turkey, and he wanted a charm to keep him safe. Such requests for protection on journeys were common and the old woman had a ready supply of amulets in her cupboard on the wall.

'Take this and hang it around your neck – then we will say a prayer together to St Christopher,' she croaked, handing him a crude *agnus dei*.

This was a small roundel of wax with a cross crudely stamped into one side and a leather lace attached to go over his head. The wax had come from stumps of altar candle that she had scavenged from the waste middens outside various Exeter churches, which she melted down and moulded to make her talismans.

'This has holy powers, man,' she assured him. 'It has a fragment of the consecrated Host within it!' A tiny scrap of the communion wafer that she had smuggled out of St Martin's made the amulet all the more powerful. She looped the thong over

177

his neck and muttered some confused words of prayer to various saints, including Christopher, James and Peter, adding Mary, Mother of God for good measure.

She forced her client to repeat them and as he was mumbling a final 'Amen' she held out her hand for her three pence fee.

'Now get you gone in safety!' she declared, opening the door and letting the sailor push past Edward Bigge, who was waiting on the step.

'What can I do for you, fellow?' she demanded brusquely. Her services were in constant demand and she could afford to dispense with courtesy and amiability.

'I have this pain in my belly and burning when I piss, mother,' Edward complained, sticking to the story that the apothecary had given him.

'How long have you suffered?'

'About four days now. I also feel feverish and sick to my stomach.'

Theophania took his roughened hands and studied the palms, then poked a finger at his face and pulled down his lower lids to look at the whites of his eyes. 'Your member stings when you pass water, eh? Have you been with dirty whores this past few weeks?'

He denied it vigorously, but the old wife sniffed her disbelief as she went to a shelf and took down a small earthenware cup. 'Here, piss into this, while I cut a lock of your hair.'

This was not what Edward was expecting, but

178

he fumbled under his short tunic to loosen the strings of his leggings. Turning his back to her, he held the cup to his loins, while the uncaring crone took a small knife and, with some difficulty, hacked off a small bunch of his cropped hair. He turned round and handed her the filled cup, some embarrassment showing even on the hard face of this rough workman. As he struggled to put his clothing back in place, she opened the door and carelessly threw most of the urine out into the lane, keeping back only an inch in the bottom of the cup. As he watched, she dropped the sample of hair into it, then went to a table in the corner where a candle was burning. She held the cup over it for a few moments until it boiled, the stench in the room becoming even more pungent. Looking into the cup, she muttered something to herself, then set it on the table while she rummaged among pots on the shelf above. Selecting one, she tipped a small quantity of brown powder from it into the cup.

'What's that, mother?' the customer grunted suspiciously, afraid that she was going to ask him to drink the mixture.

'Soil from a fresh grave, man. It has certain powers that we need.' With a piece of holly stick, she stirred the concoction, mumbling to herself. Then she advanced on him, holding the cup and stick. Edward recoiled, but she reached out and grabbed his tunic. 'Lift this up out of the way, if you want to be cured!' she snapped.

Apprehensively, he hoisted his garment to expose

his grubby belly, but was relieved to discover that all Theophania did was to dip the stick in the fluid and make a wide cross on his stomach with the odorous liquid. She repeated this three times, muttering incomprehensible rhymes under her breath. Then she repeated the process on his fore-head, before pressing the warm cup into his hand.

'Go to the cathedral and tip some drops at the north, south, east and west of the Close, saying the paternoster each time. Understand?'

He nodded, uncaring of what she told him, as his mission was nothing to do with his imaginary symptoms.

She reached for another jar on her shelf and tipped some dried flakes of crushed leaves into a scrap of cloth, which she folded and pressed into his hand. 'Mix a pinch of these in a cup of ale each morning for five days. Say prayers to five saints each day – and keep away from unclean harlots!' Holding out her hand for two pence, she opened the door and sent him out into the street.

The next morning, Matilda was still sulking with her husband, refusing to speak to him at the early morning meal. He had thought about taking Nesta's oblique advice and assuaging his wife's displeasure by at least going through the motions of holding an inquest on the death of Robert de Pridias, but his stubborn faith in the legal processes that existed in the name of his king, prevented him from carrying this through. He decided that he preferred to suffer the familiar scowls and snubs at home, rather than twist the law to his own personal advantage.

When he went up to Rougemont after breakfast, he heard from the constable, his friend Ralph Morin, that Gilbert de Bosco had visited the sheriff to demand that secular charges be brought against Alice Ailward. Although Richard de Revelle had perhaps unwisely promised his support for Gilbert's crusade, he was unable to find any specific grounds on which to arraign the woman before either the Shire Court or the royal justices, but promised the canon that he would take legal advice when he went to Winchester the following week.

Ralph Morin said that de Bosco went away in a huff, promising to bring Alice before an ecclesiastical court without delay and, if possible, hand her over to the secular authorities for sentencing. 'The bloody man sees advancement for himself in all this,' growled the constable, over a mug of ale in the hall of the castle keep. 'I hear that he has the bishop on his side, but maybe you know more about what goes on down in that nest of vipers around the cathedral.'

John promised to find out what he could from the archdeacon, as this issue was rapidly dividing opinion and heating tempers throughout the city. Although the subject of witchcraft had previously been ignored, since the canon had interfered, it was now as if a wasps' nest had been poked with a stick. Conflicting opinions were being voiced all over the city and it was the main topic of gossip in both the alehouses and the churches.

Meanwhile, another matter claimed the coroner's attention, one which potentially held more satisfaction for him. This was the arrival of the treasure chest from Cadbury, which Gwyn had escorted back to Exeter the previous evening and which now rested in the constable's chamber, at the opposite end of the hall from the sheriff's quarters.

'Does he know about it yet?' asked de Wolfe.

The big warrior grinned over his forked beard. 'I've left that pleasure to you, John! I thought you would enjoy seeing his face when you tell him.'

'Did you look inside the box?'

Ralph held up his hands in mock horror. 'No damned fear! I'm keeping well out of this one, knowing de Revelle's love affair with money. I left the chest exactly as your man brought it, tied up with cords and locked in a box. And I kept a man on the door all night, just to safeguard myself.'

De Wolfe finished his ale and with a grim smile of anticipation, loped to the door of the sheriff's chamber, at the end of the hall nearest the entrance. As usual, he marched in without ceremony and planted himself in front of Richard's table, hands on hips. For once, de Revelle was alone, without the clerks that normally buzzed around him like flies, waving their parchments for his attention.

The sheriff, who was signing warrants for this week's hangings, looked up and sighed when he saw his brother-in-law. 'Do you still stubbornly refuse to enquire into the death of Robert de Pridias, John? I suspect that this sorcerer woman that is being held by the proctors may be the one that did the deed.'

John smiled his lopsided smile. 'Yet I hear that you decline to arraign her, Richard! Very sensible, I think – you would have some difficulty in devising criminal charges in the absence of any evidence. Try that on the royal judges and they'll lock you up!'

De Revelle's narrow face flushed with annoyance. 'We'll see what the consistory court thinks of the matter first. Was there something you wanted?'

His tone was deliberately offensive, as if his visitor were some minor clerk, rather than the next most senior law officer in the county.

John ignored this, savouring the moment he had been anticipating. 'I was in Cadbury yesterday, Richard. I believe that you have leased that manor to Robert Hereward of Somerset.'

The sheriff nodded absently, still signing his documents.

'A pity you didn't keep it, for at least twenty pounds' worth of gold and silver was dug up there a few days ago!'

The quill went down on the table with a smack as Richard's head jerked up. He stared incredulously at his wife's husband. 'Treasure? Twenty pounds? On my land?'

'It's not your land, Richard. You leased it for five

years to Robert Hereward. In any case, the value goes to the King. I held an inquest yesterday and declared it treasure trove, though possibly the Chief Justiciar may award some part of it to Hereward.'

De Revelle jumped up from his chair, every nerve in his body vibrating at the thought of so much money. 'Nonsense, all that should be mine. You idiot, what right had you to declare it treasure trove? It must have been carelessly lost on my estate and must all be mine, by right of tenure.'

His previously flushed face was now pale with fear at the likelihood of losing such riches and he came from behind his table to pace agitatedly across the chamber. 'Where is this find now? I must see it and claim it before any is stolen!'

John hovered over him as he came close, a head taller and as dark and sombre as the peacock-attired sheriff was gaudy. 'It's quite safe, Ralph has it locked away. But the money – and a big gold brooch – is not yours, Richard, so calm yourself! It was not lost, it is ancient metal, all being of Saxon origin. It was obviously hidden at the time of our conquest.'

Although not a vindictive man, John savoured another opportunity to crow over his brother-in-law, who had so often cheated and embezzled the people of Devon, apart from his devious plotting against his own sovereign. But de Revelle was so obsessed by the thought of such a large hoard of gold and silver being found on what he considered to be his own land that nothing would divert him from seeing it. He hurried to the door and flung it open. 'You say it is with the constable? Is it safe? I must see it!'

With John ambling behind him, trying to suppress his glee, the sheriff stalked into the hall, pushing aside the clerks, men-at-arms and merchants who were in his way as he made straight for the constable's door. Morin's chamber was more an armoury than an office, as unlike the sheriff, he was as illiterate as the coroner. When the door crashed open, he looked up from his conversation with Sergeant Gabriel to see de Revelle, resplendent in a bright green tunic, searching the room with his eyes.

'Where is it? Is it in that chest?' De Revelle focused on a large battered trunk under the window slit, made of oaken boards and secured with a massive padlock. It was twice the size of the aumbry in Cadbury church and was used by Ralph for keeping the pay for the men-at-arms. Exeter had always been a royal castle, not the fief of a baron, which was why it was administered by a constable appointed directly by the King's Council, who sent the coin for the soldiers' wages down from Winchester. But the sheriff, often jealous of Morin's relative autonomy, was not interested today in politics, but in beautiful, shiny money.

'Open it up, it must be given into my safe-keeping!' he barked.

The constable threw a questioning glance at de Wolfe, who shrugged and then nodded. Ralph had

185

no reason to refuse, though knowing de Revelle only too well he felt a certain reluctance to let him get his hands on anything valuable. Grudgingly, he took a small key from the scrip on his belt and handed it to the grizzled sergeant, who went to a locked cupboard on the wall and took out a much larger key, with which he opened the padlock. Thrusting Gabriel aside almost before he had lifted the heavy lid, the sheriff peered inside, then hauled out the old box by the cords that bound it and dropped it on the floor. Watched silently by the others, his fingers scrabbled at the knots and he pulled off the remains of the lid with shaking hands. The sight of a mass of glinting silver and gold seemed to hypnotise de Revelle and he let coins slide through his fingers as he dipped into the treasure. As he held up the golden brooch, John heard his breath whistling out in a hiss of admiration. Then abruptly, he slapped the top back on the box and hoisted it up into his arms, uncaring of the considerable weight.

'This must be lodged in my chamber, where I can keep an eye on it!'

'Don't get any hopeful notions about it, Richard,' warned de Wolfe. 'That box and all its contents will have to be accounted for to the King or one of his ministers.'

'This was found on my land! The fact that I temporarily sub-let to someone else makes no difference. I am the owner of that ground, held in fee simple.'

De Wolfe shrugged. 'Makes no odds who owns the land. Even if you can maintain your claim against Robert Hereward, you are still a tenant-in-chief of the King. It's by that right that all treasure trove belongs to the crown.'

'It's mine, I tell you!' howled the sheriff, clasping the box to his chest as if it were his first-born child. 'It must have been lost on my property, it's not treasure trove, damn you!'

He scuttled out of the room and hurried back to his own chamber, slamming the door behind him. The three military men looked at each other and sighed.

Although Sergeant Gabriel was not of their rank, he was an old and trusted servant. Their common bond of loyalty to the Lionheart and their mutual distrust of the sheriff gave him a privileged status in private. 'I see trouble ahead over this, Crowner,' he grunted.

Ralph Morin dropped on to a bench and pulled at his beard. 'I trust you've got a detailed list of what's in that bloody box? Just in case some of it takes a walk before it gets to Winchester.'

De Wolfe nodded. 'I've got a written list, with witnesses. If any goes missing, we'll know who to blame.'

Again that was something he later wished he had never said.

On that Tuesday morning, a woman walked out of the lanes behind St Mary Arches church into

Fore Street and stopped while a large two-wheeled cart pulled by a pair of patient oxen lumbered past her. She was painfully thin and had a severe wry neck, her chin being pulled down and across almost to her opposite collar-bone. To look straight ahead, the poor soul had to swivel her eyes right up, giving her an expression of permanent questioning. Crossing the main thoroughfare, she made her way down through the lower town until she reached Idle Lane. With a couple of hours to go before noon, the Bush was quiet and Nesta was supervising her potman and maids as they changed the rushes on the floor. The Welsh woman prided herself on running the cleanest inn in Exeter, as well as the one with the best ale and food and insisted on changing the floor coverings every couple of weeks. The visitor stood at the door and watched as one of the maids dragged the old rushes into a pile, using a hay-rake made of wooden pegs fixed into a long cross-piece at the end of a handle. Old Edwin was using a pitchfork to load it on to a barrow, which was tipped on to the midden on the waste ground at the side of the tavern.

The woman, who looked about thirty, tapped on the panels of the open door and twisted her head to look across at the landlady. Nesta had seen her about the streets, but did not know her name. Coming across the taproom, she asked what she wanted, sympathy in her voice as she acknowledged the good-wife's disability. Accustomed to using her deformity to the best advantage, the caller rolled her eyeballs even farther than necessary and managed to look piteously at the tavern-keeper.

'My name is Heloise, wife of Will Giffard, a porter. I have several grave problems, good lady,' she croaked. 'But could we talk about them privately?'

Nesta already had a good idea what one of these problems might be and, having had the same dire trouble recently, was even more sympathetic than usual. 'You'd better come up to the loft, away from these ruffians!' Edwin and the maids had started an acrimonious shouting-match over who should push the barrow out to the midden and Nesta beckoned to the woman to follow her up the broad ladder to the upper floor. Here she led the way to a corner partitioned off from the rest of the spacious attic, where a dozen straw pallets were scattered around to accommodate lodgers.

Opening the door of the small room, she waved Heloise to a stool, while she sat on the edge of a wide bed. This was raised on legs, a rarity in Devon, where most folk slept on a pallet on the floor. The porter's wife introduced herself in a sad and downcast manner, wringing the loose end of her shabby belt between her thin fingers.

'I have heard that you have the gift of healing, mistress. I have three problems which ail me,' she began, rolling her eyes upwards and sideways to keep Nesta in view. 'Firstly, I have had this affliction of my neck since I was a child. Is there anything you can do to help me?'

Nesta smiled wanly at the woman, but shook

189

her head sadly. 'Much as my heart aches for you, Heloise, that is beyond me – and, I suspect, beyond even the most skilled physicians in the land. I have no special powers, you know – only what my mother and her sisters passed on to me when I was younger. They were just wise women in our village in Wales, we made no pretence at having anything more than a knowledge of common cures, passed down through the generations.'

The other woman tried to nod, though she could manage little more than a slight bobbing of her deflected head. 'Then maybe you can do something about these?'

She held out her hands, palms down, and Nesta saw that on the backs of her fingers and knuckles were a dozen small but unsightly warts.

The Welsh woman smiled. This was one of the most frequent requests and there were literally dozens of recipes for curing warts, ranging from the mundane to the bizarre. She got up from her bed and reached up to a shelf on the wall, where a dozen small pots were arranged.

'Take this, there's enough left in the bottom. I must make some more, as warts seem rife in Exeter this year.' She handed a pot to the bemused Heloise, who asked how to use it. 'Rub some on the warts morning and night. It's only willow bark pounded in vinegar, but it will rid you of those lumps in a fortnight. Better than some cures, like rubbing them with the blood of a beheaded eel, then burying the head in the churchyard!'

Nesta suspected that the first two requests were really excuses leading up to the real reason for her visit, although at the time she was unaware of the true nature of this deception. 'And your third problem? Is it what I suspect?'

Her sister's promise of a reward had improved Heloise's acting ability. She dropped her twisted gaze in a parody of chagrin. 'Yes, mistress, I am with child again. My poor body will not stand yet another carrying. It will kill me this time, as it almost did last year.'

This was a bare-faced lie, as she was totally barren, in spite of her husband's incessant attempts to father a child on her. Nesta, mindful of her own very recent crisis, was full of sympathy, but this was one thing that she would never contemplate.

'I cannot help you there either, good woman,' she said softly. 'I can help with warts and fevers and croup, but I have neither the skill nor the courage to rid you of that burden.'

Heloise offered no argument, but stood up and fingered the small purse that dangled by its drawstring from her belt. 'What do I owe you for the ointment?' she asked woodenly.

Nesta shook her head. 'Nothing at all, I can make plenty more. Use it and rid your fingers of those abominations. I am only sorry I cannot do more for you on those other serious matters.'

Moments later, the porter's wife had gone and Nesta went back to haranguing her servants, forgetting the woman's visit almost immediately. But

Heloise smirked as she threw away the pot of ointment as soon as she was around the corner of Idle Lane – the silver pennies she would get from her sister for acting out this charade could buy better medicine than willow in vinegar, even after she had bought her new shawl.

That evening, Matilda was in a neutral mood during supper, seeming to have exhausted her grumbling about his failure to further investigate the death of Robert de Pridias. However, she had heard about the unusual arrest of Alice Ailward by the cathedral proctors and scathingly remarked that it was good to hear that someone in the city was taking the menace of witchcraft seriously. Her husband rode out her criticism in silence, and when Mary had cleared away the debris of the meal, which tonight had been a rather tough boiled fowl, he announced that he was going down to visit the archdeacon.

As it was the truth – although he intended going on to the Bush afterwards – she could hardly complain about his attending upon such a senior man of God and as soon as she had lumbered up to her solar and the attentions of Lucille, he called Brutus and walked the few yards down Canons' Row to the house of John de Alençon.

Leaving the dog to lie in the evening sun outside the door, he went inside to share a flask of wine with his friend. In the archdeacon's spartan room they sat for a while, savouring the latest product of the Loire valley. This evening the coroner seemed to sense a certain excitement in his friend, as if he had good news which he was keeping in check. When he asked de Alençon whether he had something new to tell him, the canon's lean face broke into a smile, but he tapped the side of his nose and told John to divulge his own business first.

'Nothing pleasant, I'm afraid. I want to pick your ecclesiastical brain about this poor woman who was captured by your proctors.'

The archdeacon's smile faded. 'Ah, Gilbert de Bosco! I knew that man would cause more trouble.'

'Does he have the right and the authority to arrest a woman and cast her into a cell?'

The priest sipped his wine and replaced the pewter cup carefully on the table between them. 'You should really ask, who is there to stop him? It seems your brother-in-law didn't object. I presume the bishop could intervene, but he also seems happy to sit on the same wagon which is rolling on this matter.'

'Can you do nothing about it yourself?'

De Alençon shook his head slowly. 'Gilbert de Bosco is a canon of this cathedral, just like myself. My post as Archdeacon of Exeter involves administering the priests of the churches in this part of the diocese – it gives me no authority over my fellow-canons.'

'What about the authority of the chapter?'

'It's none of their business, as it does not concern the running of the cathedral. Gilbert de Bosco has done this in his own capacity as a priest, not as a canon. Chapter has no say in diocesan affairs, they are solely the prerogative of the bishop.'

There was a silence as each man pondered over his wine.

'So what is the attitude of the Church to allegations of witchcraft?' asked John, still worrying at the problem.

The other John shrugged his narrow shoulders within his cassock. 'Until now, I was not aware it had one! Though it condemns heresy and generally frowns upon anything which is ungodly, the question of witchcraft has never formally arisen here, until this interfering Gilbert made it an issue.'

'What will happen to this unfortunate woman, now that de Bosco has her in his clutches?'

'I presume he will cause her to be brought before the consistory court, as I fail to see what other measures can be taken.'

He refilled his friend's cup and then his own.

'Tell me about this court of yours – how does it operate?' asked de Wolfe.

'The Holy Church is jealous of its independence from earthly princes and misses no chance to assert that autonomy,' began the archdeacon, making his guest wonder whether he was to launch into a sermon.

'Thomas Becket went too far down that road!' grunted de Wolfe.

'Yes, and remember how Rome made old King

194

Henry pay for that! In fact, he had to reconfirm the right of the Church to keep all its clerics from the secular courts and try them itself in the consistory courts. William the Bastard himself established those with a charter at the time of the Conquest.'

'Your lot keep these bishop's courts very close to your chest! We laymen never get to know what goes on in them,' complained the coroner.

'There's no secret about them, John. We just don't like washing our dirty linen too publicly. They are convened as required in every diocese on the order of its bishop.'

'Does he adjudicate in them himself?'

The priest gave a wry smile. 'Good heavens, no! A bishop is too high and mighty to concern himself with such matters, which often involve dull charters or drunken and licentious clerks. He appoints a chancellor to run the proceedings, aided by the proctors and some senior priests.'

'So could Henry Marshal appoint Gilbert de Bosco as chancellor?'

De Alençon nodded. 'There is no reason why not – and if I read the politics of the situation right, it seems a distinct possibility.'

The coroner grimaced, though not because of the wine he had just sipped. 'Very convenient for them! And does this bishop's court have jurisdiction over all matters, even this ridiculous accusation against this Alice Ailward?'

'It would be a strange remit for a consistory court, which normally deals with disciplinary matters concerning the clergy, as well as a host of legal affairs to do with Church property, charters, contracts and anything touching upon the internal administration of the diocese.'

John de Wolfe continued to worry away at the issue like a dog with a bone, sensing that the bishop, sheriff and some of the canons were manipulating this situation for their own devious ends. 'If it is so dedicated to Church affairs, how then can it be used against the common people?'

De Alençon once more topped up their cups before replying. 'We live in a Christian state, John, where all our activities are, at least in theory, governed by the tenets of the Church. Even kings and emperors wield their power at the behest of Rome, much as they kick against the pricks at every opportunity.'

De Wolfe felt another sermon approaching, but his friend came rapidly to the point.

'The King's peace and the secular courts govern most of the lives of people not in holy orders, but the canon law which rules we clerics reaches out over everyone when it comes to matters of faith. I have seen the ecclesiastical courts deal with offences such as blasphemy committed by the lay public and have heard of trials for heresy elsewhere, though admittedly they are uncommon.'

De Wolfe digested this before asking his last question. 'So are you saying that the only charge that could be brought against an alleged witch is one of heresy?'

The archdeacon rubbed the curly grey hair that rimmed his tonsure as if goading his brain into action. 'No, for the consistory court to find guilt they must be convinced that some form of criminal damage has been caused, even if it's only the death of a pig or the failure of a cow to give milk. But no doubt idolatry, apostasy, sacrilege, blasphemy, disobedience to the true God and following other gods – in this case the Devil – could be squeezed into the arraignment, if the evidence warranted it.'

'Evidence!' snorted de Wolfe. 'From what I've heard, it is a pack of scandalous lies, deliberately whipped up for some underhand reason.'

'We can only wait on events, John. Let us tackle each problem as it arises – though I fear that this case will not be the last.'

As if to turn the tenor of the conversation in another direction, the canon poured them both more wine and settled back in his hard chair with a smile. 'After all that gloomy talk, John, I have something more pleasant to tell you. It concerns your clerk, my nephew Thomas de Peyne.'

John's black eyebrows rose. For months he had been trying to find some way of restoring Thomas to better spirits, as the little clerk had sunk to such depths of despondency that he had even tried to kill himself by jumping from the roof of the cathedral nave. His hopes of re-entering holy orders after his unfrocking two years earlier, had been repeatedly blocked by senior priests, mainly as a gesture against his master's steadfast adherence to King Richard and his dogged opposition to the cause of Prince John.

'You have news that he might be received back into his beloved Church?'

De Alençon raised a hand to cool his friend's eagerness. 'We are not there yet, John, but I have had encouraging words from Winchester. In fact I heard some weeks ago that there were certain enquiries going on there, but I held my tongue until I had further details, not wanting to raise false hopes in Thomas's breast.'

'So what have you heard?' demanded John impatiently. He found the archdeacon almost as slow in imparting information as the infuriating Gwyn.

'We all know that Thomas was accused by a girl being taught her letters by him, in the school attached to the cathedral there. She claimed that he made indecent advances to her, and as she had influential parents in the city, the whole thing was blown up into insinuations of attempted rape.'

'Bloody nonsense. That feeble little fellow hasn't got it in him,' growled the coroner. 'It was her word against his!'

'Be that as it may, she's done it again,' said the archdeacon. 'She recently entered a priory there as a novice and last month accused one of the lay brothers of interfering with her. But this time, unknown to her, there were two witnesses who swear that no such thing occurred. When challenged by the prioress, she broke down and confessed that she was lying.'

De Wolfe thumped the table with his fist, making the wine cups rattle. 'Ha! So now you think Thomas's disgrace might also be challenged?'

John de Alençon smiled his sweet smile. 'Matters have already gone farther than that. Thankfully, someone there remembered the allegations against him and told the prioress. She taxed this girl with it and in her shame and remorse she also recanted her accusations against my sad little nephew.'

The coroner smacked his hands together in delight. 'This calls for another cup of your excellent Poitou red, John! What happens next?'

'I have already sent a message to the proctors in Winchester and to several of the canons whom I know, as well as to the chancellor of the court which found him guilty. I will be going there myself in a few weeks, and will pursue the matter vigorously.'

'Have you given the good news to Thomas yet?'

'No, I thought I would leave that to you, as he seems so devoted to his master. When you agreed to my suggestion that you take him on as your clerk, you earned his lifelong gratitude, John.'

'Well, the poor fellow was destitute and nearly starving. What else could I do?' grunted the coroner.

'You are too modest, my friend. Under that craggy shell you call a body, there is a compassionate heart. But when you tell my nephew of this, impress on him that there is still some way to go before he can expect to hear anything of being received back into the religious fold. Though Winchester might be amenable, nothing has changed here in Exeter, where you have stubborn adversaries, John.'

De Wolfe finished his wine and stood up to leave. 'I'll be circumspect in what I tell him – but the poor fellow needs to have some hope in his life, so I'll give him the news in the morning. Meanwhile, keep an eye on this mad canon and let me know if he gets up to any further mischief!'

As John had expected, the next morning Thomas went into ecstasies of delight when his master gave him a cautious account of the archdeacon's news. The bluff Gwyn, whose teasing of the little clerk was a cloak for his affection and concern, was equally rapturous. He seized Thomas by the waist and held him squealing over his head in their chamber in the castle gatehouse.

Back on the floor, Thomas alternated between laughing, crying and crossing himself. 'My constant prayers have been answered, Crowner! Truth will out in the end. May God forgive that girl for the torment she has caused me!'

As Gwyn dived for his cider jar and mugs to celebrate, de Wolfe wagged a finger at his clerk in mock admonishment. 'As your uncle told you at the time, God also sent you a message when you tried to end your own life! See now how you were saved for better things.'

John had no real conviction regarding the power

of prayer – his religious beliefs were born of child-hood conditioning and adult conventions – but knowing of Thomas's strong faith, he pandered to the spirit of the moment. He was referring to the failure of Thomas's attempt to kill himself when his forty-foot fall had been broken by his gown being snagged on a projection halfway down. The archdeacon had prudently impressed on his nephew that this was a heavenly sign that he was meant to survive and not try *felo de se* again.

In spite of his dislike of cider, the joy of the moment caused Thomas to join the others in a celebratory drink and over the rim of the grubby pot he looked with dog-like affection at these two large, gruff men who had saved his life in more ways than one.

'Even when I am reordained, Crowner, I shall continue to serve you. I owe you everything and I can only try to repay you by giving you what little help my poor brain and my pen can offer!'

De Wolfe gave one of his throat rumbles to cover what came too close to a display of emotion to suit him. He scowled and gave his clerk a fero-cious glare from under his heavy brows.

'We'll see about that, Thomas, when the time comes. This will not be a hasty business, but when you are restored to your true status, we will discuss it again, together with your uncle.'

He tossed down the rest of his drink in a gesture of finality, while a grinning Gwyn gleefully regarded his little friend's suppressed delight. 'I'll be the first to come and take confession with you, Thomas – to tell you what a feeble little turd I think you are, who can't even get your leg across a horse, let alone a woman!' His tone removed any offence from the teasing words and, to confirm his affection, he gave the clerk a slap on the back that almost knocked the former priest off his stool.

De Wolfe glowered at them. 'That's enough, you pair of fools. Let's get back to work.'

8

In which Crowner John rides off with a lady

Like Alphington, the village of Ide was within sight of Exeter, across the river to the west. Belonging to a manor owned by the bishop, it was a rather obscure hamlet with no claims to any fame, other than having a cunning woman with a wide reputation for her healing powers. Her name was Jolenta and she was no old crone, but a handsome woman of about thirty years. Her mother and her grandmother had both the same name and a similar reputation for their gifts, being consulted not only by supplicants from neighbouring villages, but even from the city itself.

Jolenta was unmarried, an unusual state for a good-looking woman, preferring to keep house for her father, who was the village cobbler and harness-maker. Her mother had died five years earlier and she was content to live quietly, adding the few pennies she made from her potions and liniments to the wage her father earned from his leather-work.

On the morning that Thomas de Peyne was rejoicing about the news from Winchester, a cart drawn by two sturdy oxen rumbled slowly into the village and followed the only street until it reached a small wooden bridge over a stream. Here, where the road bent to the left, it stopped outside the only alehouse to let off a man and a woman who had hitched a ride on the back. The cart was empty, having returned from taking a load of vegetables into Exeter at dawn, for sale in the markets. Having thanked the driver, the man vanished into the tavern, leaving his wife standing uncertainly at the edge of the dusty road. A moment later, he reappeared, having received directions, and, grabbing her arm, he pointed to a shack almost opposite, which had head-collars and girths for oxen hanging alongside the door.

'Now do exactly what I told you!' hissed Edward Bigge into her ear and, with a quick push to set her on her way, he vanished back into the doorway to fortify himself with ale.

Reluctantly, Emelota Bigge crossed the road and rapped on the panels of the open door. A strong smell of tanned leather wafted out at her as the tapping of a hammer ceased and a man came from the depths of the workshop. He was in late middle age and had a lined face surmounted by an almost bald head. Rubbing his calloused hands on the long leather apron that was hung around his neck, he asked what she wanted.

'I was told that a wise woman called Jolenta lived here,' she said, with partly feigned trepidation. The older man stared at her, taking in her worn kirtle of faded brown wool and the Saxon-style head-rail of frayed white linen that came down low on her forehead. Sometimes, rich women came here from the city, but he calculated that this one would be good for only a couple of pennies. He jerked a thumb along the front of the whitewashed building. 'There's a door on the other end. She's in there cooking my dinner.'

He turned back to his hammering and Emelota walked past the blank face of the cottage to the end. Her husband had promised her five pence for a new dress if she did what she was told, as the apothecary had told him that for the fee he had paid for Edward to implicate Theophania Lawrence, he also expected the participation of Edward's wife. Around the corner, she found a garden with a goat and a milk cow tethered and some rows of vegetables growing in the croft behind. It was something of a luxury for a dwelling to have two doors, but she reasoned that Jolenta wanted to keep her sorcerer's business separate from her father's cobbling.

This time her knocking on the door was answered by a good-looking dark woman about her own age, with her hair hanging in two braids down the yellow kirtle that accentuated her full bosom and narrow waist. Jolenta looked almost too well groomed for an obscure village like Ide, and Emelota guessed that she must have a healthy trade in customers for her magical talents. Following the story with which Edward had primed her, his wife explained that she was from Exeter and that she had heard that Jolenta was expert in retrieving missing valuables.

'What is it you have lost?' Jolenta asked, inviting Emelota into the relative gloom of the cottage. It seemed clean and tidy, although barely furnished with a couple of stools, a bench and a table, at which Jolenta had been preparing some food.

'I fear it has been stolen by one of my neighbours – but I need to know which one, so that my husband can confront him with the theft.'

Jolenta took in the shabby clothes of her visitor and wondered what she could have possessed of any value. 'So what is it that has vanished?'

'A silver belt buckle that was left me by my mother, God rest her soul,' said Emelota piously, although in fact her mother was hale and hearty and lived next door to her. 'My father was a miner on the moor and over the years collected enough silver from among the lead to fashion a good heavy buckle. It is the only thing of value I possess and must be worth several shillings, but it disappeared last week from the place in my dwelling where I hide it. Only a few neighbours knew anything of it.'

Jolenta nodded her understanding, as this was a common enough request, the finding of missing objects or even persons. She went to a shelf above the table and took down a ragged book, the parchment pages fraying at the edges between the battered leather covers. She could not read it, but that was no bar to its usefulness. Coming over to the woman who stood alongside the dead fire-pit in the middle of the room, she opened the book, revealing a rusty key in the middle.

'Take this psalter, shut your eyes and place the key between any of the pages, then close the covers.'

Emelota did as she was told and waited for the next instructions.

'Now we will pray together to St James and St Jerome that they will help us reveal the truth.'

With her eyes still closed, Emelota repeated some doggerel chanted in a mechanical voice by Jolenta, calling on a variety of holy persons to assist them in their quest.

'Now, hold the holy book at arm's length and say out loud the names of those neighbours who you think may be guilty of this theft.'

Emelota mumbled at random the names of half a dozen of her neighbours in Exeter, careless of what result there might be. Nothing happened and Jolenta commanded her to hold the psalter higher, level with her forehead, which made her grip upon it less secure. Halfway through the second recitation of the names, there was a dull clink as the heavy iron key fell to the hard-packed earth of the floor.

'There, that fell as you said the name of William Hog. He is the one who stole your buckle.'

Her voice was so definite and matter-of-fact that the impostor almost believed her, until she reminded herself that the theft of the buckle – and even its very existence – was completely fictitious.

'Is there anything else?' asked Jolenta, as she retrieved the key and put the book back on the shelf. Like Nesta, she was well aware that clients often used one request as an excuse for introducing something more personal, once they had got themselves inside.

'I suffer from heavy courses each month,' murmured Emelota. 'It weakens me and they are getting worse as time goes by.'

For the first time she was telling the truth and this was an opportunistic addition that her husband had not schooled her to use. If she was to pay this woman a couple of pence, she might as well get Edward's money's worth – or rather, the apothecary's money's worth.

Jolenta nodded, as this was yet another common complaint. She went to a box on the floor and lifted the lid to reveal a number of bags and pouches of various sizes. Taking one, she opened the drawstrings at its neck and took out a few pieces of dried stick, each a few inches long.

'These are blackthorn. Scrape off the outer bark with a knife and discard it. It is the white pith of the under-bark you need. Pound it in the milk of a one-coloured cow and drink some every morning. When it's gone, you can easily find more blackthorn in the hedges. In a month or two, you will be relieved of your problem.'

Emelota placed the twigs in the purse dangling from her girdle and offered some pennies from the same pouch. Jolenta took two.

'That's for the theft of your buckle. The blackthorn and my advice are free.'

Feeling somewhat guilty, Edward Bigge's wife left the cottage and walked back to the alehouse to join her husband.

Several days passed in relative peace, with little to disturb the normal rhythm of life in the city, although the undercurrent of dispute concerning cunning women continued unabated in the taverns, the workshops and in the gossip along the streets. On Sunday, more of the parish priests preached sermons condemning all forms of heresy, apostasy and sacrilege, as Canon Gilbert had been around as many as he could to remind them forcibly of the bishop's concern on the matter.

Most of this passed over John de Wolfe's head, as he had a number of deaths to deal with, one drowning in a mill-race taking him away for the night, as he had to ride to a village near Totnes. As usual, this earned him more scowls and sarcasm at home, Matilda insinuating that it was an excuse for him to spend the night whoring and drinking. He would not have minded so much if it had been true, but in fact he and Gwyn had spent an uncomfortable night huddled in their riding cloaks in a barn, as there was no inn in the village.

The other days were taken up with an alleged rape in Clyst St Mary, another village to the east of Exeter, and a near-fatal assault in the Saracen alehouse in the city. This tavern, run by Willem the Fleming, was the most notorious inn in Exeter, being a rendezvous for thieves and harlots, providing a regular supply of knifings and head injuries for the attention of the city constables and coroner.

To assuage Matilda's bad mood, that Sunday John allowed her to drag him to Mass at St Olave's. He succumbed to this about once a month, although he flatly refused to attend confession, especially as Julian Fulk, the fat, oily priest of St Olave's, had been one of his murder suspects not long before. De Wolfe found it bad enough having to endure Fulk's sermon, full of exaggerations about witches and wizards and their supposed communion with the Devil as they went about their business of eating infants and flying through the air. Although John disliked the priest, he knew he was a well-read, intelligent man, unlike many of his colleagues, so he failed to see how he could have been persuaded to peddle such fanciful nonsense, unless it was to curry favour with his ecclesiastical superiors.

However, Matilda seemed impressed by his diatribe, as she had always favoured Julian Fulk with her admiration, rating him a potential archbishop, if not a pope. On the short walk back to their house in Martin's Lane, she ranted on about the iniquities of the cunning women in their community, putting herself firmly in the camp of Canon Gilbert, Cecilia de Pridias and all the witch-hunters of the city. Her husband wisely kept his mouth firmly closed, letting the tirade flow over him, as any contradiction of her bigoted views would serve only to start them up afresh, at an even higher level of vituperation.

That evening, he escaped to the Bush and spent a pleasant and passionate few hours with Nesta. As they lay in bed in the languid glow that followed their lovemaking, she idly mentioned that she had used the room to counsel the strange woman Heloise, who had such a peculiar affliction of her neck. Although her account of the meeting seemed innocuous, something about the incident started a little niggle of anxiety within de Wolfe's mind.

'Nesta, my love, with all this present unrest about sorcerers and folk healers, it would be best if you kept well away from such matters for the time being,' he advised sternly. 'This business with Alice Ailward shows that this crazy man de Bosco is quite willing to use false testimony to trap unwary women.'

Nesta, always an independent spirit, argued against him for a while, but his obvious sincerity and concern for her eventually caused her to promise to avoid employing her gifts again, until the present hysteria had died down.

The matter worried away at him during the night and, the next morning, at their habitual second breakfast in his chamber, the coroner mentioned Nesta's client to Gwyn and Thomas.

'I've seen that woman with the twisted neck about the town,' rumbled his officer. 'She's from some hovel in Bretayne. I know nothing of her, except that her sister is a whore who works out of the Saracen.'

Although this did nothing to lessen John's unease, the fact that the woman was a relative of a harlot seemed to have no real relevance to his concerns until he noticed Thomas looking rather uneasily at him.

'Do you know anything of this woman?' he barked.

The clerk shifted uncomfortably on his stool. 'I'm sure it's of no importance, but I have seen that woman with the wry neck walking in the town with a painted strumpet, who Gwyn says is her sister. It's just that I remember our friend Sergeant Gabriel pointing her out to me in the castle bailey one day, saying that she was one of the sheriff's whores.'

It was no particular secret that Richard de Revelle was fond of low company in his bed, as his glacial wife Eleanor almost never came to Rougemont, preferring to live at their manor near Tiverton. In fact, the coroner had once caught his brother-in-law in bed with a harlot and on another occasion, had rescued him from a burning brothel.

'Can't see the connection,' growled Gwyn. He was aware that something was bothering his master and tried to put his mind at ease.

De Wolfe chewed the matter over in his mind for a moment, then shrugged. 'I expect you're right. I'm getting unreasonably anxious with all this nonsense about witches in the air.'

'I hear that the consistory court sits tomorrow on this poor woman Alice Ailward,' said Thomas, who knew everything that went on within the confines of the cathedral Close. As well as eavesdropping on the gossip of the canons' servants in the house where he lodged, he knew most of the vicars and secondaries, many of them accepting him as if he were still in holy orders himself.

'Are you sure that this bishop's court has the power to try such women?' demanded de Wolfe, mindful of his discussion with the archdeacon.

The ever-knowledgable Thomas was only too happy to air the fruits of his recent researches among the books in the cathedral library and conversations with his priestly aquaintances. 'Generally, the Church shows little interest in the transgressions of cunning women,' he said. 'Though there have been various pronouncements on the issue for centuries.' He warmed to his theme, the latent scholar in him bubbling to the surface. 'The Synod of Elvira in 336 punished apostasy by refusing to offer communion. Then the Frankish bishops at Worms in 829 stated that it was the Devil who aided witches to prepare love potions and poisons and to raise storms. The Synod of Reisbach in 799 demanded penance for withcraft, but no actual punishment . . .'

'For Christ's sake, clerk, will you stop lecturing us,' boomed Gwyn. 'We're not pupils in your cathedral school!'

John was more sympathetic and motioned for Thomas to continue. He poked his tongue out at the Cornishman and carried on.

'When the issue is forced upon its attention, the

Church prefers to divert it to the manorial courts – or presumably, here in Exeter, to the burgesses' courts. Only if some conspiracy to cause criminal damage is evident will the consistory courts intervene – and even then, they always hand over persons they convict to the other courts for sentencing.'

'You should have been a bloody lawyer, not a priest, Thomas!' growled Gwyn with mock sarcasm, as he was really quite proud of the little man's erudition.

'What do you mean by criminal damage?' demanded the coroner.

'Well, in the villages, if a mare drops a foal or the chickens stop laying, then the owner may claim he has lost profit because a witch cast a spell on them, at the instigation of some neighbour who holds a grudge.'

'Where I come from in Cornwall, the folk don't bother with all that nonsense,' boomed Gwyn. 'They just form a lynch-mob and hang the suspected culprit from the nearest tree!'

'We all know what tribe of savages you hail from!' squeaked the clerk, dodging a playful swing from Gwyn, which would have knocked him from his stool if it had connected.

'Calm down, you childish pair!' snapped de Wolfe. 'Where and when is this court being held tomorrow, Thomas?'

'It will be in the chapter house, after terce, sext and nones. But it is a closed hearing, Crowner, only churchmen will be admitted.'

'I am the coroner for this county, damn it!' roared John.

Thomas shook his head. 'No matter, sir. The secular powers have no jurisdiction there. Not even the sheriff could attend.'

'Can you worm your way in, Thomas?' asked Gwyn.

The clerk managed to look both sly and sheepish. 'I had thought of slipping into the back row. My usual garb and my tonsure often make me inconspicuous in such company.'

'Do that, then let me know straight away what transpires there,' commanded his master. 'It's a damned scandal, having a secret inquisition. Even our sheriff's court, for all his corruption, is at least open to the people.'

Walter Winstone's intention was to use Edward Bigge to fabricate a story to incriminate Theophania Lawrence and to make similar accusations against Jolenta of Ide through the false testimony supplied by Edward's wife, Emelota. Both these were to be fed through to the obsessively receptive ears of Gilbert de Bosco, so that as with Alice Ailward proceedings could be taken against them in the bishop's court. Unfortunately, the apothecary had unwisely paid half Edward Bigge's fee in advance, the other part to be given once he had given his lying evidence to the canon. On Monday morning, with twenty pence in his purse, Bigge decided to celebrate and went drinking, first in the Anchor

Inn on the quay-side, then at the Saracen on Stepcote Hill, so that by noon he was uproariously drunk.

A surfeit of ale and cider always made Edward Bigge loquacious, usually at the top of his bull-like voice and he reeled out of the Saracen shouting to the world at large that he had had a narrow escape from the Devil. The inhabitants of the area around that disreputable alehouse were all too familiar with noisy drunks and normally no one would have taken any notice of the slurred ranting of yet another inebriate. However, as Edward weaved his way up to Smythen Street, the continuation of Stepcote Hill, he came across an unfortunate old fellow who was looking into the open front of one of the blacksmiths' forges that gave the street its name. Pinning the man against the door-post, he leaned towards him and uttered a confidential whisper that could be heard twenty paces away. 'I saw Satan, as plain as I see you now,' he hissed. 'Huge and black he was, with horns on his head and red fire coming from his nostrils!' His voice rose as got into his drunken stride and three men and a woman coming down the street stared at him with curiosity. 'She conjured up Beelzebub as plain as the nose on your face,' he roared at the disconcerted old man. 'This cunning woman over in Bretayne can kill cattle ten miles away and put a spell on husbands so that they leave their wives and cleave to another woman! I saw her bewitch someone myself, with the bats flying out of a great book she had there!'

One of the men passing by stopped at this, then turned to the woman and yelled at her. 'I told you it was a curse, you damned fool! I was bewitched when I took up with that girl!'

The woman gave him a shove in disgust, but he was already moving towards Edward Bigge, shouting as he went. 'What cunning woman is this? They should be struck from the earth for the evil they wreak.'

The drunk turned and looked blearily at the newcomer, giving the terrified old man the chance to slip away. Two smiths and three of their customers came out from the interior of the forge to see what all the commotion was about.

'I said, who was it?' demanded the passer-by. 'I live in Bretayne and similar magic has been worked on me, I swear!'

Even though his wits were slowed by ale, Bigge preened his new self-importance. 'I went to her just for a potion for stomach-ache – but she raised the Devil and frightened the life out of me, so I ran!'

'What was her name, damn you?' yelled the exasperated questioner.

'Theophania, she was. Theophania Lawrence.'

One of the smiths lumbered up closer to the pair. 'I went to her some months back, with a flux of my bowels. Two pence she took from me, but nothing did she do for my guts.'

Almost as if by another sort of magic, a small crowd began gathering, like iron filings to a lodestone. People came out of the adjacent forges and from some vegetable stalls opposite, to listen to what was going on. Inside a minute, three more people began telling of their good and bad experiences with cunning women and Edward Bigge, encouraged by the attention, spiralled into more and more fanciful accounts of his session with Theophania.

'The room went dark and there was a smell of brimstone. She grew twice as tall and green lights came from her eyes like rays!' he ranted, his imagination fuelled by the Saracen's strong cider.

The man who had demanded the witch's name became caught up in the excitement and turning to his sceptical wife, took her by the shoulders and shook her. 'See, I told you it was not my doing with that girl. I was bewitched! She should be stopped, that bloody hag.'

By now more than a dozen people had congregated in the street, many primed by the sermons they had heard in the city's churches the previous day. With the priests' exhortations fresh in their ears, they were easy prey for the infectious hysteria that started to ripple through the crowd. Now everyone was gabbling about their experiences with sorcerers and memories of mere cough medicines and poultices for ulcers were magnified into spectres of goblins and huge black cats. Every ill that had befallen them in the past few years was suddenly attributed to the curses of wizards – and those who had lost silver coins, had miscarriages, watched their pigs die of a fever or had their thatch catch fire, attributed it all to the evil works of cunning women in general and Theophania Lawrence in particular.

Within ten minutes, idle gossip had passed through rumbling discontent into open hostility, a mood that fed upon itself and turned uglier by the minute. Edward Bigge, who knew that his purse had become appreciably lighter since spending the weekend drinking the apothecary's money, had enough sense left within his fuddled brain to see an opportunity to recover his funds if he aided Walter Winstone's scheme even more.

'I know where she lives, this scandalous bitch who summons up spirits from Hades,' he yelled thickly. 'We should confront her with her evil deeds and get her to repent!'

He pushed himself from the wall against which he had been leaning and stalked unsteadily up Smythen Street, shoving his way through the now fevered crowd.

'You needn't tell *me* where she lives,' screamed a toothless woman. 'I live in the next lane. She put a curse on my son so that he was born with one leg shorter than the other!'

'Ay, ask her what she has to say for herself!' shouted another.

'Don't ask her, just hang her!' screamed another, who had drunk almost as much as Edward Bigge.

Almost as if it were a living entity in itself, the crowd flowed behind Edward, who was closely followed by the man alleging that his infidelity was due to Theophania's curse. As it moved along, more people attached themselves to its margins. Most had no idea what was going on until they were sucked into the hysteria by the exaggerated explanations of the inner core. By the time the mass of people had wheeled left through a lane and emerged into Fore Street, there were more than half a hundred shouting and gesticulating citizens, with a penumbra of excited urchins and barking dogs. Crossing the main street, several horsemen and two ox-carts were forced to stop, until the mob flowed into another lane on the opposite side, below St Olave's Church, and slithered into the stinking lanes of Bretayne.

One of the town constables heard the tumult from as far away as Carfoix in the centre of the city. It was Osric, the skinny Saxon, and he hurried after the tail of the crowd as it vanished into Bretayne. Grabbing a boy who was capering along behind them, he yelled at him to discover what was going on, but got little sense from the lad.

'They've found the Devil down here, they say! They're going to hang him!' he gabbled and twisted free from Osric's hand to run after the mob.

Having unsuccessfully tried to stop Alice Ailward from being arrested a few days before, the constable had a sudden foreboding that even worse trouble was going to come of this and that again he would be powerless to prevent it on his own. He turned around and ran as fast as his long thin legs would carry him, back towards Rougemont Castle.

The crowd flowed inexorably on through the mean lanes, oblivious of the debris underfoot and the filth that ran in the gutters. Many of the locals appeared from hovels and alleys to discover what was going on and while some joined the mob, others violently defended their neighbour Theophania. Scuffles broke out on the periphery but had no effect on slowing down the shouting and chanting vigilantes.

As they reached the house where she lived, Edward Bigge threw up a hand dramatically and pointed at her front door. 'In there it was!' he yelled. 'That's where she conjured up Satan and, for spite, put a spell on me. Since then, I've not been able to satisfy my poor wife. This witch took all the manhood out of me!'

This new accusation had been suggested to Bigge by the other man's claim that Theophania was the cause of him cuckolding his wife. The clamour increased and a burly youth, who had not the slightest interest in witchcraft but who enjoyed a good fight, dashed forward and with a mighty kick, smashed open the flimsy door.

There was a scream from inside and, as several men fought to get through the door, Theophania was seen cowering at the back of the room. As if it were not enough that fate already seemed set against her, it so happened that she was in the process of changing her kirtle to put it in the wash. She stood cringeing in her thin chemise, her long grey hair unbound and uncovered, hanging down lankly over her shoulders. To cap it all, at that moment a black cat jumped from a chair alongside her and with a squeal of fright, wisely took off through the door and vanished behind the house.

'A witch, a naked witch! With a coal-black cat!' screamed the mob, in transports of delight at this confirmation of their hysterical suspicions. A surge of bodies pressed against the doorway, with Edward Bigge yelling, 'Beware of Beelzebub – she'll set the Devil upon you!'

In spite of several of Theophania's neighbours punching out ineffectually at the edge of the rabble, the leading men and several wild-eyed women burst into the room and seized the screaming old dame, who had collapsed into a corner.

With frothy spittle at the corners of his mouth, a fat man who was the sexton at St Petroc's Church, frenziedly waved his arms in the air and repeatedly howled at the top of his voice, 'The testaments demand that thou shalt not suffer a witch to live! Obey the word of the Lord thy God!'

Osric the constable nearly burst his heart in his haste to get help from the castle and the last few yards up the hill to the gatehouse had reduced him to a gasping wreck by the time Sergeant Gabriel came out of the guardroom to meet him. When his laboured breathing allowed him to speak, he gasped out his news and the leader of the garrison's men-at-arms wasted no time in getting a posse together. Turning out the four men playing dice in the gatehouse, he yelled at another three, who were passing across the inner ward. After sending the man on sentry duty at the gate to alert the coroner upstairs, he set off with his men at a fast trot down towards the town, leaving Osric to recover his breath. By the time his heart had slowed sufficiently, John de Wolfe and Gwyn had clumped down from their chamber and the burgesses' constable was able to tell them what he had seen.

It was pointless going for their horses for such a short distance, so they all loped after Gabriel's detachment and caught up with them outside Theophania Lawrence's cottage.

'No mob here, Crowner,' panted Gabriel. 'But this man says they've dragged her off somewhere.'

Several of her neighbours were looking apprehensively through the shattered door into her dwelling, where the sparse furniture had been overturned and all her pots of lotions and bundles of herbs had been stamped into a mess on the floor. The neighbour, a rough-looking man with a fresh black eye and bloody nose, had obviously been one of those who had tried to defend the old dame.

'They took her that way, Crowner, towards the city wall!' He waved his arm vaguely downhill, towards the western corner of the city.

De Wolfe wasted no more time on questions, but set off in that direction, leading Gwyn and Gabriel at a lope through the twisting, narrow alleys between a motley collection of small houses, huts and semi-derelict shacks. Faces peered fearfully from doorways and around corners, although the ubiquitous urchins danced around in their rags, hugely enjoying this diversion from their normally sordid existence. Lean, mangy dogs barked excitedly at the running men, who slopped and slipped through the running sewage as the lanes became steeper when they approached the slope down to the river. The top of the town wall was in sight over the roofs of the huts when they came upon a bedraggled figure climbing towards them. He wore a black monk's habit, although his loud cursing would have done credit to a Breton fisherman.

He held up his staff as they ran towards him, and now John could see that one entire side of the monk's clothing was sopping wet with stinking fluid and that the side of his face was grazed and bleeding.

'Those bastards pushed me over when I tried to stop them,' he wailed. 'They had some poor woman and seemed intent on doing her harm!'

'Which way did they go, brother?' shouted Gwyn.

The monk, who must have been from the small Bendictine priory of St Nicholas higher up in the town, pointed his stick behind him.

'Last I saw of the swine, they were clustering around the Snail Tower, yelling and screaming like a pack of Barbary apes. That was a good few minutes ago, so you'd best make haste.'

Again, the coroner pounded on at the head of his small posse, making for the round tower that stood at the junction of the north and west walls of the city, just above the upper part of Exe Island. It was only a few hundred paces away and as they came past the last row of dwellings before the lane that ran inside the high walls, they saw the remnants of the mob melting away into the numerous alleys and paths that ran back up into Bretayne. The noisy approach of half a score of vengeful custodians of the law had scared away the rioters, but they left behind a chilling legacy of their activities.

Turning slowly, with her feet a yard above the ground, was the body of Theophania Lawrence, hanging by a rope around her neck from an old iron bracket sticking out of the Snail Tower, which had once carried a sconce for a lighted pitch-brand.

Her head lolled sideways on to her shoulder, her face purple as a token of her slow death from strangulation, rather than a broken neck. As a final indignity, her pathetically thin chemise was ripped down from the neck, exposing her sagging breasts, between which some at least partially literate rioter had crudely inscribed with a charcoal stick a large 'W' for 'Witch'.

Whilst Edward Bigge was drunkenly involved in the riotous events in Bretayne, his wife was pursuing the other part of her husband's contract with the

225

apothecary. Acting on the instructions that Edward had laboriously dinned into her head, she dressed as neatly as she could and went to seek an audience with Gilbert de Bosco at his house in Canons' Row. She waited until after the last of the morning offices to make sure that he would be at home seeking his midday dinner – although in fact Gilbert had deputed today's attendance at the cathedral to his vicar, as he kept his hours of worship close to the minimum allowed by the rules laid down by the chapter.

When his steward came to his well-appointed study to tell him that a common woman urgently wished to see him, he was dismissive, especially as he could hear the clatter of pewter plates and the clink of a wineglass from his adjacent dining room, where his meal was almost ready to be served. But his servant's next words caught his attention.

'She says she has a complaint about a witch, Reverence. Something about being assaulted by an incubus, raised from hell.'

As the steward had expected his master to instruct him to throw the madwoman out into the street, he was surprised when the burly priest slapped down the book he was reading and curtly told him to bring the dame in to see him. When she appeared, Emelota avoided giving her husband's name, in case the fact of two members of the Bigge family giving testimony against cunning women might look suspicious. She was not to know that the precaution was unnecessary, as at that very moment the drunken Edward was precipitating the lynching of Theophania, in which the canon was not to be involved.

Gilbert remained seated as she stood before him, hands clasped demurely in front of her. His plethoric face glared at her expectantly. 'So what have you to tell me, woman?'

'I have been grievously wronged, sir. I went to a woman who I was told was a respectable healer, but found her to be in league with imps and devils, spurning the Christian ways which are so dear to me.'

The words were music to Gilbert's ears and he had a momentary vision of himself with mitre and crozier if this campaign went as planned.

'In what way were you wronged?'

Emelota launched into the story that Walter Winstone had concocted. She told how she had visited Jolenta of Ide in order to get help in ridding herself of the barrenness that had afflicted her womb these past three years, as her husband was becoming impatient at the lack of further sons. The bizarre imagination of the apothecary led her to describe how Jolenta had caused the room to be plunged into darkness, with rolls of thunder and flickering red lights, accompanied by a smell of burning sulphur. Then wicked imps appeared, climbing up her legs and tearing at her clothing, as the witch screamed invocations to Satan and all the fallen angels. Then, after Jolenta had demanded payment of five pence, she promised Emelota that she would be with child within two months. Since then, she had been visited several times at midnight by a horned incubus, who had ravished her during her sleep – and now she was afraid that if she did fall pregnant, the child would be the by-blow of the Devil.

Incredible as this story was, the eager canon welcomed it gladly, uncaring of whether it was true or not, as long as it gave him further ammunition for his chosen crusade. It seemed that his campaign to stir up the population was bearing fruit, especially his exhortations to the parish priests to whip up animosity through their sermons.

'Can you take me to this evil woman?' he demanded, thrusting his big, florid face towards the obsequious complainant.

'Indeed I can, sir. The village is but a mile or two beyond the West Gate.'

Even the prospect of a new denunciation of a sorcerer was insufficient to keep Gilbert from his dinner, as the prospect of salmon poached in butter and boiled bacon with new beans easily overcame his crusading enthusiasm.

'We will go there in two hours, good-wife. Be back here then and when we return from Ide I will exorcise these unclean spirits from your poor abused body.'

As he sat down to his meal, he sent servants to fetch two of the proctor's men and a brace of horses, so that when they set out for Ide, Emelota was perched side-saddle upon a pony led on a halter by one of the other riders.

After splashing through the ford over the Exe and making a short ride through country lanes, they reached the hamlet of Ide. De Bosco recalled with satisfaction that it belonged to Bishop Henry Marshal, which made things much easier for him, not having to deal with some possibly obstinate manor-lord. His first action when he reined up in the small village was to send for the reeve, who quickly arrived in company with the bailiff, who was doing his rounds of the manor that day.

Gilbert quickly established his authority over the men. 'I am Canon Gilbert de Bosco, here on behalf of the Lord Bishop, who has appointed me chancellor of his consistory court.'

The two men were unsure as to what all this meant, but they were not prepared to challenge anything the canon might say, if he was the spokesman for their lord, who had the power of life and death over them.

'I am here to deal with a sorcerer in your midst, a woman called Jolenta,' bellowed de Bosco, sliding from his horse.

The jaws of the bailiff and reeve sagged in dismay and several villagers who had drifted in to eavesdrop on the group began muttering among themselves.

'Jolenta, Your Reverence? But she is a good woman, one of the most useful in the manor,' protested the bailiff.

'That's no concern of yours, fellow. Just tell me where she lives.'

His tone reminded the local officials again that they had no power to obstruct this emissary of their lord and master and, reluctantly, the reeve pointed to a cottage just along the tiny street.

'That's the one, sir,' called Emelota, climbing down from her unaccustomed perch on her steed, an experience with which she would be able to regale her envious neighbours when she got home. With the locals looking anxiously on, the two proctor's men and a pair of Gilbert's own servants marched ahead of him towards the dwelling, with Emelota trailing along behind. They were followed by a sullen and apprehensive score of villagers, who had been attracted by the unusual activity in the sleepy hamlet.

The pattern of the assault on Theophania's house was followed again, as the proctors rudely pushed open the front door and thrust themselves inside. As Gilbert followed, they found Jolenta at a table, pounding herbs in a mortar, a small cauldron of scented water bubbling on a trivet over the fire-pit beside her. She swung round, her handsome face indignant at this rude intrusion. As she protested, the canon swung his saddle-crop along a shelf of pots, bringing them crashing to the floor. 'Miserable witch, your den is full of the signs of corruption!' he bellowed. 'We know of the pacts you make with the spirits of evil. You should be ashamed of your denunciation of the true God!'

Jolenta's face paled, but her spirit remained strong as she loudly denied his charges and challenged the priest to prove anything against her.

'Here's proof, you miserable hag!' he yelled, spittle appearing at the corners of his mouth as he gestured at Emelota. 'I doubt you recall this woman, amongst all the poor souls you have defiled – she is but one of those whose mind and body you have fouled with your evil spirits. She will testify as to your pacts with Satan and all your other evil works!'

He pushed his informant forward and shook her by the shoulder. 'Is this the witch you told me of, eh?'

Emelota avoided the eyes of the other woman, but nodded her head.

Jolenta looked at her treacherous client and sighed resignedly. 'You too, poor woman? Now I know how Jesus Christ felt when he met Judas Iscariot.'

The canon was ablaze with wrath. 'How do you dare utter the name of the Blessed Christ with those same fornicating lips that called up Beelzebub from the Pit?'

He motioned to the proctor's thugs with his crop. They moved forward, seized Jolenta's arms and hustled her to the door, where her cobbler father had joined the reeve, bailiff and a crowd of neighbours in growling at these intruders from the city.

Confident in his righteous indignation, Canon Gilbert thrust past the crowd, his bulk and clerical robe dissuading anyone from resisting him.

But there were guarded snarls and murmurings of discontent as the woman was hauled out into the road to where the horses were being held by another of the canon's servants.

'What's happening, sir?' asked the bailiff, the one whose relative seniority gave him the nerve to question the priest. 'Our Jolenta is a good woman, we need her in the village.'

Gilbert, even redder in the face than usual with all the excitement, put a large foot in a stirrup and swung himself up on to his mare. 'If she is innocent, then the law will find her so.'

'But she should be brought before the manor court here, sir, not dragged away like this,' objected the bailiff mulishly.

In his anger, Gilbert almost swung his crop against the man's face, but managed to restrain himself. 'You forget this is the bishop's manor – and you are his servant. I am taking her to another of his courts in the cathedral, so mind your own business or there will be ill times for you!'

With this manipulation of the law, and with silent thanks that Jolenta had not been in another vill with an independent lord, the canon pulled his horse's head around and set off down the track. Slowly, the cavalcade moved off behind him, with Emelota once more perched sideways on her palfrey and poor Jolenta walking behind one of the proctor's horses, her wrists tied and roped to its saddle.

9

In which the apothecary goes on a visit

The news of the lynching spread around the city like fire on a parched moorland and by mid-afternoon, very few in Exeter were unaware of the events at the Snail Tower. As before, the citizens were divided into two camps, those who thought it was a scandalous crime and those who felt that justice was being done in the most effective manner.

In the last group was, of course, the apothecary Walter Winstone. He was surprised by the turn of events, as his intention had been to repeat the subterfuge he had used with Alice Ailward and Jolenta of Ide, by denouncing Theophania to Canon Gilbert. He had been unaware that Edward Bigge's drinking had led to her premature dispatch, but his delight was none the less intense. Now three of these pestilent people had been crushed, and after the rest of his plans had come to fruition, there would be a powerful message sent to others to keep their noses out of his business.

Meanwhile, he had another scheme that he wished to launch, one born out of revenge and vindictiveness, as well as monetary gain. Within hours of hearing of Theophania's death and

Jolenta's arrest, he set about putting his black-mailing plan into operation. Leaving his runny-nosed apprentice to mind the shop, with threats of dire consequences if the lad failed in any way, Walter limped along the high street in the direction of the East Gate, near which Henry de Hocforde had his grand house. As he pushed through the throng in the narrow streets, where most of the folk were gossiping and arguing about the dramatic affair down in Bretayne, he reviewed his plan of action.

To someone so devoted to wealth as Walter, the arrogance of de Hocforde in demanding the return of his money after claiming that the apothecary had failed to kill Robert de Pridias was anathema itself. Since being forced to hand back the mass of silver pennies, he had racked his devious mind for a way to get his own back – literally – and he finally came up with what he considered to be a fool-proof scheme. His first action had been to bribe de Hocforde's butler into disclosing which cunning person had been employed to put a curse on de Pridias and to make the straw effigy that had been found by the coroner's officer. Although the man was reluctant at first, Walter was desperate enough to increase his bribe until the butler gave way, after reassurances that the apothecary merely wished to employ the services of such a successful witch.

As the servant palmed two shillings' worth of pennies under the table in the New Inn, where they met for their intrigue, he finally disclosed the name. 'It was Elias Trempole, who lives at the top of Fore Street.'

'A man, not a cunning woman?' said Walter in some surprise, as he usually associated witches with the female gender.

'No, he's a wizard, though some still call him a witch. He works as a tally-clerk in my master's fulling mill. His sorcery is but a profitable side-line, it seems.'

As the apothecary walked purposefully towards de Hocforde's house in Raden Lane, the most affluent part of Exeter, he rehearsed again in his mind how he was going to use this knowledge. Unless the mill-owner returned his fee, he would denounce Elias Trempole to the witch-hunting canon, on the grounds that he had been employed by Henry de Hocforde to bring about the death of de Pridias. Walter calculated that Henry would reckon that the threat of being involved in a conspiracy to murder was not worth a pouch of silver coins, which he could easily afford. And so it transpired, for at the short interview at the door of Henry's house, the owner listened calmly to the apothecary's demand.

'You will have heard that a witch was hanged by the outraged citizens, barely a few hours ago,' blustered Walter. 'There are high feelings running against such evil people – and also against those who employ them!' he added, as a final thrust.

The tall, imposing figure standing at the door of his mansion nodded gravely. 'Very well, perhaps

I was somewhat harsh with you previously – after all, the fellow is dead, whoever brought it about. Be at your shop this evening and I'll send a servant around with the money.'

With that he closed the door in Walter's face, but the apothecary was too pleased with his success to be concerned at the other man's rudeness and limped away, savouring the thought of the imminent replenishment of his money chest.

As had happened a number of times before, a store-room at St Nicholas' Priory was commandeered as a mortuary, especially as the monastic establishment was not far from the tragic scene, being at the upper edge of Bretayne. The priory was small, with a prior and eight monks living in a cramped building, which belonged to Battle Abbey in Sussex, founded by the first King William on the very site of his conquest of Harold and his Saxons.

But there were no thoughts of such history as the corpse of Theophania Lawrence was brought in and laid to rest on trestles in the small room that had hastily been cleared of garden tools and old furniture. Several of the local inhabitants, including a few close neighbours of the old woman, had carried her up from the town wall on a door removed from a nearby house, escorted by the coroner and his group. It was Gwyn who had gently taken down the pathetic body from the sconce, untying the rope that had been thrown over it and lashed to the ring-handle of the door of the Snail

Tower. Both he and the coroner had urgently looked for any signs of life, having had experience of some remarkable recoveries in their violent careers. But this time there was no doubt that the old woman was dead, even though she was still quite warm and her limbs supple, the shameful deed having been perpetrated only a few minutes before they arrived.

A middle-aged widow, a neighbour of the dead woman, chaperoned them as the body was laid out on the boards of the trestles. Tears trickled down her rosy cheeks as she arranged Theophania's hands over her chest in an attitude of prayer.

'It's a scandal, she was a good enough woman. She would do her best to heal any ills that people brought to her – and often took not a ha'penny in return.' She sniffed back her tears. 'Maybe now and then she might help some poor girl who was in the family way – and she was not above a spell to curdle someone's milk if they had fallen foul of her. But she never deserved this, poor soul! This is murder, so what are you going to do about it, Crowner?'

A good question, de Wolfe thought. He would have to hold an inquest, but every member of the lynch-mob had run away as he arrived at the scene. It was true that some of the neighbours could identify a few faces in the crowd, but no one knew – or would say – who the ringleaders were and who had actually hauled her up by the neck over the torch bracket. Edward Bigge was clearly named as denouncing Theophania, but that was not proof that he had been involved in her execution. John also knew that the folk in Bretyane were no lovers of the law officers and would suffer torture before they would disclose anything – apart from the fact that any informer would be at great risk of retribution from the other rioters.

He sighed with resignation as he set about examining the corpse. There was little to be seen, apart from the obvious signs of hanging.

'Cut right into her skin, she's a heavy woman,' observed Gwyn, with clinical detachment, as he studied the deep groove where the thin rope had sunk into her neck.

'A blue face, blood spots in her eyes and eyelids – she didn't die easily,' agreed the coroner, who since taking office almost a year ago had attended scores of hangings.

'What about a jury for the inquest?' asked his officer. 'There'll be no finding any of those bastards who did this, they'll be skulking in their holes all over the city by now.'

De Wolfe considered the problem for a moment, standing hunched over the cadaver like some grey-and-black vulture contemplating its fallen prey.

'I'm going to leave it until tomorrow. There's nothing to be gained until we've learned some of the names of those involved, if that's possible. I'll have to talk to the damned sheriff about this. It's his responsibility to curb mob violence in his own city and county.'

'He's away for a few days, Crowner,' volunteered

Gabriel. 'He's gone to Winchester to take the extra taxes that the King's chancellor demanded for the new campaign in France. And he's taken that box of treasure trove with him, so I hear.'

De Wolfe's face darkened as he forgot all about the lynching for a moment. 'Taken the treasure already? Damn him, I expressly said that the Justices at the next Assize should decide what was to be done with it. I impressed upon him that I wanted it stamped with both our seals before it went anywhere! And that only after checking that everything we counted at Cadbury was still inside! He agreed to it, the lying bastard!'

John paced up and down the small room, glowering at the floor as he considered what was best to do. He swung around and jabbed a finger towards Gwyn. 'I want you to take Thomas and the inventory we made in Cadbury of that treasure and ride to Winchester straight away. Get Thomas to seek out the chief clerk to the treasury at the castle and get him to check whatever de Revelle has delivered against the list. I don't trust my brother-in-law farther than I can throw my horse, and there's no way I'm going to let him get away with anything that belongs to our king, who needs every penny he can get!'

Leaving the monks and the motherly neighbour to cover up poor Theophania, he stalked away, suspicion about Matilda's brother hovering over him like a black cloud.

★ ★ ★

With Thomas away with Gwyn on their three-day journey to Winchester, which was England's joint capital with London, the coroner had no spy to worm his way into the consistory court on Tuesday morning. However, later that day he had a full report from John de Alençon, who made it his business to attend. Although he was the Archdeacon of Exeter, he had no special standing in the court, the sole arbiter of justice being its chancellor. It was no surprise to anyone that Bishop Marshal had appointed Gilbert de Bosco to this office and so he was effectively both judge and jury in the proceedings.

'Fair-mindedness was a scarce commodity in the chapter house today,' said de Alençon cynically, as he sat with the coroner at the table in his study that afternoon, sharing the usual flask of wine. 'My fellow-canon was puffed up with his importance and imbued with missionary zeal – so the truth was low on his list of priorities.' He took a sip of the red nectar of Anjou and shook his head sadly. ' I must give myself a penance later for my cynical lack of charity towards Gilbert de Bosco, but the whole affair was a charade, a complete travesty of justice.'

For a normally mild man, the archdeacon sounded bitter and de Wolfe pressed him for more details of what had gone on that morning in the chapter house, where Gilbert had hastily added Jolenta's case to that of Alice Ailward and tried them both together.

'The poor women were not allowed to say a word in their own defence and the couple of neighbours who were allowed to speak up for them were treated like imbeciles by the chancellor.'

'So what were the charges against them?

'Almost identical, though it mattered little as to the details, the result was inevitable. As far as the Ailward woman was concerned, that she was guilty of sacrilege in summoning up Satan in defiance of God's law, that this meant she had committed apostasy by denial of God and that there was implied blasphemy by seeking other gods but the true one.'

John scratched his head where a flea was biting his scalp. 'All that on the uncorroborated lies of an ignorant boor like Adam Cuffe? I can't believe he has the brains to invent all that rubbish about Satan. Someone must have put him up to it.'

'Quite possibly, but I've no idea who that could be – or why he did it. And as for being uncorroborated, a trio of equally great liars were called, some of them I strongly suspect from that gang who lynched the other woman yesterday.'

'Did they spin the same story?'

'More or less . . . certainly in the same vein of unbelievable nonsense about Alice's activities. Seeing her ride through the air in the moonlight, of her cat turning into a huge bat – and casting spells on men so that they lost their potency – that was a favourite among those deluded liars.' Again the archdeacon sounded more bitter than John had ever known him.

241

'But was all that sufficient for the bishop's court to find her guilty?' he asked.

The priest shook his head. 'No, as I told you before, canon law requires that some criminal damage have resulted from her actions – but that was easy for the court to substantiate, especially when the court was solely Gilbert de Bosco. That Cuffe fellow swore that he knew of a sow and a whole litter of pigs that had dropped dead because of a curse that the woman had placed on them at the instance of a spiteful neighbour. And another witness said that she knew of two women who miscarried, having been interfered with by Theophania. That was more than sufficient to constitute criminal damage.'

'And with Jolenta of Ide?'

De Alençon shrugged. 'As I said, the spurious facts matter little. There was some hint of salacious evil there, as there were allegations of an incubus being involved.'

'What the devil is an incubus?' growled de Wolfe.

The glimmer of a smile crossed the priest's face, in spite of the seriousness of the topic. 'You've already said it, John! An incubus is a masculine devil that comes at night to have carnal relations with a woman – I believe that the female equivalent is called a succubus. They are supposed to give birth to witches.'

There was silence for a moment as they sipped their wine in gloomy outrage.

'Was there nothing that you could do or say on their behalf, John?' asked the coroner, almost reproachfully.

'I could do nothing, God forgive me,' answered de Alençon, as he crossed himself. 'I had no standing at all in that court. Henry Marshal had specifically appointed Gilbert as chancellor and I was but a spectator. I tried to reason with him before the court began, but he stiffly told me that he was the bishop's nominee and to mind my own business. I had no valid answer to that.'

'So the poor women are now committed to the sheriff's court for sentencing?'

The archdeacon nodded sadly. 'At least they can stay in the proctors' cells until then and not be humiliated further by being dragged to that foul pit in Rougemont, to be mishandled by that pervert Stigand.' He was referring to the obese and mentally retarded gaoler who guarded the filthy cells beneath the castle keep.

'But it will mean hanging, John,' said de Wolfe sadly. 'When the sheriff gets back he'll take his allotted part in this rotten conspiracy.'

'I'm afraid so, there is no other penalty. Just the lies about the dead sow, the miscarriages and the ravishment by an incubus are more than enough to send them to the gallows. And many of the townsfolk are happy with this – they were clamouring outside the chapter house, waiting for the verdict, shouting and yelling, demanding death for all witches. It was disgusting!'

There was another silence as they contemplated the situation.

'One dead and two others on the way! What's going on, my friend?' asked the coroner. 'Why this sudden vendetta against old wives, when for centuries they have been left in peace to peddle their potions and mumble their spells?'

De Alençon shook his grey head. 'I just don't know, John, but I fear we've not seen the end of it yet. One wonders who will be next?'

While John de Wolfe was eating his supper with Matilda in their usual glum silence that evening, Walter Winstone was in the upper room of his shop in Waterbeer Street, looking lovingly at the strongbox where he kept his money. He had even unlocked it in anticipation of adding the cash that Henry de Hocforde was sending to him.

Outside, it was raining again, to the despair of bailiffs, reeves and the peasantry, who were beginning to accept with fearful resignation that the harvest would be dismal and that winter would again see starvation stalk the land. The apothecary cared nothing about this, as for those with money there was always food to be bought, albeit at high cost from imports from across the Channel. Impatiently, he waited for his finances to be swollen by de Hocforde's capitulation, once again cursing the man for not accepting that his poison was the cause for the other mill-owner's demise.

There was a gruff shout from below and Walter

hurried to the top of the ladder that led down to his storeroom. He had given his apprentice a rare evening off, to prevent the nosy youth from over-hearing any talk about money, so the voice had to be that of the promised messenger.

'Have you brought me a package, fellow?' he called down.

A burly figure appeared at the foot of the steps and stared up at him.

'Are you the apothecary? Henry de Hocforde sent me with this.' He was clutching a large hessian bag which he hoisted up to show Walter.

The apothecary nodded. 'Leave it there. I'll fetch it up in a moment.'

'No, the master said you were to count it in front of me,' growled the messenger. 'He says he doesn't want to be accused of short-changing you – and I don't want it said that I dipped my hand into it on the way here.'

The thought of losing some of his coins made Walter stump down the ladder, his stiff leg clacking on the wide rungs as he went. As he reached the bottom, the man reached into the bag, but pulled out not a handful of silver pennies but the head of a pole-axe with a sawn-off handle. On the reverse of the axe-blade was a wicked spike as long as a hand, and before the apothecary had time to under-stand what was happening, it was buried deep inside his skull. Hugh Furrel, the supposed messenger, was in fact a professional slaughterman from the Shambles and was used to swinging a full-length pole-axe at cattle, so dispatching a small man with a shorter one posed no problem. In fact, this was the second this evening, as he had come directly from Fore Street, where he had performed the same service on the wizard Elias Trempole, leaving his body in a pool of blood in his back yard.

Dropping his truncated weapon back into the bag, Hugh Furrel went cautiously to the door of the shop and peered out. When he was satisfied that no one was near the house, he slipped out and sauntered along to his favourite haunt, the Saracen, where he celebrated his success by spending some of Henry de Hocforde's blood-money on a few quarts of Willem the Fleming's ale.

The bodies were found almost simultaneously, less than an hour later, but the coroner was first called to Waterbeer Street. Without Gwyn or his clerk he felt vaguely incomplete, but made do with the two burgesses's constables, Osric and his plumper colleague, whose name John could never remember. The downtrodden – and now unemployed – apprentice had discovered the murder when he returned from his unexpected break and had hared off around the corner to the Guildhall, behind which the constables had a small hut as their head-quarters. Osric had summoned de Wolfe, but by this time a trio of excited townsfolk had run up from Fore Street to report that their neighbour

Elias Trempole had been found dead in his yard by his wife, when she returned from visiting her sister in Curre Street.

When the constable arrived in Martin's Lane, John was about to take his hound for a convenient walk in the direction of the Bush inn, as Matilda had already retired for the night. However, his irritation at the frustration of his amorous intentions faded when he realised that not only was the first victim one who was Canon Gilbert's supporter in the witch-hunt, but that Elias Trempole, according to Osric, was a well-known cunning man. The coincidence was further strengthened when he was told that the mode of death in both cases was identical.

In the back room of the apothecary's shop, which was now being guarded by the other, fatter constable, he found the remains of Walter Winstone lying crumpled at the foot of the ladder. On the top of his head was a large circular hole, from which blood and brains welled out. There were no other injuries to be seen, and on the apothecary's face was an expression of utter astonishment, the eyes being open and staring almost beseechingly at the coroner, asking for some explanation of this highly inconvenient event.

The apprentice was shaking in the background, his face ashen, as if he half expected to be accused of killing his master. It was common knowledge in Waterbeer Street that he hated the apothecary for the way he was treated, but de Wolfe sensed his fear and reassured the boy that he was not a suspect. He knew nothing of any visitor that evening, but the very fact that he had been sent away by his master suggested to John that someone had been expected.

'Best have a look around,' he growled at the constables, once they had looked at the body. There was nothing to be seen out of place in the storeroom or back yard, and when they climbed the ladder, the upper rooms, though dismal and untidy, seemed undisturbed.

'That chest is unlocked,' quavered the apprentice, who had followed them upstairs. He pointed to the stout box, which had the lock lying open on the top. 'The master never leaves it like that!'

Knowing of the apothecary's reputation for covetousness, Osric suggested that he might have been robbed, but when the coroner lifted the lid he whistled in surprise at the sight of so much money. 'Selling pills and lotions must be a profitable business!' he commented. 'Whoever came to slay him certainly didn't commit armed robbery.'

John saw the lad gaping at the mass of bags and loose silver, more money that he was ever likely to see again for the rest of his life. On impulse, de Wolfe bent and grabbed a handful of coins, which he stuffed quickly into the boy's pouch.

'You're out of a job now, so this will tide you over.' He glared at the two constables. 'You didn't see that, understand? Now put the lock back on the chest and keep your mouths shut, both of you.'

He marched back to the ladder and climbed down, calling up orders to Osric. 'Send someone up to Rougemont and get the guards to take the corpse up there. I'll hold the inquest tomorrow.'

There was no way in which he could cram it into the storeroom of the priory, both because it would be indecent to lodge it with a female body – and because the prior, a miserable man at the best of times, had already grumbled about the frequency with which his premises were being used as a dead-house.

'We'll have another corpse to house very soon,' said Osric, as they set off for Fore Street. 'It's been a busy day!'

As Thomas was absent, the coroner was glad to see a familiar figure coming towards them as they turned into Northgate Street, garbed in a black Benedictine robe. It was Brother Rufus, the rotund priest from Rougemont who acted as the garrison chaplain at the chapel of St Mary in the inner ward. He was an amiable if garrulous fellow, who seemed to have a fascination for the investigation of crime and who had several times latched on to de Wolfe's inquiries, to the annoyance of Thomas, who was very jealous of his own position.

'Just the man I need,' shouted the coroner. 'One who can write for me on a parchment roll!'

He explained his lack of a clerk to record the events of the evening and the priest was more than happy to oblige. As they had to go past St Olave's on the way, Rufus went in and persuaded Julian

Fulk to loan him a quill, ink bottle and a sheet of parchment. The chaplain was agog to know what was happening, and John gave him a summary as they hurried on down to the next scene of death. He was glad to hear that the chaplain was strongly against this persecution of witches and had condemned Gilbert de Bosco's obsessive campaign.

'I used to be a village priest in Somerset, before I became chaplain at Bristol,' he explained. 'I soon learned there that these women – and a few men – were invaluable in such places, far from apothecaries or monkish infirmaries.' He puffed a little as he tried to keep up with the coroner's long strides. 'It's true that sometimes they got up to no good, with a little sorcery against other village folk – but it was all in the mind of the victims. If they knew that a "hex" had been put upon them, they persuaded themselves that they were bewitched – all the rest was mere mummery!'

His lecture was cut off as they reached the house, where Osric stood gesticulating outside. He had gone ahead when Brother Rufus had stopped off to get writing materials and was now pushing back a small crowd of sightseers from around the door. The house was on a narrow plot, its single room built of stone, with a high-peaked roof of wooden shingles. There was a bare yard of beaten earth at the back, reached by a narrow gap between the house and the next-door building. Here a wooden lean-to shed provided the kitchen and the usual privy and pigsty lined the back fence. The coroner pushed his way past the onlookers, some of whom were shoving at Osric and making threatening noises.

'Good riddance to another bloody witch!' shouted one man, who promptly got a buffet on the head from another, who yelled back, 'What evil did Elias Trempole ever do you? He healed up the ulcers on my legs and charged me nothing!'

A scuffle broke out, with abuse and counter-charges from both men and women in the crowd, which was rapidly attracting more people from the surrounding streets. John cursed himself for not wearing his sword, though he rarely needed to carry it within the city. Instead, he grabbed Osric's badge of office, a wooden staff with a metal band at the top, and began laying into those in the crowd who seemed to be the worst troublemakers. With a series of smacks and prods, he roared at them to be silent, and such was the power of his dominating appearance that they all subsided into a glowering, muttering but more docile mood.

At this point, the other constable, who John now remembered was called Theobald, came running up and Osric commanded him to keep everyone out of the plot, while he accompanied the coroner and Brother Rufus around the side of the house to the yard.

Here they repeated the routine they had followed in Waterbeer Street, as the body of the more elderly Elias Trempole had an identical wound in the same place on his head and no other injuries. The castle chaplain poked about in the other sheds in the yard, then sat on the seat of the earth closet in the privy with his piece of parchment spread on the blade of a wooden shovel placed across his lap. As John prepared to dictate what Rufus should write as the coroner's record, he admired the monk's adaptability, though he recalled that Rufus had acted as a priest in several French campaigns and had learned to be as flexible as the soldiers to whom he administered.

'You had best first set down the facts about Walter Winstone,' he suggested to his new scribe and proceeded to give a quick summary of the apothecary's death. Then he described the sparse findings concerning the alleged wizard of Fore Street, as he stood stooped over the man's corpse.

'Had you better have a look inside, Crowner?' suggested the chaplain, cocking his head towards the back of the house, from which came wailing and weeping. He gathered up his writing materials and followed de Wolfe through the door in the lean-to addition at the back of the building. Inside, it was more of an alchemist's den than a kitchen, with a clutter of flasks, pots and pestles and mortars on several benches and a haphazard collection of plant and animal remains hanging from the shelves and rafters. Bundles of herbs and strange dried plants competed for space with mummified reptiles and strips of fur and leather.

'Best keep those troublesome folk outside from seeing this collection,' grunted de Wolfe. 'It'll only make them more convinced than ever that someone else was in the habit of raising Satan in his kitchen.'

'Especially if they see these,' added Rufus, drawing John's attention to something on one of the littered tables. He pointed to two small straw figures, which John recognised as being almost identical to the one found under the saddle of Robert de Pridias. They had no cloth or hair attached, but near by were a couple of crude metal spikes similar to the one he had seen in Alphington. Like many in the city, the chaplain knew all the details of de Pridias's death, as his widow had proclaimed them loudly around the town.

The coroner's brow furrowed as he tried to assemble the significance of today's events in his mind. Two identical murders, but no apparent connection between the victims other than a tenuous thread concerning witchcraft. What could an apothecary have in common with a fulling-mill worker, other than Elias's reputation as a male witch and Walter's support of a mad canon's crusade?

Shrugging off the puzzle for the moment, John followed the sounds of distress in the next room and pushed his way through a leather flap that shielded the doorway between the kitchen and the hall of the little house. Here he found the widow of Elias, a large woman whose ample bottom flowed over the sides of a milking-stool, being comforted by a daughter and a neighbour, both of whom were wailing almost as loudly as she. This was a scene that John hated, as any form of emotion embarrassed him and drove him into an even more gruff mode of speech. Luckily, the big monk had no such problem and his sympathetic spirit burgeoned as he went forward to soothe and comfort the women, using his best pastoral manner to calm them down.

He spoke to them in his avuncular way for a few moments, then came back to John and beckoned him out into the kitchen-cum-sorcerer's den.

'They know little of any significance, Crowner,' he announced, unsuccessfully trying to conceal his delight at being involved in a murder investigation. 'The wife came home from visiting a relative to discover Elias dead in the yard, just as we found him. Nothing seems to have been stolen, though there seems little of any value here, unlike the apothecary's dwelling.'

'Does she or the daughter know of anyone who might be his enemy?'

The monk shrugged his ample shoulders. 'They admit he was never loath to sell a charm or a curse to those who wanted them and may well have upset those who thought they were the target of his necromancy. But they know of no one in particular who may have taken umbrage sufficient to want his death.'

Osric had sidled up to hear this part of the conversation, having left his colleague Theobald outside to keep out the sullen crowd still clustered round the gate. 'Remember, Crowner, that he worked at the fulling mills on Exe Island,' he said quietly. 'His master was Henry de Hocforde.'

As de Wolfe digested this, he caught the eye of Rufus, whose eyebrows rose on his moon face. 'There seem to be threads connecting each other like a spider's web, Sir John,' he observed. 'He was the merchant that Cecilia de Pridias accused of wishing for her husband's death.'

The coroner ran his fingers through his long black hair in a gesture of exasperation. 'But why would he want this wizard dead now, so long after the deed was done? And anyway, we sane people know that the fellow died of a seizure. Straw dollies are just a bloody nonsense and an irrelevance. And what in God's name could that miserable little pill-pusher have to do with it?'

Brother Rufus shrugged. 'You said that he was treating de Pridias for an ailment in his belly, but that tells us nothing.' He blew out his breath like a tired horse to express his frustration. 'All I do know is that the witch-hunting canon has caused a great deal of trouble, including a few deaths. I pray that God will forgive him when the day of judgement comes.'

10

In which two witches meet on marshy ground

In the late August dusk, an elderly woman picked her way slowly through a maze of muddy paths on Exe Island, outside the western walls of the city. The river flowed swiftly a few yards further on, its water swollen by the rains on Exmoor, though it had not yet flooded over the wide marshy area above the uncompleted bridge. Avelina Sprot, the dairy wife from Milk Street, lifted the hem of her brown woollen kirtle to keep it out of the mire, though her wooden clogs were caked in the tenacious clay that lay between the patches of coarse grass that dotted the flats. Muttering under her breath at the foul place that she needed to visit, she threaded through the reens and leats of the marsh, aiming for a rickety hut that stood on its own, out near the main river bank. Although there were many other shanties and shacks dotted across the island, housing the poorer labourers and wool porters that served the mills further upstream, the one she was seeking was even more ramshackle.

When she eventually slithered up to it, she saw that the occupant needed all the magic she could muster to prevent the hut from falling into the river, as it leaned at a precarious angle, its rotting boards and mouldering thatch needing but a good push to tip it over.

The householder was obviously at home, as smoke was filtering from under the eaves, as well as from many holes in the walls, and the battered hurdle that served as a door was lying on the littered ground outside. She called out to attract attention.

'Lucy! Are you there, Lucy?'

For a few moments there was no response, then an apparition shuffled to the doorway and peered out, the eyes blinking behind inflamed lids as she strained to see who was calling her.

'It's Avelina, Lucy. Avelina Sprot. I must talk to you.'

Even though she had known Lucy for years, the visitor had not seen her for some months and was sad to see how she had deteriorated lately. Lucy was of indeterminate age, but looked at least a hundred, thought Avelina. Her thin grey hair was matted and filthy and her back was so bent that she had to stretch her neck up to look ahead. But her most remarkable feature was the growth of long grey hair over most of her face and neck, leaving only the skin around her eyes and forehead visible. She wore a grubby and shapeless black garment which hung from her gaunt frame like a curtain, and she shuffled along with the aid of a knobbly stick. Her eyes were filmed with cataracts and she had to come close to peer at her visitor to make sure of her identity.

'Avelina Sprot! What brings you here, sister?' Compared with the rest of her decrepit appearance, her voice was unexpectedly strong. She was not claiming her as a sibling, but part of the loose sisterhood of cunning women.

'Have you not heard of what is happening in the city and around it?' asked Avelina. 'We are being persecuted, with one already dead and two more condemned.'

Bearded Lucy, by virtue of both her age and reputation, was considered by those who possessed the gift as being their unofficial leader, much as the apothecaries looked to Richard Lustcote as their figurehead.

Lucy beckoned for Avelina to come inside, but the visitor shook her head. She had seen Lucy's dwelling once before and was in no hurry to repeat the experience. 'I've no time, I must get back for the skimming. But I wanted to warn you and to ask if there is anything that can be done to stop this madness. Half the city is out for our blood, even though in a month's time they will regret it.'

Bearded Lucy sank slowly on to an empty box that lay among the debris outside her hut and leaned forward, clasping her gnarled hands on her stick. 'I have heard some of this, but I get out very little now. Kind folk bring me something to eat now and then. I hope to die soon,' she added simply.

'Nonsense, you can't die yet, we have too much need of you,' snapped Avelina. She proceeded to tell Lucy all that had been happening in the last week or so and the old woman listened in silence.

'You say that the witch-hunter is this priest, this canon?'

'Yes, Gilbert de Bosco. But he was put up to it by the widow of this merchant and an apothecary, Walter Winstone, who was jealous of our healing skills.'

Lucy screwed up her red-rimmed eyes and sat in silence for a moment.

'We'll have no more trouble from him, he has just died,' she said in a matter-of-fact way.

The other woman stared at her with some unease, as the old hag had not set foot off the marsh that day, so how could she know? She herself had only heard of Walter's murder half an hour ago, from the gossip on the streets as she was on her way here. But she returned to the big problem.

'Be careful for yourself, Lucy. There have been efforts to deal with you before this, as you well know. We are all at risk until this danger passes, as pass it must.'

The crone opened her eyes and nodded. 'I care little for myself, it is the fate of the younger women that distresses me. Poor Jolenta of Ide, she was the most promising of those with the gift. And she is young and comely, yet you say they are going to hang her, along with Alice?'

'Yes – and the mob strung Theophania from a sconce on the Snail Tower today. False witness was given against them all, but we do not know where it came from. The sheriff and the bishop are against us too, so they say.'

'Have we no just men who will speak up for us?'

'I hear that the coroner, Sir John de Wolfe, is an even-handed man. He has a reputation for being stern but honest, which is more than can be said for most of them.'

Lucy nodded. 'I have had dealings before with the crowner and his leman. Maybe I will go to see him tomorrow.'

They talked a little longer, until the approach of dusk made Avelina concerned that she would be unable to navigate the treacherous paths across the marsh. She left in the twilight, leaving the bearded old woman still sitting with her chin on her hands, staring at the ground as if she could see visions in the mud.

With the sheriff away, as well as Gwyn and Thomas being absent, John had a difficult few days ahead, though thankfully there were no sudden deaths, rapes, fires or catches of royal fish for the rest of the week. Even Matilda could find no excuse to nag him about being absent for most of the time and their routine settled into a dull round of silent mealtimes and even more silent bedtimes. Each evening he made his usual excuse of taking Brutus for a long walk through the city, which both of them had tacitly come to accept as a euphemism for visiting Nesta at the Bush. However, there was no chance of his snatching a night with the buxom

Welsh woman, which he could sometimes manage when he had been travelling outside the city.

He was uneasy about a number of matters, though the heat seemed to have gone out of the witch-hunting, at least until the sheriff came back to hold the court that would send them to the gallows. But he was concerned about the treasure trove, as Richard de Revelle's sudden departure with the box of gold and silver was very suspicious. This was one thing he was not going to let his brother-in-law get away with this time. On several previous occasions, Matilda's intercession on behalf of her brother had persuaded John to save him from disgrace and perhaps even execution, but enough was enough. If anything was missing from the chest when it arrived at Winchester, then he knew who to blame.

On Wednesday, the day after the killings of the apothecary and the wise man of Fore Street, he held inquests on the bodies. He could not rely on Brother Rufus to act as his clerk this time, though no doubt the big monk would have been happy to do so if his other duties allowed. Instead, de Wolfe recruited Elphin, a reliable clerk from the castle, one of the literate men in lower clerical orders who kept the records in the county court. With Ralph Morin's consent, he also appropriated Sergeant Gabriel and one of his men-at-arms. They began at the ninth hour at Rougemont, where one of the cart-sheds against the wall of the inner ward was acting as a temporary mortuary. Here the corpses of Walter Winstone and Elias Trempole were lying side by side under a canvas sheet alongside the massive solid wheel of an ox-cart. Earlier that morning, Gabriel and his man had rounded up a number of men and boys from Fore Street and Waterbeer Street to act as juries, in the hope that some of them might have information about the killings.

The coroner took over the empty shire courthouse for the proceedings, the few people present rattling around in the bare building. On the raised dais, John sat in the sheriff's chair and Elphin, an intense young man with a bad hare-lip, spread his parchment and inks on a trestle behind him.

Without Gwyn to act as coroner's officer, John dispensed with the formalities, such as the opening declaration and the presentment of Englishry. Although neither of the deceased was Saxon, he had no village to lay the murdrum fine upon, so again he preferred to ignore the matter. The first inquest was on Elias Trempole, and Gabriel sent the soldier to bring the corpse from the cart-shed, so that the jury could view it. It arrived lying stiffly on a plank laid across a large wheelbarrow, with the canvas thrown over it during its short journey. The dead man's brother and his weeping widow both confirmed the identity of Elias, then John stood at the edge of the platform and directed the dozen men and lads to file past it and look at the large wound in the head.

'Does anyone here recognise what weapon might

have caused that?' he demanded. Twenty years' experience in bloody campaigns in Ireland, France and the Holy Land had made him an expert in fatal injuries, but though he suspected what had caused these deep punctures, it was not a military weapon and he wanted confirmation from the locals.

A tall man wearing a long leather apron spotted with bloodstains spoke up. 'I know what did it, Crowner – and I know who did it!' he said laconically.

There was a buzz of agreement amongst some of the jurymen picked for both cases and another older man spoke up from the back. 'No doubt who did this one, Sir John – the same fellow that slew the apothecary with the same implement.'

De Wolfe looked around the group of men in some astonishment, then gave one of his rare grins. 'Looks as if these will be the shortest inquests I've ever held – and the most helpful!' He motioned to the man in the stained apron. 'Come on, then, tell us all about it.'

The tall fellow pointed a finger at the crater in Elias's almost bald head. It formed a narrow cone, going deeply into the skull, with fragments of bone crushed around the edges.

'Could only be a pole-axe, sir. I know because I use one every day.'

John nodded, as he had come to the same conclusion, unless there was some unusual foreign foot-soldier's pike loose in Exeter. 'Agreed, you can tell that from the wound. But how do you tell who did it, from looking at the wound?'

The butcher rubbed his long nose before replying. 'I can't tell from the wound, Crowner. But I know it was Hugh Furrel that did it, for I saw him in Fore Street that night – and now he's disappeared, along with one of the pole-axes from our killing shed.'

There was a murmur of agreement from the other jurymen and again someone else spoke up. 'And I saw him on the corner of Waterbeer Street and Goldsmith's Lane that night, carrying a hessian bag that had something damned heavy in it, for it banged against my leg as we passed.'

De Wolfe rubbed his black stubble with his fingers as he considered this. 'We all walk the streets of the city, as we live here,' he objected. 'Doesn't make us all killers, though I admit it seems he was in the right places at the right times. But you say he's vanished?'

The slaughterman nodded. 'He lived down in Rack Lane with a doxy, but he's run off. His woman came to the sheds today to ask after him. She said he came back home last night drunk, bragging about how much money he'd made. No one has seen him since, except the porter on the South Gate, who said he went out of the city as soon as it opened at dawn today.'

The next inquest, on Walter Winstone, lasted but a few moments, as the evidence was the same. There were no relatives to identify him, but Richard

Lustcote, the nominal master of the city apothecaries, was present to confirm his name and agree that the cost of burial would be borne by their guild. There was no alternative but to order the jury to agree to a verdict of murder by persons unknown, even though it seemed evident that Hugh Furrel was the perpetrator of both crimes.

Amid much muttering at the unsatisfactory outcome, the court was dissolved and the jurors and the few spectators drifted away. The coroner shared in the general discontent, as it was frustrating that a double murder had occurred and that the culprit was generally known but beyond retribution. However, his main concern was the motivation for the murders, which had occurred so close in time and by the same hand. There must be some common thread linking them, especially as it seemed that robbery was not the reason. As he sat alone in his chamber afterwards, missing the company of Thomas and Gwyn, he pondered the fact that it was unusual for someone like an apothecary to be slain. Most murders occurred during drunken brawls or in robberies with violence, when they were not domestic disputes within families. But for a professional man to be murdered in his own premises, with nothing stolen from his treasure chest, was a very peculiar situation.

Drumming his fingers irritably on the trestle table, John turned the matter over in his mind for a while, then got up and went out into the city in search of some explanation. He knew that the few apothecaries in Exeter looked to Richard Lustcote as their father figure. He was a man he had met several times at guild banquets and festivals, as well as when he attended Winstone's inquest. Making his way to Lustcote's shop in Northgate Street, he found the man upstairs, grinding some special salve for the wife of one of the burgesses, who suffered from weeping ulceration of her lower legs.

Lustcote greeted him civilly and put away his pestle and mortar to pour them both a cup of wine, while he listened to the coroner's questions.

'As both were slain by the same hand, the very same day, I find it hard to find a link between a lowly labourer who dabbles in charms and a respectable apothecary, a trained and educated man,' John explained.

The chubby pill-purveyor nodded sagely, glad to be of help to the law officer. 'There is a connection, Crowner. Now that poor Walter is dead, I feel I have no reason not to divulge some of his confidences. He came to me recently, complaining bitterly about the cunning men and women in and around the city, who he felt were taking some of his trade away.' Lustcote sipped his wine before continuing. 'Truth to tell, Walter Winstone was very keen on his money. If it were not speaking too much ill of the dead, I might say that he was a mean man, obsessed with squeezing every last ha'penny from life, even though he lived like a destitute monk.'

De Wolfe's black brows came together in puzzlement. 'But why should that lead to his death? If he was so much against witches and wizards, he would be more likely to do them violence, rather than the other way round.'

Richard shrugged his rounded shoulders. 'There you have me, Sir John. Again, though I should not say this, though I am no priest in the confessional, but Winstone's reputation as an apothecary was not unblemished. He came here under rather dubious circumstances and the whisper is that he was suspected of some unprofessional practices in his former town of Southampton. Nothing was proved and I declined to pursue the matter when he came to Exeter, but it is possible that he made some enemies here – though how on earth that could tie in with the death of a cunning man, I have no idea.'

John grunted into his cup. 'Unprofessional practices, you say? Can I take that to mean ridding unfortunate women of the unwanted burden of their husband's lust?'

'That at least – and possibly relieving unwanted persons of their lives!'

'You are being very frank with me, Richard,' said John, in some surprise.

'Only because Walter Winstone is now beyond the retribution of us all, except Almighty God. We can do him no harm now and he has no family upon whom any stigma might fall.'

The coroner fell silent for a moment as he sipped

the excellent wine, but his mind was working methodically. 'Tell me, what methods might an unscrupulous apothecary employ to secretly get rid of such an unwanted person?'

'There are many poisons which could be incorporated into pills, draughts and potions. Some are from certain herbs and plants, others are mineral in origin. Why do you ask?'

'To be successful in a slow, secret poisoning, the victim would have to be a patient of that apothecary?'

Lustcote nodded. 'It would be very difficult to administer the poison otherwise. Most have a hellish taste and so could not be added to food or drink by the one who commissioned the deed. But as medicines are supposed to function better the nastier they are, then almost any foul-tasting substance can be given under the guise of a medicament.'

The germ of an idea began forming in de Wolfe's mind. 'Tell me, are there any particular signs that would suggest that someone was slowly being poisoned?'

The master apothecary sighed. 'You ask a question with a very long answer, Crowner. All kinds of symptoms may appear, but none are very specific. Wasting, belly-cramps, purging, vomiting, the yellow jaundice, bleeding spots in the skin and eyes – the list is long, but so many mimic natural disease.'

'Would fouling and darkening of the gums with loose teeth suggest anything?'

' So many people have terrible mouths and most lose their teeth eventually. It could be scurvy in those who are starved – but you say darkening as well?'

'Yes, virtually black, an inky line along the roots of the teeth.'

Richard rubbed his chin reflectively. 'That could be plumbism, of course. The administration of sugar of lead – *Plumbum acetas* – over a period can do that. It's an effective poison which has no obnoxious taste and can fatally weaken the heart and brain if allowed to build up in the body.'

John elaborated no more on the matter to the apothecary, but he now fitted some more facts into place: Winstone was de Pridias's physician, the man had blackened gums after death, and his widow Cecilia vehemently claimed that he had been done to death by the intervention of a cunning man or woman. He had no means of proving it, but as he walked back to Martin's Lane the coroner wondered whether Henry de Hocforde also fitted into the pattern he was constructing in his mind.

Late in the afternoon of the following Monday, a small cavalcade clattered across the drawbridge at Rougemont and passed under the arch of the gatehouse. The sleepy sentry snapped to attention and saluted with his pikestaff, for the first rider was Sir Richard de Revelle, the county sheriff and nominally his lord and master. He was followed by a couple of his clerks, his steward and four men-at-arms who had escorted him on his journey to Winchester. The guard noticed that the sheriff's thin face, never much disposed towards amiability, was darkened by a scowl as he trotted his horse into the inner ward and made for the keep on the other side. A trumpet-blast from one of the soldiers caused a flurry of activity around the wooden stairs that led to the entrance on the upper floor. A pair of ostlers scurried out from the undercroft below and several servants burst out of the main door to stand waiting on the platform at the top of the steps. As an ostler grabbed his stallion's head, Richard slid from the saddle and stalked without a word to the keep. Ignoring the greetings of his servants, he stamped up the stairs and marched into the hall, pulling off his riding gloves and slapping them irritably against his thigh. Inside, he turned left around the screens to go towards his chambers, but then stopped dead as he saw who was sitting at a nearby table, drinking ale with the castle constable.

'De Wolfe, damn you! I want to talk to you – now!'

His high-pitched voice was vibrant with anger as he glared across at the coroner, who stared back with infuriating calmness. 'And a very good day to you, brother-in-law!' he replied sarcastically, not moving from his bench.

De Revelle wheeled around and strode to his quarters, slamming the door behind him in the face of his apprehensive clerks, who had followed him into the hall.

John rose languidly from the table, picking up his ale-pot and leisurely finishing the contents. 'I'd better see what the bloody man wants,' he muttered to his friend, the fork-bearded Ralph Morin, who had watched the little scene with interest.

'Is it what you think might have happened, John?'

The coroner tugged his sword-belt to a more comfortable position. 'It may be – but almost everything upsets that man these days! I've been waiting for him to come back, as I've a few matters to tax him with myself.'

He loped across the rush-covered flagstones, aware of a sudden hush as a score of curious faces watched him, wondering what had put the sheriff into such a foul temper. Walking in past an anxious-looking guard posted outside, he was met with a further furious command. 'Shut that damned door behind you! I don't want every nosy swine in the castle listening to what I've got to say to you!'

De Wolfe kicked the door back with his heel so that it slammed into its frame. 'You seem out of sorts today, brother-in-law,' he said mildly. 'Is your arse sore with all that riding?'

'Never mind my arse! What do you mean by trying to have me humiliated before the exchequer in Winchester?'

John stared at the sheriff as the realisation that what he suspected may have happened had actually come to pass. It had been a possibility all along and de Wolfe was now thankful that he had taken precautions against it. He let his breath out slowly as he tried to anticipate where this revelation might lead. 'So, Richard, I was right in sending my officer and clerk to follow you to Winchester!'

'Officer and clerk? Whoreson liars and troublemakers, more like! But now you actually confess your involvement in this scandal?' Standing behind his table, his foxy face pale with rage, the sheriff flung his gloves down and shook his fist at his wife's husband. 'That great Cornish oaf of yours and that disgusting weasel of a disgraced priest had the temerity to go squealing to the chief clerk of the treasury with some bloody list of what should have been in that treasure box. And then the clerk complained that it didn't tally with the contents of the chest – virtually accusing me of stealing it!'

'So did you steal it, Richard?' asked John stonily.

The pallor of the sheriff's face suddenly flushed to an alarming shade of red. 'Damn you, John! I'll not be spoken to like that! The list was patently false, a tissue of lies! You've done this to trap me – you've been plotting my downfall for months. But this time, you've gone too far. I'll have you thrown out of office for this – or worse!'

De Wolfe advanced to the table and stooped to lean his fists on the edge, bending forward to come face to face with the now-incandescent sheriff, who stood a head shorter than the coroner. 'Be careful what you say about being thrown out of office, Richard. You may have sailed too close to the wind once too often this time.'

Revelle beat his fists on the boards in a raging

temper tinged with fear. 'Thanks to those God-accursed servants of yours, the chief clerk to the treasury came and alleged that there was a difference between the coinage in the box and what was alleged to be on that damned parchment that your mealy-mouth clerk brought with him. Asked me for an explanation, blast him! A mere scribbler, questioning the integrity of the sheriff of one of the biggest counties in England!' He wiped some spittle from the corner of his mouth before continuing to rant at his brother-in-law. 'And anyway, the bloody treasure is mine by rights, being found on my land. Only your spiteful interference deprived me of it!'

John straightened up and sighed. 'We've been through all this before – the inquest rightly decided that treasure trove belongs to the King. So taking any part of it is not only theft, but treason!' He paused and then asked, 'How much of it did the clerk say was missing?'

The sheriff's features were by now dangerously purple. 'Nothing was missing, damn you! Your so-called inventory was obviously deliberately falsified by you, to discredit me!'

It was de Wolfe's turn to become annoyed at this blatant insult. He reached across the table and grabbed Richard by the neck of his embroidered tunic. 'I falsified nothing! It was specifically to stop you embezzling any of this gold and silver that I had the contents of the chest carefully checked.' He let go of the tunic and pushed the sheriff away contemptuously. 'Every coin in that box was care-fully counted and the witnesses included the priest at Cadbury, my clerk, the reeve and even the manor-lord, who was able to sign his own name on that list. Do you really think that all those would conspire to perjure themselves, just to discomfort you?'

Richard jerked his garments straight again after being manhandled. 'Then the treasure could only have been pilfered between Cadbury and Exeter,' he brayed triumphantly. 'And the only man who had care of it during the journey was that sham-bling giant of yours, that Cornishman Gwyn!'

'Are you now trying to shift the blame by accusing my officer?' roared John, flaring into anger again at this slur against his oldest friend.

Now that the idea had taken root in his mind, de Revelle nurtured it enthusiastically. 'Of course I am! The bastard obviously couldn't resist dipping his hand into the box as soon as he was out of sight of Cadbury.'

'Nonsense, you're just trying to cover up your own dishonesty!' raged the coroner, now furious at himself for failing to foresee this loophole that his crafty brother-in-law had seized upon. He should have had the treasure recounted when it arrived at Rougemont to save Gwyn from this now all-too-obvious accusation.

Richard sensed John's unease and immediately capitalised upon it. 'Yes, by Christ's knuckles, that's the only explanation!' he exulted, seeing a chance to turn the tables on what could have been a disastrous situation. 'And I'll have that whoreson thief as soon as he returns from his disgraceful escapade in Winchester. He'll be arrested the moment he sets foot in the city – and I'll see that he's hanged for it!'

De Wolfe slammed the table-top with his fist. 'Don't be so damned foolish, Richard, you've not a scrap of proof that he stole anything!'

The pointed beard of the sheriff jutted defiantly out at the coroner. 'You produced the proof yourself with the claim that the inventory was correct. If the contents were so grandly certified in Cadbury and some was missing by the time it reached Winchester, then only that bloody officer of ours had the opportunity to pilfer it, as the rest of the time it was in my care!'

'Exactly – and it was in your care a great deal longer!' retorted John, bitterly.

The sheriff, now feeling quite on top of the situation, sneered back at him. 'Either you withdraw your claim that the list was accurate, or I'll have that officer of yours, John. With a body as heavy as his, his neck will stretch delightfully on the gallows!'

De Wolfe knew that the vindictive sheriff would be as good as his word when it came to taking his revenge on Gwyn and cursed himself again for not being more careful. What had been an impending disaster for de Revelle a few moments ago was rapidly turning into a triumph for the devious sheriff.

'I'll see you in hell first!' retorted the coroner, but his tone betrayed his lack of conviction. The word of a servant would be of little avail against that of a knight and county sheriff. Either John had to withdraw his accusation that there had been a shortfall in the amount of treasure or risk Gwyn's neck. Although Richard might be in real jeopardy if the theft was eventually brought home to him, the delay in toppling him would be of little use if the sheriff's county court declared Gwyn a felon the following week. But John's iron sense of justice was totally against this scheming villain getting away with it yet again.

'Five pairs of eyes counted that money, damn you!' he shouted across the table. 'They couldn't all be blind – and I've no doubt that what's missing is not ten paces from where we stand!'

Richard de Revelle glared back at him. 'Then if you persist in this insulting accusation, John, that red-haired villain will be arrested the moment he shows his face in Exeter. In fact, I'll give strict orders to the constable and the guards to throw him into Stigand's tender care as soon as he appears!' He sat down and leered up at his brother-in-law. 'So make up your mind, John. Is it to be me – or him?'

The guard at the top of the drawbridge at Rougemont rarely had occasion to defend the castle against intruders. Apart from a few urchins and pedlars who now and then tried to get in, the last time the drawbridge had been raised and the portcullis lowered for defence had been over fifty years ago during the civil war between King Stephen and the Empress Matilda. This morning, the day after the sheriff returned from Winchester, was no exception and the only event to keep the man-at-arms awake after the previous heavy night's drinking was the appearance of a walking scarecrow on the ramp that crossed the wide ditch of dirty water that was the moat. She was halfway up, stumbling slowly as she hoisted herself painfully along with the aid of a stick, when the sentry yelled at her to clear off.

Although his voice was not too unkind, she stopped and scowled at him. If he had been nearer, he may have been discomfited by the angry glint in her eyes and flinched under her oddly penetrating gaze. 'I must speak to the crowner, boy!' she called, in a voice that was unexpectedly deep and strong, coming from such a decrepit frame.

'He's not here, mother – and even if he was, I couldn't let you in.'

There was no real reason why he should keep her out, as the inner ward contained St Mary's chapel, the courthouse and a number of lean-to dwellings built against the curtain walls for a few military families, though most lived in the larger outer bailey. However, he had standing orders to keep out vagrants, vagabonds, pedlars and beggars. The old woman's ragged clothing and frightening facial hair seemed to put her in one of those categories and he advanced to the centre of the archway to emphasise the prohibition.

Bearded Lucy stared at him for a moment, as if contemplating putting a curse on him, but as the soldier seemed emphatic that the coroner was not there, she shrugged her rounded shoulders and stumped slowly back down towards Castle Hill, her stick tapping on the hard ground. The guard watched her go, uneasy at that final look she had given him – if he had been Thomas de Peyne, he would have crossed himself.

The old woman knew that Sir John lived in Martin's Lane and slowly made her way there through the crowded high street, indifferent to the rude comments and occasional jeers of passers-by, especially those who came too close downwind of her unwashed body and filthy clothing. Even in a community where bathing was an eccentric perversion, the odours that came from old Lucy were unusual in their intensity.

At the corner of the narrow lane which led through to the cathedral Close, she hesitated, uncertain of what to do next. She was well aware that she would be unwelcome in any decent dwelling, but she had an overriding need to speak to Sir John. In her previous dealings with the coroner, she had found him to be a dour and rather forbidding man, but one who was unusually honest and compassionate, a rare quality in the Norman aristocracy, who were more likely to use their whip on her than a civil tongue. Peering down the alley, she saw the three tall, narrow houses on the right, the furthest one being that of the coroner. It was opposite the entrance to a livery stable that lay behind the Golden Hind tavern, which fronted on to the high street.

She began shuffling down the lane, still uncertain as to how she could get to speak to him, when her problem was unexpectedly solved by the appearance of two men from the stables. One wore the leather apron of a farrier, scarred with scorch marks from fitting hot shoes, but the other was John de Wolfe himself. She hobbled forward and accosted him as deferentially as her stubborn nature would allow.

'Sir John, please! Can you spare an old woman a moment?'

The farrier gave her a contemptuous look and vanished back into his stable yard, leaving de Wolfe to deal with this untidy apparition.

'Do you remember me, Crowner?' she asked. 'I have had dealings in the past with the landlady of the Bush.'

John knew very well who she was and nodded gravely. 'You are the lady from Exe Island, I believe.'

It was a very long time since anyone had called her 'lady' and her faith in this man was strengthened further. She moved closer and was gratified to see that he did not flinch. 'Can I speak frankly to you, sir? There is no one else in this city that I would trust.'

In spite of himself, John gave a furtive glance at

the front of his house, to make sure that Matilda was not standing on the doorstep. The only window-opening was shuttered and anyway, at this time of day, his wife was still probably dozing up in her solar.

'What is it, Lucy? Are you in trouble of some sort?' He had a suspicion of the nature of her problem, but waited to hear it from her own mouth, which twisted wryly at his question.

'Trouble? We are all in trouble, we cunning women. We are being persecuted and it will surprise me if I live to see the end of this month, along with some of my sisters.'

He listened gravely while she made an impassioned condemnation of the wave of hatred that was sweeping the city against her kind – and the injustice of the hysterical mob violence that had been drummed up by Gilbert de Bosco and those whom he had influenced.

'Poor Theophania Lawrence has already paid the price, along with Elias Trempole – and Alice Ailward and Jolenta of Ide will undoubtedly soon be hanged. I fear for more of us poor souls, though I care little for myself. But I would warn you, Crowner, someone very close to you may also be at risk.'

His scalp prickled at the slow but deliberate way in which the deep voice rolled out these portents of doom, especially when her last words could refer to no one else but Nesta.

'What have you heard, Lucy?' he snapped

urgently. 'Is there a threat to my woman in the Bush?'

Her heavy lids lifted as she looked up at him, her sharp eyes intense within their reddened rims. 'It is more what I feel in my old bones, sir, than what I have heard. We sisters often hear each other in our heads, without the need to shout. I knew what had happened at the very second Theophania died – and I know that the Welsh woman may also be betrayed.'

De Wolfe chewed at his lip, intensely worried by her words. He felt the conviction of her belief, though he usually had little time for sooth-saying and fortune-telling.

'Did you seek me out to tell me this?'

The old woman shrugged. 'In part, Crowner, for you have both been tolerant of me. But also, I beseech you to do what you can to stop this oppression. You are a just man and a powerful law officer. Surely there is something you can do to cool this madness?'

John looked at the bizarre face, and saw a strength of character that fleetingly, was almost regal as the old woman stared at him in hope. He only wished there was something he could say which could assuage her fears. 'I have been greatly concerned myself at this misplaced crusade,' he growled. 'But you must understand that, regrettably, there is very little I can do. The mob responsible for Theophania's killing melted away before they could be caught – and catching them would not bring her back now.'

He gripped her arm, not shying away from the feel of a skeletal limb beneath the grimy cloth. 'As to the others, I cannot yet fathom why Elias was murdered. And the other two women were brought before the bishop's court, over which I have not the slightest influence – in fact, the very opposite, as many in the cathedral have little love for me.'

Lucy nodded sadly, but persisted. 'I believe you, sir. But those two women cannot be hanged by the Church. I hear they will be sent to the Shire Court for sentencing, so have you no power to see them shown some mercy there?'

Again, de Wolfe had to shake his head. 'I fear that the sheriff is strongly on the side of the crusaders in this matter, for his own personal reasons. He also detests me, and if I tried to intervene it would merely harden his attitude towards them, just to spite me.' He rumbled in his throat, a sign of his emotions. 'I have every sympathy with your feelings, lady – but would advise you to keep yourself well out of the public eye at the present time, as there are many who would gleefully see you sucked into this tragic situation. Your reputation as a cunning woman marks you out too well for attention and I am surprised that you have not been accosted already!'

The hairy face stared at the ground as she leaned forward on her stick. 'As I have said, I fear nothing for myself, but wish to do all I can to save those of my kind who will surely perish if this madness goes on. Is there nothing you can do, Crowner?'

There was a grating sound behind him and, turning guiltily, he saw that his front door had opened. Thankfully, it was only Mary, who stood there, frowning at the pair in the lane.

'I will do what little I can, Lucy,' he said. 'I have already spoken to the archdeacon, who is wholly against this campaign of his fellow-canon. But others there support it, along with the sheriff and some of the merchants. It was the death of one of the guildmasters which started all this, as his widow stirred up the trouble in the first place.'

He moved away from the old woman and she bowed her head to him. 'Thank you for listening, Crowner. It now seems that I will have to do what I can myself, though God knows it will be little enough.'

De Wolfe stared at her in alarm. 'You be careful, now. I have told you to keep well out of sight until this blows over. Thank you for your warning concerning my friend at the Bush – but it is yourself who is in most danger at the moment!'

He nodded his head at her brusquely and loped away to his front step, where Mary was still standing with a disapproving look on her face.

As the heavy oak door closed with a squeal from its leather hinges, Lucy stood for a moment staring at it. 'Now I know what I must do,' she muttered to herself. 'And may God protect me – or at least receive me into his arms!'

★   ★   ★

Later that morning, Lucy stumbled wearily up Fore Street, her arthritic joints protesting at the slope as she laboriously hauled herself along with the aid of her stick, which was almost as gnarled as herself. She had no need to jostle through the folk on the road or those who loitered around the shopfronts or the stalls. They stood aside and gave her forbidding appearance a wide berth, her lank grey locks falling in a tangle over the shoulders of her dirty cape and the red-rimmed eyes peering from the weird face with its profusion of coarse hair. She wore no cover-chief or head-rail, but a rag was tied around her forehead like a grubby coronet. Mothers pulled their children close to their skirts as she passed, especially as her mouth was set in a ferocious scowl.

Lucy was in crusading mood, angry and morti-fied at the persecution of the other cunning women who were being set upon just because they had the gift of healing and sooth-saying – a gift that had been tacitly accepted and welcomed by the poorer people since time out of mind. She felt compelled to do what she could for them, what-ever the cost to herself – though she was largely uncaring as to her own fate, often feeling that the sooner her own miserable existence was ended the better. She was old – she could not remember how old. She was poor to the point of destitu-tion and lived in utter squalor, often hungry and usually in pain. Even her own few herbs and potions could no longer keep at bay the ache in her hips and knees and the torment from her bowed back-bone.

Lucy had had a family once – even a husband half a lifetime ago, until he had been killed in the quarry where he toiled. That was before the hair had started to grow on her face, as her skin thickened and her eyes weeped. Almost destitute, she had eked out an existence – one could hardly call it a living – by selling her gifts of healing and the herbs she collected for half-pence. She squatted in the ramshackle hut on Exe Island, built from scraps with her own hands. Now she was tired and ready to go to God, in whom she believed fervently, in spite of her familiarity with the ancient wisdom. That was why it was so unfair, so evil that the other cunning women were being persecuted on the grounds that they were sacrilegious unbelievers and heretics, denying God, Christ and the Holy Spirit. In fact, they were all white witches, and blasphemous thoughts never crossed their minds.

Lucy rolled all these matters around inside her head as she stumped up the last stretch of Fore Street and reached the central crossing of Carfoix, where High Street continued straight ahead and North and Southgate Streets dipped away down on either side. It had been a busy junction for most of the last thousand years and today was still as active, with ox-carts, horsemen, porters, packmen and barrow-men all jostling with pedestrians and the flocks of sheep and goats being herded by farmers and slaughtermen to the nearby killing grounds of the Shambles.

The old woman stopped near the corner to get her breath back, standing in front of a booth selling meat pasties, the other shoppers diverging around her like a mill-stream flowing around a post. The stall-holder stood frowning under his striped awning, waiting for the disreputable old hag to move away and stop scaring off his customers. When she failed to move on, he shouted rudely at her, but fell silent when she turned and fixed him with a stare from her inflamed eyes.

A few yards away, right on the corner of the crossing, a small empty cart stood idle, the shafts for the ox propped up while the carter took the beast away to water it. Lucy trudged across and with some difficulty, sat on the tailboard and with much grunting and panting, hoisted her legs up. Then she clawed her way to a standing position by grasping the side rails and moved to the front, where she found herself a couple of feet above the people thronging the junction of the roads. A few heads turned at this curious sight, but far more paid attention when the apparition began shouting in a voice than was surprisingly strong, coming from such a decrepit body.

'Listen to me, people of Exeter! Listen to Lucy, who has helped many of you who were in trouble over the years . . . if you have any gratitude at all, listen to me now!'

A score of people stopped what they were doing

and turned to stare at this old hag, bellowing from the back of a cart. Customers at the booths stopped feeling in their purses and even the stall-holders stood gaping at this weird old woman. Most of them knew who she was, even though in recent years she had rarely left her muddy island.

'What the hell is Lucy ranting about?' called a pie-man to the fish-seller in the next booth.

'God knows, the old witch is off her head,' he replied sourly. 'She should be locked up, along with those other two down in the cathedral.'

The whiskered face under the ragged headband slowly scanned the upturned faces below her. 'Shame on those who persecute those who cannot help themselves!' she bellowed. 'Why are so many of you turning against those whose only aim is to cure your ills, to solve your problems and to give you that help which you have sought from us for generations?'

It was quickly apparent that the division of opinion in the city was equally present in the crowd around the crossing at Carfoix. Some looked sheepish, others sympathetic at her words, remembering how cunning women had helped them find lost possessions, bring back errant husbands and given succour to their infants with loose bowels or a croupy cough. But a sizeable number, especially those who had been harangued by their parish priests the previous Sunday, glared angrily across Carfoix, and a few shouted at her and shook their fists.

Heated disputes began, both between the moderates and the sympathisers, but also among the more hawkish faction, who started to call for action against the hag.

'Get down, you evil old woman!' yelled a meat porter. 'Clear off or you'll go the same way as Theophania Lawrence!'

Lucy ignored them all and continued to shout her defiance and pleas for understanding. 'Why are you suddenly against us, when we have done nothing to harm you? We respect the Church and are good Christians, which is more than can be said for some of you intolerant murderers!' She gripped the rough wood of the cart's head-rail and shook herself against it in a paroxysm of emotion. 'Do not persecute us so unjustly – we are the same people that you have lived alongside all your lives. Unscrupulous people are using you as a tool for their own purposes and you let yourself be led by the nose like sheep to the knife!'

This really annoyed the more bellicose of her antagonists in the street. 'You cheeky old bastard, keep a civil tongue in your head or we'll cut it out for you!' yelled a red-faced shopkeeper, who was a verger in St Pancras's Church.

Someone threw a rotten cabbage that he picked up from behind a booth. It missed Lucy but disintegrated against the side of the cart. As if this were a signal, the verbal battles between citizens flared into brawling and several men began slugging it out with others over their differing opinions on cunning women. Old ladies began screaming and young mothers hastily gathered their children to their skirts and tried to get out of the way of the scuffles that were breaking out across the street. From their lair behind the Guildhall just up the street, the two constables heard the uproar and hurried down to Carfoix, but two men armed with staves were ineffectual against the spreading mêlée that confronted them.

The anti-witch faction were in the majority and more ambled out of the nearby alehouse, attracted by the noise, adding their drunken prejudices to the disputes that were raging. Osric, the lanky constable, rapidly summed up the situation and again wisely decided not to try to quell the developing riot, but to try to remove the cause.

'Let's get the old woman out of here, before they hang her too!' he hissed to Theobald, who was more slow-witted than the Saxon.

Together, they edged their way around the shouting, brawling throng to reach the ox-cart, where Lucy was still waving her arms and declaiming the innocence of her sisters and herself, though no one could now hear her above the tumult in the street. Osric reached the back of the cart without many in the crowd taking any notice of him and he rapped on the floorboards with his staff to get her attention. She turned at the noise, without breaking off her repetitive speech, but when she saw who it was she turned her back on him again.

'Come on, woman!' he called urgently. 'Get your-self away from here or they'll string you up, just as they did Theophania.'

He reached out with his staff and ungallantly poked her in the back with its end. She turned again, looking uncertainly at him this time. 'I have business to attend to, man. I care nothing for this rabble.'

'You'll do little business dangling at the end of a rope, so come on, damn you!' he said desper-ately, as he saw some of the truculent crowd staring at them, some even breaking off their wrestling and shoving to see what was going on at the cart. Theobald had seen it too and he clambered up on to the wagon and grabbed the bearded hag by the arm. 'Lucy, they'll kill you if you stay here. Come away now, for pity's sake!'

The little tableau on the back of the dray and the sudden cessation of her strident voice began to attract attention and more faces were being turned towards them. 'There's the root of the trouble!' yelled a florid-faced pie-man from Butcher Row, shaking his fist at Lucy.

Others took up the cry and part of the crowd began moving towards the wagon, abandoning most of their scuffles with the other faction.

'Pull the old fool off, Theobald!' hissed Osric, fearful of a repetition of the awful event down in Bretayne. The other constable grabbed Lucy's other arm and with some ripping of the rotten fabric of her cape pulled her protesting to the tailboard.

Another missile, this time a small turnip, caught her on the side of the head and this decided Lucy that it was best to run and fight another day, if she could. She half fell from the cart, being caught by Osric, and with the two constables dragging her, she hobbled across to the mouth of High Street. Her two protectors shouldered their way through a gathering crowd whose hostility was increasing, and hands stretched out to try to grab her, as insults and curses were thrown at the old crone. One wild-eyed young woman, who seemed already to be in some sort of hysterical frenzy, screamed abuse at her and grabbed a handful of her hair, until Theobald roughly pushed her away.

Barging their way forward, the constables forced a way through the main ring of protesters and hurried as best they could up the street, pulling the old woman by brute force, as her legs would not support her at that speed, especially as she had lost her stick.

'This is the wrong way to get me home to Exe Island,' she gasped. 'Where are you taking me? To gaol?'

Theobald shot a sideways glance at Osric. 'Just where the hell are we going, anyway?'

The other man had not really thought about it; all he had wanted to do was to get her off the cart and away from the angry crowd, who were now trailing after them, resentful at having their prey snatched away from them so abruptly.

'What about our shack? Can we put her in there

until we get help from the castle?' suggested Theobald.

'This mob would kick it to pieces in minutes, the mood they're in now,' grunted Osric, panting with the effort of half carrying the smelly old woman.

'The crowner!' she said suddenly. 'Take me to the crowner's house. He promised to help me.'

Theobald began to protest at this liberty, but Osric, mindful of the angry mob almost on their heels, was in no mood to argue, especially as Martin's Lane was now only a few yards away. As a few more old cabbages, turnips and a stone or two were hurled at their backs, together with a rising clamour of indignant abuse, he stumbled along with the other pair, pushing aside more curious onlookers in the main street, who were not yet aware of the cause of the disturbance.

When they came to the narrow entrance to the lane, he dragged Lucy around to the right and dived down the alley towards the second tall, narrow house. As they reached the blackened oak door, the horde of witch-haters appeared in the throat of Martin's Lane, but slowed down as they saw that the constables were beating on the door of Sir John de Wolfe. Most of the citizens of Exeter were somewhat in awe of the coroner, not only out of respect for his office and his reputation as a soldier, but because he was also a tall, grim authoritarian, who did not suffer foolish or impudent behaviour gladly and was likely to respond with a heavy cuff from his large fist.

As they hesitated, the door was opened by Mary and before she could open her mouth Osric had bundled Lucy across the threshold into the vestibule. 'Call the crowner. This old woman is in danger from that rabble!' he snapped, then pulled the door shut and stood outside it alongside Theobald, their staves at the ready to defend the house.

The crowd advanced cautiously, the red-faced verger and the pie-man in front, the rest pressing behind, uttering threats and recriminations against the evil women who, with the aid of Satan, rode broomsticks and roasted babies.

'Get away from here, you'll not repeat what happened at the Snail Tower,' yelled Osric.

'That was none of our doing, though it was well intentioned,' retorted the pie-man, brandishing a large knife. There was no way of telling whether he had been with the lynch-mob down in Bretayne or whether this was a spontaneous demonstration, fanned into activity by the parish priests and possibly other agents of the witch-hunting canon.

'Get her out of there, we want to teach her a lesson or two about curses and spells, the evil old hag!' bellowed a massive black-bearded fellow, who worked in the tannery and smelt far worse than Lucy.

Others took up the cry, some of the worst insults and foulest language coming from women, both young and old, who formed a rearguard to the men in the front.

As the clamour increased, the door was suddenly thrown open again and the forbidding figure of the coroner stood in the opening. He wore his long grey tunic and a ferocious scowl on his lean face, framed by the jet-black hair that fell to his shoulders. Hanging from a wide belt, supported by a baldric strap over his right shoulder, was a lethal-looking sword that had seen action across half the known world. With a hand on its hilt, he glared around the crowd clustered around his door.

'Get away from here, all of you – or I'll attach you all for riot and conspiracy to murder!' There was a growl of angry protest and he slid his blade a few inches out its scabbard, as the two constables waved their staves and used them to prod the nearest malefactors in the chest. 'Come to your senses, for God's sake!' he roared. 'There'll be no repetition of the lawlessness down in Bretayne the other day! I know many of you, so be warned.' His long head swung from side to side as he scanned the crowd and called out names of those he recognised. 'Arthur of Lyme, is it? And you, Rupert Blacklock from Butchers' Row – and you, James the miller! I know you all, and I'll see you suffer if you persist in this madness. Who's behind it, I want to know?'

His gaze darted around the mob, looking for any agitators, but there was no sign of Cecilia de Pridias or any of her family. He did not expect to see Gilbert de Bosco, but thought that perhaps he had sent some proctor's servants or a servile priest to egg on the protesters.

'We have the right to punish evil witches, Crowner!' called the verger, bolder than the others.

'You have no such right at all, damn you!' bellowed de Wolfe. 'The only right to punish is vested in the courts of this land, all of which ultimately answer to King Richard. Now clear off, all of you. Osric, get yourself up to Rougemont and call on the castle constable to send down a posse of men-at-arms with whips and staves to clear this rabble from my doorstep!'

With that, he stepped back inside and slammed the door.

11

In which Crowner John confronts the sheriff

John de Wolfe could hardly have left Bearded Lucy in the lane, with an increasingly angry mob at her heels, but allowing her into the house brought down almost as much trouble on his head as if he had laid about the rabble with his sword. As soon as the stout wooden latch on the front door had clacked down into place, the smaller one on the door to the hall jerked up and Matilda stood framed in the gap. For a brief moment, she stared at the little tableau in the vestibule, with Mary hovering uneasily in the background. Then a roar burst from her thin-lipped mouth as she pointed a quavering finger at the old woman.

'What is she doing in my house? Get her out of here at once!'

Sadly, Lucy turned to the door and reached for the latch, but John laid a restraining hand on her arm as he scowled ferociously at his wife.

'Wait. Matilda, there is a mob outside pursuing this poor old woman. Do you want another Theophania Lawrence on your conscience?'

'That's none of my concern – nor is it yours!' she spat in reply. 'I'll not have that foul witch in my house. Canon Gilbert was right when he quoted the Old Testament. They are evil unbelievers and should be dealt with accordingly – besides which, she stinks!' she added inconsequentially.

John's relationship with his wife habitually swung wildly from one extreme to the other and sometimes he even had a grudging respect for her. But at that moment his feelings for her reached an all-time low as her religious prejudices seemed to have overcome any trace of compassion. He stepped forward and confronted her, almost nose to nose as she stood above him on the step into the hall.

'You are a hard-hearted, intolerant bitch!' he yelled at her. 'It may have escaped your notice, but "your house", as you call it, was paid for by me out of my booty from the second Irish war. And I fully intend to invite anyone I wish into it. Is that understood?'

Matilda shook both her clenched fists in his face, her square face red with anger, though she knew that John in this mood was not to be provoked too far.

'Then drive the dirty old cow around to the yard, where she belongs! She'll set foot in the hall only over my dead body!'

'That can be arranged, too!' yelled her husband, sliding his sword up and down in its scabbard with an ominous metallic rasp – though they both knew full well that his threat of violence was an empty gesture, as, unlike many other men, he had never so much as laid a finger on his wife.

'Go on then, kill me, you great coward,' she screamed, playing along with the charade that was being fuelled by their mutual anger. 'Go on, skewer me on that sword that has murdered so many others!'

With a gesture of disgust, he slammed the hilt fully back into its sheath and turned away. 'Don't be so bloody foolish, woman! All I'm doing is trying to keep the King's peace in the streets of the city – a task your brother is supposed to fulfil, but he's always too busy filling his own purse at the expense of the county!'

Before she could start a new tirade in answer to this insult to the sheriff, he grabbed Lucy's arm and steered her to the opening of the covered passage that ran down the side of the house to the yard behind. Mary, who had listened open mouthed to this shouting match, scuttled ahead and was in her kitchen-shed by the time the old woman had shuffled through. Brutus took one look at the visitor, then slunk away to lie behind the privy. Even the maid Lucille stuck her projecting nose and teeth out of her box under the stairs to the solar to see what was going on, but withdrew them rapidly when she saw the apparition that the master was guiding into the yard.

Mary, who knew Lucy by sight and reputation, soon took pity on the old woman when John explained what had happened in the lane. She sat her down on a stool outside the cook-shed and found her a pot of ale and a piece of bread smeared with beef dripping.

'What are we to do with you, Lucy?' asked the coroner. 'I doubt that you can go home to your hut. They'll look for you there, now that they've been cheated of you here.'

The cunning woman stopped munching with her toothless gums. 'Even my talents cannot help me now,' she mumbled. 'I care little what happens to me, but I wanted to do something to help those two poor souls who will surely hang – as will others not yet persecuted, unless this madness stops.' She looked up at de Wolfe with her bleary yet riveting eyes. 'And as I have told you, sir, one of those might be very close to your own heart.'

She made him feel very uneasy with these cryptic warnings, but he still tried to reassure her. 'It will pass, Lucy. People enjoy novelty, but they soon tire of it,' he said, though he was not sure that he believed his own words. 'We need to hide you in a place of safety until this storm blows over.' He scratched his black stubble ruefully. 'But I'm afraid it can't be here. You saw what my good wife is like!'

Mary had been listening to this exchange and now spoke up. 'What about the Bush? There's plenty of room up in that loft – or better still, in one of the sheds at the back.'

This seemed the only practical solution, thought John, especially as Nesta had had dealings with Lucy before, as well as seeming to possess some of the healing talents in common with her. After the old woman had finished her food and recovered a little from her ordeal, Mary went to the

299

front of the house and returned to report that the mistress was shut in the hall with a jug of wine and that the lane was now empty of vindictive townsfolk.

John took Lucy out into the cathedral Close and headed for Idle Lane, keeping a sharp lookout and a hand on his sword. He wished that Gwyn was here to help protect them, but his two assistants were unlikely to get back to Exeter until the evening, or perhaps the next day – when another problem concerning the sheriff's threat to arrest Gwyn would have to be faced.

They reached the Bush without incident, other than suffering curious and sometimes hostile looks from passers-by when they saw the old hag shambling past – but the presence of the menacing figure of the coroner loping alongside her prevented anything more serious than muttered imprecations.

At the Bush, de Wolfe left Lucy in the yard while he went in to explain the emergency to Nesta, whose sympathetic nature made her instantly agree to shelter the old woman until, hopefully, the danger had died down. When the Welsh woman had had her own acute personal problems a few months before, the bearded crone had done her best to help her, and now here was a chance to pay her back.

'She can stay in the brewing-house for now. I'll get a palliasse from the loft and hide it behind a row of casks. I'll tell the maids and old Edwin to be sure to keep their mouths shut about her.'

John walked back to the Close in a better state of mind, feeling that yet another crisis had been overcome – and hoping that there would be a respite before the next one. Somewhat to his surprise, as he was a solitary man, he found that he greatly missed the company of Thomas and Gwyn, who though they often irritated him with their bickering, had become such a part of his daily routine that he felt almost lonely without them.

The thought of some companionship, as opposed to the frosty atmosphere that would undoubtedly reign in his house for the rest of the day, persuaded him to visit his friend the archdeacon. Late afternoon was the quietest period for the cathedral clergy, after all the many services had ended, until the cycle started again at midnight.

He spent a calming hour drinking wine and talking over the problems, though no new solutions presented themselves.

'Those two women will surely hang later this week, John,' said de Alençon sadly. 'I tried to talk some sense into Gilbert de Bosco yesterday – and I had an audience with the bishop this morning – but both showed no interest whatsoever in softening their attitude.'

'Even the bishop is against them, then?' asked de Wolfe.

'He professes a neutral attitude, saying that it is entirely a matter for the consistory court – not mentioning the fact that it was he who set it up, with Gilbert as chancellor! He also mouthed the

301

expected platitudes that the Church must be ever vigilant against heresy and sacrilege and would listen to no argument of mine that those sins were not remotely involved in the matter of these poor good-wives.' He sipped his wine abstractedly. 'This has become a political affair, my friend. The bishop sees himself attracting merit from Canterbury and even Rome by putting himself forward as a guardian of Christian doctrine – and the proud canon sees advancement for himself as a champion against the works of the Devil. Both have little concern for the actual substance of the matter, but they have a cynical self-interest in promoting their own careers. I suspect that the same goes for the sheriff, though his eyes are turned more to the Count of Mortain than towards archbishops.'

Reluctantly accepting that there was nothing more that either he or John de Alençon could do for the unfortunate Jolenta of Ide and Alice Ailward, the coroner took himself off to his chamber in the castle, rather than endure Matilda's wrath and sulks until supper-time.

He strode up to Rougemont in the early evening sunshine, for the weather had improved and manor-reeves and freemen were crossing their fingers and touching wood that there might be a reasonable harvest after all, if the rain held off for a few weeks. As he walked across the drawbridge and under the gatehouse arch, a worried-looking sentry banged his pike on the ground and stepped forward to mutter under his breath. 'Crowner, if I was you,

I'd go straight across to the keep. There's a bit of trouble going on over there!'

John's head jerked up and when he looked across the inner ward, he saw a few saddled horses near the steps up to the high entrance of the keep. One he instantly recognised as the big brown mare belonging to Gwyn of Polruan and knew that his officer and clerk had now returned from Winchester. With a groan, he realised too that his hour of respite from the recent crises was over and that his bloody brother-in-law was undoubtedly intent on making more trouble for him.

He hurried across and soon heard raised voices, indicating that the problem was not up in the keep but in the undercroft, its semi-subterranean basement. Part of this was used as the gaol serving the county court and for remanding prisoners for the Commissioners of Gaol Delivery and the Eyre of Assize, when they paid their infrequent visits to Exeter. For offenders taken to the burgesses' court, there was another foul prison in one of the towers of the South Gate – and of course, the cathedral proctors had their own cells, where the two helpless women were presently awaiting their fate.

De Wolfe clattered down the few steps and ducked under a low lintel into the gloomy cavern that was the undercroft, roofed by arched vaults of damp, slimy stone that supported the keep above. A barricade of rusty bars on the left marked off the half of the chamber that contained the prison cells. The rest was partly a store and partly a torture chamber where the repulsively fat gaoler, Stigand, extracted confessions and applied the painful and mutilating tests of the ordeal.

Today, however, the main function of the place seemed to be as a forum for a heated argument between a group of men standing in the centre of the soggy earthen floor. As John marched up to them, he saw Gwyn confronting the gaoler, with Ralph Morin, Sergeant Gabriel and two men-at-arms clustered around them. Thomas de Peyne, looking like an agitated sparrow, pattered around the group, flapping his arms and crossing himself repeatedly. When he saw de Wolfe approaching, he ran to him, his peaky face distraught with concern.

'Master, do something! They want to put Gwyn behind bars!'

Ralph Morin swung round when he heard de Wolfe coming. 'No, we don't *want* to, John. It's the last damned thing we want. But that bloody man upstairs has ordered it and I am in a difficult position, to say the least!'

'I'm not going to force my best friend into the lock-up,' wailed Gabriel. 'I'll leave the garrison and go back to being a shepherd first!'

'But that's the rub, dammit,' snapped the castle constable. 'You're still one of his men-at-arms and if you refuse you can be hanged for disobeying orders. So what the hell are we going to do, John?'

Before de Wolfe could assemble his thoughts to reply, Gwyn suddenly gave a roar and shook off

Stigand, who was trying to pull him towards the gate in the iron fence that led to the cells. 'You touch me again, you slimy bastard and I'll knock your bloody head off!' He raised his massive fist to the man, who cowered back, his slug-like features twisted in fear.

Thomas began squeaking in terror, Gabriel was yelling at the gaoler and the two soldiers were looking uncertainly at Gwyn, muttering to each other about what they ought to do. John found his voice, a deep bellow that brought momentary silence. 'All right, all right! Let's deal with this calmly, shall we? First of all, what exactly has happened?'

Gwyn, his normally amiable face creased in concern, lowered his threatening arm. 'Thomas and I got back not more than a few minutes ago and as soon as I dismounted in the bailey, these two soldiers grabbed me and said that I was wanted down here. The god-damned sheriff came and said I was under arrest for stealing part of the Cadbury treasure, but walked out before I had a chance to get my wits back. Then the constable and the sergeant here appeared and we have been arguing until you came. I'm damned if I'm going to be locked up, it's the bastard sheriff who should be jailed!'

John turned to Ralph Morin, who looked more unhappy than he had ever seen him before. 'De Revelle threatened me with this, as I told you. I didn't think he'd go through with it, though.'

The castellan turned up his hands in a gesture of

305

despair. 'He's desperate, John. I think he wants to use Gwyn as a hostage, something to bargain with for you withdrawing your claim that he dipped his hand into that box of gold and silver. I've the feeling that he's got something else nasty up his sleeve too, but I don't know what it is.' He paused and tugged at one of the points of his forked beard in an angry gesture of concern. 'Anyway, he gave me orders – point-blank orders – to clap Gwyn in a cell. As the sheriff represents the King in this county and I'm a royal appointee in a royal castle, I don't see any way of disobeying such a direct order, if I want to keep my own neck from being stretched!'

'The King, God bless him, would never sanction this,' cut in the sergeant, outraged at the whole affair.

'Nor would Hubert Walter, if he knew about it,' grunted Ralph. 'But it would take a couple of weeks to get a message to him and a reply, for he's in London.'

The mention of the Chief Justiciar, virtually the regent of England now that King Richard had gone back permanently to France, decided de Wolfe that this was probably the only course. 'De Revelle has gone too far this time. I must get word to Hubert Walter as soon as I can, but that's not going to solve our present problem.' He sighed and looked across at Gwyn, whose whiskered face showed both anger and apprehension. 'I'll have to go up and talk to that mad brother-in-law of mine and try to do some kind of a deal with him.'

Ralph Morin nodded his big head – he was as tall as de Wolfe and almost as burly as the Cornishman. 'But what about Gwyn? We can't stand here undecided all night.'

The coroner's officer solved the problem himself. 'Duty is duty, I know that very well,' he said with a sad air of resignation. 'I don't want to get my friends into trouble that could end on the gallows-tree. I'll go and sit in a cell to satisfy that swine upstairs, until the crowner sorts out this mess.' He swung around to Stigand, who was still standing a little way off, his slack mouth half open and his piggy eyes darting from one to the other. 'But only if this slobbering idiot goes and cleans out a cell of its filth and puts some clean straw in there!' He made a sudden mock leap towards the gaoler, who squeaked in fear and waddled off towards the iron gate.

'I'll bring some food down for you, Gwyn,' promised Thomas, worried out of his mind at the predicament of his big friend.

'And I'll fetch some ale,' added Gabriel. 'We can sit and play some dice until this nonsense is settled, eh?'

John felt that the others were putting a brave face on the situation for his officer's sake and although he gave Gwyn a reassuring slap on the back and bade him a confident farewell, he followed the constable out of the undercroft with heavy foreboding in his heart.

* * *

As that particular drama was being played out in the undercroft of Rougemont, Cecilia de Pridias was meeting Canon Gilbert in his house in the Close. Although he was her cousin, she was chaperoned by her daughter Avise and her dull husband Roger Hamund. They sat in Gilbert's study, furnished far more comfortably than the spartan room of John de Alençon, three doors away. Gilbert had several prebends, all serviced by under-paid vicars, so together with his perquisites from the cathedral and the rents from several properties he owned in Exeter and Crediton, he was relatively affluent and saw no reason to stint himself when it came to creature comforts. The room had an oak table and several chairs, two of which had padded seats and backs, a luxury indeed. There was a side locker with wine and Flemish glasses on top and several wall cupboards, between which hung tapestries to relieve the coldness of the stone walls. A small fireplace with a chimney rising to the ceiling was another modern innovation and the only token of an ecclesiastical establishment was a small gilt crucifix on one wall.

Gilbert's guests sat around the table and his steward entered to serve wine, then discreetly left, closing the door behind him – though he listened with his ear to the crack for some minutes.

Cecilia had no particular reason for meeting with her cousin, other than to keep in touch over their campaign, making sure that the canon's enthusiasm was not waning. She need not have worried, for once launched on this mission, Gilbert's obsessive nature fed upon itself. Even though he kept his eye upon the long-term advantages to his progress in the hierarchy of the Church, the crusade itself had gripped him, and he felt that this was a mission that had been waiting for him for years. Although not particularly devout in terms of a desperate affection for the Holy Trinity, he had begun to believe that God had marked him out for this campaign and that ridding the area of heresy and apostasy in the shape of witches was now his life's work.

His widowed cousin was equally enthusiastic and again the excitement of the hunt was for her a self-fulfilling emotion bordering on hysteria. Although her original motive had been to find and punish the sorcerer who had brought about her husband's death by putting a lethal spell upon him, this had broadened out into a pogrom against all cunning men and women. However, the death of her Robert was still to the fore of her mind and soon surfaced in their discussion.

'Do you think any of these wicked dames was responsible, Gilbert?' she asked.

The canon heaved his well-covered shoulders. 'There is no way of telling, cousin. The hanged one is now beyond any questioning and I doubt if the other pair will confess. Unfortunately, the proctors have no means of extracting the truth from them, and though the sheriff's court will undoubtedly hang them for us, they will not administer the *peine forte et dure* to get a true account of their misdeeds.'

'What about that strange episode some days ago, when that man in Fore Street was murdered?' asked Avise. Although not nearly so keen on hunting witches as her obsessive mother, she was a great gossip and liked to keep abreast of all the news in the city.

'They say that he was one of those cunning people, even though Elias was a man,' added Roger, speaking for the first and only time.

Gilbert poured some more wine. 'I heard the same rumour and I am quite prepared to believe it. All I can think of is that our exhortations, especially those I delivered through the parish priests, moved someone who had suffered from his devilish acts to take the law into his own hands, as did that crowd in Bretayne.' He took a sip of wine and added sententiously, 'I cannot bring myself to condemn either them or him, if that is what some aggrieved souls did to avenge themselves and to prevent him doing further harm to other folk.'

The quick mind of Cecilia saw a flaw in this explanation. 'But what about the killing of our supporter, Walter the apothecary? I hear that the means by which he was killed was identical – and Walter was no magician.'

'Neither was he much of a physician,' added Avise cynically, which earned her an icy look from her mother.

Gilbert's big, ruddy face creased in doubt. 'That is strange, I admit,' he confessed. 'But I doubt it is anything to do with our interests – though it is a pity that he was taken from us, as he was as keen as we to see these shameful people brought to justice.'

Cecilia de Pridias was eager to look ahead. 'Though four of these sorcerers have been dealt with, one way or another, there must surely be many more, both in the city and in the villages near by. How can these be flushed out, to rid decent Christian folk of their evil influence?'

The burly priest was glad see how keen his kinswoman was to help, and his ego persuaded him to part with a little knowledge that he had intended to keep to himself. 'Since they saw what happens to their loathsome kind, the rest are lying low, to save their own skins – and for that we must be thankful, for it helps us achieve our object of protecting the God-fearing from their satanic activities.' He smirked and rubbed his hands together in anticipation of good news. 'But I am about to come by some more information that should lead to the unmasking of another cunning woman. Our good friend and supporter Sir Richard de Revelle says that he knows of an unfortunate person who wishes to denounce someone who has wronged her. He is sending this informer down to see me this very evening.'

Robert de Pridias's widow looked at her cousin with admiration. 'May I remain while you talk to this woman?' she pleaded.

Her daughter tugged at her arm, her face showing her disapproval. 'Mother, these are not matters for a lady of your position to be mixed up with! Let the good canon deal with her.'

Cecilia shook Avise off indignantly. 'How can you say that, daughter? Your own dear father was done to death by one of these creatures. Does not the Bible say, as well as not allowing a witch to live, that revenge is sweet?'

Privately, the quite clever Avise thought that the Lord had proclaimed that 'vengeance is mine, I will repay', but she prudently kept her lips together.

Her mother turned back to her cousin. 'Who is this person that the sheriff is sending to you?'

Gilbert de Bosco shifted uneasily on his chair. De Revelle had impressed on him that his name must be kept out of this matter and Cecilia was known as an inveterate gossip, a family failing. 'I won't learn that until I speak to her. This is a delicate and confidential issue, I'm afraid. I must conduct it alone, dear cousin.'

And with that, the disappointed Cecilia had to be content.

Anger and frustration were overlaid with a nagging apprehension in John's mind as he climbed out of the undercroft, leaving Gwyn incarcerated with the rats and lice in a dirty prison cell. Unlike the time a few months ago, when little Thomas de Peyne had been locked in the same dungeon under imminent sentence of death, John could not believe that his officer was in similar danger, but he couldn't trust any of the machinations of the wily sheriff, who was as ruthless as he was dishonest. 'So let's have it out with the bastard!' he muttered under his breath, as he ran up the steps to the door of the keep, oblivious to several startled servants and clerks whom he barged aside. He marched straight to the small door to Richard's chambers, but to his intense annoyance found it locked, an unusual occurrence.

'He went out just now, Crowner,' said the nearby sentry. 'In a devil of a hurry he was too.'

Frustrated, John was at a loss as to what to do next, as Gwyn's predicament overshadowed all other issues. He brusquely questioned a few people as to where the sheriff had gone, but got no satisfaction. Just then, Ralph Morin appeared through the entrance and for want of anything better to do until de Revelle showed up, they sat at a bench and called for jugs of cider from one of the castle servants. The hall, another bare chamber of reddish-grey sandstone, took up most of that floor of the keep, the quarters of the sheriff and constable occupying the remaining third, apart from a small buttery at the far end, where the drink was kept.

After they had once more gone through a futile catalogue of de Revelle's misdeeds and how he had managed to get the upper hand over them in this latest episode, they fell silent, wondering how Gwyn was coping with imprisonment below their very feet.

313

'At least he's got Thomas to tease and Gabriel to win money from at dice,' said Ralph, trying to lighten the mood.

John nodded abstractedly, looking around at the crowd that milled around this busy place, without really seeing them. Idle men-at-arms, anxious stewards clutching lists of stores, merchants hoping to bribe favours from officials, clerks scribbling on parchments and servants carrying pots of ale or trenchers of food from the kitchens in the inner bailey – all the familiar sights of a busy castle failed to displace Gwyn's anxious face from his mind's eye. 'There must be something we can do to defeat this crafty swine!' he grated angrily, banging his mug on the table.

'He's looking for a quid pro quo, a deal that will get him off the hook at Winchester,' said the constable. 'How was the situation left there, as far as his guilt was concerned?'

'I've had chance only for a brief word with Thomas. He says that the Treasurer will want me to swear to the truth of that inventory from Cadbury before they will indict anyone for the shortfall in the treasure, which it seems amounts to twenty bezants.'

Ralph whistled through his remaining teeth. 'Twenty of those big gold coins! That's a lot of money to go missing.'

'And I've got no means of proving that de Revelle took it,' snarled John bitterly. 'And if I can't prove it, then I either drop the accusation or let a sheriff's word stand against that of a mere servant.'

The constable took a swig from his jar, then fixed John with his steady blue eyes. 'I suppose there's no possibility that . . .'

'Don't even think it, Ralph! I've known Gwyn for almost twenty years, there's no way in which he would have taken that money. And anyway, what in hell would he do with twenty bezants – buy a new leather jerkin in place of that one he must have been born in?'

They both grinned in spite of the seriousness of the situation, then buried their faces in their ale-pots.

'Where in God's teeth can the bloody sheriff have got to?' demanded John, when he came up for air.

'Here's my steward passing, perhaps he will know,' said Ralph. He called out to a prematurely bent grey-bearded man, who was mumbling to himself as he short-sightedly scanned a tattered roll of parchment held in his hands. 'Deaf as a bloody mill-stone!' growled the constable, jumping up and tugging at the man's faded brown tunic as he passed the end of the table. 'Samuel, do you know where the sheriff has gone?' he shouted at him.

The steward was not as deaf as Ralph made out, but his attention was always buried in his documents about soldier's pay, garrison stores and duty rosters. He stopped and stared at his master as if he had never seen him before, until he managed to drag his mind away from the crabbed writing on his rolls. 'The sheriff? Haven't seen him these past few hours, sir. But I've been busy with these accounts. I'll have to go through them with you tomorrow, just to check everything.'

Ralph Morin groaned. As illiterate as de Wolfe, he found the thought of sitting for an hour while Samuel droned through every item mortifying. 'When I die and go to hell, it will be this man who Satan will send as my torturer, by reading his accounts to me for eternity!' he said mockingly. 'But he's the world's best steward, nothing gets past him.'

Samuel's wrinkled, intelligent face creased into a smile at the compliment. 'I do my best, Constable, I do my best.' He cocked his head towards the main door. 'What was all that commotion down below, may I ask?' He was not only a meticulous record-keeper but another incorrigible nosy parker and a fount of information on everything that went on in Rougemont.

Ralph was as relaxed with his steward as John was with his officer and he told him about the impasse that had landed Gwyn in Stigand's cells.

Samuel looked from one to the other with an expression of astonishment. 'But why didn't you ask me, master?'

De Wolfe and Ralph Morin suddenly tensed at his words.

'Ask you what, man?' snapped the constable.

'About what was in that box that you kept in your chamber until the sheriff took it away.'

The coroner stared at Samuel, almost afraid to ask him the next question. 'You mean you know what was in there?'

'Of course I did – I'm the constable's steward, it's my duty to check everything,' he answered impatiently. 'I have access to all the keys and I naturally made a full inventory of the contents. What else would you expect?'

De Wolfe leapt to his feet and threw a long arm around the startled clerk's shoulders, much to the mystification of others in the hall. 'Samuel, if you weren't such an ugly old devil, I'd kiss you!' he boomed. 'Now tell me, please God, that you've still got that list.'

The steward looked affronted. 'Of course I have, Crowner! I never get rid of anything until I know it's not needed. It's in the constable's chamber.'

Morin was on his feet now, his granite face beaming with delight and pride at the quality of the man he relied on every day of his life. 'Take us to it, Samuel! This might be your finest hour!'

De Wolfe checked his impatience with a final word. 'Wait, we need the original tally from Cadbury to check it against. Thomas should have a copy in that big bag of his. He's down below now, with Gwyn.'

Morin sent a servant running to fetch the coroner's clerk and a few moments later, they were all hunched around Samuel's writing desk in the cluttered room that the constable used for his official duties. An excited Thomas de Peyne fished out a piece of vellum from his hessian shoulder pouch and spread it on the table, alongside another palimpsest that the steward had produced. Although the written words meant nothing to Morin or de Wolfe, they stared down at the documents with mounting anticipation, waiting for the two clerks to pronounce on the result.

Samuel ran his finger down the short column of writing on his parchment, murmuring under his breath, while Thomas did the same with the list from Cadbury. Then they looked at each other and nodded.

'God's blood, are you both struck dumb,' exploded de Wolfe, unable to contain himself any longer.

'They are the same, Crowner,' said Thomas exultantly. 'That which we certified in Cadbury is identical to what Samuel here recorded when the chest was in this chamber!'

The meticulous steward insisted on itemising the contents. 'Four hundred and eighty-six silver pennies, fifty-two gold bezants and one golden brooch. I remember them well.'

John turned triumphantly to Ralph Morin. 'We've got the whoreson thief! Let him try to wriggle his way out of this! I've put up with a great deal from that bastard, for his sister's sake, but stealing from his own king is beyond any forgiveness.'

He swung around to Samuel and gripped his arm. 'My own clerk is a treasure himself, but you must be his equal!'

Both scribes flushed with pleasure, the more so

because the coroner was known to be a hard man who rarely paid any compliments.

'What's to be done now, Crowner?' gabbled the excited Thomas. 'Can we go down and get Gwyn out of that verminous place?'

Ralph gave de Wolfe a questioning look. 'Can we do that or should you confront de Revelle first?'

'Set him free now,' answered the coroner impatiently. 'With this new evidence, there's no reason whatever that he should be under any suspicion. Richard won't get away with it this time. But where the hell has he got to?'

The sheriff was in fact, just pulling on his fine wool leggings as he sat inelegantly on the edge of a whore's mattress. The red-headed strumpet sat with her back propped against the wall of her mean room in Rack Lane, down towards the Watergate, which was convenient for the seafaring customers who came to her from the quay-side. However, still being young enough not yet to have suffered the ravages of her profession, Esther's good looks had attracted several of the leading citizens to purchase her services, including de Revelle.

Tonight he was here with a double purpose, as although he wanted to slake his lust, which had not been satisfied since he had visited a stew in Winchester, he also wanted to make sure that Esther's sister had embarked on the mission that he had commanded. Heloise, who lived in this mean room as well and who kept out of the way when her sister was conducting her trade, had been sent to complete the task that she had begun when she visited Nesta at the Bush tavern some time before. She had been carefully coached by Esther, who in turn had been instructed by the sheriff, who wanted to stay anonymous as far as Heloise was concerned. The girls were well paid for their collusion and their avaricious minds were too concerned with the money to ask any questions.

'She has gone with that tale to the canon, then?' he asked once again, as he threw down a few pennies on the rumpled and grubby blanket covering the hay palliasse on which they had coupled.

'I told you three times now, yes!' snapped the young harlot. 'I did exactly what you told me and she is there in the Close now, telling that priest that pack of weird lies you wanted.'

She climbed naked out of bed to get dressed and go to the Saracen to seek her next client, as de Revelle pulled on his boots and furtively left the house to return to Rougemont. His lust satisfied for the time being, he felt able to face going to Revelstoke on Thursday to endure a few days with his frigid wife Eleanor, whom he had not seen since before he went to Winchester. As he strode along the high street, loftily deigning to acknowledge the bobbed heads and pulled forelocks of the citizens, his agile mind turned to the close shave he had had with his damned brother-in-law. He cursed the day the previous autumn when Matilda had persuaded him to support de Wolfe's election to the new coronership in the county court – although realistically, there was no way that John could fail to be nominated, given the virtual order that had come from Hubert Walter, with the personal recommendation from the King himself. Since his brother-in-law had taken office, he had been a constant thorn in his side and twice before, he had uncovered schemes of the sheriff's which came perilously near to treason. Now he had done it again and the fact that the Chief Justiciar had revived the old Saxon post of coroner partly as a check on the rapacity of all sheriffs, was no comfort to a man who had his sister's husband breathing down his neck all the time. If the damned fellow had been corruptible, like most public officials, it would not be so bad, thought Richard – but de Wolfe had this abnormal streak of honesty that made him impossible to deal with. Vindictively, he was determined to strike him where it hurt most, and tonight's scheme was the first blow in this campaign. If he could turn this treasure fiasco into another strike, that would also be satisfying – he knew that John would not risk letting his old retainer Gwyn be hanged, and if he could then somehow expose the coroner's inevitable retraction of that list of treasure trove as a falsification for personal reasons, maybe he could bring about his disgrace and even his downfall. However, doing so might risk exposing Richard's own theft and he was pondering some devious way of getting round this problem when his feet delivered him to the castle gatehouse.

Ignoring the salute from the sentry he hurried to the keep, stamped up the stairs and turned into the hall. The first thing that confronted him was a group of men clustered around the nearest table, some standing, others sitting down, but all looking expectantly at him as he entered, for one of the servants had signalled his arrival in the inner bailey. Their attitude was unnerving, and among them he saw John de Wolfe, Ralph Morin, the chaplain Brother Rufus, Sergeant Gabriel, the poisonous little coroner's clerk and Morin's steward Samuel. His eye was caught by someone sitting with his back to him, unmistakable from the shock of unruly red hair that sprouted from his massive head.

'What's that man doing here?' he yelled, his anger flaring at the same time as an awareness of imminent disaster. There was something about the way these men were waiting for him which frightened him, but he put on a bold face, relying on his pre-eminence in the county to carry him through. 'Morin, I ordered that he be locked up! Are you disobeying my direct order?'

It was his brother-in-law who answered him, his dark face glowering across at the sheriff. 'Do you want to continue this in private or are you content to let all these hear our discussion?' He jerked a thumb over his shoulder at the score of people in the hall, who were straining their ears to pick up any juicy bits of scandal from the row that was so obviously brewing.

Not deigning to answer, de Revelle wheeled

around and walked stiffly to his door, which he unlocked with a key taken from his pouch. Although he made no invitation for them to follow, he left the door wide open and they all trooped in and stood in a half-circle around his table, reminding Gabriel of a pack of hounds holding a deer at bay.

Richard jabbed a finger towards Gwyn, who was back in his usual amiable mood. 'I asked, why is this thief still at large? You'll answer for this, Constable – and you, Sergeant, if you've flouted my orders!'

'Stop this nonsense, de Revelle!' said the coroner, in a tired voice now that the crunch had come. 'You've been caught red handed and you may as well drop this pretence of innocence and prepare yourself for what must inevitably come, when the King and his council get to hear of it.'

Richard continued to splutter indignantly and try to shout down his brother-in-law's measured words, but John turned to the clerk Samuel, took two parchments from his hands and laid them on the table before the sheriff. 'These are quite short – and you always boast of your prowess in reading, Richard. So compare the two and tell me how a written, witnessed inventory of the contents of the Cadbury treasure chest made in this very keep happens to be identical with the list made in Cadbury?'

As de Revelle rapidly scanned the brief documents, his face became ashen, but he still didn't give up. 'This must be some forgery – you are determined to ruin me, by whatever foul means you can devise.' He seized the list made by Morin's clerk and tried to tear it half. 'This is what I think of this imposture,' he snarled, but the tough sheepskin refused to rip and only crinkled in his hands. Furious and desperate, he held it to the flame of a small lamp that burned on his table for melting the wax for his seals, but again the leathery membrane only curled up and shrivelled in one corner.

De Wolfe leaned over and pulled it from his fingers. 'Stop wasting our time, Richard. That's but an attested copy, made in the last hour. The original is in safe-keeping, ready to be taken to the King's treasurer and the justiciar.' He regarded the sheriff with something akin to pity, until he recalled how much mischief he had caused. 'This is the end, Richard. There is no way in which I can overlook your stealing from our king. You must give up your shrievalty immediately and I will get the Shire Court to appoint a caretaker sheriff in your place until the will of the King is known.'

The unspeakable prospect of being ejected from the most powerful post in the county, with all the power and perquisites that it carried, galvanised de Revelle into action. His dandified figure almost danced with rage behind his desk as he screamed vilification and denial at the sombre group around him. 'Give up my position? Are you raving mad, man!' he screamed. 'I am the sheriff, I am paramount in this shire! No one can displace me here, no one but the King himself or the greatest men in his Council!' He waved a shaking fist at the coroner and swung it to include the other disciples of doom clustered around him. 'So get out of here! I am the sheriff and will stay the sheriff until Winchester or London decide otherwise. You have no authority over me, de Wolfe, you're a mere coroner. You are as nothing, your useless job is to prod corpses and examine ravished women. And you, Ralph Morin, are just another soldier, my servant, a spear-waver, who has no say whatsoever in the running of this county. Get out, the lot of you, and keep out of my sight!'

There was a silence. All looked at John de Wolfe to see what he would do or say.

'Bluster will only delay the evil hour, Richard. I suppose I could have you dragged to the gaol where you were so keen to put Gwyn here. But I will content myself with attaching you to appear before the royal justices, when they next come to Exeter, charged with theft and treason, which is inevitably a hanging matter. However, no doubt before then Hubert Walter or perhaps the King himself will decide what should be done, as I will send word to London as soon as possible.' He stood back and waved the singed parchment at de Revelle. 'Until then, I suppose you may as well stay here and play at being sheriff, though I will at once make soundings as to who might take over as locum tenens.'

As he walked to the door, de Revelle's voice followed him, hissing like a snake, full of evil and spite. 'You're going to suffer for this, John! If I fall, then I'm taking you down with me!'

12

In which Crowner John visits his mother

DeWolfe walked back to Martin's Lane with mixed emotions churning in his head. He was a straight-forward type of person, not overly blessed with imagination and certainly lacking the devious, crafty mind of his corrupt brother-in-law. He derived no joy from what looked like the final downfall of Richard de Revelle, but his somewhat blinkered loyalty to his office and his king made it inevitable that he go through with it. He knew that Matilda would be devastated and, strained as their relationship was, he had no desire to cause her any more grief than was necessary. She had looked up to her brother for most of her life until recently, with the hero-worship of a sibling five years older, one who had climbed to the elevated heights of county sheriff, rich from his marriage to the daughter of a wealthy Somerset baron. Matilda had closed her eyes to his misdeeds for several years, but since her husband had become coroner, his exposure of de Revelle's repeated skirmishes with treason and his dishonesty had gradually caused the scales to fall from her eyes. Ironically, it was she who had persuaded John to accept the coronership, as she wanted to use his position in the governing hierarchy to elevate her position in the social scale, little knowing that his uncompromising honesty would be her brother's undoing.

Now, as he loped along towards their house, John knew that this would be the final straw that would shatter what little remained of her faith in Richard. He was sorry for her, but it would be kinder if she heard it from him rather than through the snide gossip of her friends at St Olave's.

His readiness for such compassion almost evaporated as soon as he put a foot through the door of his hall, as she immediately put her head around the wing of her hearth-side chair and attacked him. 'So, I hear you took that dirty old crone down to the Bush. Now there are two evil witches in that den of sin!'

John clamped his lips shut to keep in an angry reply and went to a side table, where he poured himself some wine from the jug that Mary had placed there for them. He filled another pewter cup and held it out towards his wife. When she rudely shook her head, he nevertheless advanced on her with the wine. 'You'd better take it, Matilda,' he said gravely. 'I have to tell you something that may distress you.'

'There's little that can distress me further,' she snapped sarcastically. 'You've already done everything imaginable to hurt me.'

He lowered himself into the seat opposite and

took a long sip of his wine. 'This is not about me, wife. Once again, it's about your brother.'

The mention of her former paragon of Norman manhood brought her up short and she dropped her usual carping manner and stared at John uneasily. 'What about my brother?'

He returned her gaze steadily, nerving himself to drive home the dagger. 'In the past, usually at your pleading, I have turned a blind eye to Richard's failings – even when my loyalty and duty should have prevented me. But this time the matter is out of my hands, as even the King's exchequer is aware of it.'

Her hand fluttered to her throat, to lie on the silken wimple that enveloped her face. She knew from the gravity of his tone that this was no ploy in the eternal battle of words between them – this was reality. 'Tell me what has happened, John,' she said in a low voice, a tear already appearing in anticipation in the corner of each eye.

He explained calmly and with no elaboration, how the sheriff had filched part of the Cadbury treasure, unaware that a detailed inventory of it had already been made – and when challenged, had tried to lay the blame on Gwyn, putting him in danger of a death sentence.

Even at this eleventh hour, Matilda fought for her brother's reputation. 'But Cadbury is part of his estate – the treasure should be his!'

John sighed and patiently explained once again that all England belonged to the Crown and that tenants, be they barons or bishops, had no claim to abandoned gold or silver left in the soil.

'Then these lists must be in error!' she cried wildly.

He shook his head. 'They were checked by no less than six people, four of them literate. I myself was present at Cadbury, and though I may not be able to read and write, I can count coins put in piles of ten.'

Matilda was silent, her face drawn and ashen. 'What will happen to him?' she asked in a low voice.

'That's up to the chief ministers – Hubert Walter, the treasurer and the chancellor, though undoubtedly the King himself will be informed about such a serious matter involving one of his sheriffs.'

'And the penalty?' she whispered

John shrugged, not out of indifference, but because he genuinely did not know. With Richard's ability to squeeze out of tight corners, given the powerful friends he had in Prince John and some of the bishops, he might get off more lightly than he deserved. 'There is no way in which he can continue as sheriff,' he said slowly. 'It depends on what the Curia Regis think of the matter when they consider it – and what the Lionheart wishes. Strictly speaking, Richard has committed treason, by stealing from the King. Added to the seditious leanings he has displayed in the past, his political career is finished – at least under the present monarch.'

Matilda sat silently, a tear now coursing down each side of her nose.

'I gain no pleasure from this, lady,' John said suddenly. 'I wish I could spare you the sorrow that it must bring. But the matter is not in my hands, the exchequer clerks must deal with it now. However, I am duty bound, as the next most senior law officer in Devon, to deliver the attested list of the treasure to Winchester, otherwise your brother's false claim that it was stolen could lead to innocent men being blamed.'

Matilda made no reply, but a moment later rose from her chair and made her way towards the door. 'I must go to Richard and talk to him. I need to hear from his own mouth that what you have told me is the truth.'

He followed her to the screens that sheltered the door. 'You have not yet eaten, Matilda. Wait until after supper and I shall escort you.'

She shook her head, not looking at him. 'I am not hungry. I will call Lucille and she can walk with me up to the castle. It will not be dusk for some time yet.'

She left, and he sat down in the gloomy hall to finish his wine and wait for Mary to bring supper. Tonight even the prospect of going down to the Bush seemed less inviting than usual, though he must go to make sure that Bearded Lucy was still hidden safely away in the brewing-shed.

His old dog sensed that something was amiss and came to rest his drooling mouth on John's knee.

'It's a strange world, Brutus,' said his master with a sigh, as he stroked his head. 'Why does everything always have to be so bloody complicated?'

When de Wolfe returned later that night, just as the last traces of daylight were fading in the western sky, Mary told him that his wife had sent Lucille home with a message that she would be staying the night with her cousin, a widow who had a small house in the town. There was nothing unusual in this, but John suspected that she wanted to avoid him for the time being. Whether this was to hide her despair about her brother or because she suspected him of plotting the sheriff's downfall, he could not decide. In any event, he found his way to their lonely bed in the solar and fell into a troubled sleep, partly because of concern about Nesta and the veiled warnings that Lucy had offered about his mistress's safety. All had been quiet at the Bush that evening and the old crone seemed content to hide away behind a row of ale casks, comfortable enough on a straw mattress, with ample food coming from the cook-house a few yards away. In fact, she was much better housed and fed than she had been in her miserable shack down on the marshes at Exe Island.

There was no sign of the mob that had chased Lucy earlier in the day, and John hoped that some of the novelty of witch-baiting was wearing off as time went on. What they were going to do with the old woman in the long term was something else that worried him, and he wondered whether the nuns at Polsloe Priory, a couple of miles outside the city, might be able to give her refuge, if she was cleaned up a little.

Eventually he fell asleep and woke as usual some time after dawn to the novel luxury of being alone on the big feather-stuffed mattress on the floor of the solar. As there was nothing that morning which demanded his early attention, he lay indolently under the single summer blanket until he heard the cathedral bells ring for prime, soon after the seventh hour. He dressed in his linen undershirt and pulled on a pair of breeches instead of his usual hose, as he thought he might take Odin for a canter around Bull Mead, the tournament ground outside the city walls. He searched in his oak chest, which was the repository for his few clothes and took out a clean black tunic, a plain garment that reached from his shoulders to just below his knees. Buckling on the wide belt that carried his dagger and purse-like scrip, he slipped his feet into house shoes and went down the outside stairs to Mary's kitchen-hut, where she lived with Brutus for company.

A handsome woman in her late twenties, she was not married, a fact that John often thought strange, but he was thankful that she remained as the mainstay of their household, as Matilda was indifferent to any form of domesticity, being concerned only with her social life, her devotions at St Olave's and an occasional bout of needlework.

Being alone, John ate his breakfast in Mary's kitchen, squatting on a milking-stool before the small table where she prepared the food. She had been out early to the stalls and had brought back several fine sea-fish, caught during the night from boats that worked the estuary between Topsham and Exmouth. Grilled and laid on a thick slab of buttered bread, they were delicious, especially when followed by a couple of new apples and a quart of best ale.

The dark-haired maid stood over John and watched him eat with the satisfaction of a woman that knew she could please a man not only in bed, but also at the board. However, it had been a long time since they had lain together – and since Nesta had monopolised his affections, she was content to keep him at arm's length, even though now and then he caught her in a quiet corner and gave her a good kissing.

This morning they talked of recent happenings and John, who trusted her discretion, told her about the scandal that was soon to break over the sheriff. Mary had known that something was in the wind when Matilda, with a face like stone, had hurried away to the castle late the previous evening and had not returned.

'The mistress will take this very hard, after the previous troubles with her brother,' she observed. 'She has been loyal to him against the odds for so long, but this will finish it, I fear.'

De Wolfe nodded and wiped the last of the grease

from his mouth with the sleeve of his tunic. 'I feel very sad for her, poor woman, even though she makes my life a misery. I would not wish this disillusionment upon her, but the bloody man had gone too far this time – it's out of my hands now.'

When he had finished, he went to the vestibule and pulled on a pair of riding boots and attached his spurs. Crossing the lane, he went into the stables and chatted to Andrew the farrier while one of the grooms saddled up Odin, his massive destrier. Although he had no wars to fight now, John was used to the feel of a broad warhorse beneath him, and since the tragic death of Bran, his previous stallion, he had developed a similar admiration and affection for this twelve-year-old grey, who had been pensioned off from the French campaigns.

When the ostler led him from his stall, John hoisted himself up into Odin's high saddle and turned his head to the lane, but just as he was moving off, there was a deep bellow from outside and Gwyn came panting in, his face almost as red as his hair from the exertion. 'Crowner, for Christ's sake, come quickly! There's a mob at the Bush, intent on serious mischief!' For once the Cornishman had abandoned his usual long-windedness, the urgency raw in his voice. 'There's about fifty of them, some with burning brands – and that bastard canon is among them, egging them on!'

De Wolfe felt his heart thump with anxiety. 'Did you see Nesta there?'

'No, I was just on my way there for a bite of food, but the sight of that rabble clustered around the front and back sent me haring up here. There was nothing I could do on my own.'

John's warrior nature quickly took control and he snapped out orders. 'Andrew, take a horse and fly up to Rougemont and get the constable and Gabriel down to Idle Lane with some men. Tell them it's a matter of life and death!' He looked down at Gwyn. 'Run over to the house and get my sword, I've only got a dagger with me.'

It was quicker to send him than to dismount and get back up again and, within a minute, his officer was back with John's broad-sword hanging from its baldric, which he kept hanging in the vestibule.

As he threw the strap over his shoulder, he motioned for Gwyn to get up behind him on Odin. With no stirrup to help him, the ostler bent double for Gwyn to put a foot on his back and with a heave, he was up behind his master, just as the desperately impatient John touched Odin with his spurs. Though the stallion was built for brute power, rather than speed, they were soon cantering through the Close, the great beast not seeming to notice the substantial extra weight on his back.

The coroner yelled hoarsely at anyone who seemed likely to get run down in the narrow lanes that led to Southgate Street, but the thunder of the destrier's hoofs was enough to scatter any bemused loiterers in their path.

'Were they after Lucy, d'you think?' he howled over his shoulder, as they hammered downhill towards the tavern.

'Couldn't tell, they were shouting for the witch!' bellowed Gwyn. 'I didn't wait to find out more, I needed to get you down there!'

As they entered Priest Street, the slope became steeper and John slowed Odin to prevent him slipping, but also because increasing numbers of people were hurrying down to where Idle Lane turned off to the right.

They were attracted not only by the hubbub of shouting and yelling, but also by an ominous plume of black smoke that was rising into the still morning air. Any fire in a city was a danger to all its inhabitants, especially when the majority of buildings were still built of wood and many of the roofs were of thatch or wooden shingles.

'Holy Mary, the place is afire!' yelled Gwyn in his ear as they turned the corner. Before them the Bush sat isolated on its patch of waste ground, but clustered around the front and up the side to the back yard was a mass of people, being added to as a flood of sightseers and fire-fighters streamed towards it from both Priest Street and Smythen Street on the other side.

Now able only to go at a trot through the press of people, Odin barged his way towards the tavern, his nostrils flaring and his ears going back at the unwelcome smell of smoke. There were dull red flames licking up at several points around the edges of the lofty thatched roof and smoke was billowing out in ever-increasing volume from under the eaves and filtering through several places on the thatch itself.

Yelling at the top of his voice in a mixture of anger and anxiety, John forced the stallion through almost to the front door, where the mob appeared to be most excited and aggressive, shouting and screaming abuse and shaking their fists. They were being forced back from the front wall, which carried the door and two unglazed windows, as strands and clumps of burning straw were beginning to drop down from the edge of the thatch above. The eaves were almost low enough to be touched by a man standing on tiptoe, the large space in the loft being made by the steep pitch of the roof.

Just over the doorway, from which smoke was billowing, was the inn sign, a large dried bush hanging from an iron bracket sticking out of the wall. Someone had already thrown a rope over it with an ominous noose on one end, although the act was futile, as the bush had just caught fire and the rope was already smouldering. Still, the memory of Theophania Lawrence hanging from the bracket on the Snail Tower was still fresh in John's memory and his rage increased when he thought of Nesta and Lucy still inside the building.

With a roar, he turned Odin to face the rabble, keeping his rump well clear of the falling hot debris. With an almost maniacal flourish, he drew his sword, the three feet of steel making a chilling scraping sound as it came out of the scabbard. As he held it aloft, he felt Gwyn sliding off the horse, a long club in one hand and his dagger in the other.

Afterwards, he could not recollect what he was shouting at the mob, but with the flat of his sword he lay about those within reach, as Gwyn beat a path through them and vanished around the side of the inn.

Odin was in his element, for he had been trained for close combat and neighed and tossed his head and kicked out with his great feet, with devastating effect on those who were unwise enough not to scatter out of his way. De Wolfe made for a man who still held a burning brand in his hand and felled him with a sideswipe of the sword against his head. The torch fell against two others, who screamed as their flesh began to burn, and set up a ripple effect that caused the mob to move outwards in a panic-stricken circle, like a stone thrown into a pond.

Several men made half-hearted attempts to strike John or pull him from the horse, but they were rewarded either with a ringing blow from the flat of his sword or a thwack from the saddle-stick that he carried in his other hand, having hooked the reins around the pommel, as Odin needed no guiding in a situation like this. Thankfully, almost none of the crowd was armed with anything more than their usual dagger, as they had turned out to burn and hang an old woman, not to fight.

Most of them made no attempt to oppose the coroner, who was an almost demoniacal figure himself, clad all in black, bellowing in fury and laying about him with a great sword from the back of a monstrous horse.

The crowd broke up as they scattered from his path and suddenly he found himself looking down at the cassock-clad figure of a priest. Gilbert de Bosco glared back at him, yelling something that in the clamour and crackle of flames John did not understand – not that his powers of comprehension were working well, such was his anger.

'Damn you, you malicious meddler!' he yelled. 'Is this how you serve God, by persecuting defenceless women, you evil coward!' He raised his sword high and only an ingrained respect for the priesthood stopped him from slicing off the canon's head.

Gilbert stared up in momentary terror, but when he saw that John was instinctively unable to strike a member of the cloth he instantly regained his arrogance and pomposity. 'Threaten a member of the cathedral chapter, would you!' he shouted. 'You'll be brought to account for that, Crowner!'

For answer, the enraged coroner grabbed Odin's reins and hoisted the beast back to rear up so that his great fore-feet lashed the air momentarily in front of de Bosco's face. With a scream of fear, the priest stumbled backwards to escape the menacing hoofs and crashed against a man behind, falling heavily backwards to the ground.

De Wolfe brought the stallion back to earth and glared down at the priest as he lay ignominiously in the dirt. 'If anyone dies or is badly injured in this tumult that you have provoked, my inquest will indict you. Your claim to benefit of clergy may save your neck, but I will personally plead with Archbishop Walter for you to receive the harshest punishment known to the Church!'

Pulling Odin around, he turned to far more urgent matters, the burning of his beloved Bush and the safety of those inside it. Sick with concern for Nesta, he urged the horse along to the corner of the tavern and scattered the now sullen crowd so that he could reach the gate in the fence that led to the yard. The original rioters had now been diluted with ordinary citizens who were both agog with excitement and concerned with controlling the fire. Most were men, but there were a few women of all ages and, although it hardly registered, given the turmoil in his mind, he saw that one of them was the thin woman with the wry neck that Gwyn had said was sister to a harlot.

Thankfully, as the inn was on a wide patch of waste land, created by previous fires some years ago, there was less risk of the conflagration spreading, though sparks and burning straw borne on the wind could still travel many yards and set other roofs on fire. Some men were running with leather and wooden buckets, water slopping from their sides, but it was a futile gesture given the height and size of the roof.

Sheathing his sword, de Wolfe slid from the saddle and in a lather of anxiety rushed through the gate into the back garden of the Bush. The rear part of the roof was not yet on fire, as the arsonists had thrown their torches up from the lane in front, but smoke was starting to wreathe up from under the eaves. There were a dozen men in the yard, several struggling with buckets from the well and he saw the two serving maids standing outside the kitchen-shed, sobbing and wringing their hands.

'Where's your mistress?' he roared, shoving aside anyone who got in his way as he made his way to the back door.

'Gone inside, she went after the old woman!' screeched Adele, pointing at the door. 'And Edwin is in there, too.'

John ran to the doorway, from the upper part of which black smoke was now staring to waft lazily upwards. Keeping his head low, he dashed inside, wondering where in hell Gwyn had got to and now desperately worried about his mistress's safety. Mercifully, the first thing he saw through his stinging eyes was the large figure of Gwyn, shepherding out Nesta, both of them covered in smuts and coughing like a pair of sick horses. Grasping her by her other arm, he steered her to the back door and fresh air. The two serving maids ran forward and helped to carry her off to the security of the kitchen-shed, which certainly, until the back of the inn caught fire, was beyond immediate danger.

'I'm well enough, John,' Nesta gasped between coughs. 'But where is Edwin? Please find him!'

Gwyn had slumped to sit on the ground, coughing violently and gasping. He had black smudges on his face and bits of straw, some still smouldering, stuck in his dishevelled hair. 'Give me a moment, Crowner, to get my breath back – then I'll be with you!' he wheezed.

'You stay there until you've recovered!' commanded John. 'But have you seen the old potman?'

'He's still in there somewhere,' croaked his officer. 'And that mad old woman.'

De Wolfe crouched low and dived below the coils of smoke now billowing from the back door. Almost on all fours, he scuttled into the large taproom that occupied the entire ground floor. Tables and stools had been overturned when the patrons had jostled their way out at the first shouts of 'Fire'. Although at ground level the air was relatively clear, he heard a crackling noise and saw that the tinder-dry planks of the ceiling that formed the floor of the loft were burning in the centre, where a patch of flaming thatch had fallen as the roof began to give way. As he desperately looked around for any sign of the one-eyed potman, part of the ceiling fell in a shower of sparks and stirred up the smoke so that great wreaths eddied down to the ground. He knew he could not survive in that and tried to hold his breath. At that very moment, he saw a leg sticking out from under a fallen table and, tugging at the foot, slid the owner from under it. Almost on his bottom, he scurried backwards, hoisting the leg, his eyes running and aching and his lungs almost bursting. Just as he thought he would either faint or have to let go, he felt the weight lighten as someone crawled in beside him and grab the other leg. Not until they reached the patch of daylight that was the back door could John's bleary eyes see that, of course, it was the faithful Gwyn, still coughing and snorting like a grampus. At the door, other hands helped them out and a moment later, they staggered up to lean against the wall of the brew-shed as two other men and a woman tended to Edwin. He lay on his back having his face wiped clean of thick soot with water from one of the fire-buckets by an iron-smith, who was one of the regulars at the Bush.

'Is he still alive?' wheezed John.

'Yes, he's poorly, but I think he'll do,' said the smith, feeling the heartbeat of the old man.

'Did you see any sign of Bearded Lucy in there?' persisted Gwyn, who was rapidly getting his breathing back to normal. 'I'll swear I saw her by the ladder to the loft.'

'She's supposed to be in here, dammit!' grunted John, his own heart thumping like a war-drum. He slapped a hand against the brewing-shed, which was supporting him.

Gwyn hauled himself off the wall and stumbled to the door of the hut, opened it and looked in. 'She's not here – but I need a drink to wash the ash from my throat.'

He stuck his head into the nearest open tub and drank the half-brewed liquid like a horse at a trough. Seeing an empty jug near by, he dipped it in and came out to give it to de Wolfe. The coroner took a deep draught, then spat it out on the ground. 'God, that's horrible! Now I'm going to see Nesta.' He stumbled across to the kitchen-hut and, wiping his running eyes, leaned against the door-post to look in at Nesta, who was sitting on a stool, crying. Her two maids hovered behind her solicitously, trying to comfort her.

'All that work, John, in vain! My Meredydd's efforts at first, then all your help, going up in smoke!'

'We will see it built again, Nesta!' he assured her, using the Welsh tongue that they habitually spoke. 'The stone walls will stand, we can have a new floor and roof on them within weeks.'

He looked over his shoulder and saw that there were still people milling about outside the yard gate. 'Where the devil is Ralph Morin and his men-at-arms! That crowd is still there and that bloody priest! Keep yourself quiet in here, don't show yourself at all.'

He pulled the door shut and moved towards the back of the inn, but now black smoke was belching out of the rear door and there was no chance of getting inside to look for Bearded Lucy. Gwyn had rapidly recovered and, grabbing his arm, de Wolfe hustled him towards the side gate. 'I don't trust this damned mob, especially if that bastard canon is still among them.' Drawing his sword again, he first checked that Odin was safe and was relieved to see that the horse had wandered across the waste ground and was unconcernedly cropping at some rank grass and weeds, well away from the crowd around the alehouse.

'Let's get around to the front again,' he commanded, and stalked around the side of the building, pushing aside anyone who got in his way. The original few dozen agitators were now well outnumbered by more reasonable citizens, but there was still a lot of shouting and abuse with scattered scuffles going on. As the coroner and his officer forced their way towards the front door, there was a ragged cheer, mixed with cat-calls, as the crowd saw a posse of soldiers come trotting around the corner from Smythen Street. Led by Ralph Morin on foot, also waving a large broadsword, there were a dozen soldiers with pikes and staffs, Sergeant Gabriel bringing up the rear, brandishing a fearsome ball-mace.

They dived into the mob, roughly pushing them aside, and soon split them up into smaller groups, men-at-arms separating each faction. The castle constable thrust his great bulk through them to stand alongside de Wolfe. He stared in astonishment at the stricken tavern. 'There's no saving this now, John,' he rumbled in his deep voice. 'Has everyone got out? Where's Nesta?'

'All are safe, thank God. But that old woman Lucy has vanished, we don't know if she's still in there.'

345

Morin looked around at the crowd, who were now reduced to a muttering, growling rabble. 'Who did this? Do you want them arrested?'

'That swine of a canon, Gilbert de Bosco! He's over there, still trying to egg them on. A few louts had torches, but I doubt we'll find them now – apart from one whose head I hammered.'

There was the sounds of hoofs from the direction of Priest Street and, turning, they saw a horseman clattering towards them.

'It's the sheriff. What the hell does he want here?' marvelled Morin. It was indeed Richard de Revelle, in his dandified green tunic, sitting on a smart dappled palfrey.

Any further speculation was abruptly halted by a loud crash behind them. They turned back to look at the inn, where a large segment of the roof had fallen in amid a huge gush of sparks and flame. The smoke was now ascending in a great plume, almost straight up because of the lack of any breeze on that sultry day. All faces were turned up to watch, a morbid fascination with fire gripping most of the bystanders.

The quarter of the roof that had fallen was mostly in flames, but the collapse had also torn down an intact section that had been resting on the side gable. In this fire-free area against the wall, a frightening figure now appeared. Bearded Lucy staggered to the edge of the loft floor, which was burning behind her, and looked down on the crowd, who were struck dumb by the apparition. The hair on her head and face was singed, with smouldering straw entwined in it, and the hem of her flowing garment was on fire.

Swaying on the very edge of the boards, she held up her arms like some Old Testament prophet and then swung them slowly around, her forefingers outstretched, to encompass the crowd, who were transfixed with emotions varying from terror to hatred.

'Jump, Lucy! Quickly, we'll catch you!' yelled one more kindly voice. She shook her head slowly, her fingers clawing at the air as the flames licked closer.

'Burn, then, as you deserve, you bloody old sorcerer!' screamed another.

A deeper voice boomed out, from the throat of Canon Gilbert. 'The Lord said thou shalt not suffer a witch to live – so die, woman, and may God have mercy on your soul!'

The red-rimmed eyes of the hag up on the doomed building swivelled to rest on the priest. Her pointing finger followed, then that on the other hand tracked across to transfix the sheriff on his horse. 'I curse all who have brought this about! I curse those who have persecuted my sisters! And I especially curse you two evil men, who have cast out all compassion from your hearts to make way for ambition!'

There was a creaking noise from behind her head and another section of roof fell in a cascade of sparks and smoke.

'I curse you, I curse you, I curse you thrice!' screamed Bearded Lucy, the skirt of her filthy gown now being licked by flames. 'May the evil that you most fear, befall you before the next full moon!'

Then, with a massive crash, almost the entire rear half of the roof fell downward and forward as the heavy ridge timber burnt through.

A mass of flaming hazel withes and the burning thatch that it had supported fell on top of Lucy. There was a heart-rending scream, then silence.

A huge mushroom of black smoke, almost like a thundercloud, puffed up as the roof hit the remnants of the loft floor and from more than a hundred throats an awe-struck gasp went up with it. John, by no means an imaginative man, later swore that for a fraction of a second he saw the swirling cloud form the image of a young woman's face, comely and free from hair – but unmistakably that of Lucy of Exe Island.

The collapse of the roof and the horrible death of the old woman ended the last vestiges of the riot. The crowd became subdued, both those who had first gathered to revile and threaten, as well as those who came to watch. They soon began to drift away, urged on by Gabriel and his troops, who ungently shoved and prodded any stragglers until Idle Lane was almost empty. One who was not ushered away was Gilbert de Bosco, who in spite of the awful drama at the end, had regained his bluster and arrogance.

Ralph Morin and John de Wolfe closed in on him in a threatening manner and the coroner laid a hand on his arm, which the priest angrily shook off.

'When – or if – we recover any of the remains of that poor woman, I will hold an inquest, and you will be a witness!' grated the coroner.

'You have no power over me, I am a cleric and a member of the cathedral chapter, as you well know.'

The sheriff, who had dismounted and come across to the group, brayed his agreement. 'Leave well alone, John, you have no jurisdiction over this good man.'

'And you have no jurisdiction at all – or soon will have none!' retorted John. 'He is not in the Close now, he is in the city and at the very least was a witness to one death and a number of injuries, for several fellows have received burns. The pot man is alive, I hope, but only just!'

'You are thrashing at the wind, John,' snapped de Revelle. 'Why waste your time? The bishop will soon intervene in this.'

'I care nothing for the bishop, except to censure him for allowing this man to cause so much trouble. My task is to record everything for the King's justices and see that they are made aware of all that has gone on in Exeter this past week or two.'

De Revelle, who had regained his colour after blanching at the old crone's curse, paled again at John's pointed allusion to informing London of his own misdeeds.

Ralph Morin caught the change and mischievously turned the screw. 'How long to the next full moon, John, d'you happen to know?'

The canon affected contempt, but his face had a film of sweat. 'Pah, what damned nonsense! This is the very thing that we must stamp out in this county, this ungodly superstition.'

'Stamp it out by hanging or burning every poor wife who sells a charm for a ha'penny?' snarled de Wolfe, sick to his stomach with this contemptible, unrepentant bigot.

'Yes, if necessary! God's work is the reason for the Church's existence, and those who let it go by default are unworthy to wear the cloth.'

This man is impossible, thought John, grinding his teeth in frustration. He knew that the sheriff was right, in that nothing could be done to Gilbert, who could always shelter behind the impassive face of the Church and its bishop. But Hubert Walter, who was Archbishop of Canterbury and thus Primate of England, as well as being the Chief Justiciar, would get some straight talking from de Wolfe, as soon as he could get to see him.

'What brought you down here, Sheriff?' asked Morin. He had to be circumspect with de Revelle, as long as he was still nominally sheriff, as although Ralph was the King's nominee, the sheriff was his master when it came to everyday matters.

'What brought me down? God's garters, those men of yours made enough noise to be heard in

France when they left Rougemont. I came to see what had happened, in case it was an invasion!'

John knew he was lying, as he never turned out for any other emergencies, but he could not guess at the reason.

'I'm going back to the Close now,' announced the canon, in a voice that suggested that he would make trouble for anyone who tried to detain him. 'I've seen that at least one of the Devil's disciples has suffered her just deserts.'

With that cryptic remark, he walked away with Richard de Revelle, a soldier following with the sheriff's horse. The last John saw of them was as they turned the corner into Smythen Street, still deep in conversation.

'Those two had been plotting something – neither of them was here by chance,' said Ralph. 'It's obvious that the bloody priest deliberately organised this riot. But how did he know Bearded Lucy was hidden here?'

'He has spies all over the city,' said John. 'But I wonder if my dear wife said anything to him when she went to him last night? Anyway, the damage is done now. Somehow, I feel that old Lucy was glad to be finished with life, but perhaps not in that dreadful fashion.'

Gwyn had been listening in the background and now his smutted red face was crinkled in thought. 'What did that whoreson priest mean when he said that "at least one has suffered her just deserts"? Who was the other one, then?'

Ralph and John stared at each other for a moment. 'The man's right, what did he mean?' asked the constable.

John rubbed his cheeks, the soot on top of the stubble giving added weight to his nickname of 'Black John'. 'Lucy warned me several times, in her odd fashion, that Nesta was at risk, as she dabbles a little in herbs and remedies.'

The fleeting memory of the woman with the wry neck came back to him and he slammed a fist into his palm. 'That damned woman, what was her name, Heloise! Last week, she came to see Nesta on some pretext or other. I saw her again here, among the mob in the lane!'

'What about her?' asked Morin, mystified.

'She was sister to a doxy of the sheriff,' explained Gwyn.

'I'll swear he arranged that, just to get false testimony against her, the same as happened with Jolenta of Ide and Alice Ailward,' fumed John. 'If it's true, then breaking the bastard will not only be a duty, but a great pleasure!'

Gwyn was still worried. 'If it is true, then Nesta is still in danger. That bloody canon could still get the woman to come forward and denounce Nesta, the same as with the others.'

Morin nodded his big head. 'If I were you, John, I'd get her away from here for a time, until things settle down. With the Bush burned to the ground, there's nowhere for her to stay, nor anything for her to do in Exeter.'

With a new worry to burden him, de Wolfe paced up and down for a moment, until he came to a decision. 'You're right, the risk is too great, until I've had a chance to deal with those swine. I'll take her to my mother in Stoke-in-Teignhead. She'll be safe there and well looked after.'

Morin agreed, but added a caution. 'Try to keep it secret, John, in case those persistent devils try to find her. I'm sure you and Gwyn can find a way.'

The coroner resumed his pacing, deep in thought. Then he came back and gave Gwyn a broad smile. 'I have a feeling that this afternoon, we will be called out down Sidmouth way to see a dead body. Make sure that Thomas turns out with that mangy pony and that ridiculous side-saddle, fit only for women!'

It would take more than a day for the ruins of the tavern to cool sufficiently for a search to be made for any remnants of Lucy's poor body and there was nothing to be done about the place until then. Later that morning, de Wolfe and Nesta stood at the door of the kitchen, which thankfully, like the other outbuildings, was undamaged. They sadly surveyed the wreckage, which had stopped flaming and was now a sullen, smoking heap of charred wood and thatch. He thought of the comfortable French bed that he had bought for his mistress and vowed to get another as soon as the place was rebuilt. John solemnly promised Nesta that he would personally pay for the rebuilding out of his considerable profits from the wool-exporting business that he shared with his friend Hugh de Relaga. She agreed, on condition that it was to be a loan, repaid out of the future profits of the inn. This had happened once before, when she was left almost destitute on the death of her husband. The tavern had done so well under her enthusiastic management, with her excellent cooking and superb brewing skills, that she had given him back his money within a year.

With Gwyn's help, he arranged the covert escape of Nesta from the city and went home briefly to see whether Matilda had come back from her cousin's house. There was no sign of her, and John confided in Mary the details of the plan, telling her to let it be known when the mistress returned home that he had been called to a suspicious death near Sidmouth. This was in the opposite direction from Stoke-in-Teignhead, though he doubted that Matilda would be fooled for long by his subterfuge.

About noon, Nesta set off with one of her serving maids, allegedly going to stay with the girl's cousin in the village of Wonford, just south of the city. She dressed in dull, inconspicuous clothes borrowed from her other maid, who lived in Rack Lane, and carefully hid her red hair under a coverchief. They mingled with a group of pilgrims as they went out through the South Gate and walked a couple of miles down the Topsham road into open country. Here, they met up with the three members of the coroner's team, waiting with their horses in the shelter of a wood at the side of the road. Thomas de Peyne was almost in tears of relief as he greeted Nesta, safe and sound. He had a dog-like devotion for the Welsh woman, who was always kind and concerned for the poor waif's well-being. He gladly handed over his side-saddled pony to her and brushed off her apologies for making him walk back to Exeter. He would willingly have crawled back on his hands and knees, if it would help her in any way. Nesta hoisted herself into the saddle and with John and his officer flanking her on either side, set off for Topsham, another couple of miles away, while Thomas and the maid began trudging back to the city.

At the little port of Topsham, where the Exe widened out into its estuary, they crossed the river on the ferry and made for the line of low hills that ran down to the sea at Dawlish. Here Nesta grinned secretly to herself, in spite of her sadness, as she saw de Wolfe, with exaggerated nonchalance, look neither right nor left as they passed through the seaside village. She was well aware that Thorgils' wife, the delectable blonde Hilda, was an old flame and still an occasional lover of his, but she was now confident enough of his true affection to realise that Hilda was no threat to her.

By early evening they had forded the Teign near where it flowed into the sea, having to wait an hour for the tide to drop sufficiently. Less than another hour later they were in the small village of Stoke-in-Teignhead, where John had been born.

It was in a small valley, neat strip fields and some common pasture sweeping up to the trees that surrounded it on all sides. Nesta had been here once before and again received a warm welcome at the small manor house at the far end of the village. John's widowed mother, Enyd de Wolfe, was a small, sprightly woman with red hair only slightly sprinkled with grey. Her mother had been Cornish and her father was from Gwent, the same Welsh princedom as Nesta herself, so they had much in common, as well as a common language. John's sister Evelyn was also happy to see Nesta, who was only a few years younger than herself. She was a plump, homely lady and, like her mother, preferred John's mistress to his wife, who had always treated them with a supercilious disdain, thinking them country yokels and Celtic barbarians. Although Matilda had been born in Devon and and had spent only a month of her life with distant relatives in Normandy, she always considered herself one of that superior race of conquerors.

John's elder brother William, who ran the two manors to John's financial benefit, was as usual out supervising the business of the estate, this time at Holcombe, their other manor north of the Teign. Gwyn was hustled off to the kitchens, where eager serving maids made his life complete by plying him with food and drink until he was fit to burst, while the women took John and Nesta into their comfortable hall and sat them down with refreshments, to hear all their news of the big city. They listened with fascinated horror to the tale of woe that their visitors related, especially the burning of the Bush tavern.

'But it will be rebuilt – and very soon!' vowed John. 'The stone shell is still sound and all the outbuildings are intact, so all it needs is a new floor and a roof.'

Nesta looked at him with a mixture of affection and doubt. 'That will cost a great deal of money, John. And how am I to live until then?'

Evelyn laid a hand across hers. 'You'll stay here until it's done, my dear. You don't eat much, that I know – and if you want to earn your keep, John says you brew the best ale in Devon, so you can give us all a treat!'

John smiled for the first time in days. He almost wished that he could be like his brother and settle for the quiet life in the countryside. Although William looked almost identical to John, they were not twins and had totally different natures, his elder brother being a quiet, gentle fellow who loved farming and hunting, unlike the restless warrior John.

'As for the rebuilding, we can get timbers hauled up from our woods at Holcombe, as well as straw for the thatch. There are carpenters and thatchers amongst the patrons of the Bush who will be happy to lend a hand, especially if it means getting their favourite tavern back into action, so they can drink Nesta's famous ale again.'

The evening sped by and though John had

intended to travel back to Exeter the next day, he succumbed to his family's entreaties and left it until Friday before he and Gwyn saddled up and trotted back up the valley, with Thomas's pony on a head-rope behind them.

'She's in safe hands there, Crowner!' said his officer reassuringly. 'Even if those bastards in Exeter discover where she is, I doubt they'll do anything about it, with your family and the whole village around her.'

John prayed that he was right, but he had misgivings about what was likely to happen in the city over the next week or two, given the turmoil that awaited them there.

13

In which Crowner John hears a confession

In the late afternoon, the two men rode in through the South Gate and as they walked their tired horses up the hill to Carfoix, John sensed that many of the people they passed seemed either to shy away or give them uneasy stares. They were not hostile and some gave a civil touch of the hand to their temples, but it was as if they expected that the return of the coroner would start some new crisis in the city. Gwyn felt it too and looked up questioningly at the clear sky. 'Feels like we're waiting for a thunderstorm!' he grunted. 'What in hell's the matter with everyone?'

They got at least part of the answer when they came level with the new Guildhall in High Street. Standing outside, talking to his clerk, was the flamboyant figure of Hugh de Relaga, one of the city's portreeves and the active partner in John's wool venture. Dressed in a bright red tunic with a vivid green surcoat over it, he usually had a smile on his tubby face, but today he looked decidedly unhappy. He stepped into the narrow street and held up a hand to the coroner. 'You're back, John. Many wish you hadn't left the city these past couple of days.'

DeWolfe stared down at him, uncomprehending. 'What's happened?'

'That underhanded scut of a sheriff has hanged them already! As soon as your back was turned, he held a special court yesterday, to which the cathedral proctors delivered those two women. He convicted and sentenced them within ten minutes and they were taken to Heavitree this morning.'

Heavitree was where the huge gallows stood, at the far end of Magdalen Street, a mile east of the city. John groaned and Gwyn spat out some of the foulest language he could muster.

'The evil turd!' snarled the coroner. 'His days may be numbered, but he's making as much trouble as he can before he goes. Did no one try to stop him?'

'What could anyone do?' wailed the portly burgess. 'He's still the sheriff and shows no sign of stepping down. Ralph Morin was outraged, but he said he was powerless to stop it. I saw the archdeacon arguing with Canon Gilbert, but obviously to no avail.'

'De Bosco? Trust that madman to be there – why in God's name doesn't the bishop intervene? Is he totally spineless?'

The portreeve clutched at the feather in his velvet cap as a sudden breeze whipped up the canyon between the buildings. 'I have heard a rumour today that Henry Marshal may have lost his appetite for witch-hunting, after all these deaths and the fatal fire at the Bush. We burgesses sent a deputation to him yesterday, complaining about the disorder and the danger from such fires. The whole city could be burned to the ground if we get more of this rioting.'

John tried to suppress his anger and swore to stamp out the evil that seemed to be infecting Exeter over this issue. 'I'm taking this higher than a bloody bishop,' he ground out grimly. 'I'm reporting all this to the Chief Justiciar. Hubert's the only one who can bring this to an end swiftly.'

'Do it, John – and quickly! Though it will take at least another week to get a response from Winchester, if the justiciar is still there.' He thought for a moment, his amiable face wreathed in a frown. 'Look, I've got a fast messenger going to Southampton at dawn tomorrow, with an order for a ship's master sailing for Flanders. He could easily ride on to Winchester in a few more hours. He reckons on riding forty miles a day, with changes of horses – far quicker than the usual carrier. If you get your clerk Thomas to write a full account of the situation, I could add my portreeve's seal to it, to ensure that it gets proper attention.'

John accepted the offer gladly and after some more words of wrath and commiseration, rode on to the castle gatehouse. Gwyn carried on through the East Gate to go home to his wife in St Sidwells, who saw less of him than Matilda saw of her husband.

Inside the inner ward, he met both Gabriel and Brother Rufus, both of whom gave him the same news with long faces. Most people had never expected the convictions in the consistory court to end in the death sentence for two women – and certainly not with such unseemly haste, which John strongly suspected was due to the sheriff's desire to act while the coroner was away. He was very unhappy about this, but felt no personal guilt. It was de Revelle who had hanged them, not John – and his first duty had been to ensure Nesta's safety.

His simmering anger was such that he did not trust himself to confront the sheriff just yet, until he had cooled down. He gave Odin to a groom in the castle stables, with orders to get him fed and watered, then climbed to his chamber, where he found the industrious Thomas laboriously scribing on his rolls. He too was saddened by the death of the cunning women, but happy to hear that Nesta now seemed to be well out of harm's way.

'Give that up for now, Thomas, I've got important work for you,' commanded de Wolfe, and for the next hour the clerk wrote at John's dictation, translating Norman French directly into perfect Latin. The coroner recorded everything that had transpired during the past weeks, especially the perfidy of the sheriff, the obsessive mania of Gilbert de Bosco and the intransigence of the bishop. When it was finished, Thomas read it back to him and, after a couple of additions, it was ready for delivery to Hubert Walter or one of the members of the Curia Regis, if the justiciar was absent.

'Add a copy of that treasure inventory from the constable's clerk,' John instructed. When Thomas had rolled up the parchments and tied them securely with tape, he impressed his seal upon some wax melted across the knot. He did this with his signet ring, which carried the same snarling wolf's-head device that was on the battered war shield hanging in his hall at Martin's Lane.

By the time he had sent Thomas off to Hugh de Relaga with the precious manuscript, he felt that he was ready to face his brother-in-law. As he stalked across the inner bailey with a face like thunder, people scurried out of his path even more readily than usual. However, when John clumped up the steps and marched to the sheriff's door, once again he found it locked. He spotted one of de Revelle's clerks trying to pass through the hall without being noticed, but yelled at him, demanding to know where his master was.

'He's gone to his manor at Revelstoke, Crowner,' answered the man nervously. 'Be away a few days, I reckon.'

'Yellow-bellied son of a goat!' muttered John. 'Afraid to face me, the bloody coward. But he has to come back – unfortunately – then I'll get him!'

Frustrated on this front, he walked back down to his house, knowing that he now had to face Matilda, who would undoubtedly want to know why he had been away for two nights. He was in no mood for conciliatory excuses and walked into the hall prepared for a blazing row. To his surprise, he found her silent and subdued. She sat in her usual chair, staring at the pile of unlit logs in the cold hearth. Given her strong views on the biblical treatment of witches, he doubted that her depression was due to the hangings that morning. He had not seen her since she left the house two evening ago, after he had told her bluntly about her brother's latest misdemeanour, so he had no means of knowing how she had reacted to the further fall of her idol.

'I hear Richard has gone to Revelstoke for a few days,' he muttered gruffly, for something to say to break the silence.

'Gone to escape your persecution, no doubt,' she answered in a dull voice.

This was too much for her husband, who had been prepared to be conciliatory when he saw her low spirits. 'My persecution, by God!' he exploded. 'What do you call his strangling of those two pathetic women this morning? No wonder he's fled the city, he's not man enough to face me, after doing that the moment my back is turned!'

Matilda made no reply for a moment. Usually well dressed, with hair stiffly primped by Lucille, today she looked limp and bedraggled, her hair straying untidily from beneath her cover-chief. At forty-four, this evening she looked a decade older, but when she finally turned her head and looked up at her husband hovering over her, there was still fire in her eyes. 'I cannot decide who I hate most, my brother for his determination to fall from grace – or you, who hound him at every turn!'

De Wolfe jabbed his fists on his hips and bent lower to put his face closer to hers. 'It was not I who dipped my hand into that treasure chest, woman! Nor did I plot against the king who appointed me to office. And who was it who paid his whore's sister to give false testimony? And whose name has become a byword in this county for underhand dealings and embezzlement?'

He paused to draw breath and pulled himself upright. 'And it will not be me who sits in judgement on him, Matilda. As before, when he was removed from office in '93, it will be the King's ministers who decide his fate. So don't say that I hound him. In fact, I should be ashamed of myself for avoiding my legal duty by not exposing him in the past – which I did at your pleading, may I remind you!'

He stalked to the door, full of righteous indignation, but as he reached the screens he heard a stifled sob and, turning round, saw that her head had fallen forward on to her hands. Her back was heaving with suppressed grief and the sight of such a broken woman suddenly changed his simmering anger to guilty compassion. Walking softly back to the fireplace, he bent and placed his arm around her bowed shoulders.

'Easy, wife, easy! You know that Richard can't continue to act in this way. If it stops now, then he will probably be allowed to go back to his manors and live a quiet life. If he does not, then sooner or later he will surely hang. This is for the best, you will see!'

The sobbing faded and for a brief moment one

of her hands reached out to squeeze his wrist. 'Leave me now, John. You should not see me in this state.'

She said no more and, confused and embarrassed as he always was by strong emotion, he went slowly out into the lane. For the next hour he sat alone in the nearest tavern, the Golden Hind, and meditated deeply over a quart of cider.

De Wolfe, tired after his previous day's riding, rose well after dawn the next day. He left the solar quietly, not to awaken Matilda, who was snoring. He had heard her whimpering in the night as they lay back to back with the width of the wide mattress between them and now she slept the sleep of the exhausted.

After breaking his fast in Mary's kitchen, he had his customary Saturday wash in a bucket of lukewarm water and shaved with the little knife of Saracen steel that he kept specially honed for the purpose. Then he walked down to the cathedral and went into the huge, dim nave, which was completely empty, although a service was taking place in the choir beyond the screen. He stood waiting, listening both to the distant chanting and prayers and to the chirping of birds that flew in and out through the unglazed windows high up near the beamed roof.

He could see figures indistinctly behind the carved woodwork, dressed in white surplices covered with long back cloaks, even in the summertime warmth.

Soon, prime, the first of the daytime offices, was over, and John saw the participants begin to stream out through the passages on either side of the screen. There were few of the twenty-four canons there, their place being taken by their vicars and John was relieved to see no sign of Gilbert de Bosco, as he would not trust his temper to let him pass unchallenged. The precentor, treasurer and succentor were followed by a couple of punctators, who kept a record of those present, as those absent without good cause were disciplined – and missing canons forfeited their daily ration of bread from the bread-house near the West Front. Behind them came a group of younger vicars, eager to get something to eat before the next service, followed by the even more youthful secondaries and the jostling, restless choirboys. Finally, with a slow gravity befitting their seniority, came a trio of archdeacons. One was an older man, Anselm Crassus, Archdeacon of Barnstaple, another John FitzJohn, Archdeacon of Totnes, and the third John de Alençon, for whom de Wolfe was waiting. When he saw the coroner standing in the nave, he made his apologies to his companions and came across, his ascetic face even more grave than usual. 'You have undoubtedly heard what happened – I'm sorry, I did what I could, but to no avail.'

'I'm sure you did, friend. I only wish I had been here myself, but you know what happened down at the Bush?'

The archdeacon nodded sadly. 'Everyone in

Exeter knows of that murderous scandal – including the Lord Bishop, who seems to have taken fright at what he too readily condoned.'

'Thank God some good has come of it, though it needed a martyr in that poor old hag to bring it about. Do you think this will see the end of this madness now?'

The two men started to walk towards the brightness of the door in the West Front. 'I sincerely hope so – I doubt that Henry Marshal will pursue this crusade as actively now, if at all. And the town seethes with rumours that Richard de Revelle is on the slippery slope, though no one yet seems to know why.'

John explained to his friend what had happened, confident that his words would be as safe as if they were uttered in the confessional.

'But what of this crazy colleague of yours, Gilbert de Bosco?' he asked the priest. 'If I read his nature right, he'll stubbornly dig in his heels and try to carry on with his ill-conceived campaign.'

De Alençon reluctantly agreed. 'You may well be right, but he'll have precious little support now. I have made it my business to go around the parishes in the city and make it clear to the priests that they have more important pastoral duties than inflaming people against a few cunning women.'

Out in the early sunlight, they paced the few yards to Canons' Row, where their ways parted. As they walked, de Wolfe told him of the uncompromising message he had dispatched that morning to Winchester.

'That should see the matter of the sheriff settled,' observed the archdeacon. 'But as for our bishop, he is a powerful man with powerful friends, notably Prince John himself. It will take a lot to shake his foundations, especially as our king, God bless him, seems to have an unfortunate soft spot for his rebellious brother.'

De Wolfe knew this to be true, as the Lionheart had repeatedly forgiven John's treachery and even restored many of his forfeited possessions.

The priest went off to his house before the meeting of chapter and then the next services of terce, sext and nones, while the coroner strode up to a house near St Catherine's Gate, another exit from the Close up a lane beyond St Martin's Church. Here lived Adam Kempe, one of the regular customers of the Bush, a master carpenter who employed several men. Adam was also shocked and angry at the burning of the inn, especially as, like so many other men, he was an admirer of Nesta and her brewing. He readily agreed to go with John to view the ruins and they spent an hour surveying the wreckage, which had now cooled down. There was no sign of any remains of Bearded Lucy, but John did not expect any until the charred timbers and ash were removed.

The carpenter agreed to supervise the rebuilding, which would be at John's expense, the first task being to get a team of labourers to clear the site and dump all the debris on the waste ground alongside. As John wanted to hold an inquest on Lucy,

369

they would begin later today to try to recover any of the poor woman's bones.

Adam Kempe gave a rough estimate of how much new timber would be needed and John promised to contact his brother William to organise the felling and trimming of sufficient trees from their manor down near the Teign.

'A month should see it roofed and after a couple more weeks the lady will again be selling the best ale in the city,' promised the craftsman, optimistically.

With that reassurance ringing in his ears, de Wolfe went back to his chamber in Rougemont, for the morning ritual of bread, cheese and cider with his officer and clerk. For once, all seemed quiet, as there were no outstanding deaths, rapes or assaults to be dealt with, though Thomas had a never-ending series of rolls to be completed, for presentation either to the regular county courts or to the next visitation of the Commissioners of Gaol Delivery, judges who came at irregular intervals to try criminal cases. The General Eyre, which was a much greater visitation to look into the whole administration of the county, as well as to try criminal and civil cases, came at even more infrequent intervals but the coroner's cases had to be recorded for this as well, so the clerk had the endless job of making duplicate or triplicate copies on his sheets of parchment.

'What happens next, Crowner?' asked Gwyn, from his usual seat on the window ledge, where he could look down on anyone approaching the gatehouse from the outer ward.

'I can do nothing until the sheriff sneaks back and I can roast him with my tongue,' answered de Wolfe. 'Though it may give me some satisfaction, it cannot bring those poor women back to life.'

'Do you think that Winchester will take action over your message?' said his officer, with doubt in his voice.

'I bloody well trust so!' snapped the coroner. 'Hubert Walter is already well aware that de Revelle is a liability, from previous scandals. If he doesn't act this time, then I'm going to give up this appointment in protest. We'll find ourselves a war somewhere and clear off out of this rotten city!'

These were empty words and they all knew it, as John was getting too old to go off roistering to France, leaving behind Nesta, his house and his wool business. For a while they continued to talk over the present problems and discuss the rebuilding of the Bush, until their peace was broken by the sound of feet clattering up the stone stairs of the tower. Osric's ungainly figure pushed through the curtain, seemingly all arms and legs. 'Crowner, this city's getting beyond! Another attack, one that looks like turning into a murder, unless God wills otherwise!'

De Wolfe's stool grated on the floor as he stood up abruptly. Three faces stared at the constable in expectation, as he gabbled on.

'Henry de Hocforde is bleeding in the house of Cecilia, Robert's widow. Looks like she stabbed him!'

★ ★ ★

The de Pridias family had a house in St Mary Arches which befitted a wealthy mill-owner. Built of stone, it was double fronted, with a room either side of the door and two rooms upstairs. In one of the downstairs chambers the coroner found Henry de Hocforde lying on the floor, with a folded blanket under his head and a bemused Roger Hamund squatting alongside him, looking as ineffectual as usual. From the other room came the sound of female voices, one wailing, the other trying to pacify. Several servants stood around, looking helpless.

John and Gwyn crouched alongside the injured man, whose hands were clasped over his belly, blood oozing between the fingers. His blue tunic was soaked in blood over his lower chest and stomach. He was conscious, but rambling and muttering, his face deathly pale in contrast to his usual high colour. De Wolfe gently moved one of his hands and saw a small slit in the dark and sodden cloth above his belt. There was a pool of glistening blood-clot around it and John put two fingers into the rent in the tunic and gently ripped it wider, to get a view of his skin. Beneath, he had a fine cambric undershirt, equally saturated. When the coroner tore this apart in a similar way, he saw a narrow, oval wound in the skin, one end rounded, the other sharp. It was slowly welling blood, but de Wolfe knew from his years of experience on the battlefield that what was leaking out was probably but a fraction of the internal bleeding.

He looked up at Osric, who was hovering behind them.

'Run to St James's and get Brother Saul, quickly. If anyone can deal with this, he's the man.'

Saul was a monk in the tiny infirmary attached to St James's Priory near the East Gate, the nearest Exeter had to a hospital. John felt sure that this was a futile gesture, as Henry looked likely to be dead before the monk arrived, but he felt he had to make every effort to save the rival miller and weaver. For the same reason, he now grabbed the right hand of the late Robert de Pridias's son-in-law and pressed it over the wound, much to Roger's horror.

'Just keep some pressure there, until help comes,' he grunted. He leaned his face over the victim's and spoke to him, but got nothing but a few rambling words in response. He glared at Roger Hamund. 'So what happened?'

'He came here an hour ago, demanding that Cecilia should begin arranging the sale of our mill to him. He claimed that my father-in-law had promised to sell, just before he died, which is a damned lie!'

'Were you here then?' snapped John.

'No, my wife was with her mother, but I only arrived a few minutes ago, after this accident had happened.'

'Accident? A knife in the belly is a strange accident!'

'I know nothing of it except what the women-folk told me. They say it was an accident.'

De Wolfe climbed to his feet and beckoned to Thomas, who was lurking near the door, as he had no stomach for blood. 'Stay with him and try to comfort him. I fear he is beyond anyone's help,' he added in a low voice. The clerk's pastoral instincts overcame his squeamishness and he dropped to his knees alongside the injured man, making the sign of the Cross and murmuring a litany under his breath.

De Wolfe jerked his head at Gwyn. 'Let's see what the women have to say about this.'

Before they left the room, the Cornishman drew his attention to a dagger lying on the floor, near Henry's left leg. He bent to pick it up and held it out to his master. 'Must be his, his scabbard is empty.' He turned it over in his hand. 'But there's not a drop of blood on it and the blade is too wide to have caused that wound. Besides, this has two cutting edges, so it couldn't have slit the skin like that, with one blunt end to the wound.' As usual, he competed with his master over their expertise in the interpretation of lethal injuries.

John shrugged. 'I didn't think he had stabbed himself anyway,' he said, moving to the door.

In the other room, beyond a heavy hide flap that closed off the doorway, they found Cecilia de Pridias on a stool, slumped over a table, with her daughter Avise standing alongside her, looking defiant and defensive. Cecilia raised her head and showed reddened, tear-laden eyes. John suspected that her weeping was not for the man lying in the other room, but for fear of her own predicament. 'He attacked me, Sir John! He came here demanding that we give up our business to him. The very man who brought about the death of my dear husband!' Her voice was quavering, but still held anger.

'Why should he do that, if he came to do business, however unwelcome?' asked John, trying keep the sarcasm out of his voice. This was the woman who had helped to hound four women to their deaths.

'Because she told the swine what she thought of him,' spat Avise, her eyes glittering with hatred. 'He killed my father for the business and he tried to do the same to my mother.'

'Just tell me what happened,' said John patiently. 'Were you there all the time?'

'I was indeed,' replied the daughter. 'De Hocforde became abusive when my mother continued to refuse to have any dealings with him and when she loudly accused him of bringing about my father's death by having a curse placed upon him. He became angry and violent and pulled out his dagger, waving it about.'

This sounded unlikely, but de Wolfe kept his temper. 'Madame, your husband did not die as a result of magic.'

The fury that Cecilia had held for Henry de Hocforde now transferred itself to the coroner, for confounding her beliefs. 'You have kept trading me that lie from the beginning! I tell you, he did not die of a seizure!' she shouted.

375

'I agree with you,' said John. 'I now believe that he was deliberately poisoned with sugar of lead.'

Cecilia's rage collapsed like a pig's bladder pierced with a needle. She stared at him open mouthed. 'Poisoned? By whom?'

'The apothecary, Walter Winstone – though he is now in no position to admit or deny it.'

The sharp-witted widow rapidly collected her senses. 'Then it was at the behest of de Hocforde, if you are right. Why else should an apothecary want to kill a good customer?'

De Wolfe did not want to be sidetracked from the stabbing. 'How did he come to be injured?

The daughter broke in rapidly here, too quickly for John's liking. 'We told you, he burst into a flaming temper and advanced on my mother with his dagger. I screamed, but there were no servants within earshot and my brave mother was forced to pick up the knife she used to cut threads for her embroidery to defend herself.'

'He stumbled in his rage and fell upon the blade that I was holding out to ward him off. My knife was very sharp, it has to be for the work it does.' Cecilia pointed to a corner of the room, where a small, narrow knife lay on the floor, its blade red with blood.

De Wolfe thought the whole story a complete tissue of lies, but Avise stoutly supported her mother. 'I saw it all, it was just as she described,' she said vehemently. 'He is a violent madman, who uses violence to get whatever he desires. My mother was in fear of her life and was defending herself!'

They both stuck resolutely to their version of events, and John saw that it was pointless to keep badgering them at the moment. 'We'll see what the victim has to say about it,' he grunted and took Gwyn back with him to the other room. It was much too soon to expect any sign of Osric coming back with Brother Saul and they found Thomas solicitously holding a cup of brandy-wine to the lips of the mortally injured man.

'I thought it might help him,' muttered Roger, who looked very uneasy at the situation, with his wife and mother-in-law obviously lying through their teeth.

John crouched again by the victim's side and saw that his pallor had worsened and that his breathing was becoming more rapid and shallow. Although he was no physician, he had attended enough mortally injured men to recognise the agonal stages. He felt Henry's pulse, which was thready and feeble. Thomas, who also knew a dying man when he saw one, looked up quizzically at the coroner and murmured that they needed a priest.

'You are a priest, man – or soon will be again! Do what is necessary or it will be too late. But let me speak to him first.'

He bent over Henry and spoke his name in a firm voice, asking whether he could understand him. Somewhat to his surprise, de Hocforde rolled his eyes towards him and nodded. 'Am I dying?' he whispered.

John felt under no obligation to lie. 'Yes, Henry. We have sent for a physician, but I have no doubt that you will soon be in the next world.'

The man gave a faint sigh and closed his eyes. 'I have brought it upon myself. Greed has laid me low.' His lids rose again and he looked at Thomas. 'Is that a priest there?'

'Yes, he will be with you at the last. But now that you accept that you have no hope of living, have you anything to tell me? About your dealings with the de Pridias family or Walter Winstone?'

De Wolfe was being legally correct, as a dying declaration was valid in a court only if the victim had no expectation of survival, when the law assumed that it was the truth. There was a silence, then another whisper, though it was clearly heard in the quiet room.

'I paid that knave of an apothecary well to do away with Robert de Pridias, but he was useless. I had to employ a sorcerer to curse him to death.'

'And who was that?' asked John grimly, avoiding putting a name into the man's mouth.

'Elias Trempole, God rest him.'

'And did you have him and the apothecary killed?'

There was another pause and sweat appeared on the pallid brow of the dying man. 'I had to do it. Winstone was threatening to expose me. Trempole had to go too.'

'And who did you employ to slay them?'

'Hugh Furrel – but the fool made it too obvious

that the deaths were related. I have been dogged by fools all along.'

He gave a sudden cough and closed his eyes again.

'He's going soon, master,' Thomas warned, and started to administer the last rites. These included the seven interrogations required by the Church to ensure that the dying person was a true believer and sincerely regretted his sins in order to obtain the final absolution – but it was too late. Although Henry was still alive, his brain had faded from want of blood and Thomas got no response. However, he continued to recite the Latin monologue of extreme unction and when Saul arrived a few minutes later was still doing so, with Henry's heart still beating, albeit little more than a flicker.

John abandoned the task of getting more information and went out into the street with Gwyn.

'We'll never know now, will we?' grunted the ginger giant. He looked at his master with a sly grin. 'You asked him all about his crimes first, Crowner. Maybe if you'd started with who stabbed him, we'd know now.'

John scowled at him. 'Are you accusing me of something, you old devil? I don't like that malicious old bitch in there, but that bastard Hocforde had no less than three people murdered to suit his own ends.' They stood waiting for Saul and Thomas to come out to tell them that the mill-master was finally dead. 'At least we can clear up a few unfinished inquests now. I'll leave the widow Cecilia to God and her conscience, if she possesses one!'

By noon, when like most people, he took the main meal of the day, John was again alone in his hall. Mary said that Matilda had gone off in a sombre mood to pray at the cathedral, a sure sign of the seriousness of her devotions.

He ate in solitary silence, apart from the panting Brutus, who sat slavering under the table, waiting for scraps. It was a scorching day outside and the old hound felt the heat – as did many a manor bailiff and village reeve, looking hopefully towards their fields of grain.

A man bleeding to death made no difference to John's appetite and he made short work of a wooden bowl filled with mutton stew, taking his small eating knife from his belt to spear the solid lumps and drinking the liquid with a horn spoon. A piece of boiled salmon followed, all too common a fish on most dinner tables but by Matilda's orders, strictly limited to once a week in the de Wolfe household. Some dried figs and raisins made up the dessert, brought back from Normandy on one of the ships that had taken a cargo of their wool to Caen.

His stomach satisfied and his mind glad of some peace without his wife glowering at him across the hearth, he sat and finished another pint of ale, while Brutus crunched contentedly on a piece of bone that John had fished out of his stew. He stared unseeingly at a faded tapestry hanging on the opposite wall, which vaguely depicted some biblical scene, as his mind reviewed the events of the last day or two.

The Bush was destroyed, but already its rebuilding was in hand. Nesta was safe and could remain out of sight until this present madness had been resolved. It looked as if Gilbert de Bosco's obsessive campaign was grinding to a halt, if the archdeacon's view that the bishop no longer had any stomach for it was correct. The burgesses weighing in with their concerns about the effect the unrest was having on commerce was also significant, as they were a powerful lobby, which even the Church could not totally ignore.

The death of Henry de Hocforde was something of a side issue now, but at least it cleared up a few murders and unfinished inquests. John doubted that they would ever see Hugh Furrel again, but if he showed his face in Devon he could now be hanged fairly rapidly.

The unknown quantity was still outstanding – the matter of Richard de Revelle. Although his cumulative misdeeds were enough to have him dancing at the end of a rope, he was a slippery customer and his fate depended partly on how heavily his powerful friends would weigh against the attitude of the King's men in Winchester. If Hubert Walter was away and some lesser chancery clerk or a minor baron dealt with the message that John had sent, then perhaps very little would happen. De Wolfe scowled to himself at the awful thought that no significant censure would come back from Winchester and that the sheriff would remain in office to crow over John and make his life unbearable. If that happened, John vowed that he would either ride off with Gwyn to find a war somewhere – or elope with Nesta and go and live in Wales.

He prayed that the Chief Justiciar would send someone with sufficient clout to attend to the situation in Exeter – at least one of the Justices of Eyre or a member of the Curia Regis.

If Richard de Revelle was ejected from office, there would be the problem of a successor, perhaps a temporary caretaker until King Richard could be consulted as to his permanent representative in the county. The last time that Richard de Revelle had been ousted from the shrievalty, back at the time of the Prince's rebellion in '93, his place as sheriff had been taken by Henry de Furnellis, an elderly knight from Exeter. His father, Alan de Furnellis, had been sheriff twenty years earlier, but had died in office within a year. Henry was a dull, pompous man who did as little as possible to exert himself, but as far as John knew he was honest, which would be a welcome change in a county sheriff. If de Revelle was ousted, then he grudgingly accepted that de Furnellis would be acceptable as a stopgap, at least until a better long-term candidate could be found.

His musings were interrupted by voices in the vestibule outside and he half expected it to be the usual visit by Gwyn informing him that some new corpse had been found or a woman had been ravished. But Mary put her head around the screens to announce that Adam the carpenter had called to see him. John went out to the vestibule to meet the stocky, almost bald craftsman, who stood holding a hessian sack in his hands.

'I got my journeyman and two apprentices to start clearing the wreckage as soon as you left, Crowner,' he explained. 'And almost straight away, when they dragged off the main ridge beam, I saw this lying among the ashes.'

With Mary and Lucille peeping in horrified fascination around the corner of the passageway, Adam Kempe upended the sack and tipped the contents out on to the beaten earth floor of the vestibule. Amid a shower of charred wood fragments and burnt straw, a blackened skull and several fragmented bones spilled across the ground. The skull had burned through over much of the cranium and what was left was fragile and brittle, as were several segments of leg bone and some vertebrae.

'There were more bits there, but we thought this was enough to show you. The lads are collecting the rest of the poor old hag as they move away the rest of the debris,' said the carpenter, with morbid satisfaction.

John bent and picked up the skull, turning it over in his hands. The best-preserved parts were the few teeth that were left in the old woman's jaws, though even they were blackened and cracked.

'Well, at least the inquest jury will have something to view!' grunted the coroner. 'It's too late to arrange today and tomorrow's Sunday, so it will have to be on Monday. Whoever found this will have to attend the inquest. I'll hold it in the Shire Hall at Rougemont.'

He scooped up the bone remnants and dropped them back into the sack. Adam departed, leaving Mary to cluck her tongue at having to clean up a pile of ash and some small fragments of Bearded Lucy from her clean vestibule floor.

The next day Matilda was still subdued and hardly spoke a word to her husband, except to ask him civilly whether he would accompany her to church that morning. Feeling sorry for her low spirits and unaccountably slightly guilty – although he knew no real reason why he should be – he agreed and, both dressed in black, they walked to St Olave's, where he endured a long-winded Mass and an oration from Julian Fulk. He was thankful that at least the unctuous priest had dropped the witch-craft theme and suspected that John de Alençon had been firmly countermanding the edicts of Gilbert de Bosco on that score.

However, that particular canon seemed unde-terred and had thrust himself upon the priest at the church of St Petroc in the high street, almost belligerently announcing to the man that he would give the sermon today, as if this were some great favour.

Having heard that the archdeacon had been undermining his crusade and in spite of learning of the bishop's new coolness regarding the issue, Gilbert stubbornly persisted in his mission. However, still fermenting in the back of his mind was the image of the burning Lucy and her last words cursing him. Like John, he had a fleeting vision of something strange and unearthly at the moment the roof crashed upon the old woman, and he had been uneasy ever since. Each evening, he could not prevent himself from looking up at the sky and checking on the size of the moon, which was now at least three-quarters full.

The previous day, he had felt a burning sensation around the back of his neck and by evening he had a hot red swelling chafing against the collar of his cassock. His steward had put hot clay poultices upon it, but by this morning he had four egg-sized lumps pouting under the skin and a visit to the cathedral infirmarian had confirmed his diagnosis of a series of boils, amounting to a carbuncle.

'They'll have to get more proud than this, before they burst!' cackled the infirmarian, an old Benedictine who had been retired from Buckfast Abbey to look after the health of the Exeter ecclesiastics.

Gilbert now had a long length of coarse flannel cloth wrapped around his neck, covering a foul sticky paste applied by the old monk. What with the heat of the day and the internal heat of the inflamed tissues, he was most uncomfortable and could hardly turn his head. He refused to believe that this was anything to do with the curse, but part of his mind could not help recalling the seven curses placed on Egypt in the Book of Exodus, one of which was a plague of boils.

Worse was to come, and a genuine fear descended upon de Bosco, which only his deep faith managed to keep at bay. At St Petroc's, when the time came for him to stand on the chancel steps and deliver his sermon on the iniquities of cunning women and their heresy and sacrilege, he suddenly felt a most peculiar feeling spreading down the left side of his body. He opened his mouth to speak, but it drooped down to one side, spittle running out of the corner. At the same time, he felt his left arm go numb and found he was unable to move it.

Desperately afraid that he had suffered a seizure, he tried to speak, but only gargling noises came. The congregation, standing below him, looked on curiously until the parish priest, aware that something was wrong, came across and led him back to a chair at the side of the chancel. Here Gilbert sat in dizzy terror until the incumbent had rapidly brought the service to an end and dismissed the intrigued congregation.

'You had better sit there awhile and I will send down to the Close for the infirmarian,' ordered the priest. A few minutes later, the monk who had been treating his boils arrived and, after prodding the canon, pumping his arms and legs, then pushing up his lids to stare into his eyes, he suggested that a litter be sent for to carry de Bosco back to his house. By now Gilbert was feeling better and though his speech was still affected by the drooping lip and numb tongue, he had only a tingling sensation in his left arm and leg, their mobility appearing to be almost normal.

'I can make my way upon my own feet, thank you,' he mumbled ungraciously and, leaning on the infirmarian and his own steward, who had also been sent for, he managed to stumble back to Canons' Row.

For the rest of the day he lay on his bed, anxiety gnawing at him like a cancer, but as the hours went by, he seemed to recover almost completely, except for a slight floppiness of the left side of his mouth. The carbuncle progressed, however and the boils began to erupt like angry little volcanoes, oozing thick pus into the bandage around his neck. As he lay on his pallet late that evening, he could look out at the darkening sky through the window, unshuttered because of the heat. He dozed off and when he awoke a little later, he saw an egg-shaped moon, a little larger than the previous night, mocking him from above the cathedral towers.

On Monday morning the sheriff still had not returned from his manor at Revelstoke, which was on a lonely part of the coast a few miles east of Plymouth. John wondered whether Richard had decided that the game was up and had retired permanently to the country, leaving the shrievalty vacant, but on reflection rejected this attractive notion, as the wily sheriff was not one to abandon all his privileges and rewards without a fight.

John's own functions had to carry on and he dispatched Gwyn to round up juries so that he could hold his inquests upon Henry de Hocforde and Bearded Lucy, as well as reopening those on Robert de Pridias, Walter Winstone and Elias Trempole. This should be a day to clear up a record number of cases, he thought with sombre satisfaction. By the ninth hour, all the jurymen and other witnesses were assembled in the barren chamber of the Shire Court, with John sitting on the low platform in the sheriff's chair. Thomas was at a trestle table to one side, armed with quills, ink flasks and a pile of palimpsests, previously used parchments from which the old writing had been scraped off and the surface dressed with chalk. The coroner had no expense budget, having to find everything out of his own pocket, so his thrifty clerk rarely bought the much more expensive new parchment or even more costly vellum.

On the other side, Ralph Morin, John de Alençon and the castle chaplain sat along one of the benches. They had no official reason to be there, but the archdeacon felt that, given the circumstances, the cathedral chapter and the bishop should be represented, if only to show their concern. The castle constable was there in case there might be some further disturbance – and Brother Roger was just plain nosy. Gwyn lumbered around the people in the hall, like a sheepdog herding his flock, and

388

Gabriel stood at the back with a couple of men-at-arms, keeping a wary eye out for any trouble.

Eventually Gwyn strode to stand on the dusty floor below the coroner and opened the proceedings with the formal calling summons, bellowed at the top of his voice. '*All ye who have anything to do before the King's coroner for the county of Devon touching the deaths of various persons, draw near and give your attention!*'

De Wolfe's first inquiry was into the death of Henry de Hocforde. His wife had died in childbirth many years before and his two adult sons stood at the back of the hall, apparently not in any deep state of mourning and anxious to get back to the mill, which was now theirs. The coroner avoided the issue of 'presentment of Englishry', as although it was patently obvious that de Hocforde was of Norman, not Saxon, blood, it would be impossible to levy a 'murdrum fine' on the whole of Exeter, as would have been done in a village.

The 'First Finder' was accepted as Avise Hamund, as although technically the first person to see Henry dead was Brother Saul, she was there at the moment of the fatal knife thrust. Of course, by definition, Cecilia was also there, as she held the knife, but de Wolfe thought it better to distance the culprit as much as possible.

The jury consisted of a dozen men and boys from the streets around Cecilia's dwelling, where the death had occurred. John called the widow, her daughter and son-in-law, who all stuck firmly to their account of Henry's angry descent on their household and his unprovoked assault upon the wife of Robert de Pridias, over the dispute about disposing of their mills. Thomas de Peyne and Gwyn of Polruan attested that the deceased man had made a dying declaration, but had not said anything that indicated that he had been attacked by Cecilia.

There being no further evidence, the jurors were marched out to one of the cart-sheds that leaned against the wall of the inner bailey, where they solemnly paraded past the body of Henry de Hocforde, which lay on the floor under a canvas sheet. Gwyn whipped this off and they were shown the fatal wound in his chest.

Back in the hall, John de Wolfe told the bemused twelve that death was undoubtedly due to a knife wound to the belly and that there was no evidence to contradict the story of the family witnesses that it was inflicted in self-defence. In tones that suggested that any argument would not be acceptable, he directed them to bring in a verdict of 'justifiable homicide', and after a few seconds of whispered discussion the man appointed foreman agreed and they left the court with signs of obvious relief.

The inquests on Walter Winstone and Elias Trempole were taken together and were equally brief. The jury included the First Finders and those who saw Hugh Furrel in the vicinity of Waterbeer Street and Fore Street around the times of the attacks, together with the same jurors who had been empanelled for the indeterminate first inquests. Once again, Gwyn and Thomas were called to verify the dying declaration of de Hocforde and to confirm that he admitted paying Hugh Furrel to murder them.

Both victims had been buried some time ago, but the same jurors had viewed the bodies at the earlier inquests, which satisfied the legal requirements. With no difficulty, the verdicts were returned as wilful murder by Henry de Hocforde and Hugh Furrel – and in due course the latter would be declared outlaw at the county court, except in the unlikely event of him showing up there.

Now trickier matters had to be settled. The first hitch was when the coroner enquired of his officer why Canon Gilbert de Bosco was not visible in court, as he had been requested to attend the inquest on Lucy. In answer, a young priest approached the dais and looked up nervously at John de Wolfe.

'I am Peter de Bologne, vicar to Canon Gilbert de Bosco, sir. He has instructed me to tell you that he is not well enough to carry out your summons to attend this court – but also that, even if he had been in good health, he would have refused to come, as you have no jurisdiction over a member of the cathedral chapter.'

He stood back warily, as if afraid the messenger might be punished for bringing unwelcome news. John, with a face like thunder, pondered this for a moment. He did not know whether Gilbert's impertinent claim was true or not, as he had never before needed to summon a senior cleric to an inquest. He turned to de Alençon, who sat near by. 'John, what do you say to this?'

The wiry archdeacon shook his head. 'The Church lawyers have not yet caught up with this new office of coroner. You must admit, the Article of Eyre that promulgated it last year was more than a little short on detail. It ran only to one clause, you know!'

'But can this bloody man just thumb his nose at the King's courts like this?'

'He cannot be tried by any of them, that's for sure, being able to claim benefit of clergy. Whether or not that extends to inquests, where no one is actually being tried, I suspect no one yet knows. Perhaps this is the first test case?'

John made his rasping throaty noise, which he did when he could think of nothing civil to say, but the archdeacon carried on.

'In any case, the man is ill, there's no doubt of that! The whole town knows that he was struck by a minor seizure when he stood to preach yesterday. What with that and his carbuncle, everyone is whispering about the hag's curse!'

John sighed and had to accept the inevitable, which was to adjourn the inquest on Bearded Lucy, whom he referred to as 'Lucy of Exe Island', remembering then that the town constables had reported that after the fire at the Bush, part of the mob had gone down to the marsh where she had lived and tipped her pathetic dwelling into the river, where it broke up and floated downstream to the sea.

It was not only Gilbert's absence which decided him to wait until another day, but also the failure of the sheriff to turn up. He wanted him present when he interrogated Heloise and her immoral sister, to establish that Richard de Revelle had had a hand in the attack on the Bush.

All that was left was the much-delayed inquest on Robert de Pridias, for which Cecilia had been pressing since his death. Her own narrow shave with a murder charge made her less triumphant than would otherwise have been the case, but she still managed a smirk of satisfaction when she heard the coroner call the matter before the court. He used the same jury as for the last cases, as it was impractical to get a score or even a dozen men in from Alphington at that time on a Monday morning, but Gwyn had got Gabriel to send a couple of soldiers to fetch in the two men who saw Robert drop from his horse and the ale-wife who announced that he was dead.

They gave their simple testimony, then John called Richard Lustcote, the master apothecary.

'This blackening of the gums, especially around foul teeth – what can that signify?' he asked him.

The benign seller of pills and potions beamed at him, as if this were some kind of riddle.

'Almost certainly plumbism – which means lead poisoning, Crowner.'

'And could that occur in any natural way?'

Lustcote shook his head. 'Impossible! The poison would have to be given in repeated amounts over a period. Something like sugar of lead, also called *Plumbum acetas*.'

'Could this be given in food? Is it tasteless?'

'It has no particularly obnoxious taste, but in any case, if supposed medicaments were being administered, it could either be added or even totally substituted.'

'And could it cause sudden death, as in this man who tumbled from his horse?'

The apothecary looked dubious. 'It would be unusual, though I hesitate to say impossible, never having killed anyone with lead myself!'

He thought for a moment. 'But of course, if a man already had some disorder of his humours or a weakness of his heart, then I suspect that plumbism might finish him off.'

With that John had to be content, and he shied away from any suggestion that necromancy may also have contributed, much to Cecilia's disappointment. Still, she was satisfied that she had had her inquest after all, and vindicated when the coroner brought in a verdict of murder by the hand of Walter Winstone, at the instigation of Henry de Hocforde – both of whom were beyond earthly justice, whatever awaited them in the valley of death.

14

In which Crowner John sees justice prevail

The rest of the week following his inquests seemed interminable to John de Wolfe. The weather remained hot and sultry and on Wednesday there was a brief thunderstorm, with torrential rain for an hour, then the heatwave returned. He had a few new cases, including a man who was caught in the cogs of a watermill when he was oiling them. The mill-master fled and sought sanctuary, because he thought he would be held responsible for the death. He later abjured the realm, but when the case came much later to the justices, they absolved him and the King's pardon had to be sought to allow him to return home from Scotland.

Apart from this the week was quiet and every morning John looked anxiously for any signs of a messenger from Winchester. Even though Hugh de Relaga had claimed that his courier was faster than any other, it was well over a hundred miles to the city, which shared capital status with London. Even an almost immediate turn-round there – an impossibility, as John was well aware of the bureaucracy that reigned in such places – would still require a full week for the return journey.

By Thursday his patience was wearing thin, especially as Richard de Revelle had not shown up at Rougemont. He half hoped that news would come from Revelstoke that the sheriff had taken the honourable way out and fallen upon his own sword to escape the shame of being disgraced and dishonoured. This had happened two years earlier, when Henry de la Pomeroy, Lord of Berry Pomeroy near Totnes, had fled from Richard the Lionheart's retribution for supporting Prince John. He had gone to St Michael's Mount in Cornwall on hearing that the King had been released from captivity in Germany. The constable of the Mount had dropped dead of a heart attack on hearing the famous message 'Beware, the Devil is loose!' and de la Pomeroy had made his surgeon open the veins in his wrists so that he bled to death.

But de Wolfe knew that his brother-in-law would never take that way out – he must be waiting for some news or other, possibly for messages to go to the Prince or others among his supporters, to gather ammunition to fight back against any censure from the royal council.

Unable to sit idle any longer, after dinner John left the morose Matilda and walked through the clammy afternoon heat to Hugh de Relaga's house in High Street. He found him in a purple silk robe, sitting in a chair in his solar, cooling himself with an oriental fan made of woven palm fronds.

'No news from Winchester, I suppose?' John

asked. 'When do you expect this Mercury-heeled messenger back?'

The rotund burgess wiped the perspiration from his face with a linen kerchief. 'Expect him back? Not for another week, John. He's riding to Rye and Dover after Southampton, with letters to other ship-masters.'

Crestfallen, the coroner explained that he had hoped for some response very soon and thought that Hugh's courier might have brought back at least some indication of whether the justiciar intended acting on the urgent information.

'Be patient, John,' advised the placid portreeve. 'Maybe the first you hear will be Richard Coeur de Lion's hoofbeats coming up the street!'

De Wolfe went home and continued to be fretful about the complete lack of any activity in this tense situation. His brother-in-law, the sheriff, was on the verge of disgrace and possibly a charge of treachery which would carry the death penalty – but he had vanished.

Canon Gilbert was lying low, refusing to see anyone, according to the archdeacon, on the grounds that he was ill. John de Alençon said that the infirmarian confirmed that his carbuncle was in a horrid state of weeping purulence, but that his minor stroke seemed to have resolved itself almost completely.

De Wolfe was also anxious about Nesta, though he knew that she was safer with his family than anywhere else. However, he missed her, not only for the adventures in the now incinerated French bed, but for her pleasant, loving company, not to mention her cooking and superb ale. He also missed the Bush, which had become more than a second home to him. There was nowhere quite the same when he wanted an excuse to take the dog for a run or to have a quiet quart of ale or cider. He took to going to the Golden Hind or the New Inn in the high street, but he felt a stranger there – and the ale was far inferior. However, he went out each evening, mainly as a respite from the silent, withdrawn Matilda, who spent most of her time either in her solar or in church.

Gwyn and Thomas felt the tension in their master and did their best to humour him, with little success. As the coroner's work had declined that week, Thomas suggested that he might help de Wolfe with his reading lessons, which had recently fallen by the wayside.

John had no great appetite for this, but as he did not want to snub his little clerk, he made a few half-hearted efforts to master some of the work that the vicar in the cathedral had been trying to din into his head for the past few months.

Thomas had his own preoccupations, too, though he was wise and considerate enough not to burden his master at the present fraught time. He was still yearning for news of any restoration of his ordination, following the revelations at Winchester. It would be too much to hope for that the response from that city to the coroner's urgent message might also contain some reference to Thomas's reinstatement, but nevertheless he could but hope.

The weather continued to suit their tense mood, as every day was hot and still, without a breath of wind. The sky was a glassy blue, although on the far horizon, when seen from high up in the gatehouse tower, a line of piled-up dark clouds gathered towards evening and during the clammy nights the growl of thunder could be heard far away.

It was late afternoon on Friday before the impasse was broken. John was at his table with Thomas at his shoulder, laboriously writing his name repeatedly on a scrap piece of parchment. He had managed it six times, one after the other, his tongue outside his lips, moving in time with the scratchy pen, as the clerk twittered encouraging noises.

The peace was broken by the familiar clump of boots on the stairs and the hessian curtain was jerked aside by Gabriel's head, flushed with heat, exertion and suppressed excitement.

'He's back, Crowner. Just ridden in with some fellow who looks like a minor lord from somewhere. Not from these parts, talks like he might have come from Gloucester or the Marches.'

John threw down his quill and jumped to his feet. 'Is he in his chamber?'

'Yes, Sir John. By the state of his horse, he's ridden up from Revelstoke without drawing breath. Poor beast is near dropping in this heat.'

Gabriel caught Gwyn's eye, as the redhead sat on his window ledge, whittling a stick with his dagger. The eyes swivelled to the cider jar in the corner, but de Wolfe was already starting down the stairs.

At the keep, he thrust open the sheriff's door and barged in to confront his brother-in-law. Still dusty from his journey, Richard was pouring wine into one of a pair of pewter goblets. The other cup was not in expectation of John's visit, but for a man who lounged in a leather-backed folding chair placed in front of the desk. De Wolfe had never seen him before, but he was about thirty, of slim build and elegant in his dress. Black haired and clean shaven, he had a sallow, almost Spanish complexion, his face long and smooth with high cheek-bones. Although he was not wearing clerical dress, he had a small gold cross on a chain around his neck.

De Revelle's head jerked up at the sudden intrusion and he scowled at John, although the look was mixed with wary apprehension. 'Do you never knock at a door, Crowner?' he snapped.

'I probably will when the next occupant is here. It seems likely to be Henry de Furnellis once again.' Courtesy inhibited John from starting his tirade against the sheriff in the presence of a guest, so he began cautiously. 'I hear you have ridden hard from Revelstoke today.'

The stranger picked up his goblet and languidly intervened. 'We have ridden from Glastonbury – we left Gloucester yesterday.'

Richard scowled, having been caught out in a

400

lie before he had even opened his mouth. He had been nowhere near his manor in the west, but had ridden north a week ago. John immediately realised what was going on, for Gloucester was now Prince John's principal house in England. He had been given no less than six counties, including Gloucestershire and the county of Mortain in Normandy, by his recklessly generous brother at the time of Richard's accession in 1189. They were taken from him after the abortive rebellion, but recently Gloucester and Mortain had been restored to him. It was obvious that de Revelle had hurried to the Prince's nearest domain to rustle up support in this latest crisis, and his next words confirmed it.

'This is Roscelin de Sucote, who, though in holy orders, is also a lawyer and an aide to the Count of Mortain. He has come to give me some advice and bring support from his lord.'

The man nodded at John condescendingly, but made no effort to rise to his feet. 'Prince John is at present at his court in Normandy, but I can speak for him on virtually every issue,' he said smoothly.

De Wolfe grunted back at him and decided that he had no need to offer this rebel lawyer anything more than basic civility. He turned to his brother-in-law. 'I wanted you at an inquest this week, Richard. If you feel you can vanish from the county, after giving a false account of your movements, and ignore your responsibilities for a week, then

401

it seems an added reason for it being high time for you to relinquish the shrievalty.'

'You have no authority to even suggest that Sir Richard should give up his office,' cut in de Sucote. 'And it is both ill mannered and possibly treasonable for you to speak to the King's representative in that way!'

John rounded on the man, his long face dark with annoyance. 'When I want your opinion, clerk, I'll ask for it – though bulls are more likely to give milk before that happens. And if we're talking of manners, it would do you well to stand when you speak and address the King's coroner as "sir"!'

The lawyer's sallow face flushed, but he made no effort to rise. John swung back to the sheriff, who stood behind his table, looking nervously defiant. 'Come, John, there's no call to be offensive to a guest. I'm sure these recent difficulties can be dealt with in a civilised way.'

'Bollocks, you devious, lying bastard! And if you take offence at my words, I'm more than happy to meet with you with horse, shield and lance down on Bull Mead.'

He was on safe ground here, as the last thing Richard de Revelle would accept would be a challenge from the battle-hardened coroner. John plunged on, ignoring the look of outrage on the face of the Prince's emissary. 'You have even more to answer for now than before you slunk away to your rebel friends. I know now that you paid your whore's sister to falsely denounce the landlady of the Bush. That led to a death and a major fire in the city, both of which you will be called to account over, when I can finally drag you to an inquest!'

De Revelle made loud protestations at this and the lawyer-clerk finally jumped to his feet to add his outraged denials. John shouted them down at the top of his voice, to the delight of a cluster of people outside the ill-fitting door. 'So add manslaughter and conspiracy to arson to your existing crimes of stealing the King's money, Sheriff!' he yelled. 'You're still on probation for treason, aiding and abetting the King's enemies. Explain all that to the royal justices when they get here! You'll need more than a Gloucester lawyer to wriggle out of that!'

Not trusting himself to avoid physically assaulting his brother-in-law, de Wolfe stalked to the door, went out and slammed it behind him with a force fit to knock it off its hinges. Scattering the eavesdroppers outside, he marched out of the hall, his temper subsiding sufficiently to hope to God that someone in Winchester had taken notice of his urgent message.

By Sunday morning de Wolfe's patience was in shreds and he even considered sending Gwyn riding out on the high road to the east to see whether there was any sign of emissaries from Winchester. He soon realised that this was a futile gesture and turned his attention instead to Nesta, wondering if he should ride to Stoke-in-Teignhead to see if all was well there. This idea in turn was rejected, in case someone from the capital should arrive in his absence. Instead, he restlessly alternated between his chamber in Rougemont and the taproom in the Golden Hind, where he drank more ale than his bladder could cope with.

At noon, he had another silent meal with Matilda, his efforts at conversation being largely unsuccessful. He had told her about her brother's return on Friday and the fact that he had been in Gloucester, not with his own wife at Revelstoke. He also described the lawyer-priest that Richard had brought back with him, but she seemed uninterested. John had expected her to go up to visit Richard again, but she seemed indifferent to the man who had been for so long her paragon of success and virtue. After the meal, she took herself off to the solar and, feeling that he had done all he could for her in this time of her despair, he whistled for Brutus and went down to Idle Lane to inspect the work that he was paying for. During the past week, Adam had organised more men and now the site was virtually clear of debris. Edwin, the potman, had recovered from his ordeal and, though he was coughing like an old horse, he was comfortably housed in the brew-shed, acting as watchman over the building works. The two serving maids had gone home to stay with their families in nearby streets, with the promise that they would be re-employed as soon as the inn was back in business.

John walked around the remains of the tavern and saw that the masonry of the front and back walls and the high gables on either side was now intact. Where stones had been pulled down by the fall of the rafters and roof beams, Adam had employed masons to mortar new blocks into place. The stumps of the logs that had held up the floor of the loft had been removed and the holes cleaned out, ready to receive new timbers. John was eager to see these first beams brought up by teams of oxen from Holcombe, as they would surely bring news of Nesta, probably in a note penned by his literate sister Evelyn, which Thomas could translate for him.

On the way back, he called in at Canons' Row to see John de Alençon, mainly to ask him whether he knew anything about this Roscelin de Sucote, the priest that Richard had brought from Gloucester.

'I have heard of him by name, no more,' replied the archdeacon. 'He is part of Prince John's entourage and spends more time in Mortain than England. He is an ordained priest, but seems to play no part in religious affairs. He is an aspiring politician and presumably is looking ahead to high office under John, when, God forbid, he takes over the throne from his brother.'

'In that, he has much in common with de Revelle,' said de Wolfe, cynically. 'But what's he doing here? Can he really get Richard off the hook, merely because he is a creature of the Prince?'

De Alençon shrugged over the wine that he had as usual produced for them both. 'A desperate situation calls for desperate remedies, I suppose! I know that this Roscelin went with the sheriff for an audience with the bishop yesterday. No one knows what was said there, but I get the impression that Henry Marshal is not too keen to openly associate himself with potential rebels these days – just as he has distanced himself from the witch-hunting campaign.'

'Our bishop was never one to be seen backing the losing side,' observed John, sarcastically. 'What's happened to that bloody fellow-canon of yours, Gilbert de Bosco?' he asked, changing the subject.

'Lying low, as far as we can tell. It seems that he has been afflicted by all manner of ailments, which most folk – including himself – put down to the witch's curse!'

'What's wrong with him now? I heard he had some sort of seizure.'

'That seems to have righted itself almost completely, so my steward tells me, as Gilbert refuses any visitors. But he still has a stinking mass of corruption on his neck – and now he has a red rash over all his chest and belly, which the infirmarian tells me is probably some sympathetic reaction to the purulence of his carbuncle.'

De Wolfe could not restrain a lopsided grin, even though his Christian duty was to feel sorry for the canon's afflictions. The man had obstinately encouraged a period of hysterical madness in the

406

city, which had led to a number of deaths, and John found it hard to forgive him.

'So Bearded Lucy did have some powerful magic, after all! She was not a woman to be crossed – alive or dead!'

This earned him a disapproving look from his old friend, whose Christian concepts of the after-life did not include dispensing seizures and carbuncles. 'I despair of you, John,' he said with mock severity. 'You are still a heathen at heart!'

With another grin, de Wolfe sank the last of his wine and left for the castle. Here he found his two servants in their usual postures, Thomas scribing at the table and Gwyn perched in the window embrasure, staring idly down into the outer ward.

Silence reigned for a time, as the coroner tried to concentrate on a piece of parchment that Thomas slid in front of him, a revision of some simple Latin sentences. His heart was not in it, however, and he kept churning over the various problems he had, especially the failure of anyone to show up in answer to his message.

Suddenly, out of the corner of his inattentive eye, he saw Gwyn stiffen and lean forward as if to get a better view from his window-slit. 'Who the hell's this?' growled the Cornishman. 'I know that fellow, I'm sure I do! And the other one, of course!'

John rose but, before he could get to the other window, Gwyn gave a shout. 'By Christ, it's the Marshal himself! Riding alongside Walter de Ralegh.'

With an excited Thomas trying to peep under his arm, the coroner's officer kept up a running commentary on the men now riding slowly up Castle Hill to the drawbridge below. 'William, the Marshal of England, by damn! I thought these days he was always with the King in France.'

By this time De Wolfe was also looking down and could confirm Gwyn's words. Two tall erect men, with light surcoats over their tunics, rode finely caparisoned horses up the slope, followed by a pair of esquires and six mounted soldiers. The latter wore round iron helmets, but none of the party wore mailed hauberks or aventails, which would have been intolerable in this hot weather. The surcoats of the men in front bore armorial devices, which were repeated on pennants attached to the lances carried by the two leading men-at-arms.

De Wolfe almost leapt to the doorway and clattered down the steps at a speed that risked his neck on the steep, twisting stairway.

At the bottom, he was just in time to meet the riders as they came under the gatehouse arch, where Sergeant Gabriel, almost speechless at this sudden visitation, was sending his guards to fetch ostlers and take a message to summon Ralph Morin.

John saluted the two men, both of whom he knew well. They hauled themselves wearily from their horses and greeted him with a grasp of the forearm.

'I'd kill for a jug of ale, John,' were the first words of William Marshal, Earl of Pembroke, Lord of Striguil and the most powerful soldier in England and Normandy. The other man was Sir Walter de Ralegh, a Devon man who was now one of the King's judges and who had led the last Eyre of Assize in Exeter only a couple of months previously.

'Come across to the hall, you can take your ease there,' said John, still reeling from the seniority of the men who had come in response to his plea.

'Is that bloody man de Revelle there?' barked de Ralegh, an elderly man whose face seemed carved from granite.

Before he could answer, pounding feet brought the castle constable across the bailey. Ralph Morin was as dumbfounded as John by the exalted visitors who had just arrived. He also knew both men, as in the past they had all served in the same campaigns.

Ralph had heard the last remark and, after a hasty greeting, waved them towards the keep. 'The sheriff went to Tiverton yesterday, he dare not neglect Lady Eleanor any longer. He said he would be back in the morning.'

With the two squires in tow and the men-at-arms taken off to barracks to eat and drink, the party made their way to the keep, through a ragged line of soldiers and their families, who came out to doff their caps, touch their foreheads and even give an odd cheer, as William Marshal had long been a popular figure in the land, especially among the military. Now in his late forties, he had already served two kings well – and if the future could have been foreseen, was to serve another two, as well as becoming Regent of England. He had a long face, like his younger brother, Bishop Henry Marshal, who owed his ecclesiastical promotion to royal gratitude for his sibling's ability.

They went into Morin's chamber at the other end of the hall and sat down, servants crowding in after them with wine, ale and food. There were too few seats for everyone and the squires, silent young men with blond hair, went back out into the hall to take their refreshments.

'I'll arrange for your accommodation, though this bloody place is so small,' apologised Morin. 'You can have my quarters, Lord William, and I'll find somewhere for you, Sir Walter.'

The Devon-bred baron held up a hand. 'No, we'll not stay here. I've been to Exeter often enough as a commissioner or a justice to know that the New Inn is the best place, not this miserable stone box. It might have been good enough for William the Bastard years ago, but times have moved on!'

William Marshal agreed, after sinking at least a pint of ale in one long swallow. 'In any case, I don't feel it politic to share our lodgings with the man we've come to investigate.'

As the ale and wine flowed and the plates of meat pastries and chicken legs emptied, John learned how these two senior men had come to travel to Exeter at his behest.

'Your letter arrived and thankfully Hubert Walter was still in Winchester. He thinks well of you, John, and knew that you were not one to cry "wolf" where there was no real need.'

Walter de Ralegh, another tall man with iron-grey hair, took up the tale. 'The justiciar called me to him and told me to get down here to see what was going on, as I am familiar with the area and certainly have my own knowledge of de Revelle from some of his past escapades. Hubert said he would have come himself, but he was committed to going to Northampton and then on to London and Canterbury this week.'

The Marshal's cool grey eyes fixed on the coroner. 'You are well known for your faithful service to King Richard, de Wolfe. You proved this in Palestine and when you did your best for him in Vienna. Not many men would have got the Chief Justiciar to consider coming at your call.'

John warmed at the words, but they prompted a question. 'Thank you, but how did you become involved in this?'

William gave a wry smile. 'By being in the right place at the wrong time, I suppose! I am with the King in France for most of the year, but try to get back to Chepstow now and then to see my wife Isobel and attend to my lands in Wales. I was just returning to Normandy, having to go to Winchester on the way – and walked into this problem of yours. Hubert suggested that I take the sea route from here or Plymouth, instead of

411

Portsmouth, so that I could accompany Walter here on his mission.'

'And maybe call upon your brother at the same time,' added de Ralegh, rather mischievously.

William grunted. 'I'll call upon him, surely. But in the course of duty, rather than fraternal affection. Henry and I do not often see eye to eye.' He belched after his hasty consumption of rich food and ale. 'In fact, I will call upon him this evening, to see what the fellow has been up to this time, before we begin our deliberations tomorrow.'

For the next hour, de Wolfe recounted all that had been happening in Exeter over the previous few weeks, repeating and expanding upon the facts that he had given in his letter to the justiciar. The two barons listened gravely and had a number of penetrating questions for John, which showed that they were well aware of the seriousness of the situation. At the end, when they were ready to go down to their lodgings in Exeter's largest inn in the high street, William Marshal leaned forward and tapped de Wolfe on the knee. 'Crowner, I think you should get this knight, Henry de Furnellis, along in the morning. It looks to me as if by tomorrow Devon might be needing a replacement for its sheriff!'

The proceedings on that fateful Monday were fragmentary, as the varying issues needed different people at different venues.

They began in the morning with William Marshal

412

and Walter de Ralegh going to see the bishop. This was a private meeting at the bishop's palace behind the cathedral and although John de Alençon and several other canons, including the precentor, succentor and treasurer, were called in later, the coroner could only guess at what transpired. Even his good friend the archdeacon was placed under a constraint of confidentiality, so that he could not divulge anything to de Wolfe. One result of the meeting was that Gilbert de Bosco was forced to appear at the coroner's inquests later in the day.

Richard de Revelle rode in during the morning and though de Wolfe deliberately kept well clear of him until the formal proceedings began, he learned later from Ralph Morin that the sheriff was shocked to learn that no less a notability than the Marshal of England had arrived to enquire into his misdeeds, together with a senior royal justice.

De Revelle attempted to speak privately with them, but like the coroner, they declined to compromise themselves with him until the matters were dealt with officially. Richard then shut himself in his office with Roscelin de Sucote and refused to see anyone.

At breakfast, John told his wife about the arrival of the men from Winchester, but the news seemed to send her deeper into her apathetic gloom. Normally, the arrival in the city of a baron as famous as William the Marshal, especially as he was brother to the Lord Bishop, would have made her demand of him every detail of his dress, his appearance, his entourage and any other titbit of gossip, so enamoured was she of the Norman aristocracy. But now it was as if she realised the enormity of her brother's problems, that such exalted figures should be sent to investigate him.

William Marshal and de Ralegh came back to the New Inn around the tenth hour, having completed their business at the cathedral. They sent a message for de Wolfe to meet them there and within minutes he had made the short walk down the hill to their lodgings. In a room set aside by the innkeeper, they sat with some wine and told John that the inquest into the fire at the Bush and the death of Lucy could go ahead, as Canon Gilbert would now appear before them. As members of the Royal Council and as King's judges, both were also de facto coroners, but they directed him to preside over the proceedings.

'Once that's complete, then we will be in a better position to decide how we view the behaviour of both this damned priest and your dear brother-in-law,' explained Walter.

John had already primed Gwyn to get everything ready for an inquest in the Shire Hall immediately after the midday meal and when he returned to his chamber he sent his officer with messages to the sheriff's steward and down to Canons' Row to demand the attendance of both, on pain of the King's displeasure. The archdeacon had already called on Gilbert to deliver the bishop's orders

414

and though the canon still pleaded sickness, de Alençon made it crystal clear that this was a command that could not be disobeyed, even if they had to carry him to the court on a hurdle.

As always in Exeter, news travelled not just fast but almost instantaneously and a large crowd had converged on Rougemont by the time the inquest began. The sergeant-at-arms called out all his men to keep order and a line of soldiers pressed back the onlookers inside the court, so that a large enough space was left in front of the platform for jurors and witnesses. Another row of helmeted men blocked the arched entrance to keep out those who clustered around to listen from outside.

For a jury, Gwyn had collected almost thirty men, as although the minimum was accepted as a dozen there was no maximum. In fact, the law stated that in the countryside, every man – which meant all over twelve years of age – from the four nearest villages should be empanelled. This was physically impractical, and in towns and cities impossible. The men Gwyn had rounded up were from among those who had been at the Bush when it was besieged and burnt. Some were mere spectators, others helpful fire-fighters, but some of the instigators and rioters were also reluctantly present. One of them was the man with the torch whom John had felled with the flat of his sword, who appeared with a grubby bandage still around his head.

One of the last to arrive was Gilbert de Bosco,

on his own two feet, rather than a hurdle. He looked awful with a red, swollen face, dotted pustules around his jaw and a wide bandage swathed around his neck. His stroke seemed to have subsided, although there was a slight droop to one side of his lower lip. He was helped into court by his vicar and steward, who found a stool for him at one side of the hall below the dais.

On this low platform were already assembled a few chairs, some benches and stools, with a trestle table where Thomas de Peyne was already settled with his writing materials. The ubiquitous Brother Rufus was lurking at the back along with a few clerks from the castle and the cathedral, none having any business there apart from their own curiosity.

Then the official party arrived, the men-at-arms thrusting the crowd back with their staves, to leave a path for the coroner, who led the King's Marshal and Walter de Ralegh to their chairs. Behind them came Hugh de Relaga and Henry Rifford, the city's two portreeves and in the rear the tall figure of Ralph Morin, guardian of Rougemont.

As agreed, de Wolfe took the central chair, flanked by the two visitors from Winchester, the others finding stools and benches on either side.

'Where's Richard de Revelle?' demanded Walter de Ralegh, glaring around the spartan hall. As if his words had conjured him up, the sheriff appeared at the door, dressed in his finest outfit of green linen, gold embroidery at the neck, hem and wrists, with a blue silken cloak draped over his shoulders, secured across the breast with a gold chain. At his heels was Roscelin de Sucote, wearing a plain but elegant black tunic with a gold cross on his breast.

De Revelle stalked in and, without looking to right or left, made to step up on to the dais, until a barked command from William Marshal stopped him in his tracks. 'You are a witness in this matter, sir. Your place is down there!' William pointed to the double line of jurors and witnesses who stood shuffling between the line of soldiers and the front of the platform.

Richard coloured instantly and protested. 'I am the sheriff of this county, sir! This is my court and indeed that is my chair you are occupying!'

William Marshal was not one to be contradicted. 'A court is not a building, it is a legal device which is constituted according to its function. Today, you are in the same position as any other of the King's subjects.' He relented a little, for the sake of Norman solidarity. 'However, you may have a stool to take your ease, if you so wish.'

De Revelle's fury increased and he turned to glare at Roscelin, who stepped forward towards the platform. 'I must protest, sir! Sir Richard is the King's representative in this county and it is intolerable that he should be treated in such a way.'

'The King's representative, as you put it, appears to have been embroiled in instigating a riot that ended in arson and a death. So be quiet, or I will have you put out!'

So much for being asked to conduct the proceedings, thought de Wolfe wryly – so far he had not had a chance to say a word.

Now the slighted lawyer was as angry as the man he was there to protect. 'You cannot speak to me like that! I am Roscelin de Sucote, a priest and an advocate, chamberlain to Prince John, Count of Mortain and the King's brother!' he shouted.

'And I am William, the King's Marshal, Earl of Pembroke and Lord of Striguil. Now be quiet, d'you hear?'

It was not strictly accurate for him to call himself Earl of Pembroke, but no one was likely to object. It was true that the King had given him the hand of Isabel de Clare, daughter of 'Strongbow', Earl of Pembroke, but as the lands were to be kept in royal hands for another ten years, William was not yet entitled to the earldom. Still, everyone knew him by this name and a Devon inquest was not the place to dispute it.

Glowering, the two men subsided and stood trying to strike a defiant pose while Gwyn yelled out his opening lines.

John rose to his feet and declared that he was enquiring into the death by fire of one Lucy, a dweller on Exe Island. 'And as coroners are obliged also to enquire into fires in a town or city, whether or not there is a death, that is also an issue,' he added. Glaring around the packed court, he carried on in his deep, uncompromising voice. 'As to a First Finder, it cannot apply to the fire itself, as this conflagration began before the eyes of half a hundred people. As to the death, then I call Adam Kempe, a carpenter of St Catherine's Gate.'

The craftsman came to the front of the court, as the coroner's officer humped the sack of bones to dump on the earth at his feet. Then Gwyn rooted inside the bag and pulled out the scorched skull and a couple of bones, which he held out to Adam. The man studied them and nodded. 'Yes, Crowner, these were the remains which I recovered from the ashes of the Bush.'

As Gwyn paraded along the row of jurymen, displaying the grisly relics almost as if he were offering them for sale, de Wolfe continued. 'It is well known, and witnessed by a hundred pairs of eyes, including my own, that the woman known as Bearded Lucy was in the tavern during the fire. No one else is missing and therefore I am satisfied that these remains belong to her.'

Once again he ignored the issue of Englishry and proceeded to the cause of the fire. 'The conflagration was started deliberately and maliciously by rioters in the streets, some of whom flagrantly carried burning torches. I personally felled one of those miscreants!' He scanned the hall with piercing eyes and then jabbed a finger at someone trying to look inconspicuous as he edged towards the entrance archway. 'Hold that man!' he bellowed, and Gabriel and two soldiers forced their way towards him and dragged him before the coroner. 'You were that man, damn you!' he shouted at the fellow, whose dirty bandage wrapped around his head was now like a badge of shame. 'You were not the only evil-doer that day, but you will do! I commit you in custody to the next session of Gaol Delivery. Sergeant, get this wretch to the cells, my clerk can record his details later.'

As the man was dragged away, hollering with fright, as he would surely be hanged in due course, de Wolfe called for his next witness. 'Where is Heloise, wife of Will Giffard?'

There was a scuffle towards the back of the hall and several people prodded the skinny woman with the wry neck, who at first refused to move, until another man-at-arms went and pulled her by the wrists to the front. She stood shivering before the coroner, her eyes swivelled up to regard him fearfully. Her husband, a burly man with a pugnacious expression, pushed through the crowd to stand behind her.

John glowered down at her, aware that this was the creature who had tried to add Nesta to the list of women who went to the gallows. 'Heloise Giffard, did you visit Nesta the landlady of the Bush Inn several weeks ago, on the pretext of seeking a cure for the affliction of your neck?'

'It was not a pretext, sir. I wanted a cure. And I had warts on my hands.'

'Did she offer a cure? And I want the truth,

woman, not a litany of lies about devils and goblins, or it will be even worse for you!'

The twisted wife peered furtively to left and right, but whoever she was seeking had made themselves scarce. 'She said she could do nothing about my neck, sir. But she gave me a salve for my skin.'

'Did she demand money from you for this simple service?' snapped John. Heloise hesitated, then shook her head, a strange movement given the angle of her neck. 'No, sir!' she whispered.

'And did anything untoward happen when that good lady did her best to help you, without so much as a ha'penny fee?'

Again the woman wagged her head. 'No, Crowner, nothing.'

De Wolfe's voice rose into a roar. 'Then how was it you told Canon Gilbert that when you visited the tavern, that the woman conjured up black mist out of which came a hellish devil with fire coming from its mouth – and that she and this apparition performed lewd and obscene acts upon you? Answer me, you wretch!'

Heloise fell to her knees, her hands clenched before her in supplication. 'It was my sister, Esther, sir,' she wailed. 'She persuaded me and gave me good silver coin to do what I did. It was her fault, sir, not mine. I only did what I was bid – and I am a poor woman, deformed in body.'

'This sister of yours, Esther. Is she in this court today?' John thundered.

'No sir, she left the city last week, in fear of what

might become of her after what happened. I don't know where she is. I think she may have gone to Plymouth to follow the sailors.'

'Your sister is a whore, is she not?'

Heloise seemed to shrink, like a hedgehog when threatened. 'She is, sir, God forgive her.'

'I doubt that, woman – and he will have to stretch his compassion to forgive you, too. Tell me, this harlot sister of yours, did she have regular clients in this city?'

Again, Heloise's eyes squinted furtively along the front rows of the hall. 'I don't know that, Crowner. I tried to keep clear of her immoral business.'

'I don't believe you,' snapped de Wolfe. 'Do you see anyone in this court who you know visited her often – or who she visited for carnal knowledge?'

Here Roscelin de Sucote made his first mistake. He stepped forward a pace from the sheriff's side to address the three men seated in the centre of the dais. 'As a lawyer, I must object! The woman has said she doesn't know, so why badger her further? It is not relevant.'

William Marshal leaned forward in his chair. 'If it's not relevant, why did you intervene, eh? What possible interest can you have in who might be the customer of a whore?'

The Gloucester cleric flushed and stepped back, getting a venomous look from the sheriff, whose troubles were only just beginning. The coroner dismissed Heloise after attaching her in the sum of four marks to attend the next visitation of the royal justices, then he called Richard de Revelle.

Again de Sucote intervened, to protest that a sheriff could not be forced to testify in a lower court in his own county, as he himself was the principal law officer. This time, Walter de Ralegh cut him down to size. 'You talk arrant nonsense, young man! This is the coroner's court, an office set up only last year by the King, to conduct the King's business. Have you taken no notice of his title, eh? *Custos placitorum corona,* "keeper of the pleas of the crown"!'

On the other side of the upstaged coroner, the Marshal of England spoke again. 'Your interference is doing more harm than good, sir! I would advise you to keep your mouth shut, before you do more damage.'

The said mouth opened and closed a few times like a fish, but Roscelin obviously thought better of antagonising two members of the Curia Regis any further, and stepped back.

'De Revelle, come before us!' grated the Earl Marshal, crooking his finger.

With reluctance showing in every slow footstep, the sheriff moved to stand below his brother-in-law. Although he stood in a deliberately nonchalant pose, throwing his gaudy cloak back over one shoulder, his small eyes looked up at John with pure poison oozing from them.

De Wolfe was deliberately correct and polite, doing his best to suppress his own contempt and loathing for the man in the cause of even-handed justice. 'Sir Richard, were you acquainted with Esther, the sister of Heloise Giffard?'

'Of course not, I've never heard of her!' said the sheriff contemptuously. 'Why I should know the name of an alehouse strumpet?'

There were a few cackles of laughter from the back of the court, as de Revelle's partiality for whores was well known in the city. He turned round furiously, but the culprits had ducked down out of sight.

'I fear we shall hear soon that your memory is failing you, if you continue to claim that she was unknown to you. I suggest that you paid this woman to get her unfortunate sister, who arouses sympathy because of her affliction, to visit the Bush inn under a pretext.'

'Absolute nonsense – or rather, malicious lies!' snarled de Revelle. 'I suggest you produce this woman to speak for herself, before you make such unfounded accusations.'

John sighed. 'I wish we could, but she has vanished – most conveniently, it seems. Now, Sir Richard, you were at the scene of the fire in Idle Lane, why was that? It's not your habit to attend criminal events.'

'I was riding in the city and heard the commotion and naturally went to investigate,' he said loftily.

'It would be the first time you've ever investigated anything,' observed John, cynically. 'Where were you riding that you could hear what was going on in Idle Lane? It's not a part of the city that a busy sheriff normally frequents.'

'Were you expecting something to happen there?' cut in de Ralegh.

'Of course not – I tell you, I was riding down the high street and heard this rumpus.'

'He must have had bloody good hearing!' muttered Gwyn to Gabriel, at the side of the platform.

The sheriff stonewalled all further questions with flat denials and, however unconvincing he sounded, there was nothing further to be obtained from him. When the coroner curtly dismissed him, Richard stared haughtily at the three men above him. 'If you have no further need of my help, I will return to my chamber and get on with the more pressing business of administering this county!' He turned and, head held high, strode towards the doorway.

'Don't go too far, Sheriff,' called William Marshal after him. 'We have much more to say to you later.'

Ignoring this, de Revelle stalked out, Roscelin de Sucote falling in behind him as the men-at-arms cleared a path for them through the gawping crowd.

The last witness was Gilbert de Bosco, now a different man to the arrogant, blustering fellow of a couple of weeks earlier. He looked ill, he was hunched and his face had an unhealthy fullness about it that was worsened by the rash around his jaws and the bulky dressing around his neck.

De Wolfe motioned to his vicar and steward to

help him from his stool and settle him back upon it below the centre of the dais. Having salved his conscience by deferring to a sick man, he then treated him as any other witness. 'Canon, did you instigate, foment or encourage the attack upon the Bush inn by that mob?'

De Bosco raised his head slowly and painfully to the coroner. 'I did my duty as a Christian and a priest, in that I sought out necromancy, witch-craft and those consorting with the Devil.'

'That's not an answer to the question the coroner put to you,' snapped Walter de Ralegh. 'Did you stir up a riotous assembly?'

'I received information that two daughters of Satan were hiding in that den of iniquity and acted accordingly.'

'What d'you mean "hiding"?' barked William Marshal. 'One of them was the landlady, she owned the bloody place!'

'And from where did you receive this information, as you put it?' asked the coroner.

The priest looked uneasily across the front of the hall. Seemingly reassured by the absence of Richard de Revelle, he replied. 'I had a message from the sheriff, through one of his clerks, that the old witch from the mud flats beyond the West Gate was being sheltered there. It became well known that she was a disciple of the ungodly, probably their leader in these parts.'

'And what of the other, the ale-wife known as Nesta?' interjected the marshal.

'Sir Richard had already directed a woman to me. The one with the deformed neck, who had been a victim of that tavern-keeper. She told me of the hellish practices that she suffered when she visited her for some simple remedy.'

'And you believed her?' snapped de Ralegh, incredulously.

'Today, she admitted that everything was a tissue of lies, you gullible fool,' shouted William.

John, again excluded for the moment, steered the questions back on to the original path. 'So how was it that a rabble appeared in Idle Lane, with you virtually at their head, some carrying flaming torches?'

Some of the old defiance flowed back into Gilbert de Bosco. With an effort, he stumbled to his feet and his head rose, despite the pain in his inflamed neck. 'Yes, I walked the streets that day and preached a crusade against them, calling on good men to help cleanse the stables of God. I sent two proctors' men to proclaim that witches lurked in the lower town and when enough good folk had assembled we marched there, intending to seize and arrest them and put that house of shame to the torch. It was not intended that anyone should be burned alive.'

'No, you wished to save them for your own court, so that you could hand them on to your fellow-conspirator, the sheriff and have them hanged. Dead either way, the fire or the rope!' boomed de Ralegh, his face as hard as a Dartmoor rock.

The canon remained silent, but his face bore a sullen defiance, almost a martyred resignation that these heathen would never understand his dedication to the protection of the Holy Church.

De Wolfe waved him away in disgust and his helpers led him away to the side again, while the coroner addressed the jury. 'You have heard the evidence and indeed a confession from this priest. There is no doubt that both on the matter of arson and of the death of Lucy of Exe Island, the cause was a riotous assembly, whipped up by Gilbert de Bosco in an insane, misplaced campaign of hate against harmless women who use their gifts in traditional practices.' He glared along the line of jurors. 'The verdict you must return is clear – malicious fire-setting and manslaughter, for we must accept that the immediate object was not to cause death by burning.'

He paused and looked sideways at the two justices. 'As to who is responsible, I am in a difficult position at an inquest, which is not a trial. One of the obvious culprits is a priest, over whom I have no jurisdiction when it comes to attachment on a criminal charge – that is a matter for the bishop. Similarly, it is unique for another suspect – for he declined to admit any guilt – to be the county sheriff. I therefore defer any action on him to my seniors present here today. I have attached the woman Heloise Giffard to the next visit of the royal justices and if her sister ever shows her face, she will go the same way.'

After this long speech, he directed the jury to return the verdicts he had set out, giving them a ferocious glare that defied them to contest or even question his decision. They all hurriedly assented and the Shire Hall broke out into a hubbub of excited gossip, as the men on the platform filed out and went to the castle keep for well-deserved refreshment in the sultry heat.

The next act in that day's drama was held not in the public eye, like the inquest, but in the privacy of the sheriff's chamber. This time, Gabriel and two soldiers guarded the door and others formed a line some yards away, to keep those using the hall well out of eavesdropping range. Inside the large room that was the sheriff's office were assembled those who were to decide his future. The Earl of Pembroke, Lord of Striguil, sat behind de Revelle's table with Sir Walter de Ralegh. At one end was one of the clerks who had come with the Marshal, ready with his pen, ink and parchments to record the deliberations.

An empty chair stood on the other side of the trestle, facing the august pair. At the back of the room, against the shuttered window-slits, sat Constable Morin, John de Wolfe and a large, elderly, florid man with a flowing white moustache. This was Henry de Furnellis, who had occupied this room as sheriff for a short time two years earlier. He had bristly white hair and bags under his pale eyes big enough to accommodate hen's eggs.

'Get him in here,' ordered William Marshal and the constable went to an inner door that led to the sheriff's private quarters, a pair of rooms behind his office. He knocked, went in and returned with Richard de Revelle, followed by Roscelin de Sucote. They were dressed as they had been in the Shire Hall, but de Revelle's colour was different, in that he had rosy patches on his narrow cheeks and he seemed slightly unsteady on his feet, evidence of the brandy-wine that he had been drinking in the back room. He dropped heavily into the chair set for him, with his acolyte near by.

'Get on with this charade, then!' he said thickly. 'I still deny the right you have to invade my privacy and subject me to this discourtesy. Prince John will hear of this, as soon as a messenger can reach Normandy.'

William Marshal regarded him coldly. 'If the Count of Mortain objects, he can petition the King about it. But as long as the Lionheart is in France, the administration of England is in the hands of the Chief Justiciar, the Chancellor and the Royal Council.'

Walter de Ralegh glared at the smooth-faced lawyer standing stiffly behind the sheriff's chair. 'Why does this fellow have to be here? This is a confidential matter.'

'Sir Richard has requested that I advise him as to his legal rights and to report what transpires to Prince John, the future King.'

De Ralegh recognised the veiled threat in

Roscelin's words and responded harshly. 'The sheriff is an officer of the present King, not a future king, though even that is not a foregone conclusion! With God's grace, Richard will be on the throne for very many years to come.'

William Marshal flapped his hand at the cleric from Gloucester. 'Oh, let him stay. Though it does go to confirm with whom the true sympathies of de Revelle lie.'

He shuffled some parchments before him, though this was mere habit, as, in spite of being one of the most powerful men in the Plantagenet domains, he had never learnt to read either French or Latin.

'We will keep this short and to the point. Your fidelity and allegiance to the king have long been suspect. The Chief Justiciar himself, when he visited this city some months ago, was apprised of various matters which gave him great concern and which have been discussed in the Curia since then. Only the reluctance of your brother-in-law to press the matter left you in a state of probation, rather than suspension – possibly by the neck!'

De Revelle opened his mouth to deny this, then found he had nothing useful to say, so shut it again.

'This time, you have been caught out once more in shameful activities. You recently brought treasure trove to the exchequer and claimed it was as intact as when discovered, yet it has been proven that you removed a substantial portion for your own purposes.'

He pushed some documents across to Walter, who could read, although he had already been through these inventories of the cache found at Cadbury.

'Those documents were falsified. It was part of de Wolfe's scheming to bring about my ruin!' cried the sheriff.

'We challenge the authenticity of those lists and the trustworthiness of those who wrote them,' brayed de Sucote.

William slapped the table with a large hand. 'Be silent! We have made all necessary enquiries to show that they are genuine and were made in good faith. We interrogated not only the treasury clerks in Winchester, but stopped at Cadbury on the journey here to confirm with the manor-lord and his priest the amount of coin originally found. Here we have checked with the constable's steward that he accurately confirmed the contents of that chest, before you made off with it, in defiance of the coroner's legitimate ruling that the decision upon its disposal be left to the next Eyre of Assize.' De Ralegh jabbed a forefinger at the discomfited Richard. 'And not only did you pilfer the hoard, but you attempted to put the blame on an honest coroner's officer and even had him arrested on a felonious charge, to cover up your own crime!'

De Revelle began muttering some feeble excuse about a terrible error, but the Marshal overrode his words. 'Not content with that, you attempted to silence the coroner's promise to expose you by

432

veiled threats to cause harm to a woman, who, not to put too fine a point on it, was his favoured mistress.'

'Sir Richard strongly denies that!' broke in de Sucote.

'Let him speak for himself, his mouth has been active enough in other directions!' rasped Sir Walter. 'He may deny it all he wants, but what we heard in the court today convinces me that he set a trap for Sir John de Wolfe, paying his whore to get her sister to falsify evidence of witchcraft to that gullible canon.'

As the catalogue of de Revelle's misdeeds was expanded, the sheriff seemed to sag in his chair, convinced now that all was lost and that he would end on the gallows, perhaps after being mutilated and disembowelled for the greater crime of treason. Walter de Ralegh's finger went down a list on a parchment roll, stabbing a series of items that recorded actual and suspected misdemeanours on the part of Richard, the most serious being his involvement some months earlier in an abortive rebellion on behalf of Prince John, in which the de la Pomeroy family were once again embroiled. When his finger reached the bottom, Walter threw the list aside with a flourish and leaned forward threateningly towards de Revelle.

'Do you call that honourable behaviour for a Norman knight, and a servant of your king, to whom you swore an oath of allegiance when you were elected sheriff, eh?' He leaned back and looked across at the Marshal, as if handing over the baton to him.

William shook his head sadly. 'I cannot tell what is to become of you, de Revelle. We know you claim to have influential friends, some right here in Exeter and perhaps some in Mortain. But I can assure you that you have none in Winchester or London.'

He drummed his fingers impatiently on the table, his long face grave as he stared at the stricken Richard, much as a ferret immobilises a rabbit before pouncing.

'We have discussed this matter with others in the council and have their full authority, especially that of Hubert Walter, to act as we see fit when we have heard all the evidence here in Exeter.' He paused and looked at de Ralegh, who gravely nodded his assent. 'What happens to you eventually will depend on further deliberations between the members of the Curia and ultimately what the King wishes to be done. In that, I have no doubt that your own sponsors, if they do not cast you aside, might have some say. That is none of our concern today, whether you ultimately live or die!' His voice hardened even more. 'But what is crystal clear and as certain as night follows day is that you are no longer fit to be sheriff of the county of Devon.'

He rose to his feet, a tall, spare man, with an aura of authority about him that had fortified him in the special role he had played in the history of England.

'Richard de Revelle, from this moment forth you are no longer the King's representative in this county. Henceforth, you will have no more authority or privileges than any other man in the city streets. The justiciar has given me the power to appoint Sir Henry de Furnellis as sheriff, until such time as the will of the King and his council is known as to a permanent successor.'

He sat down heavily, leaving a paralysed de Revelle sunk on his chair.

'This is not the end of the matter, sirs,' brayed Roscelin. 'The Prince will soon hear of this.'

William Marshal flung an arm towards the inner door. 'Just get out of here – and take him with you!' His eyes dropped to meet those of the deposed sheriff. 'And if you take my advice, you will collect your chattels from here and quickly get yourself to one of your manors and lay as low as you can, for as long as you can! Maybe then they'll forget to hang you!'

As the room cleared in an atmosphere of suppressed embarrassment and excitement, John de Wolfe felt one major emotion – not elation at the final defeat of his long-term adversary, but anxiety about how he was going to report this to Matilda in a way that would cause her the least anguish.

John was not present at the last chapter of that Monday's climactic story, but had to rely on his friend the archdeacon for an account of what went on in the bishop's parlour at the palace. In the evening, when the oppressive heat seemed even more cloying than before, the three archdeacons who happened to be in the city, plus the more senior members of the cathedral chapter, were called to the palace to witness their prelate deliberate on the behaviour of their fellow-canon, Gilbert de Bosco.

The sun had set when the coroner called upon John de Alençon at his dwelling in the Close. The approaching dusk was made more gloomy by black clouds that had rolled in from the Channel and, as on many of the previous days, a grumble of thunder rolled in the distance every few minutes.

This evening they sat in the small garden behind the house. Although the usual outhouses and privy were farther down, de Alençon had had a small area fenced off with woven hurdles, where sparse grass grew and a couple of benches flanked a small table. It was an unusual elaboration for a yard, which was usually just a functional addition to a house, frequented only by servants, but the archdeacon had once lived in a priory where gardening was considered a virtue and solitude a blessing.

They sat at the table to drink wine and talk, giving the occasional glance up at the heavens to gauge whether they needed to run from a sudden thunder-shower.

'This has been an eventful day, John,' observed the priest. 'We have lost one sheriff and gained

436

another. You have cleared up several slayings in the city – and we now have another vacancy for a canon in the chapter.'

De Wolfe rubbed his stubble wearily. It had certainly been a stressful day. He had just left Matilda, who took the news of her brother's disgrace stoically at first, then retired to her solar, where through the slit that joined it to the hall, he heard her sobbing as if her heart would break. She had slipped the bolt on the door, so he was unable to go in to try to comfort her in his stiff, awkward way and he decided it would be best to leave her alone, until she was ready to face the world again. He knew that her loss of prestige among her many friends, now that she was no longer the sister of the sheriff, would hurt her cruelly, but there was nothing he could do about it now.

'So what happened to the witch-hunter?' he asked de Alençon.

The archdeacon turned his wine cup delicately with his long fingers, as he recalled the scene in the palace an hour or two earlier. Henry Marshal had entered his parlour, the large room where he held all his audiences, in a black cassock with a large silver cross on his breast and a round cap on his head. Gloved and beringed, he sat on an ornate chair placed on a dais at the end of the room. His chaplain, a young priest destined for rapid advancement in the Church owing to his high family connections, stood behind him ready to attend to his every wish.

Facing them in the room on hard benches were Thomas de Boterellis, the precentor, John FitzJohn, Archdeacon of Totnes, Anselm Crassus, Archdeacon of Barnstaple, John of Exeter, the cathedral treasurer, and archivist Jordan de Brent, as well as several of the older canons, including Roger de Limesi and William de Tawton. Two of the proctors and their servants stood at the back of the room, having already led in Gilbert de Bosco, who sat in the centre of the front row of benches.

'He looked dreadfully ill, but his spirit was as stubborn as ever,' said de Alençon to his friend. 'I don't know if as a true Christian I should believe or reject these notions of the supernatural, but I suspect that there are few in Exeter who believe that his recent afflictions were not the work of Lucy's curse!'

De Wolfe agreed that in court that day the canon had looked in bad shape. 'His stroke seems to have healed, but his affliction of boils seems worse. What was the outcome?'

'Like your account of the sheriff's dismissal, John, it was short, though by no means sweet. The bishop allowed him to remain seated owing to his parlous state of health, but that was the only concession he made. He roundly condemned him for excessive zeal, which he said was grossly misplaced.'

The coroner drank and set down his cup. 'Yet at the start the bishop seemed Gilbert's staunch ally in his crusade against these cunning women. How could he turn around so completely?'

'I'm sure his brother gave him a good talking-to, when he visited. Though to the people at the cathedral the bishop is only one step down from God Almighty, to William the Marshal he is just a younger brother!' The priest wiped the sweat from his brow, the atmosphere seeming to press in on them, before continuing. 'Though no one knows what was said between them in private, I suspect that William offered very robust opinions on Henry's covert support for Prince John, as well as about his aligning himself with crooked sheriffs and dangerously obsessive canons!'

A large drop of water plopped on to the table between them, followed by another. Looking up, John saw that the roiling clouds were moving across the darkening sky, the large moon appearing in the gaps and then disappearing again.

'Best go inside, John, the heavens may empty on us in a moment.'

They moved indoors, and sat in the archdeacon's study, a three-branched candlestick on the table between them.

'So what happened to Gilbert?' persisted the coroner.

'Henry Marshal upbraided him for being too gullible in accepting the unproven accusations of those who denounced the various women. He blamed him for persuading the parish priests to give inflammatory sermons, encouraging unruly mobs and inciting riots which ended in the deaths of two citizens.'

'What did de Bosco say to this?'

'He fought back valiantly, but the bishop hardly let him speak. At one point I feared he might call the proctor's men over to shut him up! Endless denials, rambling excuses and an attempt to justify his great crusade seemed to be his object, but his speech was not that clear and, as I say, the bishop rode roughshod over him.'

There was a long rumble of thunder outside and they could hear the patter of rain beginning to fall outside the window.

'You had better stay here a while, John – in this, you'll be soaked just crossing the Close,' said de Alençon, kindly.

'If you've more of this particular wine, I'll gladly stay all night,' replied the coroner with a grin, the first he'd managed that day. As his cup was refilled from a jug, he continued his quest for news. 'So what was the outcome? He deserves to be hanged, but that never happens to those of your cloth!'

'No, we don't go that far, thank God. At the end of it, Henry Marshal delivered a homily for our benefit, as well as for Gilbert, on the perils of taking anything to extremes. He paid lip-service to Gilbert's good intentions in safeguarding the Holy Church, but condemned him for not seeking support and advice from wiser and cooler-headed counsellors.'

'That's bloody hypocrisy, considering that he strongly encouraged the man at the start,' growled de Wolfe.

'That's as maybe, but the upshot of it was that he deprived him of his several prebends, so he has no living to support him or his vicar, and he is therefore no longer a canon of Exeter Cathedral, which means that he will lose his lodging in the Close. He applied no other penalty or stricture, but said that he would send Gilbert as priest to some remote parish in the diocese, where he would have time and space to reflect on his misplaced zeal and to pray for forgiveness for the damage he has caused.'

The coroner grunted in disgust. 'So he gets away with having caused at least four deaths and goes off to sit in the sun in the countryside for a few years! As I said, he should have been hanged, like the poor women he betrayed!'

'That would never happen, given benefit of clergy. And don't think de Bosco saw it as an easy forfeit, John. When the bishop announced his decision, he howled like a dog and began raving about injustice. But Henry just motioned to the proctors and left the room. Gilbert was hustled away by them, still ranting at his unfair treatment and accusing everyone of conspiring against him.'

There was a flash which lit up the bars of the shutters on the window and, a short moment later, a loud clap of thunder.

'At least this will cool the air – though the farmers and peasants will not welcome yet more rain on the harvest,' observed the archdeacon.

'So where is de Bosco now? It's too much to

441

hope that they locked him up until he's banished to a mean chapel on Bodmin Moor or somewhere equally dismal.'

John de Alençon shook his head, the pink skin of his sunburned tonsure glistening in the candle-light.

'They took him home and called the infirmarian to attend to his carbuncle and to cool his mania with a sedating draught. We look after our own, John, even if they have fallen by the wayside.'

As another peal of thunder shook the house, the archdeacon's steward tapped on the door and put his head around it. 'Pardon, sirs, but there's someone who wishes to speak urgently with you. It's Peter de Bologne, the vicar to Canon de Bosco.'

He stood aside and the young priest who had appeared at the inquest hurried in, rain dripping from his dark hair and shoulders. 'Archdeacon, please, can you come? My master is behaving in a most strange manner. I fear for his safety.'

The two Johns rose and went to the door, which opened on to Canons' Row. The huge towers of the cathedral rose in front of them, the dark bulk of the building black against the last of the western twilight. It was sheeting with rain, which fell almost vertically, with little wind to deviate it.

'This way, he's at the end of the Close. He'll catch his death in this, given his state of health.'

The vicar hurried anxiously away, looking back to see whether they followed. The archdeacon

442

looked at the coroner and shrugged. 'Not much choice, have we?'

His steward tried to offer him a cloak, but he waved it away. 'Better that only my cassock is soaked, rather than that as well. Come on, John.'

They both set off in the gloom, trotting through the downpour after the younger cleric. A hundred paces away, they passed de Bosco's house, but the vicar kept going until he reached the foot of the city wall at the end of the Close. The fortification, which stretched all around Exeter, was about twenty feet high here, with a walkway along the top, reached by stairs built into the masonry at intervals.

At the foot of the nearest, the vicar stopped and pointed upward. 'He went up there – I fear he must be confused in his mind, with the fever from the infection in those awful boils.'

The rain eased a little; it had seemed impossible that it could continue with such intensity for long. De Wolfe shook the water from his beetling eyebrows and began to climb the slippery steps. At the top, he looked right and left, then gazed down, to where the two priests were following him.

'To the right, Crowner,' called the vicar. 'I saw him go towards the South Gate'

The wall here was a long uninterrupted stretch that overlooked Southernhay, the gardens and fields immediately outside the city on that side. It ended against the large bulk of one of the towers of the South Gate, which housed the burgesses's gaol.

It was now virtually dark, thanks to the massive clouds that had rolled in from the sea, but occasional breaks fleetingly allowed moonlight to strike through. During one of these John saw a figure, almost invisible in black, standing still about two hundred paces away.

Then the light vanished, but a second later a flash of lightning lit up the whole scene and confirmed that it was Gilbert de Bosco, his arms upraised to the heavens.

'It's not safe,' wailed the vicar, who now also stood on the wall, with de Alençon behind him on the top of the stairway. 'He could fall, especially in his condition!'

'Maybe that's what he intends!' said the archdeacon, gravely.

Suddenly, the clouds parted again and full moonlight fell on them. They saw that Gilbert had his face upturned, as well as his arms. He reminded de Wolfe of a church wall painting he had once seen, of some Old Testament prophet communing with God on a mountain in Sinai.

'We must get to him before he falls or jumps!' he snapped, starting to step along the walkway, which had low castellations on the outer side. It was narrow, dark and wet, so he moved carefully. The light brightened slightly as a wisp of cloud moved away, and he looked up. The orb above was an almost perfect circle – it was the night of the full moon.

'De Bosco, keep still, man. I'm coming to get

you,' he yelled. Behind him, the archdeacon called out that he was following and John turned momentarily towards him. That probably saved his life and certainly his eyesight, as an explosion like the end of the world erupted near by, with a flash that would have seared his eyeballs if he had been looking ahead. A blast of air hurled him to the stones and only a crenellation on the outer side of the wall stopped him from being pitched over into Southernhay.

There was a sulphurous smell as the rain miraculously stopped and an eerie silence enveloped them.

'Oh, good Christ, he's gone,' cried the vicar tremulously, pointing along the wall, where now nothing could be seen except a wreath of smoke ascending from a patch of fused sandstone where de Bosco had been standing.

John, shaken but unharmed, ran along the wall and looked down. There was nothing on the outer side but on a patch of waste ground at the foot of the wall on the city side, he saw an inert body.

They ran back to the steps, hammered down it and then along to where the canon lay. The coroner pushed the others aside and looked at Gilbert. His clothing had been rent into strip-like rags, singed and smoking and there was a fern-like pattern of pink lines across the skin of his exposed chest and belly, typical of other lightning strikes he had seen abroad.

The man's mouth and eyes were wide open, as

if he were staring and shrieking at the full moon above. John looked up at the wall from which he had been thrown and saw smoke still wisping up from the stones. Maybe it was the shock of almost being struck himself, but just as he had imagined when the roof of the Bush fell in he thought that, just for a split second, the smoke formed itself in the moonlight into an image of a bearded face.

HISTORICAL POSTSCRIPT

The use of real names in historical fiction is a matter of debate among writers, but for the sake of authenticity I prefer to adopt them wherever possible. However, in this story, although the name of every Exeter canon in 1195 is on record, there was no Gilbert de Bosco. I felt that, even after more than 800 years, it would be unkind to so deeply blacken the memory of a real person – although all the other senior clerics existed and held the offices described.

I had no such qualms about Richard de Revelle, as history records (though only in few words) some odd facts about his shrievalty. He was appointed at Christmas 1193 but almost immediately Henry de Furnellis took over. At Michaelmas 1194, de Revelle again is recorded as being sheriff, but in late 1195 he vanishes again and Henry de Furnellis becomes sheriff until 1198. Although no explanation is offered anywhere, it is tempting to associate his exclusion with the Prince John rebellion. It is known that Bishop Henry Marshal was a supporter of the Count of Mortain at that time. Richard de Revelle was still alive in

1225, as his name appears on a document relating to his manor at Revelstoke, near Plymouth. In 1200, a Ralph Morin was made sheriff of Devon, but it cannot be our Ralph Morin, as this one was given the shrievalty as a reward for his support of the rebellion, when John came to the throne in 1199.

We have no knowledge of the names of the early Devon coroners before about 1230, but all the names used for other characters are authentic for the period, being taken from the records of the Devon Eyre held at Exeter in 1238.